D1528614

MIND BURN

BOOKS BY RHETT C. BRUNO

STANDALONE NOVELS WITH T. E. BAKUTIS

Mind Burn

STANDALONE NOVELS

The Roach
Vicarious
Operation Bushfire
The Luna Missile Crisis

BLACK BADGE WITH JAIME CASTLE

Cold as Hell
Vein Pursuits

THE ASCENDANT WARS

Hellfire
Brimstone
Ashes

THE BURIED GODDESS SAGA WITH JAIME CASTLE

Web of Eyes
Winds of War
Will of Fire
Way of Gods
War of Men
Word of Truth

CHILDREN OF TITAN

Titanborn
Titan's Son
Titan's Rise
Titan's Fury
Titan's Legacy

THE CIRCUIT SAGA

Executor Rising
Progeny of Vale
Earthfall

RHETT C. BRUNO

MIND
BURN

T. E. BAKUTIS

BLACK
STONE
PUBLISHING

Printed in the United States of America

First edition: 2023
ISBN 979-8-200-99642-1
Fiction / Science Fiction / General

Version 1

Blackstone Publishing
31 Mistletoe Rd.
Ashland, OR 97520

www.BlackstonePublishing.com

PART 1

01

COWAN

Ventura Visions was an office like any other in San Diego, an orderly mess of tinted glass, polished metal, and stark concrete.

Cowan Soto's first partner waited outside, smoking a texture cigarette as if there wasn't a rush at all. Cowan supposed there wasn't. Their clients were already dead.

Standing over two meters tall, Detective Forrester was built like a linebacker. He wore dark slacks, a sterile blue blazer, and a long graphene trench coat that wasn't standard, but didn't break any regulations. He had a prosthetic hand and a clean bald head that glistened in the afternoon light.

Cowan looked to Forrester, then back at the office. He didn't want to go inside. He didn't want to be here at all, honestly, but he'd met all the requirements, passed all the tests, and signed a corporate contract saying he'd investigate cybercrimes for the Cybercrimes Investigation Division, or CID.

So, here he was. A trainee investigating his first crime.

"Follow me," Forrester said. "Our killer's inside."

Cowan followed until he smacked into a wall of stench. The coppery, sewagey smell only got worse as the lobby's automated doors closed behind him, cloaking the office interior in near dusk. His eyes watered, and his nostrils burned. The interior lights rose to reveal pristine white walls, a marble desk missing a large chunk, and the body. Her body.

Cowan stared at the corpse, a seventeen-year-old woman who'd just committed the first mass shooting in twelve years. Someone who'd had a whole life ahead of them and didn't now.

Sheila Fisher. His first case.

"Look at her, kid," Detective Forrester said. "Tell me how she died."

Cowan was twenty-six, about as far from a *kid* as you could get by anyone's standards, but he let the implication slide because Forrester was much older—fifty-two, according to his file. What bothered Cowan more was that Forrester had tagged this atrocity as a cybercrime. How could *this* be a cybercrime? There was way too much blood.

Cowan couldn't breathe. He needed to breathe. He ordered his PBA (Personal Brain Assistant)—a cybernetic implant at the base of his *real* brain—to alter his senses and make the smell more tolerable. When he finished, the air smelled of drying laundry instead of corpse stink.

"We already know what killed her," Cowan said, after drawing a breath of now fragrant air. "Chopgun blast to the head." Even with his senses altered by his PBA, the sewage smell lingered in his mind. He'd have to redact it later, when he wasn't on the job.

"I don't need my partner regurgitating the scene report," Forrester said. "I need you thinking for yourself, drawing your own conclusions."

"I can do that." Cowan took in the nested letter *V*s behind the desk—the Ventura Visions logo—as well as the plush couches along the lobby's sides and the freshly waxed, white floor. "What do you want to know?"

"How you think. First, I want you to forget the last thirty minutes. I don't want what you read in the scene report to influence your conclusions, so you're doing this blind."

Cowan flipped to his head desk—a floating screen he could see when he closed his eyes and focused on the virtual world created by his PBA—and reviewed his memory timeline for the day. He selected the thirty-minute stretch leading to the present, a long ride in a low-slung autocar, and placed a temporary block on that period of time. Finally, he saved his changes.

When Cowan opened his eyes again, he no longer remembered what he'd read on the drive over. He didn't even remember the ride. He simply knew he was standing at a crime scene, with Detective Forrester, staring at a killer named Sheila Fisher.

"What now?" he asked. He knew he was supposed to ask for instructions now, though he didn't quite remember why.

"Examine the body on the floor of this building and tell me what you think happened here," Forrester instructed. "This is a test, but in the real world, with real consequences. If it helps you focus, remember that body isn't a person any longer. It's evidence. Just a gruesome work of art."

That was a terrible idea, but it gave Cowan a better one. Instead of acknowledging that he was still in meatspace—what everyone now called the real world—what if he pretended he was in the Sim, the online virtual world he and 90 percent of the world's population escaped into every day? That would make this just a splatterhouse simulation, a pleasurebox filled with violence, murder, and other horrors of the Internet Age. Cowan knelt beside Sheila and examined her feet first. Her feet hadn't been blown in half.

Sheila's boots were military style, brown leather laced with barbed wire. What kind of lunatic used barbed wire to lace their boots? She wore grimy cargo pants, ragged hems chewed up by the years.

Cowan forced his eyes upward, past her worn leather belt and a bright yellow tank top soaked in dried blood, to her head—or what was left of it. Cowan couldn't tell if she'd had a pretty face, or the color of her eyes, because most of her head was missing. Whatever had killed her had sheared off everything above her jawbone. He could see right down her throat.

"Some kind of heavy weapon took her out," Cowan said, when he knew his voice still worked. "The separation is really clean, like a blade cut through or something, which suggests a chopgun round." Sheila's lower jaw still had all its teeth. "Either her nutrition was poor, or she drank too much black coffee. Her teeth are stained yellow."

"Staining is common with closed circuits." Detective Forrester meant the stubborn holdouts who refused PBAs. "Comes from eating processed food. It's the artificial flavoring."

Cowan would never understand people who refused to install PBAs in their heads. Why refuse the wonders of modern technology? Why wade in the grime and the ugliness when life could be so much easier?

"Why do they eat that stuff?" he asked.

"They don't have PBAs to make everything taste like bacon."

Right. Only someone without a PBA inside their head could walk in here and murder people. People like Cowan and Detective Forrester— people with PBAs, networked to each other through the Sim—couldn't hurt or kill another human being, ever. If a person's PBA ever detected hostile intent directed at another person, the PBA prevented its user from hurting that person, by force if necessary.

Cowan examined the red couches again. Three holes in the back of one sprouted tufts of yellow foam. In the corner, a toppled potted plant drowned in its own dirt.

"Why did she pick this building?" Cowan asked. "Was this personal? Where's the people she killed?"

"Her victims are all around you, kid," Forrester said quietly. "Did you disable your mental health filters?"

"Shit." Cowan felt a hot blush. "Sorry."

He culled his mental health filters—programs in his PBA that seamlessly replaced things he saw in the real world with photorealistic models—even though he dreaded what he might see. The only reason his PBA would use augmented reality to alter what he saw was if it had determined seeing *un*augmented reality might harm his mental health.

And it did. Oh, it did. Three more savaged corpses appeared, innocents who probably had families crying over them at home. Blood spatter painted the not-so-white walls in a gruesome mosaic. And the floor? There was blood all over it, and gray bits, and worse.

A dead woman in a black suit slumped on the red couch. Another woman in a crimson skirt and blouse lay crumpled behind the desk. Next to the desk, sprawled out face down on top of the toppled plant, a janitor leaked his brains into the dirt. Cowan took in slack jaws, sightless eyes, gaping wounds, and gray matter. Just more works of art.

"Three victims." Cowan trembled as he spoke and didn't stand up, couldn't stand up, because he didn't trust his legs. "Our killer got three people before someone got her."

"Seems like it," Forrester said.

"How could this happen? Massacres like this don't happen anymore."

"That's why we're here. To find out *what* happened."

"Right." Cowan could see inside that janitor's skull, see red blood smeared on ripples of gray brain matter. "So . . . how do we do that?"

"You've archived the scene," Forrester said, calmly enough that he'd probably firewalled his emotions, allowing him to remain calm. "Run a simulation using the scripts the CID installed this morning."

Cowan focused on scripting. He could deal with scripting. He blinked over to his head desk and selected every important detail in the lobby: the blood spatter, the bodies, the couch, and the fallen plant. He dumped those details into the CID's simulation program and activated it.

———

Cowan sees the lobby from a top-down, three-fourths perspective, like in a classic '90s video game. The lobby doors open. A red female mannequin slides in on motionless legs, like a robovac. The red mannequin's arm rises, holding a black arrow. Yellow flashes from the arrow, and a blue mannequin tips over on the couch. Victim Number One.

The red mannequin spins like a compass pin, yellow flashing from her arrow. Another blue mannequin behind the desk pops backward. Victim Number Two.

A blue mannequin by the desk slides off. Yellow flash. The blue mannequin drops and scrambles, flailing limbs like a dog on a freshly waxed floor. Some simulations abstract participant actions so as not to damage the psyche of the reviewer.

The red mannequin vacuums its way over, arm lowered and arrow pointed. Flash. Flash, flash. The last blue mannequin goes still. Victim Number Three.

A green mannequin with a G above its head slides into the lobby, holding another black arrow. That arrow flashes as the red mannequin turns. She spins like a top at superspeed, then topples.

———

Cowan blinked back into meatspace. The CID's scripts had created all he just saw from the evidence remaining in this lobby. Had the program in his head used the placement of the bullet holes? The patterns of the blood spatter? How had the program decided who the killer shot first?

"Kid?" Forrester asked. "What happened here?"

"If the reconstructed simulation is correct," Cowan said, "Sheila walked inside and just started shooting."

Cowan pointed at the dead woman on the couch. "Sheila shot her first. Then the receptionist. There was a janitor by the receptionist . . . they were talking, maybe . . . and he tried to run. Sheila shot him in the back, walked over here. Finished him off."

"Then why is our killer dead?"

"One of the building's synthcops responded to the situation, balanced possible solutions, and solved the problem."

Synthcops were robots controlled by VIs (virtual intelligences) that could make simple decisions within parameters defined by their programmers. VIs were not actually sentient, no matter what the conspiracy buffs on the darkSim claimed, but they were creative problem solvers.

"You've established a chain of events," Forrester said, without nodding, "but anyone can do that. What we do . . . what this job is about . . . is figuring out what's missing."

So this was like solving a puzzle. Cowan enjoyed puzzles. He flipped back to his head desk and reviewed the end of the simulation, with the fallen mannequins, from his own perspective—his own eyes. He ordered his PBA to project the simulation he'd previously seen inside his head in the real world, then compared the position of the computer-generated bodies (created by augmented reality) with the real bodies in the real world.

Cowan saw it then. The missing piece. "Sheila's body is in the wrong place."

"Is it?" Forrester waited.

"She's in the middle of the lobby." Cowan looked at where Sheila should be, then where she should not be. "The synthcop shot her over there, not here. Did someone move her?"

"What do you think, kid?"

Cowan's stared at Sheila Fisher's *simulated* body, the body his PBA had used augmented reality to place next to the dead janitor, and traced the trail of bloody boot prints leading from Sheila's simulated body to her *real* body. The corpse with half a head lying right beside his feet.

"Jesus," Cowan whispered. "She walked over here after she got shot."

Forrester crossed his arms. "With her head missing?"

"She didn't do this. Someone forced her to do this."

"You think someone was blackmailing her?"

"No, not that kind of forcing." God, this *was* a cybercrime. "Someone puppeted this woman in here, made her shoot these people. Uploaded her every move."

"How? Sheila Fisher didn't have a PBA installed."

"She did have a PBA, Detective. She had to. The only way she could still walk over here after that synthcop blew her head off is if the brain in her skull wasn't the brain controlling her body."

Cowan shined his narrow flashlight down Sheila's blown-open throat. He focused on the charred flesh at the base of her neck. Just a trace of metal glistened there, the edge of a quarter-sized circle. The edge of a black-market PBA.

Cowan's throat clamped up. He regretted every unkind thought as he mourned this woman, this hostage locked inside her own head by some sick fuck with an urge. Forced to watch, unable to act, as her puppeted body committed atrocities.

Sheila Fisher.

Victim Number Four.

02

COWAN

Once they were back on CA-14 in a CID autocar, Cowan downloaded a travel estimate off the Sim and winced. Sheila Fisher had lived in Palmdale, a fenced-off reservation for closed circuits—the common term for people who refused to get PBAs installed—and it would take them at least forty-five minutes to ride there. Forty-five minutes stuck in this car, with an all-too-silent Detective Forrester, thinking about dead people.

Streetlights flashed in a steady rhythm, highlighting asphalt below and scrub-choked hills beside the highway. Cowan sat in the autocar's dark leather seat, facing forward, and Detective Forrester sat in one of the forward seats, facing him. It was easier to talk that way, but Forrester wasn't talking. He was in the Sim, eyes closed and twitching.

Something about discovering Sheila's PBA gnawed on Cowan's nerves, but nothing clicked until the block he'd placed on the last thirty minutes of his memory expired. The connection he made between what he'd known then and what he knew was a heady rush, a breakthrough, an addiction that was difficult to shake. The CID hadn't failed to find Sheila's PBA. They'd been *testing* him.

Cowan shot a query to Forrester's PBA, one that would politely page his partner in the Sim. Forrester blinked as he returned to meatspace.

"Something on your mind, kid?" he asked.

"The CID knew Sheila got puppeted before we arrived," Cowan said.

Forrester's eyes didn't widen, and he didn't suck in his breath, and he didn't do anything people did when you surprised them. He just smiled. "I think I'm gonna like you, kid."

"The team that processed the scene couldn't have missed Sheila's PBA, yet the report clearly stated she was a closed circuit. They claimed she'd refused to have a PBA installed. Why would they lie about it?"

"That's an interesting question."

"Do you always answer questions with evasion?"

"Have you ever interviewed a murder suspect?"

Cowan actually smiled back. "Fine." Forrester was training him, after all. "Tell me if I've got this right. Crime scene reports aren't publicly available, but simNews can access them with a public interest request."

"True," Forrester said.

"So, the Office of Mental Health didn't want any stories circulating about people being puppeted into shooting rampages. They edited the report to exclude that information, and then they sent us to figure out what really happened. Our reports are classified."

"I can't speculate about decisions by the Office of Mental Health."

"So is this the first time this happened? Or has the OMH suppressed other mass shootings?"

Cowan knew the Office of Mental Health could censor any simNews story—that was their job, ensuring the public felt safe—but how far did their reach extend?

Forrester watched Cowan in silence as streetlamp after streetlamp shined across his shiny head, like a marble in a code scanner. Had Cowan asked the wrong question? Was Forrester angry with him now? Cowan found his new partner all but impossible to read.

"Let's just say the director wants us browsing every lead," Forrester said, finally.

"We're partners, aren't we?" Cowan asked, a question that had been gnawing at him since the moment they got paired for this job. "Is there some reason you can't just tell me?"

Forrester shrugged. "That's another question for you to mull over, isn't it?"

Cowan wanted to be annoyed at Forrester, but was that really fair? Forrester might be a senior detective, but he didn't make policy about who got to see classified information. He followed orders, and his orders probably didn't include spilling all of Oneworld's secrets to the new guy.

"Fair enough." Cowan nodded, and Forrester nodded back. "So, while we're on the road, let's check out our victim's black-market PBA."

Cowan blinked over to his head desk and uploaded a simulation request. The autocar's VI used his PBA to create an augmented reality simulacrum in the car between him and Detective Forrester, a PBA-generated hologram that floated in meatspace. Because Forrester's PBA was networked with Cowan's, Forrester saw that simulacrum too.

What remained of Sheila's implant was still in her corpse, headed to the morgue. Before she left, the team that scanned her body archived everything that hadn't been disintegrated. The magnified projection of her black-market PBA was a charred disc with thin wires trailing off one end. Colored circles, like rounded handles, floated off each side. Cowan reached up and placed his hands on each projected handle, allowing him to rotate the hologram.

Using the handles, Cowan spun the PBA around, then zoomed in and out, but he found no corporate tag and no serial number. "This isn't any corporate model I recognize. Most smugglers buy knockoffs from the Hanyu Expanse or the Russian Freedom zone, so this is probably one of those. Maybe a Nerve Six."

"That so?" Forrester sounded amused.

Cowan examined the ripped wires trailing off the PBA's spiral stem, highlighting and isolating the broken ends with pokes of his index finger. Those wires had linked the tiny CPU in Sheila's neck to the neural netting surrounding her brain. That net grew as the brain did, lacing into everything.

"That's black fiber." Cowan was certain. "The Chinese don't like it, because it degrades inside biosystems, but the Russians love it because it's supercheap."

"You know a lot about PBAs," Forrester said. "Did you work on them before you applied to the CID?"

"I did a lot of things before I applied to the CID." Cowan could be evasive too.

Forrester smirked and sat back. He didn't ask again.

"So, assumptions are bad," Cowan said. "I get that. I'll posit a hypothesis instead."

"Let's hear it."

"Sheila Fisher wanted to be simlinked, but she was still a minor. Her parents, both closed circuits, wouldn't allow her to install a PBA, because they're morally opposed or something. So, she saved a few grand doing summer jobs, ordered a jailbroken PBA over the internet, and found a back-alley grayDoc in Palmdale willing to install."

"Why do you think her surgeon is in Palmdale?" Forrester asked.

"Too much security and too many cameras at the corporate gray-Docs, ever since those Natural Body nuts started picketing. She'd be archived by somebody on her way in or out."

"You think this underground grayDoc is involved?"

Cowan thought about it. "No. You'd never send someone you just simlinked on a shooting rampage. There's too much chance it'd get traced back to you."

"So, this surgeon's installing the PBAs, but he's not hacking them."

"Right," Cowan said. "Sheila got puppeted by someone else. The firewalls on black-market PBAs are garbage, so she was fair game the moment she connected to the Sim."

Only then did Cowan process what Detective Forrester had actually said, and he played it back on his head desk, twice, just to be sure. *"Installing the PBAs."* Cowan had been right about multiple shootings, and Forrester had just told him that. Accidentally.

As Cowan returned to meatspace, Forrester raised one bushy eyebrow. "Problem?"

"No problem," Cowan said. A man like Detective Forrester wouldn't let that information drop by accident. Forrester was skirting an order. Maybe he wasn't so bad after all.

"Since we've got some time on the road," Forrester said, "study for your first-day exam. You'll be expected to recall everything you learned this morning, without archives."

That's right. Cowan was not an actual detective yet. He was still on probation, and he'd have to pass several more exams before he could officially join the CID. The exam was a distraction, and he welcomed it.

He blinked back over to his head desk and organized this morning's memories into thirty-minute blocks. He sped over all he'd learned, paying particular attention to where the CID stood in the corporate structure of Oneworld: the singular corporation that invented PBAs and, as of twenty years ago, ran most of the civilized world.

Cowan's particular CID office handled San Diego and many of its surrounding counties, interfacing with county police as necessary. The CID's director reported to someone at the North American Office of Mental Health, and they reported directly to Oneworld. It was a simple enough hierarchy, easy to memorize and easy to understand.

Hidden somewhere inside the network of Oneworld's planetwide bureaucracy was Ellen, the woman he'd loved and betrayed one year ago.

"We are approaching Palmdale Reservation." The car's automated voice stirred him, sounding British and female. They always sounded British and female. "Two vehicles are ahead of us in the checkpoint queue. Estimated time to the Fisher residence is eight minutes."

Cowan couldn't dare think about Ellen now. That would raise his heart rate, which might make the CID think he wasn't cut out for this job.

He had a murder case to solve and a puppeteer to capture. That was the only way to get into the CID, and he *needed* to get into the CID. He needed to get Ellen back, even if she wasn't really Ellen anymore.

The reservation's three-story border wall loomed ahead. Hill-mounted floodlights lit its concrete bulk. Their autocar cruised to a stop behind another vehicle idling inside the tunnel checkpoint. This reinforced gateway was a concrete half-pipe sticking out on both sides of the wall, with expensive sensors lining its interior. An actual uniformed human sat behind bulletproof glass inside the tunnel, a closed circuit doing a VI's job.

Cowan recognized the model of the autocar ahead of them—a Hyundai Corvette—and a quick simsearch verified one could get that model with a steering wheel and pedals. He squinted at the Corvette's taillights.

"Isn't it a little late to be coming home?" Cowan asked. It made no sense for a closed circuit to be out this late. "Don't they care about the fine?"

Forrester snorted. "You give a bunch of stubborn holdouts a curfew and see how many violate it each night."

Cowan shook his head. Corporate-produced PBAs had been free for over thirty years, approved for installation as early as age two, and while holdouts in the Middle East still refused to accept mandated PBA installation, the majority of the world had been online for decades, linked in harmony by the Sim.

Sheila Fisher's parents were throwbacks who claimed exemption from the Lathan-Faulkner Act on religious grounds, like the Natural Body nuts who picketed augmentation clinics. Each year, closed circuits found fewer exemptions to claim. The only way society could be safe was when everyone in the world finally had a PBA.

Only then would all violence *stop*.

PBAs like Cowan's offered uninterrupted Sim access with all the benefits thereof, everything from a head desk and emotional firewalls to weather warnings and street closings. PBAs allowed you to visit thousands of pleasureboxes recreating every world ever imagined by man without even needing to move. For those who could afford them, skills involving muscle memory or reflex training were a download away.

How could anyone turn that down?

Sheila's parents could limit themselves to meatspace—that was their right—but walling off their child against her will? That was stupid and selfish. If Sheila's parents had just simlinked her at age two, like every other newborn, she wouldn't be lying in the lobby of Ventura Ventures missing most of her head.

"When we meet Sheila's family," Forrester said, "let me ask the questions. Dealing with folks who just lost their kid isn't a training exercise."

"Okay." Cowan remembered the bodies and clenched his fists. "I won't tell them they're fucking idiots."

Forrester gripped Cowan's shoulder with his prosthetic hand hard enough to make Cowan wince. The tunnel gate rattled upward. The guard behind the glass motioned the Corvette through.

"Cowan," Forrester said, and that sounded far different from *kid*. "What we're going to do next has nothing to do with corporate regulations or cyberization debates. It has nothing to do with your opinions or prejudices. It's about talking to two parents who just lost their only child, and us handling that conversation with compassion and respect."

Cowan felt a rush of anger and a rush of shame, and those competed until he imagined what Ellen would say right now if she were still around, the disapproving look he'd see in her eyes.

"You're right," Cowan said quietly. "I was out of line. I won't bring it up again."

Forrester sat back. "I believe you." He blinked, eyes going distant as he reentered the Sim.

As they cleared the gate and rolled into Palmdale Reservation, Ellen refused to return to the mental vault where Cowan kept her sealed away. She needed him to find her. He'd loved her and betrayed her, and she might not exist, not any longer, because of his mistakes.

Cowan knew how it felt to lose someone you loved. Someone irreplaceable. What he'd felt every day since he lost Ellen was what Sheila's parents would feel soon. A hole would open up inside them, deep and raw and cold.

So, he'd try and cut the Fishers a little slack.

03

JEB

As the autocar's headlights swept across Sheila Fisher's light gray house, CID Detective Jeb Forrester felt like he was coming home. The Fisher residence—an antiquated structure ripped from the early 2040s—reminded him of his grandmother's house. The slanted roof had red clay tiles instead of solar, and a two-car garage sprouted from the house's rectangular body. The garage even had a classic segmented door.

The house was double the size of the stack home in which Jeb grew up. Even Palmdale real estate was pricey in today's housing markets, so if Sheila's parents weren't rich, they had likely inherited the house from ancestors. For a family of closed circuits, they lived well. A thin green cypress tree shot skyward in the yard—cloned, no doubt, since the natural variety had been eaten by invasive beetles fifty years ago—and the lawn was freshly combed, smooth dirt marked by swirling patterns of colored pebbles.

This wasn't the house of a teenager who wore grimy cargo pants and combat boots laced with barbed wire.

As the autocar cruised to a stop, its gull-wing doors folded open. Jeb stepped out and watched his trainee do the same. Even this late, California nights felt hot and humid.

"CID records list Sheila's parents as Andrew and Pamela Fisher," Jeb said. "Andrew's a desalination engineer for Palmdale's city office, and Pamela chairs the local chapter of Natural Bodies." Jeb remembered Cowan's outburst at the fence. "I'll do the talking."

"Understood," Cowan said. "Mouth shut, eyes open." He ran his hands through his short hair reflexively, fixing it, even though it was already basically fixed. He seemed nervous.

Jeb smiled, but only on the inside. Cowan had the type of face that seemed both trusting and trustworthy, with a strong chin and ears that were just a tad too big. With hardened suspects, his fresh-faced appearance might hurt him, but with younger or single folks, it might actually help. He clearly had an eye for details and listened to feedback instead of fighting it. All in all, Jeb felt he had *potential*, which was more than he could say for most rookies.

What bothered Jeb at the moment, however, was Cowan's "training exercise." Jeb never directly questioned his orders—he'd been a cog in the machine too long to be that stupid—but it made absolutely no sense for the CID to give him a first-day trainee on a puppeting case. Guns had been illegal for decades now, and a puppeted shooting like this should have attracted the CID's top resources. Yet all they'd sent to investigate Ventura Visions was Jeb with a rookie rounding out his first day.

Nothing about it smelled right. Still, one mystery at a time.

Jeb waved Cowan along and led, loafers crunching pebbles on the path to the front door. His black duster drifted out behind him like a curtain, a graphene and Kevlar weave capable of stopping even metal bullets. This didn't look like the house of militant Natural Body nuts, but you never knew what to expect on a reservation. Outlawed or not, people who shouldn't always seem to get their hands on firearms.

Jeb pressed the old doorbell. A chime sounded inside, and Jeb didn't miss it when Cowan blinked like the door had yelled at him. Contemporary "doorbells" were PBA pings, so the kid probably thought an audible doorbell was rather weird. The amplifiers embedded deep inside Jeb's ears picked up footsteps beyond the door, unhurried and even, and that was reassuring.

"One moment!" A woman cracked the door and peered out. "Can I help you, officers?" If she was surprised to see two cops standing on her porch past dark, she didn't look it.

Jeb put on his most comforting tone. "Good evening, ma'am. Is this the Fisher residence?"

"It is," she said flatly.

"And you must be Pamela Fisher?"

She nodded. Then Pamela Fisher stepped onto her front porch, back straight and eyes narrow. A good sign that she did so willingly. Jeb was too tired for trouble.

Even this late, Pamela wore a pink blouse and a gray skirt with black flats. Her dirty-blond hair matched her daughter's, and she looked to be in her late forties.

Her shoulders sagged. "What has Sheila done now?"

Jeb moved closer, keeping his prosthetic hand at his side because cyberization often made Natural Body folks uncomfortable. "If you don't mind, ma'am, I'd prefer to talk inside. My name is Detective Forrester. This is my partner, Detective Soto. We'd like to ask you some questions about your daughter."

A man yelled from inside the house. "Just tell the cops we'll pay the fine! Is she spending the night in jail?"

"Missus Fisher," Jeb said, "I must insist."

"Yes, all right." Pamela smoothed her blouse and turned. "Follow me, please. We'll talk in the parlor."

This couple had a parlor? Had Sheila been rebelling against her perfect home by jumping into counterculture? Or had she simply wanted to experience the pleasureboxes her clear circuit friends raved about?

Jeb activated his archiver and entered the home. He could see a huge kitchen down the hall, with a clay tile floor and an array of black appliances. A real oven? A microwave? He felt more unexpected nostalgia. Everything he saw was being recorded, of course—the CID mandated that—but he'd delete it after seventy-two hours if it turned out the Fishers had nothing to do with Sheila's murder.

Jeb's grandmother, like many born before the creation of PBAs, had been obsessed with the Internet Age. When seen through the lens of decades, with the hard edges of global conflict and political strife filed off, it seemed like quite the time to be alive. There was something alluring about art, culture, and decisions made without the aid of scripts or archives. The creations of those decades simply screamed individuality.

Despite his mother's best efforts, his grandmother's passion for pre-PBA culture had infected Jeb. He loved manually driven cars, old detective movies, vampires, and spaceships. A hundred years ago, people had willingly filled the internet with cat pictures. There was something seductively extravagant about that.

Presently, Pamela Fisher led them into a room with light green walls and big glass windows. An ornate chandelier lit the space. The parlor held a plush white couch and two green armchairs, with a real fireplace built into the wall. There wasn't a simport in sight.

"Please, sit wherever you like," Pamela said. Her features were the very definition of polite frustration. "We're appropriately appalled by Sheila's actions. We'll pay whatever fees she's incurred. May I ask where my daughter is now?"

"Have a seat, Missus Fisher," Jeb said. "I have a few questions about Sheila."

Closed circuits lacked the ability to firewall emotions or answer questions when overwhelmed with emotion, and telling the Fishers their daughter was dead would absolutely overwhelm. Jeb had to question them first to ensure he received honest answers. This was the official CID procedure, and today Jeb hated official CID procedures.

He imagined the many questions gnawing at the inside of Pamela's mind. Is my daughter hurt? Is my daughter dead? Why are you asking all these questions about her?

Yet what if one of the Fishers had bought that black-market PBA for their daughter? What if one had gone behind the other's back? Jeb had to get a feel for their involvement and knowledge before Sheila's death destroyed them.

He had to decide if one of them already knew.

Jeb pointed Cowan to one chair, then sat in another one. "Do you know where Sheila planned to travel tonight?" He blinked, twice, to activate his facial analyzer.

A floating AR panel popped up beside Pamela Fisher, displaying heart rate, breathing rate, and other vital statistics. Using real-time facial analysis to detect lies always felt like cheating, but a young girl *was* dead. The routines in his PBA weren't perfect, and Jeb had learned not to rely on AR when his gut said otherwise. But again, procedure.

Pamela settled herself on one edge of the couch. "She told us she was going to an outdoor concert with friends," she said.

True (90.3 percent) displayed on the panel beside her face.

Andrew Fisher stalked into the parlor. He was a tall man with an athletic build and graying hair.

"I'm sorry, but is this really necessary?" he asked. "It's past curfew."

"I'm sorry as well, but we have procedures," Jeb replied, knowing a desalination engineer would understand procedures. "As soon as you answer our questions, we can answer yours."

Andrew moved past his wife and sat on the opposite end of the couch. He didn't touch her, and he didn't sit beside her. Jeb wondered if they'd had a recent argument, or if this resentment had existed longer.

"Fine," Andrew said. "What do you want to know?"

"What concert was Sheila attending, ma'am?" Jeb directed the question at Pamela Fisher.

"Some chiptune group popular in her social circle," Pamela said. "I'm afraid I don't keep up with historical music." *True (96.7 percent).*

"You don't recall the group's name?" Jeb knew it must be difficult to have to write down the names of places, people, and things instead of archiving them on one's head desk.

Andrew leaned forward. "Did Sheila get into another fight? Have they already decided to sue?"

So, the Fishers had been slapped with a lawsuit recently. Jeb filed the knowledge and continued.

"How often does your daughter get into fights, Mister Fisher?" he asked.

"The last one wasn't her fault," Pamela said. "Another girl got very aggressive with Sheila's partner. She was standing up for her." *True (80 percent).*

Jeb nodded to show he understood. He needed to stay on their good sides. "Did she and the other participant know each other before the fight occurred?" he asked. "Have they been in contact since?"

Andrew threw up his hands. "How should we know? Sheila does as she pleases, when she pleases, and never cares to inform us. Just tell us what she did and go away."

"Sir." Jeb raised his prosthetic hand, and the gleaming metal caught Andrew's attention. "I need you to answer my questions first. Answer my questions and I'll answer yours."

Andrew clenched a fist. He had a temper. Closed circuits had no conditioning, and they could still abuse their families. Another horror Jeb had seen in all those old movies.

Andrew relaxed his hand. "Very well."

Pamela hadn't flinched when Andrew clenched his fist, nor did she seem alarmed by his raised voice. So, Andrew Fisher probably didn't beat his family. One small mercy.

Jeb reengaged. "Do you have the names of those who attended the concert with your daughter?"

Pamela looked to the hall. "They're in the kitchen, on my notepad. I make sure Sheila leaves us contact numbers for everyone before she leaves the reservation." *True (92.4 percent).*

"Thank you," Jeb said. "Now, I'm going to ask you something delicate, and I need you to be honest with me."

"What the hell did Sheila do?" Andrew demanded.

"Did either of you purchase a Personal Brain Assistant for your daughter?"

The blood drained from Pamela's face. "What?"

Andrew's face flushed bright red. "Did you catch her with some uncertified grayDoc? Who did her installation procedure?" Then his eyes went wide, and he stiffened like someone had slapped him. "Is . . . is my daughter all right?"

In both real and augmented reality, their shock and fear seemed genuine. The parents weren't involved, for what meager comfort that offered. Jeb would deliver the approved story, retrieve the list of Sheila's friends from Pamela's notepad, and let the Fishers grieve.

It was time to bring in Sarisa.

Jeb checked his head desk. OMH Counselor Sarisa Bassa had arrived outside the house a minute ago, right on time. She was the best grief counselor Jeb knew, even if she did work for the Office of Mental Health.

"You're on," he said, over the wireless connection shared by their PBAs.

"On my way." Sarisa's voice sounded just as comforting in his head, and for those with PBAs wireless communication, or "wireless," was almost as common as normal speech. *"I'm sending the approved cause of death."*

Sarisa uploaded him the acceptable story the OMH had fabricated. The Fishers couldn't be trusted to keep a mass shooting secret. For that reason, they wouldn't be told.

"Is Sheila in the hospital?" Pamela asked. Her voice trembled.

The doorbell rang. Andrew jumped. Pamela did too. Neither seemed to understand where they were now.

"Cowan," Jeb said quietly. "Get the door."

Cowan hopped up like something had bit him. He strode quickly into the hallway. Neither Fisher watched him go.

"I'm afraid Sheila Fisher was struck by an autotruck while walking on the side of CA-14," Jeb said calmly, and firmly, and without any quaver in his tone. "Our medical examiner concluded she died instantly, upon impact. She didn't feel any pain." One kind lie among the cruel. "I'm so sorry for your loss."

Andrew Fisher stood, shaking his head. "No, Sheila wouldn't do that. It must be someone else." He wet his lips with his tongue. "Where is my daughter now? Do you need a DNA sample?"

Jeb stood as Sarisa strode into the parlor in a gray pantsuit and a form-fitting navy jacket. She had dark eyes, dark hair to her shoulders, and a black bindi in the center of her light brown forehead. She offered a shallow bow.

"Mister and Missus Fisher," Jeb said, "this is Counselor Sarisa Bassa, from the Office of Mental Health. She'll guide you through this development and help you adjust to your new circumstances."

Adjustment. Circumstances. Those words weren't how you described losing your only child. Those were *procedures.*

"Do you mind if I sit?" Sarisa asked. Quietly. Calmly. In a way that made you want to say yes. As always, it was a pleasure to watch Sarisa work, as much as Jeb hated the work she had to do.

Andrew Fisher's hands shook. Pamela Fisher put one hand to her lips. Jeb walked out as she started sobbing. He found Cowan waiting in the hallway, arms crossed and shoulders hunched. Looking guilty.

"Isn't there anything else we can do for them?" Cowan asked. If he still had any reservations over the Fisher's Natural Body beliefs, their naked grief over their murdered child looked to have done away with it.

"Sarisa will do all she can," Jeb said.

"But how do they deal with losing a child without emotional firewalls to dull the pain? Can't we give them . . . drugs, or something?"

Jeb frowned. "We can stop this from happening to anyone else."

"Right." Cowan nodded. "Right."

"Now," Jeb said. "Kitchen." He led the way into the Fisher's immaculate kitchen before Cowan could think much more about anything. Jeb archived each page of Pamela's notepad on his PBA. His heart ached, even through his emotional firewalls, as he imagined what the Fishers must be feeling right now. No one deserved this pain. No one deserved to bury their child, which was why he had to make sure this didn't happen again.

Notepad archived, Jeb led Cowan past the Fishers. Sarisa would help them as best she could. A barrage of questions from Cowan filled his PBA as Jeb gripped the door handle.

"Why did you spend so much time stringing them along?" Cowan asked over wireless. *"Why did we lie to the Fishers about an autotruck? Who's the Indian lady in the navy jacket?"*

Jeb sighed and opened the door. Seconds later a man beside their autocar opened fire.

Jeb spun and slammed his hands against the doorframe around

Cowan, grunting as bullets fractured violently against his back. His graphene duster kept him whole, and the grip of his prosthetic hand kept him upright. Diving aside would leave Cowan in the line of fire. Once the stinging impacts ended, his amplifiers detected the click of a magazine dropping.

He had perhaps four seconds to get Cowan back inside, find the Fishers, get them—

Cowan leaned around Jeb and fired his stunner. The stench of ozone assaulted Jeb's nostrils as his world became a dull, persistent ringing, even with the noise protection provided by his ear implants.

"He's down!" Cowan shouted, or maybe shouted. It was more lipreading than anything. Jeb turned anyway and found the shooter flat on his back by the autocar. Someone had taught Cowan Soto how to shoot.

"*Hey!*" Cowan asked, now speaking over wireless again. *"Are you hurt?"*

Cowan using wireless to communicate was smart, actually. Jeb had forgotten how stupidly loud real gunshots could be. Given the ringing in his ears, he couldn't hear much of anything in meatspace at the moment.

"I'm fine," Jeb answered, as he focused on breathing more than anything. His PBA dulled pain when necessary, but he still felt like a vengeful hockey team had slapshotted a dozen pucks into his back. *"Secure the shooter."*

"How do I secure a shooter?" Cowan sounded a bit panicked.

Jeb noticed the stunner shaking in his grip. *"Walk over to him. Keep an eye on him. If he moves, stun him again."*

"Oh." Cowan strode off. *"I can do that."*

Sarisa joined Jeb on the porch, stunner drawn, as he sat back against the doorframe.

"Same puppeteer as Sheila?" she asked, also over wireless. Neither of them wanted the Fishers to overhear this conversation.

"Might be," Jeb answered.

The ringing faded into a muted buzz as Sarisa holstered her stunner and squeezed Jeb's shoulder. *"Thank you for not dying."*

"Counselor?" A trembling voice filled the night. "What was all that?"

They turned to see Pamela Fisher, concern darkening her features. "An unrelated case, and nothing you need to worry about, ma'am," Sarisa said. "Please, let's head back inside." As she ushered Pamela back to her parlor, she pinged Jeb again. *"Any more coming?"*

"If our puppetmaster had more, he'd have sent them." Jeb hoped that was true. *"I see you called for backup?"*

"They're twenty minutes out, but I can handle things until they get here. Get that shooter out of their sight."

"Got it."

"And see a doctor, please."

"Yes, dear."

"Love to David."

Thoughts of David Forrester helped Jeb breathe. He couldn't imagine life without the man he loved, even if David was going to give an earful about getting shot. He wasn't supposed to get shot. That's why they sent synthcops on all the dangerous calls.

Jeb stumbled over to Cowan and archived the shooter. He was a Latino kid with a spider tattooed on his cheek, piercings in his nose, and another in his lip. He wore a ratty black hoodie and long cargo pants. Barbed wire laced his muddy boots, just like Sheila Fisher.

The CID sent the shooter's name a few seconds later. He was Michael Villo, sixteen years old and a closed circuit, though obviously not any longer. Michael's father was dead, and his mother worked two jobs.

Worse than all of that? His name had been in Pamela Fisher's notebook.

"Be advised other puppeted civilians might be in play," Jeb informed the CID. He uploaded the CID the complete list of Sheila's friends. Other officers would locate them at once, take them in for examination, and stop anyone else from getting shot. He hoped.

Jeb crouched and took Villo's feet, then glanced up at Cowan. "Holster your stunner, kid."

Cowan eyed his weapon, paused for a moment, then holstered his stunner and waited for orders.

"Take a good grip on both his hands," Jeb said. "Lift."

They muscled Villo into the autocar, where Jeb strapped him in and applied a blocker to the simport at the base of Villo's neck. That cut Villo off from all wireless connections, which meant he couldn't be puppeted again. Small comfort, since the OMH claimed puppeting was impossible.

"I wasn't sure I'd hit him," Cowan said. "I mean, I've played a lot of StrikeForceGo, but still . . . it's different, in meatspace."

"It is," Jeb said. "But you did good. You saved our asses."

The kid practically blushed, grinning like Jeb had asked him out on a date. "Thanks."

That was not the reaction Jeb expected, and it made him consider Cowan's origins again. How had Cowan ended up working for the CID? Had he been a troll caught in a corporate sweep, one talented enough for the classic ultimatum? Work for us or we make you into someone else?

Yet Cowan was practically the anti-troll. He apologized when he screwed up, and he seemed to legitimately care about people in a way that wasn't induced by his PBA. In Jeb's experience, trolls were borderline sociopaths who took what they wanted with no regard for those they hurt. That profile didn't fit Cowan Soto.

"Cowan," Jeb said, "this is how you interrogate a suspect." He activated his PBA's facial analyzer, creating an AR panel by Villo, and then spoke to their autocar. "Car, wake him."

At Jeb's command, the autocar dispensed a small puff of noxious wake-up gas that descended from the ceiling like a deflated balloon. Villo recoiled as the cloud reached his nostrils. He opened his eyes and thrashed in his restraints, heart rate spiking.

"The fuck?" Villo shouted.

Jeb gripped Villo's shoulder, gently but firmly, and gave it one comforting squeeze. He couldn't imagine how terrifying it must be to lose control of your own body. "Easy now, Michael. You're safe. Do you remember what just happened?"

"I shot you!" Villo trembled in his seat. "Why would I shoot you?"

"We believe someone hacked your illegal PBA." Jeb kept his voice calm, his tone even. "What else do you remember? When did you first get puppeted?"

"Shit." Villo's trembling eased. "No. No way, man. I want a lawyer. Right now."

"So we get him a lawyer?" Cowan asked, over wireless.

"His request automatically pinged the California court system," Jeb said, *"but whatever closed circuit is working Palmdale these days won't be notified until tomorrow morning. There's no reason we can't ask him a few more questions."*

"Ah," Cowan said.

With other puppeted civilians out there, possibly ready to commit more mass shootings, there was too much at stake to stop the interrogation here. Jeb had to keep going. He had to stop another young girl, or a building full of people, from getting shot to death.

"We'll get you a lawyer," Jeb told Villo, "but right now we need your help. We think your friends might be in danger."

"So." Villo's vitals were already settling, which suggested he'd been interrogated before.

"Let's start with an easy one," Jeb said. "Who installed your PBA?"

Villo batted at Jeb's hand. "Lawyer."

"Where did you get the handgun?" Jeb asked. "Did someone give it to you?"

Villo shrugged.

"Was anyone else with you when the puppeting started? Do you know of anyone else who might be armed, or on their way to cause trouble?"

Villo actually chuckled. "I'm not telling you shit. You thought police don't have jurisdiction on the reservations, and your little metal brains mean you can't even twist my arm." He grabbed his own crotch and pumped, adding, "Limp dick."

"Enough bullshit!" Jeb bellowed, and that made both Villo and Cowan jump. "Sheila Fisher was puppeted, just like you, and now her head's missing! People are dead!"

Villo's eyes shot wide. "What?" His vitals spiked.

"Someone walked her into Ventura Visions, Michael. Someone made her shoot three people, and then a synthcop pulped her head. Was that you?"

"I didn't do shit!" Villo shouted. *False (83 percent)*.

Jeb visibly bared his teeth, for intimidation factor. Villo knew *something* about what had happened to Sheila, even if he hadn't puppeted her himself. Jeb was certain.

"You're lying," Jeb said.

"Lawyer!" Villo shouted. "I want a lawyer, now!"

Jeb glanced at Cowan. "In about ten seconds, my partner will carve open the simport in your shiny new PBA. We'll watch every memory since you installed. What'll we find?"

"Um, that's not actually legal," Cowan said over the wireless. *"Only the Office of Mental Health is allowed to examine suspect archives."*

"We know that," Jeb said. *"Villo might not."*

He smiled down at Villo in meatspace. "What about it?"

Villo glared. He didn't speak.

Jeb turned to Cowan and pointed. "Cut his brain open."

"Wait!" Villo's hands shot up. *"I didn't puppet her!" True (75 percent)*.

"No?" Jeb asked.

"All I did was sell her ghostlink!" *True (98 percent)*.

Unexpected anger flooded Jeb at Villo's horrifying admission, matched quickly by PBA-induced nausea. "You ruthless little shit. You *duped* her?" Dots danced before his eyes.

Genuine anger at another human was a primal emotion, a red flag to a PBA. If Jeb didn't calm his anger soon, this nausea would grow until it became unbearable. It would get so bad Jeb couldn't breathe, couldn't think, and eventually, wouldn't even be able to see.

That was how a Personal Brain Assistant kept one person from hurting another.

Yet what Villo had just admitted was the worst kind of cybercrime. A person's ghostlink—their unique identifier—was encrypted on corporate servers, set to read-only when a grayDoc installed their PBA. One of the most straightforward ways to access someone's PBA was to physically plug a line into the simport on the back of their neck, then use a banned script to dupe their ghostlink. Doing so required your target be drugged or very, very drunk.

The Sim detected and deleted duping attempts in corporate PBAs, but unregistered PBAs didn't have such protection. Once a troll had the target's ghostlink, they could make its owner *do* things. That was one of many reasons jailbroken PBAs were illegal.

"She was a poser, man, not one of us!" Villo shouted. "I figured he'd make her shave her head, get real tattoos instead of spray-ons. Pierce her nipples or some shit!"

"You thought Sheila Fisher didn't deserve to run with you," Jeb said, creeping across the car as those dots danced, "so you sold her to some random on the darkSim. Did you want her raped, Michael? Dead?" His vision swam as his PBA ratcheted up its warnings.

"I didn't know he'd do that!" *True (42 percent).* "He'd never done anything like that!" *True (62 percent).*

"Who?" Jeb felt his anger rising and reminded himself he didn't actually plan to *do* anything to Villo. "Who had never done anything like that?" He raised his metal fist.

"Galileo!" Villo shouted. *True (98 percent)*

Jeb sat back covered in sweat, breathing hard, and let his rage drain away. He focused on the grief of Sheila Fisher's parents, the overwhelming love he felt for his husband, and any emotion but rage at this thoughtless, worthless little punk. Gradually, his nausea faded.

"Shit," Villo whispered, slumping in his chair. "He's gonna' kill me." *True (95 percent).*

"How do you contact Galileo?" Jeb asked. His desire to knock out this kid's teeth had served its purpose, even if he'd never actually do it.

"Galileo contacts us," Villo whispered. "I don't know where he lives." *True (97 percent).*

So, Galileo was their puppetmaster. With a username like that, they certainly had delusions of grandeur.

Jeb opened his head desk and queried the name "Galileo" to refresh himself. After the *real* Galileo supported the theory of heliocentrism— that the earth revolved around the sun—the Catholic Church accused him of heresy. They arrested Galileo for his blasphemy and kept him under house arrest until he died.

Galileo was the handle of someone who felt the system persecuted them, someone who saw themselves as the smartest person in a room of people standing in their way. *That* was the type of person who would puppet an innocent girl into a shooting rampage.

"You've got one chance to save yourself," Jeb said. "A name. Who installed your and Sheila's PBAs?"

Villo trembled. "Promise you'll protect me."

"You have my word, Michael. We'll keep you safe." The olive branch Villo needed. "Now. Who installed your PBA?"

Villo slumped. "Doctor Barkov. He's in the Res Mall." *True (98 percent).*

"Damn," Cowan said, over wireless. *"You're good at this."*

Jeb deactivated his facial analyzer and breathed deep. He couldn't feel sympathy for Villo—selling Sheila's ghostlink was goddamn reprehensible—but Villo had a family too. If Villo's mother was working two jobs, she was doing it to give her child a better life, and maybe their lives would be better now.

Villo wouldn't go to jail for his crimes, not like in the days before PBAs. The Office of Mental Health would simply use Villo's new PBA to forever change how Villo made decisions, making him a better person. When they were done fixing how Villo thought, he'd still be Villo, just . . . not an asshole.

"Car, open," Jeb said. Hot air rushed into the car as the doors lifted. "Cowan, out." His trainee didn't question the order at all.

"Hey!" Villo struggled as they exited the autocar. "Where are you going? I need—"

The doors sealed Villo inside. It cruised off without a sound.

"So," Cowan said as he watched the taillights recede, "he just takes our ride?"

"The VI will deliver him to our cybercriminal processing center in San Diego," Jeb said. "They'll rehabilitate him there."

"Okay," Cowan said.

"Getting arrested is better than getting dead."

"Right." Cowan stared after the autocar.

Jeb glanced at his new partner. "You morally opposed to behavior modification?"

After a moment, Cowan shrugged. "I just wonder what it's like afterward. Getting your compulsions rearranged seems like it'd cause some issues."

Behavior modification—modding—was one of the many benefits of the world of PBAs. Engineers working for the Office of Mental Health could suppress inclinations toward bad behaviors and implant inclinations toward good ones. If you liked selling the ghostlinks of innocent women on the darkSim, for example, you'd stop liking that.

While Jeb *could* have analyzed Cowan for discomfort, he'd never do that. As Cowan's superior, he had that right, but what was allowed and what was decent sometimes didn't match up in Oneworld corporation. More times than Jeb liked, if he was being honest.

"Modding is better than prison," Jeb said. "Trust me, kid. I've watched the archives from the days when we stuffed people in concrete boxes with metal bars, and it isn't anywhere you'd want to be."

Jeb flipped over to his head desk and ordered a warrant to search Barkov's office. The order cleared in ten seconds. He blinked back into meatspace to find Sarisa's autocar waiting, the letters *OMH* glittered on its side.

He pinged her. *"Borrow your wheels?"*

"Fine," she answered. A one-word answer. Sarisa must be deep into it with the Fishers.

That brought a sense of calm to Jeb's heart. Villo's thoughtless actions had destroyed the Fisher family, but Sarisa would help piece them back together however she could. She really cared.

Her autocar opened after Sarisa cleared Jeb to assume control. "Let's go." Jeb waved Cowan toward the autocar.

"We're going to the doctor's office?" Cowan asked. "Will Barkov even be there this late at night?"

"He's there, kid." Jeb uploaded the new destination to the car's VI, then sat back as their borrowed vehicle cruised off. "When else would he install black-market PBAs?"

04

COWAN

The OMH autocar cruised to a stop in the empty parking lot outside the Reservation Mall: a strip of stores that offered everything from tanning services to carpet cleaning. The AR tags floating above each shop informed Cowan that at least a third of these stores were vacant. Business on closed circuit reservations got worse every year.

A massage parlor bookended the horizontal strip of storefronts, with a doctor's office beside it. Doctor Anton Barkov, MD. They left out, *"Installer of black-market wetware."*

Cowan stepped out when Forrester did, then drew his stunner. The firearm felt heavier than in pleasureboxes, with real weight on the back end. Firing at Michael Villo had made his arms tingle, and Cowan could swear he felt the capacitor spinning in the grip.

He'd been shot at today. He could have died just like those poor people in the Ventura Visions lobby, body blown open like rotting fruit. That thought left his heart pounding in his ears and his PBA working overtime to keep him calm. He didn't join the CID for action. It was supposed to be all scripting and paperwork.

Cowan had been shot at plenty of times in theory—he played as much StrikeForceGo as anyone—but pleasureboxes didn't simulate the agony of real bullet wounds. He figured getting shot felt way worse than a bee sting. He also knew you didn't merely stand in a penalty box for thirty seconds after you died.

"Cowan," Forrester said, "everyone is nervous the first time they confront a suspect. The install you received at orientation includes a hunt-and-evade package, as well as Krav Maga training. I'm uploading the unlock codes now."

The codes arrived, encryption strings Cowan didn't read so much as absorb. His vision flashed blue, and he adjusted his arms, holding his stunner correctly. Everything clicked inside his head, and that was when he realized his new partner hadn't called him "kid."

Things were getting real now.

Cowan Soto knew what to do if a suspect ran. He knew what to do if a suspect charged or raised a weapon. He even knew how to take down a suspect with his bare hands, and that was more intoxicating than he'd expected. For once in his life, he felt like a legitimate badass.

"One procedural issue," Forrester said. "If we run into another puppeted victim, don't stun him unless he threatens your life. Run away if you have to."

"That sounds dangerous," Cowan replied. "Why?"

Forrester's response came over wireless. *"The CID has scripts that can backtrace wireless connections."*

Cowan blinked. *"That's not possible."*

"If we encounter another puppet and take him down without stunning him, I should be able to piggyback on his wireless. Find out who's pulling his strings."

Cowan felt a chill as he considered all he must not know about PBAs. He had worked on them for a living, but much of the functionality was black-boxed. *"Phoenix was right."*

"Who?" Forrester asked.

"A buddy from back in the day. He claimed VIs were sentient, and the OMH would put you on a watch list if you fucked an underage waifu. Paranoid kid."

Forrester chuckled aloud. "You know what they say about paranoia."

Cowan steadied his breathing. While he was surprised Forrester had shared this fact, perhaps his partner was starting to trust him. It meant he might be doing a good job.

"Ready?" Forrester asked.

"Sure." Cowan's nerves felt rock steady, firewalled by his PBA's hunt-and-evade package.

"You want me on the back door?" Cowan asked. It was a bit strange to say that and feel qualified to do so.

"The guilty ones usually bolt out the back," Forrester said, leading toward the office. "You comfortable taking Barkov down if things go that way?"

Cowan remembered Sheila's body and her sobbing parents. "Yeah. I'm comfortable."

Forrester thumped Cowan's shoulder and pointed left, which Cowan now knew meant "split up." He marveled at his own quiet footfalls as he walked to the mall's end. He paused outside the alley between shop rows and contacted Forrester over wireless.

"Any chance Barkov has cameras outside his place?"

"A good chance," Forrester said, *"and his building isn't connected to the Sim, which means we can't open or lock down the doors. Be ready for a runner."*

Cowan stalked up the alley, stunner down and finger resting on the trigger guard. His eyes slid between a brown dumpster and rows of grimy exit doors until he reached the door behind Doctor Barkov's office.

The door out of the back of the doctor's office was battered and blue, with an old-style keypad on the wall nearby that couldn't be controlled by PBA or over the Sim. Closed circuits lived differently.

Cowan pressed his back to the plaster wall just past the door, where he'd have a second to evaluate anyone bolting down the alley.

"Ready here," he informed Forrester.

"I'm patching you my vision," Forrester said.

The view from Detective Forrester's left eye replaced the view from Cowan's left eye. Cowan saw the front door of the doctor's office, labeled with Barkov's name and a large red cross. Forrester's prosthetic hand rapped on glass and shook hanging blinds.

No one answered. Forrester waited, rapped again. Nothing.

"Doctor Anton Barkov!" Forrester's voice boomed from their auto-car's speakers. "This is the CID! We have a warrant to search your office! Step out with your hands raised!"

Nothing from Barkov. Nothing at the door.

"He's heading for you," Forrester said. *"Be ready."*

Cowan didn't hear anything, but he didn't have Detective Forrester's aural amplifiers. It was amazing that Jeb could hear Barkov's footfalls through the closed door. Cowan should upgrade his ears someday soon. The opportunity to access police wetware was a little intoxicating.

The door handle rattled—was it locked?—and then the door swung outward. A short white man with graying hair stumbled into the alley, wearing blue medical scrubs.

Cowan holstered his stunner and engaged the man from behind. His loafer-clad foot calmly kicked Barkov's feet out from under him, and then his steady hands caught the good doctor by both arms and dropped him to his knees in a submission hold.

Cowan paused momentarily, incredulous. He wasn't even sure how he'd just performed that incapacitating move, only that he *had* done it. The fact that PBAs could download muscle memory always amazed him.

Barkov craned his head toward Cowan and shouted, "Idiot!"

Only then did Cowan notice Barkov held an object in each hand—a large black box in one hand and a tiny remote in the other. Barkov clicked the remote. Cowan's world blanked in a burst of static.

When his vision cleared, he was slumped against the wall, and Barkov was stumbling down the alley, lugging that huge black box. Cowan's ears rang and his vision swam, but that wasn't what made his stomach turn.

It was the utter silence in his head. For the first time in a long time, Cowan's PBA was deactivated. His vision blurred as the world spun around him and his nose, no longer managed by his PBA, experienced a phantom mishmash of horrible smells. Every last emotional firewall fell.

Cowan felt sick as the memories his PBA had long suppressed returned. He remembered Corporate Security smashing through the windows of his and Ellen's home off Mission Beach. His throat clamped up as he remembered Ellen screaming at him to run. He remembered her tackling a CorpSec trooper and going down in a tangle of armor and elbows, sacrificing her own freedom to save his.

He had to find a way to free Ellen, even if it killed him. But to even *find* Ellen, he'd first have to prove himself to the CID. He'd first have to capture Doctor Barkov. So, Cowan pushed away the memories he could no longer suppress and focused on his job. Doctor Barkov was still running.

Cowan should probably get after him.

Blinking back tears, Cowan stumbled down the shadowed alley, pulled his stunner from its holster, and shouted, "Stop! Or I'll shoot!"

Barkov didn't stop. Cowan did, raising his stunner in trembling hands. He pressed the trigger. His bolt charred the wall by Barkov as the bad doctor stumbled into the moonlit parking lot, hampered by his car tire–sized black box. What was he carrying in there?

As Cowan ran after Barkov, he stowed his stunner, except he missed his holster, and the firearm clattered on the pavement behind him. So what? He couldn't aim it anyway.

As Cowan chased Barkov into the empty parking lot, he realized the lights in the parking lot were out, as well as the lights in the surrounding buildings. Was this a power outage? Some troll screwing with the power grid?

It didn't matter. Barkov was at a chain-link fence now, one blocking off thick woods. Barkov tried to toss his heavy black suitcase over the fence and failed. The suitcase bounced off the fence instead.

"Shit!" Barkov spun and pulled a glistening metal object from under his scrubs.

Cowan stopped dead when he saw it, and his hands shot up. It was a real, illegal gun. An old-style, gunpowder-based revolver.

Barkov pointed it at Cowan with both hands. Cowan trembled as he stared at the weapon and the doctor. He might actually die tonight, and he wondered if that would be easier than being forced to grieve for Ellen without an emotional firewall.

"You think I'm getting mind burned?" Barkov stepped toward

Cowan with his weapon raised. "For that *cyka*? No deal! Step back, CID, or I blow a shot right through your skull!"

"Blow a shot" was a threat from someone who clearly had yet to master English. Barkov's PBA was probably down as well, including his translation routines, so he couldn't be puppeted. That was the only positive Cowan could invent for a gun pointed at his head.

"I'm not going for him!" Barkov's wild eyes twitched as his arms remained rigid as iron bars. "You see me? I'm serious!"

"You're serious," Cowan said softly. A numb calm filled him. He was terrified, and he couldn't be more terrified, and that unlocked everything he'd hidden away. Everything became so clear.

He could be shot, and killed, and never wake up, and it wouldn't be the worst thing. The worst thing had been knowing Ellen's arrest was all his fault. Cowan had called CorpSec because he had been sure Oneworld's private police would protect them both. Instead, they'd arrested Ellen and taken her away.

Dying couldn't be as bad as betraying the woman he loved.

"I get it," Cowan said, keeping his hands raised. "You're not going down for him. That's reasonable. Want to tell me who he is?"

He had to stall Barkov until Detective Forrester arrived. Detective Forrester had to still be out there, right? His partner wouldn't abandon him.

Barkov blinked rapidly. "I want immunity! Protection! Understand? No mind burn!"

"Sure," Cowan said. "Whatever you want."

A tingle told him his PBA was spinning back up, but he'd have to rebuild his emotional firewalls and reinstall his hunt-and-evade package before it could help. He also couldn't ping Forrester or the CID, which meant local wireless was down as well for some reason.

"I want a new life," Barkov said, "somewhere nice." He shuddered, blinking, and Cowan wondered if his PBA had just spun back up as well. "Canada. Send me to Canada."

"We can send you anywhere." Cowan lowered his hands a bit, and Barkov didn't shoot him. Progress. So how would Forrester handle this? The olive branch?

"We'll get you protection," Cowan said, nodding first at Barkov, then at the gun. "But we need facts first. Did you approach Galileo, or did he approach you?"

"You know of Galileo?" Barkov lowered his revolver, and then the shaking gray-haired man actually smiled. "That makes this much easier. Galileo coerced me. He—"

Barkov's eyes went so wide Cowan could see the red parts. Drool sputtered from his lips and wet stained his pants as one hand dropped from the revolver. His other kept hold of it in a white-knuckled grip as his trembling arm bent at its elbow as his arm turned.

Cowan could see his lips mouthing the word *no* as the tip of the ancient weapon settled against Barkov's temple. He was being puppeted. Doctor Barkov was being puppeted. How was that possible without local wireless?

Cowan dashed forward. "Stop!"

The bang deafened him.

———

Twelve minutes and forty-two seconds later, Cowan sat outside Doctor Barkov's office on a sidewalk, alone. Darkened storefronts loomed over him. The parking lot's overhead lights shined once more, spraying shadows across concrete.

He watched four synthcops—police models in blue and white—load a black bag into an autotruck. They were taking Barkov's body to the morgue after he "committed suicide on the reservation"—the OMH story already archived at the Palmdale Sheriff's department.

No one with PBAs worked in Palmdale. No one wanted to be around closed circuits who could rape or murder the moment their unaugmented brains got out of control. Synthcops didn't worry about their lives, didn't feel pain or fear. They leapt onto the grips of the autotruck, hanging off like garbagemen as it rolled off with Barkov's corpse.

Detective Forrester took a seat beside Cowan, wads of Kleenex balled up in his ears. He thumped Cowan's back. "Nothing you could do, kid. He set off a goddamn EMP."

That had been the contents of Barkov's heavy box. EMPs were nukes for the prosthetic age, and real nukes hadn't been a threat since the leaders of all nuclear powers installed PBAs.

Cowan's ears still rang from the gunshot, not the EMP. All Personal Brain Assistants had surge protection, but Forrester had been linked to their autocar when the EMP fired. Feedback spurting over that connection had apparently knocked him out cold.

"Anything in Barkov's office?" Cowan asked.

"Junk data," Forrester said. "Whatever cleaner Barkov installed, it cleaned."

"So there's nothing in there to tell us who he worked for?"

"Afraid not."

"Who do you think he was working for?"

"What I *think* doesn't matter. We need proof, and I didn't find any in there."

That was more frustrating than Cowan liked. "Who would install PBAs in closed circuits? Why would they be puppeting kids from Palmdale?"

"Not everyone plays by the same rules we do here, Cowan." There Forrester went, using his name again. "Hackers like Galileo will always be out there, breaking the rules and hurting people. That's why we need the CID. To stop them."

Forrester was right, of course. That was the only problem with PBAs, the reason there were still murders, even if the numbers were down. Unhinged people kept screwing with the firmware.

"Don't lose any sleep over this asshole," Forrester added. "Barkov installed illegal PBAs in innocent kids. One way or the other, this arrest was the end of him."

Cowan knew what Forrester meant and thought it wasn't any comfort. Barkov's punishment would have been what the government called rewriting, and what everybody else called a "mind burn." Setting off an EMP was a capital crime, and the OMH dealt with those by remaking the culprit into someone who could function in society from the inside out.

Modding—making minor tweaks to a person's natural impulses

using their PBA—changed a few behaviors, like making them no longer afraid of spiders. It was safe and noninvasive. A mind burn, by comparison, basically made you into someone else. It erased all you'd been and created a new person, a loyal person. A person who was not you.

That was what the Office of Mental Health had done to Ellen, Cowan's Ellen . . . though probably not anymore.

"Tell the CID about the killswitch," Forrester said. "You're the one who figured it out, so you should add it to our report."

Cowan focused. "It's a passive script, always on, triggered by an emotion or concept in the brain." What he was saying now would go into the case file they delivered to Director Stanton, who ran the CID, and probably also be reviewed by a bunch of clueless bureaucrats up and down the Oneworld chain of command. He'd have to keep this simple.

Jeb prompted Cowan for more. "And snitching on Galileo triggered this killswitch, even though his PBA was still inactive?" They'd discussed all this previously, of course, but not while Forrester recorded it.

"No, Barkov's PBA had already spun back up when he tried to tell me about Galileo," Cowan said. "A scripter with a grasp of PBA firmware must have installed a passive scan in Barkov's PBA programming. It monitored Barkov's physical brain for the firing of neurons associated with Galileo and betrayal, and when those fired together, his PBA forced him to kill himself."

"So as soon as Barkov thought about betraying Galileo," Jeb said, "the killswitch in his PBA activated. No one was puppeting him. The compulsion was already buried in his PBA's programming."

"Right," Cowan said.

It sounded so simple when Cowan explained it that way, like an experiment or an exercise. Making someone blow their own brains out wasn't an exercise. He couldn't stop seeing those gray bits flying out of the side of Barkov's head.

"Good work, Detective Soto," Forrester said. Then, after a pause, "We're done." Forrester was no longer recording their conversation.

"Great," Cowan said.

"It gets easier," Forrester said, because he was apparently a mind reader or something. "But it'll never get *easy*. If this was an easy job, we'd let synthcops do it all."

"I know."

"So, is this the job for you?"

"What do you mean?" Cowan hunched his shoulders. Had he screwed up that badly?

"I've been doing this job for twenty-nine years," Forrester said, "and in that time, you get a feel for people. My feeling? You can do this. My question is if you *want* to do this."

Cowan imagined Sheila Fisher's body lying beside all those others, Michael Villo twitching as he convulsed from the stunner, and Doctor Barkov's brains exploding from his head. What would it feel like to haul this job home every night? The blood? The tears? The bodies?

Just the horrors Cowan had seen today were too much for even the most advanced PBA firewalls to completely suppress. The reason everyone used the mental health filters Cowan had disabled earlier today was so they never had to *see* dead bodies. Without the augmented reality created by his PBA to hide things that disturbed him, how much more violence could Cowan witness without permanent mental damage?

Then he imagined Ellen, mind burned, but still alive. He knew she was still alive—the OMH had no reason to kill her—and he was completely out of leads. Public searches found nothing. Private searches found nothing. Every favor he called in on the darkSim found nothing.

The Office of Mental Health's database was the only thing left to search, and the only way into the OMH database was through the CID. If they caught him snooping, they'd toss him in a dark hole, forever, but he'd risk that for Ellen, even if she didn't remember who she'd been before. He couldn't let her spend her life in a padded cell. He couldn't live with that.

"This job isn't what I expected," Cowan said. "I don't think it's even what I wanted." He remembered Ellen's smile, her hand squeezing his . . . before he betrayed her. "But I think it's what I need to do."

Forrester clapped him on the back. "Glad to hear it."

After a moment of cricket-filled silence, Cowan spoke again. "Detective?"

"Jeb," Forrester corrected. He smiled a tired smile. "You saved my ass twice tonight, but if you're going to be my new partner, you're going to use my first name."

"Great," Cowan said. "About this Galileo guy. You think we'll get another shot at him?"

Forrester—no, it was Jeb now, according to Cowan's latest orders—frowned and stared up at the night sky. "Depends on if he wants to amend his statement."

"His statement?" Cowan asked.

"Why do you suppose Galileo sent Villo at us? Knowing Villo might give him up?"

Cowan's brow furrowed. "You think he *wanted* to be caught?"

Jeb shook his head. "Not caught. Credited. You don't puppet people into shooting rampages for the lulz. Galileo wanted the CID, the OMH, and by extension, Oneworld, to know he did this."

"Why?"

"He wants us to know he can do it again."

PART 2

05

SONNE

"So disconnect him," Sonne told the pale-faced man standing in front of her desk. "If his credit is dry, his connection is too."

Her six-inch heels pinched her toes something fierce, but Sonne could deal with discomfort. What she *couldn't* deal with was idiots.

"That's just it, ma'am." The hired help—his name was Andrew, but she didn't really care right now—wrung his hands and grimaced. "I can't."

Sonne didn't have time for this, not tonight. She had real plans, with real people, in the real world. That was why she had wriggled herself into this incredibly tight dress.

"Ma'am—"

"The process is simple," Sonne interrupted. She was going to have to do another pass on her training simulations, because obviously they weren't cutting it with the hired help. "Slide off the protective panel on the lower portion of the bed, by the power plug. Press Menu to bring up the terminal options, and—"

"Choose Disconnect, Confirm, Confirm. I've tried that, ma'am, three times." Andrew was spending an awful lot of time interrupting her. "I showed it to Mick, and he said the simBed's locked up. He sent me up here so you could authorize a link pull."

Sonne stood fast enough to send her chair rolling backward. "Don't pull client hardlinks." She was going to need to talk to Mick too. "Don't *ever* pull a client hardlink."

A vision of throttling this stupid kid flashed through her mind, along with a hint of nausea courtesy of her PBA, but this wasn't Andrew's fault. It was Mick's influence. She would have throttled Mick, too, if she didn't know he'd enjoy it.

Andrew wrung his hands. "But, ma'am, Mick said—"

"Who owns this place, Andrew?" Sonne stalked around the table, got in his face, and pointed to the roof. "You see someone else's name on that fucking sign?"

Andrew's back thumped against the door. "I know that, ma'am! I know! But the simBed—"

"Do you know what the CID would fine me if we gave someone a brain hemorrhage? Pulling a hardlink without disengaging the client's PBA clamps wouldn't just mess up the link; it might fuck up their brain!"

No, she refused to let this idiot ruin her night. Tonight was about good friends, good liquor, and at least one good lay. Even in an age where you could scratch any itch somewhere in the Sim, Sonne craved connections that were more than just data flowing through PBAs.

Andrew pressed back against the door, eyes darting like a cornered animal. As Sonne watched him, she knew she was doing this wrong. This wasn't how you fixed a problem. She ran this business—it was hers—and tearing the skin off her befuddled employees wasn't good management. She took a deep breath, then exhaled slowly.

"So long as you're working for me," Sonne said, "you will not pull anyone's hardlink. You will disconnect a delinquent customer through the terminal in the simBed, and if that terminal malfunctions, you will come get me so that I can handle it."

Sonne strode from her office, heels clicking on cheap tile. Andrew followed. The aging TLEDS in the hall flickered—was some troll screwing with the power grid again?—and Sonne wondered if the power surges in Kearny Mesa were screwing with her simBeds.

It had to be something like that. Sonne had bought half her

simBeds from a parlor in Free Russia, trading away true love scripting she now wished she'd kept for her own waifus—interactive sex dolls that existed in her beautifully constructed pleasureboxes. Even with Sonne's refurbishment skills and a factory reinstall, her simBeds remained dodgy.

She threw open the door to the most popular waifu parlor in Kearny Mesa to find Mick blocking the door. He was a tower of Austrian muscle, with a neck as wide as a melon and a brain the size of a small one. He kept simjunkies from the door.

"Which one is it?" Sonne shouted. Her clients were too deep in their waifus to care.

Mick pointed. He didn't speak. He rarely bothered using his mouth, which was one of many reasons he didn't get many dates.

Sonne strode toward the problematic simBed. Her waifu parlor was the size of a laundromat, with beige walls and ratty carpet. Thirty lozenge-shaped simBeds filled the space in neat rows. She recognized the thin, balding client as she approached.

Carl Jennings had maxed his pension weeks ago. He'd probably stolen some poor sap's credit account off the darkSim, and now the sap had cut him off. She'd be on the hook for reversed charges, but she could afford that. She couldn't afford a lawsuit.

Sonne turned sideways to kneel in her tight dress and punched in the disconnect sequence.

"Error Code 0041" flashed on the terminal's tiny screen.

She grimaced and entered the code again; 0041 flashed again. Jennings's PBA was actually refusing the disconnect request, and that wasn't Andrew's fault.

Sonne stood, sighed, and rubbed her temples. She was going to miss dinner. She was going to miss dancing. She was going to miss her really good lay. She blinked into the Sim and alerted the CID. Her whole body tingled as a return ping confirmed her call.

"Ma'am, did you just call the cops?" Andrew asked.

"You don't miss much, do you, Andrew?" She wondered if he would miss the sarcasm.

"*Why* did you call the cops?"

Sonne stared out her darkened front windows at the disturbingly empty night outside and hated her life for a moment. "Apparently, we've got a hostage situation."

06

COWAN

Two weeks after his first case with the CID, now *Detective* Cowan Soto's autocar stopped in a parking lot framed by leafy palm trees. Jeb tapped the window and guided Cowan where to look.

He rubbed his dry eyes as he peered out. A square brown building stood against a darkened sky, and floating above one suite was an augmented reality sign: *Sonne's Sanctuary*. Bulbous letters shifted pink, blue, and red within wisps of mist.

Cowan didn't often frequent Kearny Mesa's simMalls—he had a fast hardlink at home and wouldn't be caught dead outside his own firewalls—but many who didn't have his security knowledge came here. They'd drain their bank accounts for quick thrills and pleasure, and, if the proprietor who'd called them was to be believed, somehow had gotten locked in the Sim.

Cowan downloaded the business licenses for the complex. He counted four waifu parlors; two adventure parlors, which could mean anything from undersea treasure hunting to competitive archery atop dinosaurs; and two edutainment parlors. Both were empty.

The first three waifu parlors held between three and six desperate romantics noodling with artificial paramours. *Sonne's Sanctuary*, by comparison, hosted thirty occupants—its maximum capacity—and a waiting list of horny clients twice as long. Sonne, whoever they were, was doing something right.

Jeb straightened and stretched after the two of them exited the autocar. He glanced at Cowan. "Sleeping okay?"

"I'm sleeping fine." Lying got easy once you did it enough. "I told you before, I've been busy."

"Don't be. Whatever you're dealing with during your downtime, set it aside or manage your sleep cycles. If the murders are still bothering you, all you need—"

"I'm not redacting them. It's how I stay motivated." Cowan started off toward the door of *Sonne's Sanctuary*, windows tinted reflective to hide what went on inside.

"Eventually, we're going to see another murder," Jeb said. "Another dead person. You plan to carry them around with you?"

"Not your problem, is it?"

"It is if the Office of Mental Health suspends you." Jeb reached out with his gleaming prosthetic hand and opened the parlor door. "I don't want to get stuck training another new guy."

Getting suspended for persistent depression was the last thing Cowan was worried about now. He'd already betrayed the love of his life and watched her erase her own brain, but he was still chugging along. He had to keep going because he knew Ellen couldn't.

"Let's close this one out and grab dinner after," Cowan said as he strode into a humming building filled with flickering TLEDs. "*Crazy Noodles?*"

Jeb stepped into the parlor behind him. "Nutrient bars taste exactly the same."

"Texture's all wrong."

"You and your textures."

Cowan stopped walking as a woman stalked toward them, jaw visibly clenched. Saying she looked a bit unhappy would be an understatement.

Cowan archived the waifu parlor. Three rows of lozenge-shaped simBeds cut the space into five open corridors. The whole place smelled of carpet cleaner and human sweat—a stink that Cowan decided to allow through his PBA's filters. Investigating meant seeing all the grime, or in this case whiffing it. Considering what went on here most nights, the smell could be much worse.

"Finally!" The parlor's owner was shorter than Cowan, with tan skin and a bright blond pixie cut. Smeared mascara surrounded her eyes. "Where the fuck have you been?"

An AR panel flashed above the owner's head with the words *Sonne Lambda, Owner*. As a CID detective, Cowan could access all Sonne's info with a cursory request, but that felt like invading her privacy. He wondered if Jeb felt the same.

"We came as quickly as we could, ma'am." By using the projector on his artificial hand, Jeb displayed their CID's logo. "Now, what seems to be the trouble?"

"I called you four hours ago!" Sonne jabbed a finger in Jeb's chest. "Did I forget to stress the word *hostages*?"

Cowan frowned as he considered the implications. Had she really been waiting four hours for them to arrive? Dispatch had assigned them this case ten minutes ago.

"We're here now, ma'am," Jeb said. "Now, before we get started, are you certain—"

"I programmed these simBeds," Sonne interrupted. "I pulled half of them apart and put them back together with my own hands, so if I say someone is holding my clients hostage, that's what's going on."

"Understood," Jeb said. "What exactly is the problem?"

"None of my clients can disconnect. Some troll has an external signal running into my simBeds, one I can't block, and that signal is keeping their hardlink clamps locked. So, let's fix it now, please."

"We'll certainly take a look. Why don't you show us where your client is, Miss . . ."

"Sonne." She pronounced it like *sauna*, which made Cowan glad he hadn't said her name out loud. "Don't you have that on your head desk?" She spun and stalked away.

"I never assume," Jeb said.

As they followed her through her place of business, Cowan wondered if a troll really could lock hardlink clamps. A hardlink was a small, grooved prong connecting a simBed to a PBA via superfast wire. Simulating a realistic world burned a lot of data, even by today's standards, so most people used hardlinks for the best experience in detailed pleasureboxes.

After a person inserted the prong into their auxiliary port below their left ear, tiny clamps inside their PBA locked it in place. Sonne claimed those clamps were locked now by some outside signal, but that was impossible, because you couldn't lock clamps without altering a PBA's firmware. PBA firmware was scanned constantly by Oneworld's servers, and any deviation from approved firmware booted you at once.

Connecting to the Sim wasn't like it was in those cheesy old movies. People didn't get stuck there because PBA designers weren't morons. Cowan knew this because he'd designed PBAs, some of the best, for Oneworld corporation. He'd been good at that, and Ellen had been good too. Their late nights working on PBA software were when they fell in love.

"There's nothing wrong with my hardware," Sonne said, interrupting his latest melancholy. "You Oneworld guys fucked up somewhere, and I'd like that fixed, please."

"That's certainly possible, ma'am." Jeb knelt at the simBed she'd called out. "And please understand, I'm not double-checking your conclusions because I doubt your ability to diagnose what's wrong. I'm double-checking because the CID requires it. It's my job."

After a moment, Sonne crossed her arms. "Fine." She still looked annoyed, but less so.

"I'll only be a moment." Jeb opened the maintenance panel and poked inside, flashing the fingerlight on his artificial hand around. "I apologize for the wait."

The gadgets on Jeb's prosthetic sometimes made Cowan jealous. Still, he wasn't going to get a perfectly fine body part replaced like some tech junkie. A PBA made sense even if it came with a port in your head, and a prosthetic made sense if you lost a limb in an accident, like Jeb. But *voluntarily* amputating your own limbs to replace them felt wrong.

As Cowan waited, doing nothing useful, he scanned the room for traces of distress among the other clients. No one was twitching, and not one moan escaped their lips. No one seemed upset by their predicament. Had any of them even tried to disconnect? Did *they* even realize they were stuck?

Jeb nodded, still crouched. "The bed's in debug mode, as you said, and I do detect an external signal. This man's PBA isn't responding to disconnect commands." He settled, cross-legged, and rested his hands on his knees. "I'm going to try and trace the external signal through your bed. To do that, I need your wireless security key."

Sonne's scowl returned. "You want my credit feed too? How about my ghostlink?"

Cowan took the opportunity to chime in. "We'll protect your privacy, and we'll delete your codes when we're done. Promise. You can even scan my PBA afterward to be sure."

She looked him up and down, and then her lips did this derisive smirk thing he kind of liked.

"Isn't one of you supposed to be the bad cop?" she asked.

"Ma'am," Jeb said, "I must insist."

"Yeah, I get it. I know my rights." Sonne blinked over to her head desk. "Or lack thereof." She blinked again, returning to meatspace. "Please don't delete anything in there."

Jeb closed his eyes. "Cowan, I'm dropping our LAN in case the unknown signal infects me. If I start acting strange or not responding, I'd like you to call for backup."

"Will do," Cowan said. "Be careful."

"Always am."

Then Jeb's eyelids twitched, once, as he went off to trace the suspect signal to its source. Even if they didn't believe it could lock hardlink clamps, going in using wireless was still safer.

Cowan figured he might as well get more information while he waited. "Miss Sonne? You believe the signal you detected is preventing your client's hardlink clamps from disengaging. How could it do that?"

"You're asking me?" she said.

"Absolutely. You know your setup better than anyone. If you were going to break into your own system, how would you do it?"

Sonne frowned again, but thoughtfully. "I don't know. Maybe another parlor drilled in and patched into my hardline. I guess that's possible, if they did it while it wasn't here."

"Why would anyone do that?"

"Maybe they decided to hack me from inside my own firewalls, screw up my beds and get my parlor closed for investigation. Maybe they don't like me taking all their clients."

Cowan nodded. "It looks like you're doing really well in comparison, so espionage seems plausible, but corporate PBAs are secured against external tampering. You can't lock hardlinks."

She raised one eyebrow. "So prove me wrong, Detective."

"Why don't we ask someone what they're seeing in there?" Cowan glanced at the motionless man in Sonne's simBed. "Have you tried asking him what's going on?"

"Wait." She narrowed her eyes. "You're serious?"

"Even inside simulations, people can still hear voices in the real world, respond, and even move their limbs." Considering her job, she had to know that about PBAs, which made Cowan feel foolish. The way her eyes narrowed worried him, but he pressed on. "That's one of many safety mechanisms. Have you asked this man if he's having trouble disconnecting?"

"Why, Detective Soto"—Sonne's lips twisted into that smirk again— "you really don't know how it works?"

He felt an unwelcome flush on his cheeks. "How what works?"

"Making tender love to your adoring waifu." She stepped close enough that he smelled soap. "Are you telling me you've never tried it?"

"It's not really my thing," he said, flailing for the calm of his hunt-and-evade package. He'd downloaded a waifu for simsex, once, but the conversation had been lousy and the sex forgettable. It also felt like betraying Ellen, though she'd been gone for half a year.

Sonne stepped past him and pointed at the balding man on the simBed. "My clients routinely load a full stem barrier while enjoying my pleasureboxes."

Cowan blinked. "What?"

"A full stem barrier means they can't hear or say anything, and they certainly can't move their limbs."

Cowan knew that, of course. "That's insane." Loading a full stem barrier wasn't illegal, but it was incredibly stupid.

The barrier completely disconnected your physical body from your PBA, cutting off connections to eyes, ears, and limbs. Getting trapped in that state . . . Cowan couldn't even imagine the havoc that could wreak on a mind.

"Why would anyone disable their body?" he asked.

"Here's a better question." Sonne gave him a sidelong glance. "Ever had a wet dream?"

The words *POSSIBLE HACK DETECTED* popped up so fast Cowan stepped back, reflexively swiping at the AR panel. An alarm beeped in his head, but it wasn't from his reaction to Sonne's statement, nor the flash of insight when it clicked, which was gross.

Jeb had just tried to reestablish a wireless connection, but Cowan's own PBA had automatically rejected it. His personal firewalls, several levels above corporate, believed someone was attempting a hack.

Cowan suppressed the alarm and knelt beside his partner. "You there, buddy?"

Jeb's eyes stayed closed, twitching. His PBA kept hammering at Cowan's, trying to reestablish their connection, and Cowan felt a chill when he realized Jeb's brain was *winning*. The wireless link they shared was unusually vulnerable to internal attack.

Cowan blinked over to his head desk and terminated all wireless connections, even his link to the Sim and the CID. He couldn't risk getting hacked, not with Jeb already in trouble.

His PBA still functioned, and he still had all the advantages it provided. He simply wasn't online any longer. That should protect him from being hacked and ensure he stayed in control of his own body.

"What is it?" Sonne asked, from somewhere close. "Did you trace the signal?"

Cowan flipped back to meatspace and found her kneeling on the other side of Jeb. He went to talk, then gagged a bit. The stench of Jeb's fresh sweat was nearly overwhelming. Something very bad was happening inside Jeb's mind.

"Um, my partner just got hacked," he said.

Sonne stood up and stepped back. "You are shitting me."

"I think your external signal can affect PBAs even if they *aren't* connected to a hardlink."

"Fantastic," Sonne said. "So, who the fuck do we call now?"

Cowan focused. He'd been a detective for two weeks, but Jeb had always been there, guiding and helping.

"Call the CID again," Cowan said. "We need backup, and I can't risk contacting them. There's a chance Jeb might infect me."

"Sure, okay." Sonne's eyes went distant, then focused. "Or not."

"What's the problem?" There was obviously a problem.

"That external signal I mentioned? It also seems to be blocking wireless calls."

"But you called us, didn't you?"

"Sure did." Sonne tapped her chin. "That means whoever's blocking me only blocked calls *after* I called you, which means you've just walked into a trap."

"Oh." Cowan felt an irrational urge to draw his stunner.

"Not mine, of course," Sonne said, frowning as if she'd noticed his expression. "I wouldn't be that stupid. But if whoever locked down my customers knew I'd call the CID, then waited for your partner to access my network over his wireless . . ."

She was right. Cowan knew she was right about the troll blocking their communications after Sonne summoned the CID. And worse, he had no idea how this troll had hacked Jeb.

"Do you have any nonstandard wireless in this building?" Cowan asked.

"Nothing. Everything is Oneworld legal and honestly, kind of cheap." Sonne peered at him. "What about you? Feeling particularly hacked at the moment?"

"No, I cut my wireless. All of it."

"Clever boy." She smiled again, which was odd, given the situation.

"I don't need some puppet shooting me with his stunner." Sonne waved over a white-skinned man as tall as Jeb and even more muscular. "Mick! Grab the tie-downs!"

"Tie-downs?" The only way Cowan could connect to anything now was through a hardlink plugged into his auxiliary port. "Why do you have tie-downs?"

"Some of the clientele prefer them to the Sim version. Being tied up in meatspace adds to the realism."

"Being tied . . ." Cowan figured it out. "Oh." More gross.

Mick, who was apparently Sonne's bouncer or something, went into the back and returned with two sets of adjustable cuffs linked by a black cable. Each cuff was lined with fur, or what looked like fur. Cowan wasn't going to check.

Sonne pointed at Jeb. "Cuff him. Hands and ankles."

Cowan thought about protesting, but Mick's stare murdered his voice in his throat. Mick yanked Jeb's arms behind his body and cuffed him like a pro, hands to ankles. If he did get puppeted, all Jeb could do was roll around and yell.

"Get his stunner, Detective Soto. We can't touch it legally."

"Good idea." Cowan opened Jeb's holster and retrieved the firearm.

"We've got a safe in the back," Sonne said. "We'll stow it there. Mick! Keep an eye on our new client." She strode off without looking back.

Cowan followed her into the hallway behind the parlor because he wasn't sure what else he should do. What was the protocol for dealing with CID-issued stunners when an officer was disarmed? Was it legal to store them in civilian safes? He couldn't check the CID protocol manual, because he was offline. He couldn't call for backup, and he wondered then if this had been Sonne's plan all along.

Was she *playing* them?

Sonne had already admitted she had the technical knowledge to tear down a simBed and build it back up, and the fact that her waifu parlor was so popular showed she knew how to script PBA interactions. Cowan wondered how big her terrorism insurance policy was.

Cowan slammed the parlor door and locked it, blocking Mick in the main room. He raised Jeb's stunner and aimed it at Sonne's back, and his corporate hunt-and-evade package kept his arm steady. "Hold it," Cowan said. "Turn and raise your hands."

Sonne stopped. Turned. Saw him pointing a stunner and jumped. "What the shit?" Her hands shot up.

"This is your parlor, your simBeds. You called *us*. If you've somehow hacked my partner and driven me offline, you can't possibly think that you'll—"

"I didn't do any of this," she said, glaring at him, "and I'm trying to help you fix it! If we go to my office, we can use my private hardlinks to find your partner and our troll."

"And let you lock down my hardlink clamps too?" Assuming that was possible, which it wasn't. "No. Not doing that."

"The ones in the office are on a different network. I don't share a pipe with customers."

That made sense, honestly. It was what Cowan would do.

"Prove it," he said.

"How can I prove anything if you won't let me actually *do* anything?"

She had him there. Cowan was already feeling guilty about pointing Jeb's stunner on her, yet this was all too suspicious. Was he overreacting? Sonne's hands began to drop.

"Hands up!" Cowan's finger pressed against the trigger guard.

"What are you afraid of, Detective Soto? Think I'll yank a stunner out of my ass?" She dropped her hands. "I'm in sweats! Want to know what I'm *not* wearing under them?"

She was trying to distract him again. "Now, listen. I'm not—"

"You need proof I'm unarmed?" She grabbed the base of her sweatshirt and pulled up, revealing a very bare stomach. "Shall we archive a striptease into evidence?"

Cowan's PBA kept his arm steady even as his thoughts scattered in a dozen directions. "That's not necessary. Just . . . hold it there."

"You're horrible at this." Sonne dropped her sweatshirt and shook her head. "Like really, really bad." That damn smirk returned. "How long you been doing this, two weeks?"

Lucky guess or not, she was baiting him. He couldn't let her get under his skin. He couldn't trust her until he was certain she wasn't involved.

Sonne sighed. "Listen. If I really wanted to lock down a CID detective, there are much easier ways to do that. Want me to list the people you work with who are regular customers? I could take any of you, any night, alone."

That was another good point. Logging a call to the CID to get them out here was foolish when people from his office already visited while off duty. It also left a record of her call, which would look really suspicious later. Why leave evidence that would implicate you?

"What we need to do now," Sonne said, "is rescue my clients, and apparently your partner. Which we can do, probably, from my office, through my hardlinks, which have dynamically generated firewalls. I'd like to see this troll asshole crack those."

Cowan's opinion of Sonne's scripting experience spiked. If she could script firewalls that advanced, she was talented enough to work for Oneworld. So why wasn't she?

Thirty paying clients a night and a waiting list answered that. If her parlor was making that much money, money as a motive also didn't make sense.

He glanced at the closed door. No one was pounding on it, but Sonne could summon Mick over the wireless. She hadn't.

"Does anyone else service your simBeds?" Cowan asked, keeping his stunner raised.

"My employees, sure. They all have access." Sonne crossed her arms. "You going to shoot me or not?"

Cowan thought back over everything he knew about PBAs from around the time Jeb would have been connected. Some still had legacy Wi-Fi ports separated from Sim wireless, once used to update firmware. Such ports should have been deactivated long ago, but overtaxed gray-Docs sometimes missed doing that.

If someone had installed an ancient Wi-Fi router nearby, the troll on the other end of that external signal might have managed to sneak in through Jeb's legacy port. Yet it would take a human to plant a router, and working museum relics weren't common.

"Who works here?" Cowan asked. "How many employees?"

"You're thinking this was an inside job." Sonne tapped one foot as her eyes went temporarily skyward. "I've got Mick and two part-time employees, all working for waifu time. Good kids but starved for cash."

"They'd take a bribe?"

"They'd take anything that wasn't nailed down, if they knew I wouldn't delete their waifus." She turned and walked toward her office at the end of the hall. "Once we get your partner back, we can track down who trapped my simBed."

"Hey!" Cowan protested. "Hands up, dammit!"

"You're not going to shoot me," Sonne said, without looking back at him, "and I'm not taking my clothes off. So stop playing with your trigger and come help me."

Cowan ground his teeth, then lowered Jeb's weapon. As Jeb had told him many times, *"Don't pull your weapon unless you're going to use it."* He followed Sonne and tried not to look peevish.

Once he actually stepped into Sonne's office, he stopped dead. It was beautiful inside, a huge vista with a breathtaking view of a forested mountain peak. Sonne had holo-painted the walls and ceiling of her office, creating the illusion of a vast space. He'd seen work this convincing before, but only a few times, and it always inspired him.

To his left, a number of trees he didn't recognize rustled in the wind. To his right, a waterfall poured into a shallow pool so real Cowan could almost feel its cool mist. Sonne's modest black desk—one of the only nonprojected features in the room—sat in a shallow river, with a much larger waterfall pouring down behind her.

The illusion felt so peaceful. So serene. He could almost feel a breeze tousling his hair, a warm sun beating down on his face.

"Wow," he said.

Sonne pulled a door open in thin air, revealing a floating safe. "You like?"

Cowan walked over to the waterfall painted on the office wall, extending a palm until he found the invisible surface. "You modeled all this?"

Her frown returned. "You're surprised?"

"Just impressed." Cowan settled Jeb's stunner inside the floating safe, which vanished in fake water when she closed the door. "I mean, this is really good. Oneworld quality."

Sonne sat at her desk and patted the seat beside her. "Don't compare my work to that corporate dreck. Office drones paint by numbers. They don't love what they do."

"Still." Cowan sat beside her on a rolling stool that appeared to be made of solid rock. "Damn good job."

A trace of a smile softened her considerably. "Well . . . thank you. And just so you know, I tried the CID again. Nothing. I think the whole block might be jammed somehow. Do you want to jump in your autocar and see if you can get a signal?"

Cowan considered. This mysterious cybercriminal had already locked down Sonne's simBeds and hacked Jeb. Someone that talented could easily hack an autocar, and the CID model he rode here inside didn't have manual controls. Being driven off a cliff or into a building wasn't his idea of a good time. They'd try this Sonne's way first.

"So how does this even work?" Cowan asked. "How do we find one person in all your pleasureboxes?"

"I tagged your partner with a tracer program when he invaded my simBed," Sonne said. "I needed to make sure he didn't go anywhere he shouldn't."

Cowan blinked like she'd propositioned him for sex. "That's illegal!"

"So's archiving my client list without a warrant," Sonne said, "which you CID assholes have done before. Besides, I did you a favor. My tracer will lead us right to your partner."

Cowan knew Sonne was right. He was the last person to berate someone for using illegal scripts, considering how often he used them to visit the darkSim and do illegal things, and charging her could make her life very difficult. He wouldn't do that.

"I get finding Jeb." Cowan maintained his sour expression. "But what about the troll?"

"Bonus question," Sonne said. "If our troll did all this just to hack a CID PBA, where would they be now?"

Cowan was being an idiot today. He nodded. "Hacking Jeb."

"Who we'll find with my tracer. And if it'll settle your stomach, I'll give you admin access."

Cowan breathed easier. "Thanks."

"I'm only offering because you don't seem like a complete tool."

He could do a lot with pleasurebox admin access. This was as safe as this was going to get. He could prove to Jeb that he could handle himself alone. Or maybe, more importantly, prove that to himself.

"Both of us," Cowan said. "Hardlinked with admin access. We dive in at the same time."

"Deal." Sonne pulled two glistening hardlinks from under her desk, raised one tip, and smirked. "Time to go do your job for you, I guess."

07

COWAN

Cowan opened his eyes in a square room with bamboo walls. A paper door framed by light-colored wood bore an impression of a Japanese dragon. The floor was soft gray tatami mats, their crosshatched texture as convincing as any he had ever seen, and paper lanterns hung in each corner, glowing with candlelight. Outside, trees rustled.

He glanced down at his body, which *wasn't* his body, and gawked. He was wearing a beautiful pink-and-white kimono with embossed flowers. It fell open at his neck, but that wasn't what made his eyes pop wide. It was the fact that he now had breasts.

"Enjoying the view?" Sonne chuckled. Her voice had an odd echo to it.

Cowan jumped up as she appeared behind him, as a muscular man in samurai armor. Her helmet was red with thin eye-slots, flared nostrils, and teeth that leered like he'd expect. The hilts of two swords jutted from her hips, one sheath shorter than the other.

Cowan touched his head and found long hair bound into a clump with giant needles. He had no sword, no armor, and when he stood, his elevated sandals made him wobble. This wasn't really the best avatar for chasing a dangerous troll through a pleasurebox.

"Why am I wearing a geisha avatar?" Cowan's own voice echoed as well, like it was coming through a long tube, and that assured him he and Sonne were speaking on an administrator channel. No one in here could see their lips move or hear them talk.

"We're disguised as NPCs!" Sonne marched past him, armor clanking like a pile of sticks. "This pleasurebox is occupied. If my client or our troll figure out we're admins, they might disconnect before we can catch them."

"I get that, but why not—"

"If my client sees people he doesn't know in here, he'll panic. Can't have him panicking when he can't disconnect."

Cowan had boobs now. "But can't you—"

"My samurai never patrol together, so we can't both be samurai, can we?" Sonne slid the paper door aside. "And while my geisha do travel together, then I wouldn't have any swords."

She was clearly messing with him. "Are you still mad about the stunner?"

"Give 'em a squeeze if you want. I won't judge." Sonne left the door open and stalked out of sight. "But move that perky little ass! We've got a troll to slay."

Sonne already had a head start, and she knew her pleasureboxes way better than Cowan did. Best not press his luck. He followed her outside, careful not to trip in his ridiculous sandals. The world beyond was just as impressive as the room.

Sonne had modeled an entire Japanese villa with long wooden walkways lit by paper lanterns. Pictures of geisha, birds, and dragons adorned its paper walls, and freshly made spirals filled the rock garden beside the house. It was gorgeous.

Despite all the advances in photogrammetry, pleasureboxes didn't build themselves. While it was simplistic to record and transfer the signals firing inside human brains, each brain processed those signals differently. Artists had to create computer-generated environments for PBAs to project inside a user's head, so everyone saw the same thing.

Cowan hurried after Sonne—at least, as much as he could hurry in these sandals—and walked behind her at a wobbly pace.

"How long did it take you to model this?" he asked.

"A few weeks, I guess?" Sonne marched along the wooden walkway with her armor clacking away. "I didn't model the pebbles. I just modeled one pebble and cloned it using a looping script to randomize the size, dimples, and orientation."

"So there's only one model loaded in the client's PBA." Cowan knew PBAs could only render so much visual data without causing noticeable corruption in the virtual world. "Good compromise."

"Glad you think so! But keep walking, please. I've set my geisha to wander off the path every so often, but they never gawk at anything for long."

Cowan blinked as a gentle wind caressed his skin—a subtle but effective piece of simulation—and a forest of bamboo stalks swayed beyond the paper lantern light. The air smelled like rain and grass and flowers. His sandals clopped audibly, wood on wood.

"My tracer's out at the edge of the pleasurebox," Sonne said, her voice still isolated to their private channel, "by the hot springs. Porting would assure anyone watching we're actually admins, so we've got a bit of a walk."

They passed another geisha, a simulated entity identical in appearance to Cowan. She respectfully lowered her head, and Cowan remembered to do the same. He was supposed to be an NPC, after all. "I still don't understand why you modeled all this."

Sonne didn't look back. "What don't you understand?"

"It's great. I mean, I could spend hours here. But do you really need a simulation this big so your clients can hook up with their waifus? There's not a lot involved."

"That's because you're accustomed to inferior product. That's what so many waifu parlors get wrong."

"How so?"

"You can get cheap simsex anywhere. I could point you to hundreds of virtual dolls you could down and fuck silly tonight. It gets old fast."

She was right—Cowan knew from experience—but he wasn't going to admit that out loud. One board creaked as he stepped on it, one among others that didn't, and that was another subtle touch. Sonne really did have a knack for authentic world-building.

"What keeps you coming back," Sonne continued, "is the emotional connection you form here. It isn't just sex. It's the experience. And that experience makes my clients fall in love with their waifus."

Cowan could scarcely believe that. "How do you fall in love with a VI?"

"You meet one that's convincing enough. My girls are all VI, not self-aware by any means, but they'd still ace the Turing test. My waifus adore their clients, and my clients adore them back, and the world makes it feel like a real romantic date. Not a back-alley meetup. That's my hook. That's what keeps you coming back."

Was she boasting? "Why waste that on prostitution?" Cowan asked.

Sonne's shoulders squared. "You going to moralize at me now?"

"No, I'd never do that. It just seems overcomplicated."

"Let me tell you why it's not." They stepped off the edge of the wooden platform and walked a path of white stones on black dirt. "Trafficking."

"Huh?"

"Our vaunted Office of Mental Health would love everyone to believe no one gets trafficked anymore, that our clear circuit paradise has no place for girls forced into sexual slavery. All they do is suppress the news. I give johns an alternative."

Cowan felt a pit open in his stomach. "These men are into sex trafficking?"

"I really hope not. Yet anyone can rationalize, convince themselves someone wants it, likes it, no matter the fear in her eyes. I'll build a dozen pleasureboxes to keep horny jerks satisfied if it stops one real person from getting raped."

Cowan respected the passion in Sonne's voice. Ellen had that passion, too, before she erased her own brain to save him from being sent to prison. Sonne shared Ellen's determination to make the world *better*.

"My waifus can't really experience fear, or guilt, or pain," Sonne said. "They're just simulations, and simulations don't cry themselves to sleep at night. And if any of my clients *does* do something to them a real woman wouldn't like, I report them."

"I get it," Cowan said.

"Do you?" Her voice had an edge to it.

"I do. And even if it didn't, it wouldn't be any of my business."

"Glad you think so." She didn't stop walking.

He'd probably just insulted her, again, but he'd done a pretty piss-poor job of gaining her trust already. What was one more misstep? He popped an admin screen to distract himself from overthinking it.

Options for time of day, gravity, and avatar pain threshold appeared, among dozens of others. He pulled a client list for this pleasurebox and verified he and Sonne were in admin mode. He doubted Sonne would lie, but he should have checked sooner.

His query returned three users: the two of them and Carl Jennings. There was no troll, and there was no Jeb, which meant Jeb must be hidden. Only admins could hide themselves from other admins, which suggested their troll was in admin mode as well. That wasn't comforting.

Her admin menu offered no guns, just a dagger, wakasashi, and samurai sword. Cowan wondered how well he could effectively swing that sword with his current body. This geisha avatar wasn't exactly optimized for sword fighting. Still, the sword had the highest attack power and an enchantment against spirits, so he'd summon that first if they got attacked.

They approached a forest of rustling bamboo lit by a full moon with a hint of yellow to it. Cowan considered all the tricks this troll could be using to enter this pleasurebox without appearing on the user list, and then he had a thought.

"Sonne, one question."

"Question away." If she was still pissed at him, she hid it well.

"When we were first discussing how that external signal invaded your simBeds, before Jeb got locked down, you said you thought a competitor might have drilled in and patched into your hardline."

"Sure."

"So, who are your neighbors?"

"The parlor next door caters to shooters, running boxes like Strike-ForceGo and DropForce. They do all right, but most of the gun nerds play from home these days if they can afford it."

"What about the other side?"

"That's History in Motion."

"Is that as boring as it sounds?"

Sonne actually laughed at that. "Historical recreations of presidential inaugurations and the Mars landing don't really pay the bills." She moved her armored head left and right, making a show of looking for simulated invaders. "So you think . . ." She waited for him to finish.

"Wouldn't it be perfect? Someone could break into History in Motion, drill into the walls, and patch into your lines. We know our troll is in this pleasurebox, but they don't show on your roster."

"Which would happen if they're accessing this pleasurebox, but not registered with my suite's overlord VI. They're registered next door." Sonne turned on him. "Shit, I think you're onto something. So do we hop out and break into the other parlor?"

A gust of wind caught Cowan's kimono, threatening to expose things he did not want exposed. What would Jeb do if he were here?

"No," Cowan said. "We don't risk violence in a physical confrontation. We lock our troll down here first, so we can end this external signal and call for backup."

Sonne turned back to the bamboo. "Makes sense."

"Also, what if they booby-trapped the door or something?"

"Exploding would be bad." Sonne led them toward a narrow path through the bamboo, marked by raised white stones.

Soon enough they came to a wide clearing with a large steaming bowl of mirrored water. Hot springs? Of course an environment like this would have hot springs. Still futzing with his admin panel, Cowan finally located avatar selection.

The first choice he found that seemed better equipped for their current circumstances was called "Kunoichi." He enabled it to give it a whirl. His body instantly changed to a svelte badass optimized for infiltration and sword fighting. Some class of female ninja, he suspected.

"Soto," Sonne said, and she sounded pissed again, "did you consider that our troll might be watching us right now?"

Cowan felt a hint of panic. "Are they?"

"You just revealed yourself as an admin."

Cowan scanned the trees, heart pounding, but it seemed to him he'd gotten away with it. "No worries. I think we're—"

A throwing star came flying from the bamboo.

Sonne blocked the throwing star with her drawn sword, creating a bright flash and a loud clang. Another throwing star glistened as it spun toward them. This one bounced right off Cowan's thin black clothing, making it obvious to anyone watching he was currently invulnerable. "They made us!" Sonne charged the woods. "Lock 'em down!"

Cowan sprinted toward the bamboo forest, drawing his kunoichi's balanced twin swords. At least he was ready to fight now.

Sonne swung her sword in a half-moon arc. A wave of fire roared through the bamboo, evaporating the stalks. The trees burned to ash as a distant shadow, a woman, waved open an exit portal and stepped through. She'd just jumped to another pleasurebox!

Sonne tapped at an admin panel that floated alongside her as she ran. "She portaled through a lockdown? That's darkSim-level shit!"

Something about that didn't add up, and Cowan's brain itched as he considered. "Wait!"

"Pleasurebox is unlocked! Make the jump!" Sonne opened a portal and leapt into the adjacent pleasurebox.

Cowan stumbled to a stop and stared at Sonne's portal. She had locked down the pleasurebox as soon as they arrived, with the troll inside, which meant no one could get in and no one could get out. So how had this troll opened a portal despite the lockdown?

They hadn't. Cowan knew they hadn't. You couldn't port out of a locked-down pleasurebox, and this troll simply wanted them to think he could.

Cowan flipped to his head desk and manually scripted a query for all entities currently rendered by the pleasurebox. Thousands. He filtered by those loaded when the pleasurebox spun up and found a deficit of

540, probably the bamboo Sonne had evaporated. He tallied ash piles and smiled: 542.

There were two entities in this pleasurebox that weren't being rendered by his PBA. Someone had disabled their visibility. Cowan swiped through admin panels until he found the option he wanted, and then poked "Unhide All."

A slim woman dragging a motionless geisha materialized a few meters to his right, pulling open another portal in the now *unlocked* pleasurebox. She wore a gray robe to her bare, twisted feet. Straight black hair completely obscured her face, which was just a bit unnerving. The nameplate above her head listed her as "ADMIN: Ringu Girl."

Cowan locked the pleasurebox down again, and the ringu girl's portal slammed shut. As her long dark hair turned on him, Cowan hit her with an administrative snare. She went stiff, locked in place, and dropped the limp geisha she'd been dragging by the hair: Jeb. Cowan advanced with his twin swords held out to each side, glistening in the moonlight. "This is the CID! You're under arrest!"

The ringu girl avatar vanished. She had flagged herself invisible again, but how? His administrative snare must not have stopped her from using her own admin panel, which was bad.

Cowan raised his admin panel as the ringu girl popped her thin arm right through it. Her long nails pinched and squeezed inside him, locking his heart in a vise grip. Cowan hyperventilated, panicking as all his internal firewalls dropped. She shouldn't be able to hurt him like this, but she *was* hurting him, and doing it while connected to the Sim.

This woman was a PBA hacker who'd somehow bypassed the Oneworld behavioral protocols that prevented her from hurting another human being. The changes this woman had made to her PBA's programming should have prevented her from connecting to any shared simulation, yet here she was in one, hurting him. The CID had a term for people who managed this.

This woman was a loose circuit.

"My detective is being obstinate." A creepy little girl voice whispered through her impenetrable curtain of dark hair. "Will you be more pliable?" She squeezed again.

Brambles ripped Cowan's veins, his throat, his skull. They forked and twisted and stabbed. He thrashed, shrieking, and even through the pain he knew something was very, very wrong. After what felt like an endless moment, she released his heart.

Cowan swiped desperately through his admin panel and found no relief. All his pleasurebox sliders were grayed out, including his PBA's pain threshold. This loose circuit troll had jacked it up to 10, full immersion. Nobody used full immersion, except daredevils trying to make a point.

Cowan couldn't disconnect. Somehow the troll had dropped a full stem barrier into his PBA without his permission, completely separating his mind from his physical body. None of this was possible, but it was happening, which meant it *was* possible. How could she do all this?

"She's not coming back, you know." The ringu girl was probably talking about Sonne. "She'll get back into this box eventually, but not in time to save you."

Cowan scrambled for focus. Now was not the time to consider the hows or whys. Now was the time to not get his heart crushed until he blacked out from agony.

"What do you want?" he groaned.

"CID detention records for every facility in California," she said. "You have thirty seconds before I hurt you again."

That was sadistically funny. This woman wanted access to the same thing he wanted, but Cowan couldn't risk poking around in CID records until he was certain they wouldn't detect his intrusion.

"I can't access those records," he said. "I just started two weeks ago!"

"You're lying," she said, "and I know because I can see every segment of your physical brain through the monitors in your PBA. Shall I hurt you again? I'll ask again after."

"Don't!" Cowan's avatar body seized up. "I'll do it! Just flip my wireless back on!"

He would do anything to delay more pain. Preventing people from causing pain to others was why everyone in the world should have a PBA installed, and it worked . . . except when someone hacked one.

"If you send any sort of warning to the CID," the ringu girl said, "I'll fry your brain. I can always get another detective." She flipped his wireless back on.

Cowan accessed the CID's database and initiated a detention registry download, knowing he had seconds before his request got flagged by CID leadership. As he started the download, he saw the opportunity he'd avoided ever since he was made an official CID detective. He activated the archiver in the hidden partition on his PBA and mirrored the download.

If Ellen was on that list, he might finally learn where Oneworld had imprisoned her.

The download completed, but the ringu girl hadn't tortured him despite his hidden archiver. That implied she couldn't detect what he was doing on his PBA's hidden partition, which meant he could do other things on that hidden partition too.

He quietly removed the pleasurebox lockdown.

A burning samurai sword burst through the ringu girl. She shrieked—a real, female shriek of agony and terror—and Cowan remembered then that a pleasurebox's pain threshold was global. This troll had done it to herself.

Still impaling her, Sonne dropped her armored fist on the ringu girl's dark head like a hammer blow. She ripped her sword free as Cowan's tormentor dropped. Mercifully, the girl's screams ended as soon as Sonne took her down. That meant she'd blacked out back in meatspace.

Despite what that troll had just been doing to him, hearing her very real, very tortured scream made Cowan ache with empathy.

Sonne raised her sword and staked the ringu girl to the pleasurebox floor. "Not going anywhere now, are you?"

Cowan could move again. He touched the back of the ringu girl's neck and activated the CID's backtracing program. He pulled her real name—Sarah Taggart—and the physical address off her hardlink. History in Motion, right the hell next door. He'd been right!

Sonne, breathing hard, glanced at the geisha slumped nearby. "Your partner?"

"Yeah. Nice job locking down that troll." Cowan hurried over to the naked white lady who was actually Jeb.

"How'd she get you through admin mode?" Sonne asked.

Cowan froze up. The Office of Mental Health would never chance anyone spreading the news that trolls could now paralyze people while connected to the Sim. They'd redact Sonne's memories of tonight and, most likely, throw in some behavior modification too. Modding and redactions dulled artists the worst, and Sonne wouldn't ever be the same after the OMH finished with her.

Cowan checked his wireless connection and winced. Archiving was active. The troll had likely spoofed their signals so the CID wouldn't know either of them was offline, but they knew now. Officer down. Backup would be coming from every available unit in San Diego, CID or not, which didn't give Cowan a lot of time to think. He had to think.

Cowan logged himself in, then forwarded Sarah Taggart's location and an arrest request to the CID. A confirmation that the Violent Crimes Division was enroute bounced back. He knelt by Jeb, wondering if there was any way to wake him up.

"Detective?" Sonne asked. "Soto?"

She expected an answer. So did the CID.

"It was my fault," Cowan lied, knowing the CID would archive everything he said. "I suspended my admin privileges. I wanted to test if my name would still appear in the user panel. That's when she snagged me."

There was no archive of Sarah Taggart paralyzing him through admin mode, but he had to tell the CID what had happened, eventually. Too many people were at risk. Still, by lying to Sonne right now and archiving it, he'd have a good argument for leaving her unmodded. She couldn't tell anyone what she didn't know, which might keep her safe.

"Seriously?" Sonne stomped over in her samurai armor. "You're going to bullshit me after all this?"

"It's the truth."

She glared at him, then rolled her eyes. "You're *so* lucky you were able to unlock the pleasurebox."

"I know," he said, relieved she was moving on. "Thank you for saving me. I'm sorry I can't tell you anything more. Regulations and all that."

"Whatever." She huffed again. "Who did this? What did they want from you?"

"No idea," Cowan lied. "I'd say go next door and ask her, but I don't think she's waking up for a while."

Cowan quarantined the full stem barrier afflicting Jeb: the hack that had paralyzed Jeb's body in the real world, preventing himself from disconnecting. He also made a secret copy for himself, hiding it away on the same PBA partition he'd concealed from Sarah Taggart. He couldn't let a script this impossible slip through his clutches.

He needed to figure out how this program altered PBA firmware without detection, how it evaded Oneworld's real-time scanning even while on the Sim. Cowan had spent years designing PBAs for Oneworld, considered every exploit and hack under the sun, and he had been very good at what he did.

Apparently, this Sarah Taggart was better.

Jeb opened his eyes and gasped, blinking and trembling. He saw Cowan. The flesh of his slumped avatar looked even paler in the moonlight, and his trembling eased.

"Cowan?" Jeb said.

Cowan nodded. He did still look like a badass female ninja, so he couldn't blame Jeb for confirming.

"Thanks." Jeb's voice was hoarse.

"No problem, partner." Cowan thumped Jeb's pale shoulder. "See you soon."

"Yeah." Jeb's geisha went limp.

Cowan also returned to meatspace and found Sonne sitting silently beside him, eyes staring at nothing. Probably cleaning up the mess they'd made in her pleasurebox. He plucked the hardlink from his head with a wet *pop*. His clamps disengaged without issue.

Sonne blinked. She popped her hardlink, set it aside, and frowned.

"So that's all I get, huh?" she asked. "Regulations?"

"That, and a glowing review in my official report of your role in aiding the CID." Cowan forced a smile he didn't feel. "Also, you're up and running again. So, hooray?"

———

As Cowan cruised across the Coronado Bridge at two in the morning, a glittering complex rose against San Diego Bay: Oneworld's San Diego headquarters. Corporate One was a hive of gleaming glass pyramids and blinking lights occupying the entire bay island once known as Halsey Field. Military drones patrolled both water and air around its restricted airspace.

Jeb sat beside him in silence, in the Sim, running a redaction routine that would erase his worst memories of Sarah Taggart's torture. It couldn't eliminate the trauma of that episode entirely, but it would be incredibly useful to whatever psychologist the Office of Mental Health assigned Jeb after this case. Being hurt like that wasn't something a person shrugged off.

Their autocar cruised through the maze of concrete barriers in front of the main gate, an armored behemoth with automated gun towers on each side. Beyond the gate were glass pyramids housing the Office of Mental Health, the Violent Crimes Division, the Cybercrimes Investigation Division, and Corporate Security, among many others.

Closing Sonne's case had been relatively straightforward. Cowan soon found hidden payments to Andrew West, waifu parlor employee. Andrew confessed the moment CorpSec kicked down his door, but he had no idea who paid him. The best (or worst) thing about money trading hands on the darkSim was that it remained anonymous.

Cowan and Jeb entered Corporate One, walked past a dozen milsynths—military synthetics that were mostly humanoid in appearance, like thin armored soldiers—and rode up twenty stories in a mirrored elevator. Cowan followed Jeb into a tiled, glassed-in hallway. A lone janitor in white scrubs buffed the floor, whistling.

As they passed, Cowan recognized the janitor and spun around, pinging Jeb on wireless. *"Hey, that's Michael Villo!"* The asshole who sold Sheila Fisher's ghostlink to Galileo.

"Yup." Jeb kept walking.

"They gave him a job as a janitor?"

"A good job with decent pay. Much better than a cell."

Cowan grimaced as he imagined Ellen wearing that same vacant smile. He imagined her scrubbing floors and windows in another building, modded into her own happy little world. He'd find her. He had to find her. He still had the CID's detention registry waiting on the hidden partition of his PBA but couldn't access it until he was alone. Waiting hurt.

Cowan followed Jeb through a mess of tall gray cubicles. Some were still occupied by his coworkers despite the late hour. A few people he'd met during orientation looked up, and one nodded, but Cowan didn't nod back. He hadn't joined the CID to make friends.

They entered an office with faux wood walls, deep blue carpet, and a huge oak desk. Director Ivana Stanton—or rather, a holographic projection of her piped in from the CID's corporate airship—stood behind the desk. She had a blond crew cut with bits of gray at the temples, and she wore a crisp brown pantsuit. Her mouth was a hard line.

"I've reviewed your archives of the incident at this waifu parlor," Stanton said. She had a very noticeable Russian accent, which was odd, because PBAs could erase accents so everyone in Oneworld coalesced. "I'm satisfied your report summarizes what occurred, but there is one bit on which I need clarification." She turned to Cowan. "What the fuck were you thinking, Detective Soto?"

Cowan flinched. "Sorry?"

"Did you really think allowing a troll to access the CID's detention registry was an acceptable plan?" The way she glared made him involuntarily hunch his shoulders.

"Ma'am," Cowan said, "I merely pretended to give her access. I did that so she wouldn't notice when I opened—"

"She downloaded a full detention registry."

"I'd stopped her before she could do anything with it. Once the pleasurebox was open again, I was certain Sonne—"

"Do you understand the stink a troll could raise if they published a classified list of current CID detainees on the darkSim?"

Cowan did, but he went another way. "If I may ask, ma'am, what would you have done instead?"

That only increased Stanton's glare. "You expect me to do your job for you?"

"Not at all, ma'am, but you've been doing this a lot longer than I have. I understand I acted rashly, and I apologize for screwing up. So, what should I have done instead?"

Stanton glared for another moment, then relaxed and looked to Jeb. "Good. He can be taught." She turned back to Cowan and stuck out a finger. "You're suspended for a week."

Cowan winced. Had that all been an act, to test him? It didn't matter. If they'd kicked him out, he'd never find Ellen. This was best-case scenario.

"Ma'am, if you don't like the way I handled things—"

"Figure it out," Stanton said. "When you return, I'll expect you to deliver a report of five other courses of action you could have taken, none of which compromise the CID's classified archives." She pointed to the door. "Dismissed."

"Yes, ma'am." Jeb turned as Stanton's hologram vanished. He walked out the door of her now empty office.

Cowan followed and contacted Jeb over wireless. *"Wait, that's it? She chews me out, suspends me, and assigns homework?"*

Jeb smiled. *"She can't really complain about the results. You stopped a dangerous troll, archived an unknown and highly illegal script for study, and saved your partner. Don't let an ass chewing shake your confidence. It's her job."*

"So, you think I did the right thing?"

Jeb led him toward the elevator. *"I think you did a thing, and that thing worked—this time. This job is hard calls and gut checks. No archive is ever going to show you a road map. At the end of the day, if you solve the case and come out alive, you did good."*

Maybe Jeb was right, but Cowan didn't *feel* good.

"What the hell was going on with Sarah Taggart?" Cowan asked.

"Paralyzing people over the Sim, with a full stem barrier, isn't supposed to be possible." Cowan knew it was, now, but he wanted to know how people were doing it.

"So," Jeb said.

"Do you think . . ." Cowan remembered the CID archived all wireless conversations. *"Will they let us keep it?"*

"Keep what?"

"Our memories of what happened in there?"

"If the Office of Mental Health was going to redact our memories, we'd be heading down to the rewriting center right now, not going out for noodles. We're going for noodles, so we're okay."

Cowan relaxed. *"Because they trust us to keep our mouths shut."*

"No, because they're watching us through our own eyes, monitoring everything we do on and off duty. Granting permission for twenty-four-hour in-eye surveillance was right there in the NDA you signed when you came on board. You get used to it."

Cowan's calm burned away like those bamboo stalks in Sonne's pleasurebox. *"Oh."*

———

SEPTEMBER 2, EARLY MORNING

"Lights," Cowan said. He walked into a dark room as his apartment's VI flipped everything on when he got home. It would be light in an hour, which meant he'd had a *really* long night. Of course, since he was suspended now, he'd have a week to sleep it off. Great.

"Welcome home, Mister Soto." The VI's voice sounded British and female. They always sounded British and female. "Did you have a productive day?"

Cowan's new apartment was a shoebox. The hallway led past a tiny bedroom to a single room split into living area and kitchen. There were no real windows, just a glass patio door with a great view of the apartment building across the way.

Cowan enabled augmented reality, allowing his PBA to alter his perceptions of reality. Instead of his dingy apartment, he now saw a pleasant cabin in the middle of the woods. It even smelled like cedar, thanks to his olfactory processor.

A hardwood floor gleamed in bright sun. The walls were cut logs, and huge glass windows looked onto an expanse of leafy trees. Dozens more rustled beyond his patio window. The scenery relaxed him enough to focus on the problem at hand.

The Office of Mental Health was archiving everything he saw through his own PBA, through his own eyes. They knew he'd spent the last two weeks diving into the darkSim, searching for any links to Galileo, and they hadn't come after him. Why wouldn't they?

Connecting to the darkSim was highly illegal. The CID must be collecting as much evidence as they could before dropping the hammer. Why arrest him when they could archive everything he did? He'd snitched on his darkSim friends without knowing, and he felt terrible about that.

Fortunately, those Cowan associated with on the darkSim were pranksters, and he didn't know their *real* identities. The darkSim was an independent network run out of Switzerland, a prototype Sim, and it anonymized everything. So, while the OMH had the handles of his friends and whatever avatars they'd worn there, that was nothing, really.

Still, being spied on was less than ideal. He'd never find Ellen if the Office of Mental Health was watching him all the time. It was time for a calculated risk.

Cowan got ready for bed, then accessed the private partition in his PBA. It was a partition that existed, to his knowledge, in no other Personal Brain Assistant on the planet. It was the secret that ended his and Ellen's former lives.

He climbed into bed and called up a book on his panel projector. While pretending to read, he activated the partition hidden from the OMH. He mirrored what his PBA was transmitting to the Office of Mental Health, just to check, and it was indeed everything.

He deactivated the reading panel, ordered his lights off, and closed his eyes. He archived his closed eyes on his hidden partition for a full ten minutes. Then he opened his template bin, pulled out the appropriate constructors, and scripted.

It took him almost twenty minutes to finish—for him, a long time—but the result was exactly what he needed: an endless randomized loop of his closed eyes as he slept. He swapped the loop over the feed his PBA was broadcasting to the Office of Mental Health.

No alarms sounded on his head desk. No remote lockdown took his apartment. The Office of Mental Health thought he was asleep, and they would continue to think that so long as his archive looped.

Cowan sat up on his bed, opened his eyes, and projected the enforcement registry he'd downloaded for Sarah Taggart in augmented reality. He scripted a string query, searching for Ellen Gauthier. Why had Sarah wanted this list so badly? Had she lost someone to a mind burn too?

The query would take time—the registry was heavily encrypted—so Cowan pondered all he'd seen tonight. Forcefully engaging hardlink clamps. Inserting a full stem barrier in someone else's PBA to paralyze them over the Sim without getting booted offline. How had Sarah done it?

You could knock a person out in meatspace and insert a full stem barrier over a hardlink, but that required physically disabling them. Jailbreaking your PBA to disable behavioral protocols also prevented you from connecting to the Sim. People with modified PBAs couldn't connect to other people there.

Yet Sarah Taggart had done just that.

She was a loose circuit. She had stayed connected to Sonne's pleasure-box and, through that, the Sim at large, despite jailbreaking her PBA and literally torturing both Cowan and Jeb. That was impossible, unless . . .

Cowan knew it *was* possible to connect to the Sim without active behavioral protocols because he had done it. He and Ellen had done it, together, before he betrayed her to Corporate Security. Yet the firmware they'd created was destroyed, erased, like her.

That wouldn't stop someone else from trying the same thing.

Yet even if Sarah Taggart had created another set of loose circuit firmware that bypassed the Sim's real-time scanning, she still couldn't update the firmware on another person's PBA. Doing that was the only way to insert a full stem barrier, which she had done to Cowan. Cowan's string query finished processing the CID enforcement registry, and there was no Ellen Gauthier. Not finding her hurt—failing Ellen always hurt him—but at least he knew the CID hadn't abducted her. One less horrific fate to keep him up at night.

Another name did appear on the CID's enforcement registry: Ethan Taggart. He would be Sarah's older brother, and it explained why Sarah had been so desperate to find him. The CID had arrested Ethan for identity fraud six months ago. He was still in custody.

Ethan's records showed some modding, probably so he wouldn't want to steal people's identities, but Ethan was still himself, for the most part. So why keep him locked away in a rewriting facility? Why not release him back to his family?

Cowan knew Sarah's requests to see Ethan had fallen on deaf ears. Oneworld financed the courts, and the courts supported Oneworld corporation. Cowan had learned that while failing to find Ellen in the weeks after her arrest. That didn't excuse Sarah's crimes, but it did explain her motivation. She'd lost her brother to the OMH.

Was Cowan doing the right thing, putting people like Sarah away for the CID? He couldn't know, and honestly, it didn't matter. This was the only way to find Ellen, so he'd do whatever he had to until he found her.

Morality? He'd worry about that later.

Cowan filed the CID's detention registry away, along with Sarah Taggart's paralysis scripting, in his PBA's private partition, where the CID could never find it. He and Ellen had made certain they couldn't.

The truth was, to the OMH, Cowan Soto would be considered a loose circuit. And they would burn him a new mind if they ever figured that out.

08

SONNE

The autocar dropped Sonne off at Sharp Memorial just before lunchtime, dressed for the heat in shorts and a loose T-shirt. She was there to visit Taylor Lambda, CEO of Benzai Corporation. But more than that, he was the man who'd adopted her after her biological parents died.

She finally knew why he might be in a coma.

Sonne entered the lobby and rode up a mirrored elevator, then walked down several well-lit halls. The coma unit was where Taylor had rested for the past year, living but unable to wake up. Just like CID Detective Jeb Forrester had been the night before.

Sonne slid the door to Taylor's suite open and found her sister Kate sitting in silence. Kate Lambda was Taylor's biological daughter, so she shared her father's short hair and Asian features, but the Lambda lineage was more complicated than a region. Like Benzai Corporation, the Lambdas were multinational. Kate was dressed nicely, in a dark skirt, blouse, and flats, but Kate was always dressed nice.

She looked up as Sonne entered, then smiled. "Hey, sis."

"Hey." Sonne sat by Kate and stared at their unconscious father. Taylor's once vibrant skin was pale, his cheeks sunken. His muscles had atrophied in the coma, despite a constant regimen of forced muscle stimulation. Nothing the doctors tried woke him up.

There was no physical reason Taylor wouldn't wake up. It was like someone had locked his PBA and swallowed the key.

Kate tapped her feet rhythmically on the floor. "Did you bring it?"

"Yes." Sonne popped a linkline into the auxiliary port below her left ear, then offered the other end to Kate. Kate brushed back her dark hair and plugged the linkline into her own port. With a perceptible tingle, they were connected.

I was able to keep all my logs from last night, despite those assholes trying to delete them, Sonne said directly into her sister's mind. Untraceable. *The one you'll want is Japanese Teahouse.* She uploaded that to Kate's PBA, along with all the others. *That's where last night's troll paralyzed that detective.*

Kate stared at their father. *You're sure the troll inserted a full stem barrier into the detective's PBA, over your network? Even though that's not possible?*

It is possible, because she did it. She locked them both down, Katie, and at least one was in admin mode when it happened. That's not possible, is it?

So far as we know.

But it happened to Dad.

Yes. Kate sighed and closed her eyes, recalling that awful day a year or so ago. *It happened to Dad.* She popped the linkline out and opened her eyes.

"I'll look over things tonight," Kate said, out loud this time. "If I find anything, I'll let you know."

"Thanks," Sonne said.

"I read him all the latest financials," Kate said, "like I always do. So he'll know his company's doing okay without him. So he'll know we're still alive."

Sonne squeezed Kate's hand. "I'm sure he appreciates that."

"I'm done with reports for today. Reports are dumb. I need a break."

"I'm with you. Sim time?"

"Hell yes!" Kate grinned. "Want to run the Lamia Cave in Kanthe-mar one more time?"

Sonne didn't, but she knew Kate did. "Yes. Let's."

PART 3

09

LEROY

The swampy sawleaf jungles of Arcadia Four were steamy, muddy, and crawling with spine beetles, but [N]moset—or Leroy Keller, as he was known back in the real world—wouldn't have it any other way.

Most StrikeForceGo teams hated this pleasurebox, but Team Grindhouse lived here. They knew this battlefield better than anyone, and Team FunBags would soon be praying for deliverance.

[N]moset hadn't moved for over five minutes, yet his view-stream kept growing. He was up to 9,432 on his last update, and donations kept pouring in. His loyal viewers camped with him, anticipating the moment when he'd fire his rifle and drop an enemy soldier.

"Contact." Sn0wing's voice crackled in [N]moset's ear-comm. "Three bags and a droid on the high road."

[N]moset shifted his TechSniper rifle and pressed an eye to the rubber scope. He tweaked the focus until he had a clear view of the high road, an open stretch of muddy road cutting through a jungle of purple-gray sawleaf trees. His targets came into view.

Team FunBags rounded the bend, crouching behind their Shield-Drone. The rolling robot's extended panels armored them against frontward fire, and while its big tank treads couldn't handle swamp, they worked fine on the open road. They rolled right past the bush that concealed Sn0wing.

[N]Moset's heart thumped as he activated a glowing targeting beam only he could see. Would the admins detect it? Of course not. He was way too smart for the admins.

The ShieldDrone trundled forward as the mail slot in its armor plate danced like a candle flame. Nemo adjusted his targeting beam as it locked onto one target, then another, then another, all the while threading the mail slot. He pressed his trigger.

His TechSniper climaxed with a bang that echoed across the sawblade trees. Two full seconds later, his armor-piercing round slipped through an opening no bigger than a book. Grim[Kin]'s shield vanished, and her underlying health bar dropped into the red.

[N]moset worked the bolt, ejected the round, loaded a new one, and slammed it home. His rifle followed EzChilled of its own volition as the idiot hopped atop the ShieldDrone, searching for the sniper. *Stupid kid.* [N]moset fired, and EzChilled dropped, head-shotted.

No one on his team bothered complimenting [N]moset's shots. [N]moset made those often enough that people were only surprised when he *didn't* hit something. It made [N]moset feel good to be like a god here, envied and admired across the Sim.

He had two targets left. As his finger floated above the trigger, white-hot pain tore open [N]moset's head . . .

    *&^−−−−−
    −−−−−−^&*

. . . Leroy Keller screamed. His body spasmed as shadows replaced Arcadia Four. He tumbled out of his ergochair and hit the carpet so hard spots flashed before his eyes.

He was back in his real-world apartment. Why was he in his apartment?

Someone had ripped out his hardlink! There was a shadow in his room, or no. His Kalinda-waifu-bot was in his room. What was it doing in his room? She was supposed to be on her charging station!

"Hello, Leroy." His very expensive sexbot straddled him and pushed him down, far more roughly than he was used to. "It's time to play a game."

10

JEB

"So, Cowan." CID Detective Jeb Forrester flexed his artificial hand and watched numbers tick inside the glossy black elevator. "What do you know about the VCD?"

"Violent Crimes Division." Cowan was fresh off his suspension and seemed eager to work. "All former soldiers, people whose PBAs already had a HARM switch installed."

Jeb kept his expression neutral, but it surprised him that Cowan even knew what a HARM switch was. Most didn't. Most would be kind of worried if they knew Corporate One could flip a switch in an agent's brain and allow them to harm or kill people.

Did Cowan know about HARM switches because of his work as a PBA engineer before he'd joined the CID?

"That all?" Jeb said.

"Um . . ." Cowan's eyes went distant. "Wasn't there a story years ago, about a VCD cop who went rogue? Found a way to flip his own HARM switch and killed three officers?"

"Two." Jeb turned his gaze to silver elevator doors. "One survived and put him down."

The Office of Mental Health suppressed all news suggesting you could hack PBAs, which left only one place Cowan could have learned about fratricide at the VCD: the darkSim, an enormous restriction-free network based in Switzerland. It mirrored the functions of the Sim and was illegal to visit from the United States, but Jeb knew a great many people did.

Visiting the darkSim was a moddable offense, and Cowan had just all but told the CID he'd been there. The kid really needed to be more careful, but Jeb couldn't mention that while the CID archived this case in real time, through both their eyes. He'd warn Cowan later, over noodles, on wireless.

"Who's the soldier who lived?" Cowan asked. At least he didn't know *that.*

"Captain Barondale," Jeb replied. "She's one of the soldiers we'll be working with today, actually." The elevator doors rumbled open. "Don't ask her about that incident. It's an old wound."

The last thing he needed was Naomi Barondale hearing anything Cowan had just said. The darkSim was where the person who hacked her squad got the tech he needed to do so. Since then, Naomi had been a real stickler for the rules.

They stepped into a hallway on the eighteenth floor of one of San Diego's luxury stackhomes. Gleaming silver baseboards ran along walls of padded black, with recessed lights providing a soft glow throughout. The floor was soft carpet with a winding floral pattern. If Cowan was impressed by the opulence, he didn't let on.

Jeb led them down the hallway to a door two from the end, covered in a projected Crime Scene Barrier. It cast a sickly yellow glow across the carpet. Jeb glanced at Cowan and spoke again.

"Captain Barondale's partner is Santino Zhang, a Marine. He served two tours in Peru during the recent unpleasantness and earned some prosthetic legs on the way out."

"He step on a mine?" Cowan asked.

"IED shredded his tank. He had the option to get realistic legs with synthflesh but opted for gleaming metal instead."

"Why?" Cowan asked, wide-eyed.

"He likes fucking with people who stare at his legs," Jeb said. "So don't."

"So he's a troll," Cowan said and visibly relaxed. "That's the one type of person I deal with all the time. I won't let Zhang get to me."

Jeb almost smiled. "Never had a doubt."

The text of the floating Crime Scene Barrier repeated inside their PBAs: *"Access Restricted. Trespassers Will Be Prosecuted. Access Restricted. Trespassers . . ."*

Using the projector on his artificial hand, Jeb projected the CID logo in front of the door. He simultaneously pinged the VCD's general channel over his PBA's wireless to alert those inside the room. Two-step authentication would ensure those already investigating that he was who he said he was, and that he was authorized to be here.

The metal door popped open as the barrier faded to reveal VCD Detective Santiago Zhang, oversized prosthetic boots filling the doorframe. Zhang's artificial legs started at midthigh. They looked like gleaming pistons, wrapped in rings, stuffed into metal feet. He wore shorts, a black armored vest with the letters *VCD*, and fingerless biking gloves.

"Forrester." Zhang bumped Jeb's metal fist. "Good to see you, brother." He smiled at Cowan. "Hey there, little buddy!"

To his credit, Cowan didn't react to Zhang's derisive greeting. He simply said, "Detective Cowan Soto," and offered his hand, challenging Zhang to repeat what he'd just said without acknowledging it.

Visibly thrown off by Cowan's complete lack of reaction, Zhang hesitated. Then he shook Cowan's hand. "Zhang, VCD."

"So why'd you call us in?" Cowan asked, all business.

Jeb resisted the urge to laugh at the visible disappointment on Zhang's face. The Cowan Soto who'd started working with him almost a month ago would have flubbed this hard. Jeb liked knowing he could still teach.

"The ant swarm just finished their sweep." Zhang frowned as he cleared the door. "The captain's finishing up the remote autopsy. Should have Keller's cause of death soon."

"Leroy Keller lived alone?" Jeb's briefing had specified one murder, but he never trusted briefings, especially when the Office of Mental

Health routinely suppressed facts from those who didn't need to be in the know.

"Keller's parents live in La Mesa," Zhang agreed. "They authorized the autopsy ten minutes ago."

Jeb was glad he hadn't handled that call. Notifying people their loved ones were dead was the worst part about his job. Next time he saw Sarisa, he would ask how Sheila Fisher's parents were doing.

He took a quick look around Keller's apartment. Its wide curtains hung open, allowing natural afternoon light to fill the apartment. Augmented reality evidence tags floated on the plush brown carpet, and on several rips in the black leather couches. Those surrounded a dirty glass table piled with empty food cartons.

All the evidence tags were checked out by Captain Naomi Barondale, which meant Jeb didn't have to worry about missing details. Naomi was one of the most competent cops he'd ever met, but that wasn't surprising, given her mother had run corporate contracts before the Lathan-Faulkner Act. Arcasia Barondale was practically a legend these days.

Keller's long shelves held a kitschy mishmash of action figures, glistening metallic trophies, and actual paper books. Behind those, vista windows looked out over San Diego's hazy sprawl. This was an expensive apartment. Very expensive. But pro-gamers made far better money than a twenty-year veteran of the CID. Especially those involved in StrikeForceGo.

Jeb turned to Zhang. "Any thoughts on motive?"

Zhang shrugged. "Somebody was hard up for a quick lay? They didn't crack his private safe or take any of his action figures, even the super-rare ones. Even his retro gaming collection is untouched. The only thing missing is Keller's million-dollar sexbot."

Cowan eyed Zhang. "Wait, you don't actually mean—?"

Zhang grinned like a predator spotting his prey. "Keller was loaded. Boy owned a *fully functional* house synthetic, wrapped in synthflesh with a rack big enough to—"

"We get it," Jeb said, before Cowan could get *more* flustered. "So you guys think someone murdered Keller to steal his housesynth?"

Zhang shrugged. "That's my theory, but hell, maybe somebody wanted to shake up the finals of StrikeForceGo. That'd be a real story, wouldn't it? Fixing matches by murdering pros here in meatspace?"

Cowan turned a bit less red. "Would that actually work?"

"Keller was top tier, little buddy," Zhang said. "The semis happened last night, and Keller was *destroying* the other team before he went dark. Happened right before the match ended."

"Because he got murdered," Cowan said.

Zhang nodded. "Seems like it."

Jeb considered Zhang's theory, and honestly, it wasn't as far-fetched as some might think. SimSports Pros knocking each other off was un-likely—clear circuits couldn't harm others—but there was enough money involved in pro-gaming to tempt those with means to murder. Jeb had heard betting went into the billions on a good night.

Zhang raised one eyebrow and grinned at Cowan. "Body's in the bedroom, kid. It's nasty though. Shit will blow your mind."

Cowan swallowed. "Jeb, should I—"

Jeb placed a hand on Cowan's shoulder. "Nothing you need to see." Cowan wasn't a VCD investigator, and the CID didn't handle *violent* crimes. "Log into the apartment VI and pull the visitor log."

"Right." Cowan nodded. "I'll see what I can find."

Cowan's eyes went distant, staring into space as he focused on his head desk. He was likely searching the apartment's virtual intelligence for clues.

Zhang touched his ear, a habit common among ex-soldiers when they received wireless transmissions. Jeb often saw David do the same when he was tired or distracted. Jeb's husband had been deployed in Peru as well, in one of the suppression wars waged to remove terrorists who resisted PBAs, and though David rarely talked about it, Jeb knew it had been a rough time. Fortunately, PBA redaction dramatically re-duced PTSD.

"Remote autopsy confirms the captain's theory," Zhang said.

Jeb watched him. "And that is?"

Zhang grinned wide. "Captain said not to tell you."

Jeb smiled back despite the situation. "Understood."

Naomi was testing him, a game they played whenever the CID and VCD crossed paths, but only because she respected his judgment. Naomi wanted his theory, not hers.

"What's the body look like?" Jeb asked.

"Broken fingers, gouged-out eyes, crushed balls. Pretty sick shit." Zhang led Jeb to the stackhome's single bedroom, metal legs hissing and clomping.

"The mutilation happened postmortem?" Jeb prayed the answer was yes.

Zhang cocked an eyebrow at him. "How'd you know?"

"Just a guess." Mutilating a body postmortem was rage, not greed. It implied just killing them wasn't enough. "So, who hated Keller enough to defile his corpse?"

"Lots of people hated this kid," Zhang said. "Don't you know who Nemoset is in the gaming world?"

Jeb shrugged. "My husband's the shooter fanatic in the family."

"Right." Zhang frowned and shook his head. "Leroy Keller was one of the top snipers in StrikeForceGo. Dude got accused of using marksman scripting so often he quit playing in public, just to avoid the harassment."

It wasn't uncommon with top-tier players to face cheating accusations, especially when slumming in public pleasureboxes.

"All right, so he was good," Jeb said.

"Not good. Godlike. Odds were Team Grindhouse would take the trophy this season. Nobody had seen synergy like theirs since the Death-Kittens, back before ex-military got banned from the game."

Of course Zhang would bring *that* up. David, Jeb's husband, had founded the DeathKittens shortly after the Peruvian conflict ended and had gotten banned with all the rest of the military pros when the Strike-ForceGo devs rebalanced the game for its 90 percent civilian player base.

Everything in StrikeForceGo *felt* real, giving people with real military experience a big advantage, but Jeb thought it was callous to lock veterans out of ranked play. Still, Jeb knew no one would play

StrikeForceGo if an elite group of military veterans could murder them with their bare hands.

Zhang opened Keller's bedroom. Blood and other fluids covered the carpet, and more splattered the beige walls. Enough to make Jeb's stomach turn. The silk sheets of a thick bed were matted with gore. Someone had ripped Keller's ergochair in half.

VCD Captain Naomi Barondale knelt beside their victim. She was dark-skinned, built like an Olympic wrestler, and had four prosthetic limbs. Unlike Jeb and Zhang, however, Naomi had *chosen* to replace her forearms and legs with hyperrealistic prosthetics.

Few people handled truly dangerous jobs these days, with world wars over, but those who did, like VCD officers, wanted every advantage military tech could provide. And with far fewer soldiers in need of advanced cybernetic replacements, firms who'd formerly sold millions of dollars of military-grade prosthetics were eager to sell.

Naomi wore a full carbon-plated bodysuit with flexible boots, covering everything up to her neck. Her outfit shimmered in the faint light, a sign it incorporated mimetic camouflage reserved for elite soldiers. Her eyes glowed purple, an effect of ocular implants that let her see through walls using enhanced Wi-Vi. Had she been busy peering *inside* Keller's body?

"Got a visitor log for our vic?" Naomi asked.

Jeb was careful not to step on any human bits as he entered. "My partner's working on it. Is that all you need me for?"

"I'd also like your insight." When Naomi crossed her arms, they looked perfectly human, though Jeb knew they had reinforced nanofibers inside. "What do you see in here?"

Jeb looked past the gore for puzzle pieces. Leroy Keller's body was splayed out like a paper doll. His limbs were spread evenly, like he was making a snow angel with his blood.

Jeb was glad Keller had died before this happened, not after. This killer had clearly posed him.

"This was personal," Jeb said as he strode carefully around the corpse. "The killer targeted Keller and wanted to dominate him, even after he was already dead. They probably archived this. They wanted a trophy."

"What else?" Naomi asked.

Something about Keller's neck bothered Jeb. It was puffy, like he'd been stung by a bunch of bees, and badly discolored. He knelt and stared.

"The killer strangled him," Jeb said.

Naomi nodded.

"With what?" Jeb asked. "I've never seen any neck swell up like this."

"I have," Zhang said. "Some drunk idiot stuck his neck in the claw of a construction synthetic to impress his drunk buddies, trying to be all 'mouth of the lion' and shit. Another drunk idiot tripped over the activation switch. They shut down the claw, but not in time." Zhang spread his hands. "Dude's neck swelled up like a ball sack."

Jeb ignored him and looked to Naomi, suddenly realizing why Naomi called the CID. "You think a synthetic strangled this man."

"Could it?" Naomi asked. Her face remained entirely without expression.

"No," Jeb said, "or . . . it shouldn't be able to. If a synthetic was responsible, it'd be new, and the door was intact, wasn't it? There was no way for a synthetic to get in here, unless . . ." Jeb remembered Zhang's comment about Keller's missing housesynth. "His sexbot?"

"Is that possible?" Naomi asked.

"Anything is possible, with enough evidence." Jeb took a breath. "What's yours?"

Naomi pointed at Keller's body. "His neck vertebrae were literally pulped inside his body, along with his neck. No human can do that."

"No unaugmented human," Zhang corrected. "You could pop his head clean off if he gave you reason, Cap. Or if he fell under my boot." Zhang flexed his artificial leg, twisting his foot with a *snap-hiss*.

"What kind of sexbot was it?" Jeb asked Naomi.

"A Companion Triple-F."

Jeb pulled the schematics from the CID and gave it a once over. Though the Triple-F was almost entirely fiberglass, to keep weight down, it had enough pneumatic pressure to crush a neck. It also had a hard limit on how tight it could close its fingers.

Jeb flipped back to meatspace. "A Triple-F couldn't strangle Keller.

They ship with a hardware safety. It can't close its hands tightly enough to strangle someone."

"Actually," Cowan said as he strolled into the room, "I think that—"

Jeb slapped a palm into Cowan's chest just before he stepped on one of Keller's fingers. "Crime scene, Cowan. Body parts. They're all over the place."

Cowan backpedaled. "Shit, sorry! My filters are up."

Jeb knew PBAs would warn the user if they got too close to redacted objects, via abstraction, but a severed finger might be too small to register as an obstruction.

Naomi's tone turned cool. "You were saying?"

Though he remained pale, Cowan spoke. "I think the Triple-F could do it, ma'am, if you disabled the hardware safety. I found instructions for doing that in Keller's private cloud. Step-by-step."

Naomi tapped her chin and frowned. "Why remove a safety that keeps your synth from strangling you?"

Zhang whistled and snapped his fingers. "This kid *wanted* it to choke him!"

Cowan blinked again. "What?"

"Autoerotic asphyxiation," Naomi said. "He'd be far from the first."

That actually made a lot more sense than Jeb liked. "What about the visitor logs?" he asked.

Cowan's eyes went distant again. "Keller hasn't let anyone in this apartment for weeks, and no one's left, but I did find something else. Last night, about ten minutes after Leroy Keller vanished from StrikeForceGo, someone accessed the trash incinerator tube."

Naomi glanced at the wall, probably looking *through* it at the tube somewhere beyond the wall. It was where residents in a luxury high-rise like this could toss trash and burn it away. Out of sight, out of mind.

"A housesynth would just about fit in there, wouldn't it?" Naomi asked.

"Yes, ma'am." Cowan's blank gaze focused. "I mean, Captain."

"So, wait," Zhang said. "Keller's sexbot strangled him, mutilated him, and then tossed itself down the trash incinerator tube?" He snorted. "Must not have paid it enough."

"Accessing the incinerator logs wasn't easy," Cowan said. "The apartment's VI doesn't log incinerator usage. The building's Overlord VI does that, and it's highly secured."

Jeb felt a bit of professional pride that his partner had dug so deep. "So, whoever hacked the synthetic might have assumed we'd never see that log, or know Keller modified his Triple-F to strangle him. They'd think this was a robbery gone wrong and file it as such. Nice work."

"Agreed." Naomi's tone thawed. "Did you find any other anomalies on Keller's private server or the apartment's VI?"

Cowan cleared his throat. "Well, he was logging at least twelve hours in the Sim a day."

"How'd he manage that?" Zhang asked. "Loose circuit?"

"No, it's a simple hack," Cowan said, "and anyone can do it. You down a script that sets your hardlink clock. Your PBA sets its auto-dump timer off that clock when you dive. So as far as your PBA knows, you're under your limit. Your hardlink doesn't regulate that."

Jeb considered that. Due to the extreme popularity of the Sim, the Office of Mental Health imposed a hard limit on how long anyone could spend inside the simulated reality of a pleasurebox: six hours, followed by a mandatory ten-hour break. People who stayed in pleasureboxes too long—simjunkies—often developed Simulation Disorder.

Those people often lost the ability to distinguish reality from the Sim. While clear circuit algorithms prevented them from harming others, people killed in pleasureboxes all the time. If someone in meatspace thought they were in a pleasurebox, they might not think they were hurting actual *people*, thus bypassing behavioral algorithms. That got messy.

"What was he doing?" Naomi asked. "He couldn't have spent all that time playing StrikeForceGo."

Zhang shook his head. "You kidding, Cap? Pro players live off sponsorships. If Keller thought practicing six extra hours a day would give him an edge, he'd take it."

Naomi turned back to Cowan. "What do the apartment's security archives show?"

Cowan looked at Jeb, then at Naomi. "You didn't delete them?"

"We can't even access apartment archives," Zhang said. "That's why we call you guys."

"Oh," Cowan said. "Then we have a problem."

Naomi crossed her arms again. "Our killer erased the archives?"

Cowan grimaced. "If they didn't, someone else did. What does that mean for our synthetic theory?"

Jeb held back a heavy sigh. "It means this case remains with the VCD."

Without Keller's Triple-F to examine, they had no real proof his sexbot had strangled him. Only Naomi's suspicion. Unfortunately, Oneworld's official statement insisted house synthetics couldn't be hacked. More corporate bullshit.

The VCD couldn't accept Naomi's assertion that a hacked housesynth murdered Keller without Jeb's confirmation, and now Jeb couldn't confirm anything. That meant the CID couldn't take over the case, and it meant whoever had done this could do it again. The VCD handled crime that occurred in meatspace, while the CID tackled crime through the Sim.

Letting some hacker kill people with their own housesynths wasn't something Jeb could tolerate, orders or no orders.

"What's your next move, Captain?" Jeb asked. He knew Naomi might be thinking the same thing he was. "You going to follow this StrikeForceGo theory?"

"Not much we can do, in our jurisdiction." Naomi raised an eyebrow at him. "For now, all we can do is examine our physical evidence and hope for an anonymous tip."

Jeb smirked, knowing Naomi's statement was both encouragement and permission. "Well . . . let's just hope someone calls one in."

11

JEB

When Jeb stepped out of his chartered autocar, the Americas Oneworld Megacenter sprawled out ahead of him: six glistening twenty-story buildings festooned with thirty kinds of holo-projection. Its grand plaza was even more packed than he expected. The crowd was as dense and diverse as you'd find during the Olympics, which he'd seen before, having attended once with David.

Synthcops in bright yellow stood at attention along the autocar route, armed with tasers and batons, but even they had trouble keeping the single autocar path into and out of the megacenter clear of pedestrians. The plaza itself was rife with transmitters broadcasting enough augmented reality ads to make anyone dizzy. As part of the CID, Jeb could block ads, and once he did, the plaza became vastly more comprehensible.

As he walked, he pitied the poor folks swiping away as they made their way from shop to shop, looking for the best deal on the latest addiction. Even today, there were still some things you couldn't order online, not because a drone couldn't deliver them to your house—a drone could deliver most anything to your house—only because it wasn't yet *legal* for a drone to deliver them. Even Oneworld, in all its monopolistic glory, had yet to unravel the layers of contradictory local laws passed before they took over the government.

The early twenty-first century had been a whirlwind of accelerated technological development. Virtual reality, augmented reality, dozens of unclassified chemical compounds, and everything from camera drones to sexbots all hit the market at a pace that terrified the average politician. Certain things were legal *here*, and certain things were legal *there*, and certain things were legal on certain days of the week or only if they were transported by hand, not drone. As a result, the Americas Megacenter soon became the only place near San Diego you could buy certain luxuries.

It was also the only place offering anonymous hardlink access to the Sim.

A glowing AR arrow appeared across the plaza, by a glittering silver column covered in glowing artwork. That would be David, right on time, and Jeb worked his way through the crowd until he finally caught sight of his husband.

Unlike Jeb, David Forrester had hair. Lots of it. He also had a blunt nose and a square jaw, like a military recruiting poster. He wore a loose flannel shirt and dark jeans that hugged his muscular legs.

Jeb pulled his husband into a hug and gave him a quick kiss, then stepped back and squeezed his hand. "Sorry for the short notice. Time might be a factor."

David shook his head. "A kid's dead, Jeb, and I'd be an ass if I let that slide. I brought the quiet line." He turned his head. The companion node of David's wireless linkline was already slotted into the port behind David's left ear.

Jeb popped the wireless node into his own auxiliary port, and a brief tingle assured him the encrypted connection was active.

"And you were bored, weren't you?" Jeb said over their wireless link. A wireless linkline wasn't as secure as a real one, but being tethered to each other was awfully inconvenient in a huge crowd. *"Don't tell me you weren't bored,"* he added.

David grimaced as they cut through the crowd. *"I still can't believe*

Nemoset's gone." All their communication would be wireless now, which ensured no one in the crowd could overhear them.

Trust David Forrester to cut right to the heart of today's mission. *"Leroy Keller, and yes."* He filled David in on the conversation he'd had with Naomi, Zhang, and Cowan in Leroy Keller's apartment. *"Of course, given Oneworld's official policy—"*

"We're not investigating any of this. Just out for a night of shopping," David said. *"The CID's out of the picture?"*

"We're clear for two hours at least. More than that, and they'll wonder."

One of the advantages of twenty years with the CID was that, at night, Director Stanton allowed Jeb to deactivate his PBA's surveillance when he wanted private time. Normally, he and David used that allowance for the things every other couple used it for—dinner, a streamed show, or just quality time in private without some asshole from the Office of Mental Health archiving everything through Jeb's eyes—but tonight Jeb was conducting an unsanctioned Sim investigation with an unregistered accomplice.

The risk was warranted. Whether Oneworld wanted to admit it or not, a murderer might still be out there, with the ability to hack synthetics and crush the life out of anyone. If Jeb had to, he'd get the proof on his own. He wasn't going to just go home and relax while another kid got strangled by his house synthetic.

"Tell me your theory," Jeb said as they worked their way through the crowd toward Megacenter Two. *"Why murder Keller over StrikeForceGo?"*

David had locked on to Zhang's theory as soon as Jeb called him, though neither of them had wanted to discuss it over a monitored line. Killing Keller over StrikeForceGo might be just a hypothesis, but following a hypothesis was better than sitting on his hands.

"Zhang isn't off base," David said as they walked. *"Nemoset's death completely changes the landscape of this season. With Nemoset out and Grindhouse down a pro, their match against TrollStompers could go either way. Before now, the odds were fairly locked."*

The two of them entered Megacenter Two but avoided the elevator. There was always the chance some troll could lock the elevator up and trap them inside, just for kicks. Still, it was going to be a tiring climb up fourteen flights.

"Give me details," Jeb said.

"TrollStompers were seed six and up against the top Korean team, Kudzu. Kudzu was a four-to-one favorite and lost in the last five minutes, when Garnet and Recoil went on a killing spree." David grew more animated as he summarized the match. *"They took down NumAngel, Dorfling, and MatterRat before they dropped, and LuckyBro made off with Kudzu's hostage in the cross fire. PositiveMC had a shot on Lucky, but missed. That's the third shot he's missed all season."*

"Tough luck." Jeb was lost halfway through, but he loved the way David perked up when discussing the game. His mind was already fitting facts together to see if they made sense. Could someone who favored the TrollStompers really have killed Leroy Keller to shake up the odds?

Intentionally or not, Leroy Keller's murder had caused a shift in this season's landscape. The clear favorite was now a question mark, and that left bookies raking in money. Bad for the Keller family, but good for illegitimate businesses. If Sim rivalries had finally escalated to real-world murder, that was bad news all around.

"Did Nemoset have any enemies?" Jeb asked. Ten floors to go, and his legs ached.

"None I can think of," David replied.

"Did he have any rivalries at all?"

David shook his head. *"LuckyBro trashed him before their last match, but Lucky trashes everyone, so no one considers him a rival. Nemoset had a professional rivalry with LinSpork, from Team Taco Party, but they respect each other. Also, Taco Party's out for the season, due to losses."*

Eight floors left. Jeb was already winded. *"Has Nemoset ever called anyone out, in or out of the Sim?"*

"He didn't really call people out," David said. *"He was a quiet kid who never even did postmatch interviews. DNF does the talking for his team."*

"Who's DNF?"

"Did Not Finish. It's an old racing joke. Anyway, Nemoset just let his sniping talk for him."

Jeb focused on the steps and breathing. *"So the only gripe against Nemoset is he was good."*

"Sure," David agreed. *"But with all those corporate sponsorships flying around, that might be enough to convince someone to put a hit out on him. Ever since StrikeForceGo exploded in Russia, people have been worried the Bratva might get involved."*

Jeb remembered the death of Doctor Barkov, at the end of Cowan's first case, and grimaced at the mention of the Russian mob. They, like hackers in many countries, fought a constant battle with Oneworld's engineers to bypass the safety restrictions on PBAs. No matter how many PBA security patches Oneworld put out, some hacker was always a step ahead.

Yet the Russians couldn't be behind everything. Jeb had no evidence they wanted to influence StrikeForceGo brackets. He had to follow the evidence, not speculation. By the time he reached floor fourteen, his legs and chest ached.

"Need a breather," he transmitted over wireless as he leaned against the railing.

David grinned and nudged him, entirely not out of breath. *"Need to do more cardio."*

"Some of us have jobs, you know." Jeb rolled his eyes. *"Not everyone can spend all day on a treadmill."*

With the proper equipment and safeguards, it was still possible to walk on a real-world omni-treadmill while exploring the Sim, like people had done in the early days of the VR. Jeb figured he walked enough on the job. Still, he didn't walk as much as David did while inside the Sim.

Soon Jeb had his breath back, and they were off to bend some confusing laws.

Jeb hadn't told Cowan his plan, of course—investigating a Violent Crimes Division case without their authorization—because Cowan still had the Office of Mental Health in his head 24-7. As far as Cowan and the OMH knew, he and David were still at home.

The simParlor they were heading to, simply titled *Absolution*, was one of eight slightly legitimate businesses on floor fourteen. Jeb had no doubt there were dozens of cybercriminals and possibly even some loose circuits in here tonight, conducting illicit deals they didn't want One-world to be able to trace back to them. Still, there was no better place than an anonymous simParlor to do some virtual investigation without alerting Oneworld.

And if *Absolution* was as secure as CID reports claimed, no one would ever know different. In this one case, Jeb was grateful all the an-cient local laws kept things snarled up enough that he and David had this option.

Buildings like Megacenter Two were one of the only places in Cal-ifornia where anonymous hardlink access to the Sim was still legal, a clause grandfathered in from a private deal between politicians in the early days of the Sim. Oneworld had since imposed regulations that outlawed anonymous access elsewhere. Loose circuits had their own private anonymized connections, of course, but Jeb didn't have access to an anonymized hardlink at home. That would be enough to get him fired and arrested.

The exchange with the bored proprietor of *Absolution* was simple—you paid by the hour. David paid for four hours, using one of several private accounts he had from his days investing his considerable win-nings from StrikeForceGo. They walked alone into a small gray room, together, to a single simBed with a gleaming hardlink jack.

David popped out his wireless linkline and pulled a physical linkline from his pocket, along with a splitter to merge a second line. Linklines also allowed two people to experience the Sim as one entity. The CID could detect them, but they weren't illegal . . . yet. David laid down on the bed and popped the splitter into his auxiliary port, then the linkline. He offered the other end to Jeb.

Jeb took one of the two seats beside the simBed and settled in.

"Ready," Jeb said out loud.

David leaned back, pulled the simBed linkline from its retractable perch, and plugged it into the other slot on the splitter. His body re-laxed as his eyes fluttered closed.

Jeb plugged the end of David's split linkline into his own port. The dingy little private room deformed as a tingle started at Jeb's toes and worked its way up through him, a warning his PBA was transitioning from meatspace to the Sim.

Soon he was seeing through David's eyes, feeling what David felt. Jeb's husband opened the closet in his old simPartment—one archived locally inside his PBA rather than a registered location that existed on the Sim—and scrolled through avatars. He paused on an avatar in a brown combat vest, brown-and-gray fatigues, and thick army boots.

"You sure you're okay with this?" Jeb asked over the linkline. He didn't know how David might feel, diving back into the world from which he'd been unfairly exiled.

"Like riding a bike." David reached inside his old avatar and squeezed. His body flashed, and then he was wearing his avatar from his Strike-ForceGo days. It was a rugged Army Ranger from the Internet Age.

"Still fits," David said.

Jeb chuckled. David had been a Ranger before he retired, so paying tribute to his branch of service was appropriate. Not to mention, Jeb had always thought his husband looked spectacular in a uniform.

David clicked through several subpanels until he found a bookmark for Dust, which as far as Jeb knew was a very exclusive pleasurebox favored by StrikeForceGo pros. The word *Private* flashed once. Thanks to David's status as a former top-tier StrikeForceGo player, he could access it.

"We won't get a better shot at today's pros than tonight," David said. *"With Nemoset down and the finals two days away, Dust will be packed. If you really think Nemo had beef with another pro that didn't get reported, tonight is the night people gossip."*

"And you want to blow their minds a little," Jeb said.

David grinned at his reflection. *"Maybe a little."*

Jeb uploaded the last of his stored archives to the CID, clearing his archiver. *"Just do what you'd normally do. If I want you to ask anything, I'll let you know."*

"Let's see what our pros have to say about their fallen comrade." David poked the Invite Only button.

They were immediately transported into the middle of a warzone.

David hit the dirt, which saved them from dying in a shower of shrapnel. He rose and sprinted as another shell shrieked by. He dove into a shallow crater as the shell landed.

Jeb didn't dare break David's concentration by speaking over their linkline, but what the hell had they ported into? Was this an alternate pleasurebox set up to discourage unexpected visitors to Dust?

David was up after the shell landed, charging a soldier in bright red armor. The spectral name tag floating above his head read "Recoil." He was currently crawling out a foxhole, and David caught him from behind before he could turn around.

David slammed one hand into Recoil's spine, forcing his whole body straight, then grabbed Recoil's chin with his other hand. He snapped his neck with a loud pop. Jeb had forgotten how lethal David Forrester was when behavioral algorithms weren't in play back in meatspace.

Recoil's body vanished to pixels as David seized his rifle—an AK-47, Jeb recognized—and jogged forward at a brisk but steady pace. When David glanced down, Jeb noticed his husband's armor was tinted blue.

A staccato of shots rang out as David slammed his back into the wall of a burned-out building. Cover. David peeked around the corner, spotting two red soldiers advancing on a pinned-down blue. Jeb didn't have time to scan their name tags.

David popped out and put a shot into one red soldier's head. He dropped back into cover before the other fired back, sprinting to the building's far side. He rounded it just in time to catch another red soldier flat-footed, one with "Sn0wing" floating above her head. She had her weapon strapped to her back and carried a giant blue flag.

That was when Jeb realized. The team colors, the flag—they'd landed in a capture the flag match!

Sn0wing's green-painted eyes went wide. "You can't be—"

David shot her in the face. He shouldered his rifle and picked up the flag, which turned red the moment he touched it.

"Carrier at center base!" David shouted aloud. "Need an assist!"

Another red soldier sprinted around the corner just before his chest exploded. Blue soldiers charged into view and stumbled to a halt, name tags bouncing as they stumbled to a stop. They gaped at the blue Army Ranger holding the red flag.

NumAngel, a woman wearing white-and-blue armor, literally hopped up and down as she pointed at David. Phantasmal wings sprouted from her back, drifting as she hopped. "No freaking way! It's Major F'ing Hero!"

The second soldier, MatterRat, saluted. "Sir!" His armor sported a glowing taegeuk—a red-and-blue circle similar to a yin-yang symbol—on its chest plate. "Welcome to Dust!"

David grinned at them. "You here to cover me?"

"My God, yes!" NumAngel dashed past David, onto open ground, and dropped. "Clear!"

"Move on, sir," MatterRat said. "The enemy team is respawning."

"Understood." David jogged off.

Jeb marveled at the instantaneous respect in the voices of these two pros. These men and women got paid obscene amounts of money to shoot at each other in the Sim, yet just the sight of David—or Major-Hero, a legendary avatar that still sold plenty of sports drinks—left them in awe. No wonder David still had so many sponsorships.

David spoke aloud to MatterRat as they ran together, and David breathed easily despite the flagpole's weight. "I was the commentator on your match against TrollStompers. Shame about that last shot."

MatterRat grimaced. "It sure was, sir. Still say that was some bullshit, sir."

A rifle shot cracked. Someone screamed in the distance.

MatterRat stopped running. "Lin just dropped their scout, but the other team just bought a gunboat. Grimkin's heading this way with Maidferno and Garnet on the guns."

David slowed. "Can't outrun a gunboat."

"Keep running, sir," MatterRat said. "Team Kudzu's got you covered."

"You sure about that, son?" David asked.

Matter grinned like a demon. "Fuck yeah, I'm sure."

"Good hunting." David clutched the giant red flag and ran. Another rifle shot echoed through the rolling desert, but Jeb didn't hear anyone scream.

"Why are they playing CTF?" Jeb finally asked David, over the linkline.

"It's One Flag CTF," David replied over the linkline. *"And this is how SFGo players commemorate a fallen friend. By doing what we love."*

Jeb could feel the exertion David felt, pushing his body as hard in the Sim as he would in the real world. This flagpole was heavy and running felt real. In professional StrikeForceGo, every sensation except fatal wounds approximated meatspace. Shouting and gunshots rang out, and then the shockwave from an explosion sent them stumbling. David somehow kept his footing.

They crested a hill and approached a tall, empty flag-well. A slim woman in bright blue armor camped in a nearby tower, aiming a sniper rifle as long as David. The name above her head read "LinSpork," which made her the sniper who apparently had a rivalry with Nemoset.

Someone else materialized in the tower out of nowhere, a ninja in spiky red armor. He impaled LinSpork with his laser sword, eliciting a pained cry. Then the ninja leapt off her already vanishing body and landed between them and the flag-well. His name tag read "Hampline."

A horizontal glowing visor covered Hampline's eyes. He advanced with his sword raised, then stopped. Hampline's jaw dropped.

"Holy shit!" Hampline said. "It's a goddamn honor, sir. Sorry to have to cut you down." He advanced.

"Don't apologize, son. Just get out of my way!" David charged.

Hampline brought his laser sword down right into the flagpole, which David raised like a staff. The sword didn't split it, bouncing off instead.

"The fuck—?" Hampline started, before David planted the spiked tip of the flag in his neck. There was a sucking gurgle. David heaved the red ninja aside and stomped to the flag-well.

David slammed the flag down. The desert, sand, and sky flickered as fireworks exploded as the flag turned white. The words *Blue Team Wins* arced across the sky.

"So, then he impales me," Hampline tapped his finger on his neck, "right here. With the fucking flagpole!"

The rest of the pros—MatterRat, LinSpork, NumAngel, and half a dozen others—chuckled and nodded at Hampline's tale. David sat at a wooden table inside a large canvas mess tent within the Dust Sim.

"You're enjoying this," Jeb said over their private linkline, grinning back in meatspace. *"Don't forget why we're here."*

"I won't," David said over the linkline. *"And I am."*

Once they'd officially broken the ice, they both hoped to learn as much as they could about Nemoset and his possible enemies.

MajorHero, David's alter ego, had returned to StrikeForceGo for the first time in years. He had taken down four pros in a CTF match he wasn't even supposed to play, and now the pros in this pleasurebox were lined up to get his friend link. True StrikeForceGo players didn't hold grudges.

From what Jeb gathered, David had been permitted into the game upon entry because a blue player had previously disconnected during the match, leaving the blue team one soldier down. David immediately took that slot. Too bad for the red team.

"Sir, I have to ask," Hampline began. He still had his visor on, which was apparently part of his actual avatar, not equipment. "How did you know the flagpole would block my sword?"

David glanced at him. "You ever played in Dust before, son?"

"No sir," Hampline said. "Never had the opportunity."

"Well, Dust runs SFGo Classic, has for as long as I recall. In classic, the flagpole's invulnerable."

NumAngel smacked the table. "That's right! DeathKittens versus BloodyBrawl! Snakeoil used the flagpole to block Logic's plasma rounds and plant the flag."

"Snakeoil was always doing things like that," David said. "One creative son of a bitch."

LinSpork stepped closer. "So, you know Hardcase?" With her helmet off, she had a brown pixie face and a short black Mohawk. "You've met him?"

"Hardcase?" Jeb asked David, over the linkline. It was difficult to keep track of all this lingo—he wished he'd paid more attention when David used to ramble on about the game.

"Dust's admin," David explained privately. *"He's a former pro who played with Chinese Hell."*

"We used to scrimmage all the time," David said out loud. "After the league retired us vets, Snakeoil suggested we pitch in to cover his pleasurebox. Technically, we're co-owners."

"Cool." LinSpork stomped her foot, and dust drifted up. "Think you can buy us a goddamn floor?"

The other pros laughed, and David chuckled with them. The laughter ended as an older Black man with an eyepatch approached. He led two pros: Sn0wing—the green-haired woman David shot when he stole the flag—and a heavyset white man with a thick red beard and red hair. His tag read "Peachrind."

The other pros parted. The remaining members of Team Grindhouse had arrived.

"This is it," David said privately. *"We're on. That's DNF with the eyepatch."*

DNF bowed his head. "It's a pleasure to meet you, sir."

"Pleasure's all mine," David said aloud, nodding back. "I've watched your matches, son, and you do good work." He looked to the others. "You all do good work."

Sn0wing smiled wide, and Peachrind actually blushed. Jeb remembered David shooting Sn0wing right in her pale face, but she looked honored, not pissed. Of course, getting shot here didn't involve real bullets, so it seemed unreasonable to hold a grudge.

DNF didn't smile or blush. "Sir, can I ask why you're here tonight?" he asked.

"Why I'm here?" David replied.

"Yes sir. It's unexpected."

"You're asking if I'm here about Nemoset, aren't you?" David thumped a fist to his chest. "He was a good sniper and a good player. I came to pay my respects."

"Damn," LinSpork whispered.

Everyone got quiet, people who suddenly remembered they weren't soldiers in meatspace. They were gamers, and they'd lost one of their own. Sn0wing nodded as, beside her, Peachrind dabbed at what might be a real tear. Often facial rigs duplicated the user's actual emotions.

"Thank you, sir," DNF said, for all of them. "I know Nemo would appreciate that."

"Oh, come on!" someone shouted. "Who else wants to suck his dick?"

DNF stiffened, but he didn't turn around. David watched as another soldier strolled into their canvas tent, a bronze man with a huge spike of purple hair. He had a classic troll face painted on his flak jacket, a distorted white cartoon face with an oversized grin.

"Who's the asshole?" Jeb asked over their linkline.

"That would be LuckyBro," David replied privately. *"The blue player who dropped last match."*

LuckyBro scoffed as he approached. "Some old-timer walks in here after a five-year ban, and all of a sudden it's Beatlemania?" He pointed. "You took my spot, old man."

"I pulled your weight," David said aloud. "Were you busy?"

Another pro with spiky black armor and albino skin approached LuckyBro, the man David had killed at the foxhole. "This isn't the time," Recoil said. "Knock it off."

LuckyBro snorted and shoved him aside. He stopped in front of David and leaned in, hands on hips. "You know what I think? You're aimbotting, old man. You knew you couldn't keep up with us, so you scripted your way to a cheap win."

David narrowed his eyes and said nothing. That was the way Jeb would respond to such a wild accusation. He'd dare LuckyBro to repeat it.

"You just admitted you know Hardcase!" LuckyBro shouted as he spread his arms. "Don't you noobs see it? He cheated. The old man just wants you to gobble his knob for old time's sake."

David stood. "I don't cheat," he said calmly.

"So prove it!" LuckyBro said. "Get the DeathKittens and meet the TrollStompers on a public sim. We'll whomp you back to the Stone Age."

Recoil forcefully gripped LuckyBro's arm and tugged, to no avail. "Jesus, Lucky, that's too far. Get out of here before he bans you."

LuckyBro spread his arms. "You scared, old man?"

David frowned. "Tonight isn't about you, son. It's about your comrade and friend."

"So, you *are* scared."

David stared him down. "You can't bait me. All you're doing is being an asshole, on a night when you should be honoring Nemoset's memory. The DeathKittens will never step into a box with you."

"Then you're chick—"

David cut LuckyBro off with a knifelike gesture. "Even if we stomped you into the ground, the viewstream hits would put a finals game to shame. You think I don't know what you're trying to do?"

LuckyBro tried to speak again, but David raised his hand and shut them up. He shut them all up, even LuckyBro.

"Now," David said, "you're going to walk out of this tent, log off, and decompress, and I'll forget you insulted me."

LuckyBro smiled wide. "Fuck you, old man."

"Asshole!" Recoil tore off LuckyBro's shoulder pad. Light flashed as the pad evaporated into pixels.

LuckyBro stepped back and stared at his albino teammate. "The fuck, Recoil? You're kicking me?"

Jeb realized then that Recoil led the TrollStompers.

"Should have kicked you weeks ago," Recoil said. "There's a time to talk shit, and a time to shut your goddamn mouth. You never got that."

LuckyBro flipped them off with both middle fingers as he backed away from the table, wearing a maniacal grin. "You think I can't play as a free agent? Fuck all y'all. And you know what? Fuck that dipshit Nem—"

LuckyBro froze, legs walking in place as if sliding on wet floor. He kept taking the same two steps, swinging the same two arms, taking the same two breaths. Lagged out.

Jeb had an aching premonition they were already too late. *"Touch his neck,"* he told David, over their linkline.

"Why?" David asked privately.

"Do it!" Jeb ordered.

David hurried over, grabbed LuckyBro's twitching arm, and pressed his palm to LuckyBro's now cold neck. Jeb ran the CID's tracing protocol and got his address—a house in Des Moines, Iowa. Then he sent an emergency alert to the Iowa VCD.

"Idiot pulled his own hardlink," Recoil said.

"He didn't," Jeb said privately. *"Someone pulled it for him."*

David repeated what Jeb had told him out loud for the others to hear.

"Why would anyone do that?" Hampline asked, incredulous.

"I'm disconnecting," Jeb wirelessly told David. *"I have to ping the CID from a clean line. See what else you can get out of the other pros and warn them to lock up their housesynths."*

David glanced at the crowd of confused faces, then answered privately. *"You think the same person who killed Nemoset came after LuckyBro?"*

Jeb remembered Leroy Keller's splayed-out body, crushed and covered in gore. *"We'll know in a few minutes."*

12

JEB

Ten minutes after he left *Absolution*, a report from the Des Moines CID reached Jeb's PBA. Synthcops had entered the house of Jacob Howard—a.k.a. LuckyBro—after he ignored their entry request. A well-proportioned sexbot greeted them with a baseball bat. After neutralizing it, they discovered Howard's mutilated body in his bedroom.

Evidently, Jacob Howard lived alone.

Jeb and David sat now in a round booth at a bar built into Megacenter Three, one that served real alcohol. Alcohol wasn't illegal, but it was rare. PBAs could make water taste like wine and simulate drunkenness, so few bothered with real booze these days except for purists.

"So," David said, swirling a quarter glass of real whisky. "Someone's knocking off SFGo players."

"Possibly." Jeb kept his voice low, even though there was no one near enough to overhear them. "We only have two murders, but I've already recommended Corporate One task synthcops to protect the remaining pros until the finals conclude."

David grimaced. "If teams keep losing members, there won't be any finals."

Jeb knew David was upset. Seeing LuckyBro go down had shaken them both. Jeb knew from the crime scene report that the damage to

Jacob Howard's body matched that of Leroy Keller—gouged eyes, broken fingers, crushed balls—but the difference, this time, was Jacob Howard was alive while that happened.

David took a sip of his drink before speaking again. "You mentioned darkSim betting. Do darkSim bookies murder people?"

"Never," Jeb said. "The reason the darkSim persists is because its members *avoid* corporate attention. That, and Switzerland's status as the last independent country in the world."

"So, taking out simSports players is a bad move?"

"They're Sim celebrities. It would trigger investigations. That's bad for everyone on the darkSim."

David stared at the doors of the bar, at the crowd of people wandering by outside, and frowned. "Here's another odd detail. LuckyBro wasn't actually that good."

"How do you mean?" Jeb asked.

"If you're hoping to influence this season, taking out Nemoset makes sense. But other than his shit-talking, LuckyBro was easily replaceable."

"You think that's why he talked so much trash?" Jeb asked.

"Probably," David said. "Everyone in simSports needs an angle, even the prodigies. It's all about the viewstream hits, the cash, and the sponsors that come with those."

"So how did LuckyBro's viewstream compare with Nemoset's?"

"Nemoset's viewstream spiked in big matches. Lucky's viewstream spiked before and after, when he was talking shit. He was basically a professional asshole meant to rile the opposition."

"Any other similarities?" Jeb asked. "People they pissed off?"

David's eyes went distant as he went into his head desk, and Jeb waited, keeping one eye on the rest of the bar. It was mostly empty this time of night. When David returned to the present, he stared at Jeb.

"Cheaters," David said.

Jeb didn't quite follow. "What about them?"

"That's what Lucky was going on about before he went linkdead. He accused me of using marksman scripting to automatically aim my rifle."

Jeb frowned. "Didn't he just say that to antagonize you?"

David shook his head. "There are better ways to piss me off. Accusing me of cheating doesn't make sense, because all the other pros in there know you can't cheat in StrikeForceGo."

"So what actually stops people from cheating?"

"Every official server runs random scans and complex monitoring programs," David explained. "Anyone running marksman or evasion scripts gets caught and banned, and Dust is used in official StrikeForceGo matches. It runs the same monitoring software all the time."

Jeb remembered David commiserating with the pro named MatterRat over their last match. "You mentioned a match—Kudzu versus TrollStompers. You said their sniper missed a shot at LuckyBro, near the end of a big game. Was that sniper competent?"

David nodded. "That was PositiveMC. He isn't the best, but he's a good shot. He shouldn't have missed that shot on LuckyBro."

"So LuckyBro cheated." All Jeb's instincts latched on to this theory. "If everyone truly believes you can't cheat in SFGo, someone who found a way would have a big advantage."

"And if Lucky knew it was possible," David said, "it'd be foremost in his mind. He'd really believe that's how I took down people in One Flag CTF. So, how does it factor in?"

Jeb leaned close and lowered his voice. "Nemoset was cheating too."

David took another sip of whisky and set it down. Jeb expected to see his husband's eyes go wide with shock, but he looked calm as ever.

"He did make some ridiculous shots," David agreed.

Jeb sat back and laid out his new theory. "So, let's say someone discovers players cheating at SFGo, on a professional level. They're stealing sponsorships and money. How would the other players react?"

"They'd be furious. Cheating spits in the face of every pro in the sport."

"What about the admins?"

"Many are pros, too, or retired, like me," David grumbled. "Some are also ex-military, banned but still involved. Many run pleasureboxes for official SFGo matches. If anyone could detect cheating Oneworld missed, it would be a former military-pro turned admin."

Jeb almost smiled. That sounded a whole lot like a motive. "Would this administrator, theoretically, be angry enough to murder those cheaters?"

"Maybe, but how? The military disables our HARM switches when we leave the service."

Jeb remembered discussing HARM switches with Cowan at the start of this case, and how Oneworld could flip those switches, at any moment, and allow those they chose to harm or murder people with impunity.

"Maybe one of you figured out how to flip it back on," Jeb said.

David leaned back in the booth. For the first time tonight, David looked less than calm. "Well, that's terrifying."

Jeb flipped to wireless and called Cowan. *"Still up?"* he asked.

Cowan pinged him back almost immediately, like he had nothing better to do than to wait around for more case intel. Maybe Cowan didn't.

"Here," Cowan answered. *"What's up?"*

"I need you to script a cross-ref. I'll authorize a warrant for records of all boxes that hosted pro StrikeForceGo matches this season." Jeb requested the warrant from the CID and got it quickly.

"What am I looking for?" Cowan asked.

"A box admin who's ex-military. Former SFGo player. Both LuckyBro from Team TrollStompers and Nemoset from Team Grindhouse played in their box this season."

"This is about the Nemoset case?" Cowan asked, audibly excited.

"Possibly," Jeb said, amused despite the situation. *"Can you do it?"*

"Coming shortly." Cowan went silent, but Jeb knew he'd have the info soon enough.

As Jeb waited, a courtesy ping arrived on his CID panel. Someone calling himself Cisero had just taken eighteen people hostage at a sim parlor down in Escondido, and the VCD was on the way. Wonderful. Like they needed a hostage crisis on top of everything else.

"Got it," Cowan called back over wireless before Jeb could investigate the Escondido situation further. *"There's four boxes that fit those criteria."*

"Where are they hosted?" Jeb asked.

"Two in Texas, one in Maryland, and one in California," Cowan said. *"Are the admins listed?"*

"I need another warrant for that. All the administrators are anonymous."

Jeb got it. Two minutes later, Cowan uploaded administrator names. One, Joseph Dunn, actually *lived* in Escondido, which was a bit of a coincidence given their just-announced hostage situation. It set Jeb's case-sense tingling.

"Any admins former military?" Jeb asked Cowan.

There was a pause before Cowan answered. *"Joseph Dunn was military, but anything beyond that is classified. The other three admins have no listed military records."*

That was even more odd. *"Dunn's information shouldn't be classified. Not to us."*

Jeb uploaded another warrant request and waited. Three minutes later, it was denied by MILSEC, the military component of Oneworld. That was highly unusual.

There wasn't much call for the army these days, not since milsynths. Still, all it would take is a few talented hackers to start up another situation like the Peru conflict David fought in. Before Oneworld had stopped them, rebels almost took over the Sim and, by extension, everyone connected.

So, could Dunn *be* the Cisero who'd just taken hostages? Could he have discovered SFGo players cheating and decided to take matters into his own hands? If so, why suddenly switch to hostage taking?

It was a promising theory, but thin. Jeb needed more. He wasn't getting around MILSEC without a week's worth of paperwork, but he had another way to track Dunn.

Jeb flipped back into meatspace, where David waited patiently, having nursed his drink down to only one more sip or two.

"There you are," David said, grinning.

Jeb regretted they had no more time for flirting. "I know the Rangers worked with a lot of navy in Peru. Did you ever hear anything about a man named Joseph Dunn?"

"Hang on." David's eyes went distant this time, and Jeb waited as

David's PBA searched years of records and, likely, thousands of contacts from his military days.

David focused. "Joey Dunn?"

Jackpot! "You knew him?"

"It might not be the same person, but before we officially entered the Peruvian conflict, I was involved in operations I can't discuss with a soldier by that name."

Jeb understood and waited for what David *could* tell him.

"Joey Dunn was a member of the navy's ECM squad," David said. "Most of us called them braincooks. Talented hackers who could do some sick shit to enemy PBAs, and who protected ours against the same."

Jeb beamed as another piece of the mystery surrounding these murders fell into place.

"So Joey Dunn might have the capability to hack a house synthetic," he said.

"If anyone could figure that out, it'd be a braincook," David agreed. "Best thing I can say about Joey is while he was with us, no one in my unit got hacked. The enemy, they didn't do so hot."

"Could a braincook figure out how to flip his HARM switch too?"

David finished his whisky in one last gulp. "Yeah." He set down the glass.

"There's a hostage crisis in Escondido that might be related," Jeb said. "I think us catching our killer in the act, with LuckyBro, might have spooked him. If that's Joseph Dunn, and he can hack synthetics, I have to warn the VCD before he seizes control of their milsynth backup."

"Go." David stood. "There's no record of you being in *Absolution*, and if anyone asks, I'll say the anonymous hardlink was all me. Not like they can prove otherwise."

"Love you," Jeb said, sliding out of his seat. "I'll call you when it's over."

As soon as he was clear of the bar, Jeb informed the VCD he'd received a tip about the hostage situation in Escondido, one he needed to deliver in person. Clearance arrived from Director Stanton, who dispatched a CID helo to the Americas Megacenter. An autocar would never get all the way out here and back to Escondido in time.

Jeb hoped he was wrong about Cisero and Joseph Dunn being the same person, but the way this night was going, no one seemed to be that lucky.

———

Jeb's black CID helo landed in Escondido to find Captain Naomi Barondale and the Violent Crimes Division camped outside Cisero's simParlor. Cowan was on his way, but still twenty minutes out.

simNews would be here in ten minutes. Having had a whole flight to work out possible motivations for Cisero's actions, Jeb suspected Cisero wanted simNews here before he executed the final part of his plan. Jeb had never met any zealot who didn't want some way to preach.

Naomi and her squad crouched behind recently dropped plastibarriers. Behind them stood an army of automated milsynths that served as the VCD's front line, easily twenty or more. Jeb knew he had to work fast. If Cisero was capable of turning those milsynths on the VCD, he might plan to do it in front of the news cameras.

"Captain!" Jeb hopped from his helo and jogged toward Naomi. "A word in private?"

Naomi turned and waited, cybernetic eyes glowing purple. Her soldiers were deployed, her barriers in place, and her target was ignoring all calls. She had no reason to rush.

Jeb crouched behind the plastibarrier, too low for anyone inside Cisero's parlor to see them. He motioned Naomi down. She dropped, Zhang crouching beside her.

Zhang stroked his ratty goatee. "Evening, Forrester. Married life get boring?"

Jeb plugged a linkline into his auxiliary port and spoke aloud. "Got that anonymous tip you were looking for. About Leroy Keller." He offered the other end to Naomi. He knew a skilled hacker could eavesdrop on wireless signals, but a linkline should be relatively secure.

Naomi raised one eyebrow, took the line, and plugged the other end into her own auxiliary port. The world popped.

"You know," Zhang said, "if we've got time for that sort of thing, I wouldn't mind—"

"Shut up," Naomi said out loud. *"Yes, Detective Forrester?"* she then asked over the private linkline. The linkline would keep this entire conversation inside their heads, so no one could eavesdrop.

"I might have intel on Cisero," Jeb said. *"I believe his name is Joseph Dunn."*

"What makes you believe that?" Naomi asked.

Jeb transmitted the records he'd retrieved with Cowan's help to Naomi. After a moment, Naomi took another look at the army of milsynths surrounding them. Her lips pressed together.

"If it's possible to hack our milsynths, what would you suggest?" Naomi asked.

"It's possible Dunn called because he wants to make a statement," Jeb said. *"Maybe he just wants to publicly call out cheaters in SFGo. Or maybe he wants to do something far worse, like make an example of the VCD or Oneworld. Expose a weakness in our system."*

"You really believe he has the skills to hack milsynths? I can accept a house synthetic, but our models use more advanced decryption than anything he might have hacked in Peru."

"I don't see any other reason he'd call you, Naomi. You just delivered his personal army."

Naomi tapped her fingers on one leg. *"If we send them away, or deactivate them, Dunn might suspect we've figured him out. He might start killing hostages."*

"If you don't send them away, he might start killing hostages and *the VCD,"* Jeb countered.

Naomi flipped to her full squad's wireless channel, then added Jeb through their linkline. *"We're going after Dunn now, and we're firing up the security blanket,"* she ordered.

Zhang paled. *"Why?"*

"Zhang, Sparks, Bradley, you're with me. Marquez, you're out here on crowd control. Everyone form up so I can pass out ear-comms. When I give the order, turtle up."

"What kind of a plan is that?" Zhang took another look at their army of milsynths. *"Won't the security blanket disable the bullet sponges?"*

Naomi shook her head. *"From what Forrester just told me, our target can hack milsynths. I'd prefer they don't shoot us in the back."*

Zhang actually turned pale. *"Motherfucker."*

Naomi handed out private ear-comms to her gathered soldiers and offered Jeb an apologetic look. Finally, she spoke aloud.

"I know you can handle yourself in a fight," Naomi said. "I also know you can't hurt or kill human beings, and we may need to hurt someone inside. You stay out here."

"Understood." Jeb lacked a HARM switch, which made him incapable of hurting Dunn purposefully. He could stun anyone trying to escape, however, so he wasn't deadweight.

Naomi pulled the gun from her ankle holster and handed it to Jeb. "Also, given we know our target is a braincook, I'd prefer you carry a weapon linked to our friendly fire safeguards."

Jeb focused on the gun, and his PBA identified it. It was a Glock G70, with real bullets, but he couldn't use this. Before Jeb could ask why she'd handed him the gun, Naomi spoke again.

"It's for the milsynths," Naomi clarified. "They're stunner resistant. If one comes after you, put one round through its faceplate. That should blind it, and it can't shoot you if it's blind."

Naomi was right, and having a real gun was reassuring. Jeb tucked the firearm into the back of his pants, hidden beneath his duster.

"Good hunting, Captain," he said.

Naomi stood and turned to face the darkened parlor. "We'll certainly see, won't we?"

13

JEB

Jeb waited as the VCD activated their mimetic camouflage and moved out as shimmers in the air, like heat off pavement. His own duster couldn't camouflage him, but military gear was for military people. The CID was a civilian branch of Oneworld corporation.

Jeb crouched behind the plastibarrier and sent a wireless message to the CID. *"Going dark for a joint operation with the VCD, under electromagnetic suppression."* He forwarded the message to Cowan too. No point in alarming either of them by vanishing off the Sim.

A security blanket was a very powerful jammer. It scrambled all wireless traffic, including all communication with and orders to synthetics. Only synced encrypted channels, like that on Naomi's ear-comm set, could operate while a security blanket was active.

"Going dark in ten seconds," Naomi said aloud, over Jeb's ear-comm.

Jeb knew the security blanket was active when his wireless connection slipped away. He'd been networked for almost thirty years, and being without a connection to the Sim always left him feeling like someone had wrapped a cotton blanket around his head. Every single sensation—touch, smell, taste—became muffled.

A vague female form materialized by the parlor's front door: Naomi.

She raised a hand and pointed, then vanished again. There was silence, followed by gunfire. Lots of it. Jeb winced. Who were they shooting at?

A handful of seconds later, the gunfire stopped. No one said anything.

"Naomi?" Jeb whispered over the ear-comm.

No answer.

"Sparks? Zhang?"

"They're not picking up," Marquez answered. "They should be picking up." He sounded just a little bit panicked, but he was also tech support. They stayed in the van.

With Naomi out of touch, Jeb saw no options but to start giving orders and hope for the best.

"Open a hole in the blanket and alert Corporate One," he ordered Marquez. "I'll have a look inside."

Jeb vaulted the barricade without effort and crept forward, eyes adjusted to the dim moonlight. Cotton still wrapped his head, assuring him the security blanket remained active, but this silence was wrong.

The building's doors hung open. Jeb slammed into the wall, took a breath, and dashed inside. A metal spike whizzed by as he entered, barely missing him.

Jeb fired his stunner at the shadow, but his round ricocheted off. That sound told him his target was a synthetic, and since the security blanket would keep anyone from operating it remotely, he knew this synthetic was running off its limited AI brain. With luck, that also made it rather dumb.

He dove across the room as the bulky construction synthetic opened fire with is dual nail guns. A nail nicked his calf right before he landed behind the desk. That stung.

"Marquez!" Jeb shouted over his ear-comm. "The construction synthetics in here are still active! What are the ones outside doing?"

Marquez didn't answer. Something inside this building was blocking his ear-comm. Cisero?

Jeb heard beefy metal feet advancing and holstered his stunner. He pondered pulling Naomi's Glock, but this was a construction synthetic, not a milsynth. If Joseph Dunn was watching him, Jeb didn't want to reveal his real gun.

He snapped his artificial hand open. Half his prosthetic palm folded back upon itself, exposing his shocker mount. He rose as the synthetic rounded the table and jolted it right between its boxy yellow shoulders. It dropped like a pile of smoking bricks, overloaded.

Stepping over its still-twitching body, Jeb then discovered why all the shooting had happened. At least eight domestic synthetics clutching knifes and other melee weapons littered the floor, shot full of holes and nonfunctional. There were no human bodies.

Where was the VCD? Where was Captain Naomi Barondale?

"You weren't on the guest list," a voice said over a PA system. The front doors slammed and locked behind Jeb. "Who are you?"

"Just a concerned citizen," Jeb said as he looked around for cameras.

"Good job on the security blanket," the voice on the PA said. "How'd you know I could hack your milsynths?"

"I know everything about you, Joseph." Now was the time for Jeb to test his theory about Cisero being Joseph Dunn. "You're not getting out of this. We have you surrounded. Your only chance is to surrender."

There was a pause. "Who's Joseph?"

The pause suggested Jeb's theory was right, but he kept his face a mask. He hugged the wall as he crept forward, listening for the sound of metal feet.

"What are you trying to accomplish, Joseph?" Jeb asked, using his suspect's name again in hopes of striking a nerve. "Why are you killing people in StrikeForceGo?"

Metal legs clomped ahead, and Jeb fell into a crouch, readying his shocker mount. Running was pointless, but if he could shock the synthetic before it reacted, he might be okay. Jeb jumped out to find Zhang instead, and barely avoided shocking him.

"Zhang!" Jeb hissed. "Is your ear-comm broken?"

Yet Zhang didn't answer. He simply shuffled past, eyes twitching. Each step of his big artificial legs was hesitant and uncoordinated, and a chill gripped Jeb's spine as he realized *why* Zhang looked uncoordinated.

Cisero was remotely puppeting Santiago Zhang's entire body, just like Galileo had done with Sheila Fisher on Jeb's first case with Cowan.

Zhang reached the stairs as his metal feet clomped to a stop. He craned his neck unnaturally and fixed Jeb with worried, rapidly blinking eyes. Zhang—no, the man who was currently puppeting Zhang's body—wanted Jeb to follow him.

So, if Dunn was capable of puppeting everyone in the VCD, why couldn't he puppet Jeb? How were they different? He thought about it, and one answer made the most sense.

Everyone in the VCD had a HARM switch installed. If Dunn knew enough about HARM switches to enable his own, he probably knew enough to use those switches to hack people's PBAs. Unfortunately for Dunn, Jeb didn't have a HARM switch installed in his PBA, which left him safe from being puppeted . . . but for how long?

"What's your name, Detective?" Dunn asked over the PA speakers.

"Me?" Jeb followed Zhang up the narrow stairs. "I'm just a guy having a shitty night."

Dunn chuckled. "I didn't ask you to join the party."

Zhang's puppeted body turned at the top of the stairs and led Jeb down a second-floor hallway. The window at the end was completely covered in shiny foil and metal. A door opened in the middle of the hallway, a room away from the windows. A secure room.

Jeb drew his stunner as another VCD cop stepped out, a young woman with a blond ponytail and blue eyes. He recognized her as Melissa Bradley, another member of Naomi's squad. Melissa strained, eyes wide, as Dunn puppeted her into a low bow. She straightened and held the door open.

"Come in here, Detective," Dunn said over the PA. "Oh, and hand your stunner to Sergeant Bradley. Wouldn't want me to cook anyone's brain."

Jeb handed his stunner to Bradley and entered the room. The VCD report had stated Dunn had over fifteen hostages inside his parlor, so where were they? Only the members of the VCD were inside, and all the rooms on the way up had been empty.

At least Dunn hadn't asked for Naomi's Glock. Dunn didn't know about it. Yet what good would a real gun do when Jeb's clear circuit algorithms prevented him from using it?

Bradley followed him into the room and shut the door. Dunn wanted to gloat, which meant Jeb could buy time. He had to figure something out before Dunn cooked his PBA next.

Naomi stood stiff in one corner, with Sergeant Terry Sparks in the other. Sparks was a tall, muscular man with umber skin, a crew cut, and a long scar down his stubbled face. He pointed his own Glock at Naomi's head.

Jeb kept his hands up. "Now, Joseph. Let's not do anything rash."

"How many hostages do I have now?" the PA system asked. "Six? Do I really need six hostages, or can I get away with five? Four?"

Jeb shook his head. "If you start killing hostages, the VCD will storm the building. Once you start killing people, the kid gloves come off."

He scanned the room once more, but found no one but Naomi's squad. Where *were* the rest of Dunn's hostages? Oneworld had confirmed hostages.

Dunn laughed. "There's no other soldiers outside, Jeb, though sim-News *has* just arrived. Perhaps I'll march this squad out and make them shoot each other for the cameras. That'd be dramatic, wouldn't it?" Dunn's voice grew almost fervent. "That'd make the evening news."

Jeb kept his voice as calm as he could manage. "Where are the hostages, Dunn?"

"You're looking at them."

"The others. Your clients."

"There's no clients in here," Dunn said. "I didn't have any hostages until you arrived. Are you really so inept that you couldn't figure that out?"

So, Dunn had fooled Corporate One's satellites? How? Jeb had seen the IR scans on his flight over, seen fifteen warm bodies huddled inside the building. Either Dunn *was* lying, hiding his hostages somewhere in the building, or he could manipulate Corporate One's satellite imagery. Jeb didn't know which possibility disturbed him more.

"Five," Dunn said. "Five hostages to use as bargaining chips, and one to show the negotiator I mean business."

Jeb turned as Bradley raised her Glock. She pointed it at Sparks' shaved head. Her lips trembled, and her wet eyes blinked. Sparks pointed his gun at Naomi as Naomi aimed hers at Bradley. Zhang mumbled in the corner.

"Who can they lose?" Dunn asked. "Who's the team slacker?"

Dunn wanted Jeb to beg for their lives, but Jeb knew that would only delay a good cop's death. Jeb couldn't follow Dunn's script. He had to flip it.

Jeb signaled his PBA to simulate the effects of drunkenness, as if he had indulged in a whisky with David earlier. That would allow him to cut loose. To seem unhinged in a way he naturally couldn't.

Jeb started laughing. He bent over, chuckling like a maniac. He sucked in breaths and pounded his leg.

"What the fuck are you laughing about?" Dunn sounded pissed, which meant Jeb was getting to him.

Jeb straightened, wiping his eyes. "You. You're so proud of yourself."

"Well, I did puppet an entire squad of VCD," Dunn said, audibly frustrated now. "Did I crack a nerve?"

"You didn't crack anything," Jeb said. "You're in a pleasurebox."

Mimetic camouflage outfits, like those worn by the VCD, hadn't been invented when Dunn served. Few people outside active VCD knew how they worked. There was a chance a man like Dunn had a history of Simulation Disorder. If Jeb could exploit that . . .

"Resorting to mind games?" Dunn sounded intrigued. "You convince me none of this is real and what? I surrender?"

Jeb shrugged. "I don't care what you do, because you've already given us all the evidence we need to burn you a new mind. Let me ask you this: Remember when you called us?"

Dunn said nothing.

"Remember how you waited in your little room, undetected?" Jeb asked. "The VCD showed up, twenty milsynths hopped out, and then we marched in just like you planned?"

"It was a good plan," Dunn said.

"We've been onto you from the start, Joseph! How else would I know your name? We've known you could hack synthetics since you killed Keller. If we knew that, why would we deliver twenty milsynths to your door?"

Dunn huffed angrily. "Because you're a bunch of amateurs, asshole!" He wasn't denying being Joseph Dunn anymore.

"We captured your PBA the moment you took that call," Jeb said, allowing a grim smile to cross his face. "You're in an OMH detention center, and our little fantasy is about to get a lot worse."

"You're not very good at this," Dunn said. "Let me show you who I am. Captain Barondale!" Dunn paused. "When I give the order, shoot Melissa Bradley in the head."

"Oh, and your other problem?" Jeb said. "Because we're controlling your simulation, I still have a gun."

Before Naomi could shoot Bradley, Jeb pulled out the Glock. He fought the warning tingle caused by his PBA, the nausea and blurry vision that followed any hostile intent. His vision clouded.

He reminded himself that he did not intend to hurt anyone, that what he was doing would save lives. He reminded himself that VCD body armor could easily stop a round from a Glock, even at short range. Nausea churned as his entire body shook.

Somehow Jeb shot Melissa Bradley in the chest.

The bullet struck Bradley in her vest hard enough to knock her over. She hit the floor and ceased to exist. Naomi, Sparks, and Zhang all vanished at the same time.

"What the hell?" Dunn said. For the first time, he sounded spooked.

"Here's your problem, shithead." Jeb strode for the door with a wide, predatory grin on his face. "They weren't real."

David had tested mimetic vests before he left the military and shared what he knew with Jeb. All VCD vests had an anti-puppeting safeguard. Any attack from any weapon linked to the friendly fire system made Naomi's entire squad invisible and also blocked their wireless, just in case any of them were being puppeted. Like they had been.

"Bullshit!" Dunn's voice was higher now, panicked, and Jeb's claim about this being a pleasurebox was clearly taking hold. Dunn *was* susceptible to Simulation Disorder.

"You're deep beneath Corporate One," Jeb said, sauntering out of the now empty room. "This is all happening inside your PBA, and now it's going to get real nasty."

"I shielded my hardlink!" Dunn shouted.

Jeb laughed as he descended the stairs, praying Dunn's cameras would follow. "I'm coming down to your little room now, and I'm going to do everything you did to Jacob and Leroy to you."

He used "your little room" because he knew Dunn had to be in the modest basement. This building was only two floors, and the floor plan he'd reviewed on the way over accounted for them all. The basement was where Jeb would put his security system.

"Prove it!" Dunn shouted. "Change the walls to brick!"

Jeb headed for the back of the building, the best place to conceal a trapdoor and ladder. "I'm coming for you, Joseph." He singsonged his voice. "I'm going to break your fingers, oh! I'm going to break your balls."

"Change the walls!" Dunn screamed.

The building rumbled and shook. Jeb rushed beneath a doorframe as plaster dust fell and pattered on his head. Marquez had just blown the building open, probably with the breaching charge from the VCD's truck. Sometimes tech support got out of the van.

Whatever Dunn had done to shield this building from the security blanket wouldn't work with a giant hole in it. Jeb cranked up his amplifiers and listened for the sound of any door. He detected a soft click from the hall behind him.

He spun and sprinted back the way he'd come. When he spotted the closed door, he stopped and kicked it with his boot. The door flew open with a crack. He stormed inside as Joseph Dunn emerged from the trap door, hair wild. Dunn had full body armor, thick boots, and a rifle strapped across his back. He had no helmet.

Dunn shrieked and fumbled for his rifle, but Jeb's clear circuit algorithms wouldn't let him actually shoot another human—not to kill them anyway. Jeb opened his shocker mount and shocked the piss out of Dunn instead. Totally nonlethal.

Boots thumped and people shouted in the hall as Naomi's squad closed in, finally free of Dunn's wireless puppeting. Jeb shouldered Dunn's body and walked out of the room. Weapons surrounded him as a bunch of frantic VCD cops shouted orders.

"Easy, folks." Jeb patted the top of Dunn's unconscious head. "I've got this one."

Naomi lowered her gun and grinned impishly. "Dammit, Jeb."

"What?" He frowned.

She pointed her thumb over her shoulder. "Couldn't you have shot Zhang?"

14

COWAN

"So, Melissa Bradley is a member of Team Grindhouse." Cowan stared at Jeb through a panel in his private simPartment. As it turned out, they hadn't needed him after all.

"Yup," Jeb said. "That's why Dunn called the VCD. Us interrupting him with LuckyBro made him worried we were closing in, and there was one last cheater he needed to kill before he dropped out of sight forever: VCD Sergeant Melissa Bradley. She hacked her PBA to bypass the safeguards that prevented active military from playing StrikeForceGo."

As PBA crimes went, Melissa's was minor, a misdemeanor. Given her exemplary record with the VCD, it was unlikely she'd face any real punishment. That, likely, was why Joseph Dunn wanted to *punish* her.

Cowan shook his head. "He wanted to murder her because active military are banned from StrikeForceGo? All this over a game?"

"StrikeForceGo was Dunn's life, Cowan. His church. Nemoset, LuckyBro, and Sn0wing were shitting all over that, breaking the rules he saw as gospel. They had to be punished, and I think he planned to use the distraction of hacked milsynths to escape."

Cowan snorted. "Kind of a bad plan, wasn't it?"

"Maybe," Jeb said. "But he couldn't have known David and I would figure out his identity. If I hadn't done that and been there to stop him, things would have gone very differently."

Cowan couldn't imagine going through that. "Remind me never to play poker with you."

"Kid, I'm terrible at poker. But I'll kick your ass at chess."

Another panel flashed beside Jeb's, and Cowan barely avoiding looking. He couldn't risk Jeb or the OMH finding out what he was up to. The reason he was late to help Jeb. They were monitoring him right now.

"Get some sleep," Cowan said. "You've earned it."

"You too," Jeb said. "Thanks for the assist, partner."

Cowan closed the panel and took a breath. A sigh of relief followed. The guilt would have eaten at him for a long time if something had happened to Jeb while he was here.

He reclined on his bed, closed his eyes, and activated his sleep loop. Once he was sure the Office of Mental Health was watching nothing but his closed eyelids, he rose, plugged in his hardlink, and dropped into the darkSim.

He swapped to his true avatar: Corvus, a man-sized raven wearing an oversized fez. His eyes glowed a soft red, subtle enough to be cool instead of creepy, and he rarely wore any other avatar in here. On the darkSim, as Corvus, he was kind of a big deal.

He landed on his island in the darkSim—a tropical paradise, filled with coconut trees, surrounded by a sea glistening orange in the setting sun—and opened the blinking panel. The woman who greeted him had bright blue skin, snakes for hair, and a sultry smile that made people weak in the knees. Her name was Medusa Oblongata, and she was one of the best fixers on the darkSim.

"I found the scripts you wanted, hot stuff," Medusa said.

"Both of them?" Cowan didn't bother to hide the shock in this voice. That was bad news.

He'd first contacted Medusa after he recovered the paralysis script from *Sonne's Sanctuary* and had asked her to look for places someone might buy it on the darkSim. He'd been worried Sarah Taggart might have shared her work, but if it was that widespread—

"Your paralysis script and the synthetic hacking one," Medusa clarified. "I didn't think those actually existed, but you know me. Tenacious as I am adorable." She narrowed her eyes. "I gotta ask, Cor, because this is some heavy shit. What do you want with these?"

"I want to make sure they don't hurt anyone I care about." That was absolutely true.

Medusa linked him the download. "Good enough for me."

"Thank you." He could never have tracked down either script on his own, but Medusa had connections he didn't. "How much did it set you back?"

Practically all her headsnakes *tsked* at him. "It's on me. I still owe you for your help with my psycho ex-boyfriend."

Cowan winced. "You know you don't owe me for that." Years ago, one of Medusa's cyberflings had been a bit too determined to take things to meatspace and gotten all sorts of obsessive about it. "Let me pay you something."

She beamed at him. "Not an option, love. Let it go."

"So, who was selling those scripts?" Cowan asked. He wanted her to say Sarah Taggart.

"Some guy named Cisero." Before disappointment could blossom, Medusa spoke again. "I snagged his transaction list."

Excitement made Cowan sit up straight. "Who's on it? Is there an entry for Sarah Taggart?"

"I don't know why you're so obsessed with a woman who's not me, but here. See for yourself." Another download link appeared beside the one for the scripts. "It's all there."

Cowan grabbed both links. "Love you." He meant that, but only as a friend.

Medusa laughed. "Have fun, Cor." Her panel closed.

Cowan scanned the list, and then he jumped so hard he almost swallowed his tongue. There was no Sarah Taggart on this list, but there was another name he recognized.

Galileo.

Shit! Galileo had *traded* a paralysis hack to Joseph Dunn, in exchange for Dunn's synthetic hacking script. So, either Galileo had bought that paralysis algorithm off Sarah—or she'd bought if off him. He knew which made the most sense, and he also knew he'd had it backward. Sarah Taggart wasn't the person paralyzing people in the Sim.

Galileo was. All these recent cases tied back to the mysterious hacker.

So, what other scripts had Galileo traded with Dunn? The puppeting scripts Dunn used to hack the VCD through their HARM switches? The ability to fake Corporate One's satellite imagery? A monitor script to detect who was cheating in StrikeForceGo?

It didn't really matter anymore, since the OMH was going to burn Dunn a new mind soon. Double murder was absolutely a capital crime, and in a few hours, Joseph Dunn wouldn't exist as a person. Someone new would inhabit his body.

What worried Cowan now was what Galileo's illicit trading meant for the Sim at large. If he was selling dangerous scripts to desperate people, enabling them to commit crimes far more dangerous and brazen than they could have managed without his help, the Sim could quickly descend into chaos. Now that Dunn's synthetic hacking script was out there on the darkSim as well, no one was safe, not even in meatspace.

So, what was Galileo's motivation? Money seemed simple, but money didn't explain him puppeting Sheila Fisher into a shooting rampage. There had to be more at stake here than selling people dangerous scripts, but what? What was Galileo hoping to do?

And how many more innocent people was he going to kill on his way to do it?

PART 4

15

KATE

Kate Lambda reviewed the logs from *Sonne's Sanctuary* again. The irregularities from Cowan Soto matched those logged by her father's pleasurebox the night of the attack. For the first time in a year, she had a lead on the man who had put her father in a coma.

"Opaque," Kate said, and her top-floor office windows went dark. Drones could be watching her from several kilometers away, through telescopics. Kate dialed Sonne.

A glowing window appeared above her desk. Sonne blinked with bleary eyes, wearing only a nightshirt, which meant she'd been sleeping. Not all that unusual at 0212.

"Is Dad okay?" Sonne asked. Because of course she would ask that when Kate called her at two in the morning.

"He's fine, sis." Kate leaned forward. "I've finally got a lead on who attacked him."

"Then hold on." Sonne hopped up, walked out of camera view, and came back with a steaming cup of PickMeUp. Kate let her sip and collect her thoughts. Once she was actually awake, Sonne set the cup aside and met Kate's gaze. "Tell me everything."

"I've been going over the archives from Japanese Teahouse." Kate had spent the last two hours verifying the data from the night *Sonne's Sanctuary* was attacked. "You were right. There's an anomaly in the archives."

"I knew that slick shit was lying!" Sonne said as her face lit up. "Did you find out how the ringu girl paralyzed Cowan?"

Kate grimaced. "Actually, the ringu girl wasn't the anomaly."

Sonne blinked like a cat had jumped on her lap. "What?"

"It was Cowan. His PBA doesn't read right in the Sim. It's subtle, but it matches the troll who put Dad in a coma."

Over a year ago, an attacker had paralyzed Kate's father inside his own pleasurebox, despite the fact that her father was in admin mode. Though Kate had been unable to determine who hurt her father, she had isolated a unique signature attached to the attacker's PBA.

After reviewing the logs from *Sonne's Sanctuary*, Kate had discovered the same signature in Cowan Soto. His PBA read just like the PBA of the man who put her and Sonne's father in a coma.

Sonne's hands bunched up. "So, Cowan did this."

Kate raised both hands to stop her sister from doing something violent and rash. "That's the only part I'm not sure about."

Sonne's eyes narrowed. "You're losing me, Katie."

"Just listen. I called in some favors over at Corporate One, accessed classified logs from over a year ago."

"And?"

"Cowan wasn't always with the CID. He used to work at a Oneworld subsidiary, Mind Games, as a PBA engineer. He quit a year ago with a generous severance package."

Sonne leaned closer. "Hush money?"

"It wouldn't be the first time," Kate agreed. "I think they scripted something bad over there, some script Oneworld never wanted to come to light. Maybe it got out somehow."

"A paralysis script?"

Kate shrugged. "Why not? Dad was attacked a few days after Cowan quit, and that might not be a coincidence. Maybe he didn't hurt Dad, but he might have scripted whatever did."

Sonne turned her mug in her hands. "How's Dad doing anyway?

I'm sorry I haven't called. First two simBeds blew out, and then Jennings failed his credit check again—"

"He's fine," Kate said. "I mean, as fine as a person in a vegetative state can be. He hasn't gotten worse."

Sonne exhaled slowly and looked far away, like she did when a problem stumped her. "So how do we find out if Cowan's involved in this?"

Kate tapped her fingers on her desk. "Well . . ."

"Do we fake a cybercrime?" Sonne asked. "Lure him back to the sanctuary?"

Kate winced, mentally. "Didn't you tell me you thought he was cute?"

There was a pause. Then Sonne set down her mug.

"So, that's how it is," she said.

Kate flushed. "I wouldn't ask if there was any other way!"

"You want me to go on a date with the man who may have put our father in a coma."

"Just to find out how he's involved. And besides, you wouldn't be alone with him. We'd go together, double date. I'll bring Lucy, and you invite Cowan."

"And then what?" Sonne demanded. "We roofie him and poke around his brain?"

Kate smiled her best conciliatory smile. "Maybe?"

Sonne leaned close to the vid screen and glared. "I'll kill him, Katie. If he hurt Dad, I'll fucking kill him."

Kate's big sister instinct tingled. "Don't say that! We aren't killers. We're doing this to get justice for Dad, not for revenge."

"Remind me how they're different?"

"Dad wouldn't want you to get your mind burned."

Sonne sat back and hugged herself, probably reacting to a correction from her PBA. "How do I do this, Katie? Smile at him, flirt with him?"

"Well, honey . . ." Sonne was going to like this suggestion even less. "You could start by redacting this conversation?"

"Oh." Sonne relaxed. "I guess that would work."

"Need me to script an infatuation for you?"

"Nope." Sonne's eyes went distant. "I've got this."

16

COWAN

As his autocar pulled into the parking lot out front of *Sonne's Sanctuary*, Cowan checked himself in the mirror one last time. Dark hair spiked, button-down shirt buttoned, slacks unruffled. His stomach fluttered in a way it hadn't in over a year.

He was actually doing this. A date. With dancing.

Cowan hadn't dated anyone since Ellen. Sonne had looked surprisingly relaxed when she called to ask him out, but relaxed was Cowan's nemesis tonight. This was a big step.

Jeb had told him the best way to ride was to get back up on that horse, but that was a stupid, antiquated metaphor. Sonne wasn't a horse, and he certainly wasn't riding her tonight . . . or was he? What was she expecting?

That thought made his stomach churn.

He could easily be much calmer using PBA emotional firewalling, but that felt like cheating. He needed tonight to be real and unfiltered. He needed to know if he could be with someone again, or if betraying Ellen had turned him into a relationship zombie.

He knew the autocar had pinged Sonne's PBA when it arrived, but should he get out to greet her? Would she consider that charming, or condescending? He was just about to step out when her suite's front door opened. He stared just a little bit.

Sonne wore a sparkly, tight green dress with a deep V cut and a hemline at midthigh. Gold highlights glittered in her short blond hair, and her eyelids were painted the same color.

This shockingly gorgeous woman was his date. They were going on a date now. Then there was no more time to panic, because the autocar's door swung open.

Sonne stepped in sideways, in that way women did while wearing clingy skirts. She sat down, buckled in, and smiled at him without saying a word. Her door closed. As the autocar cruised off, Cowan wondered what he should say to her. He wondered if he should have rehearsed.

Sonne peered at him. "You all right? You look a little pale."

"I'm fine!" Cowan blurted.

"Butterflies?"

He exhaled through his teeth. At least she understood. "Just, full disclosure: I haven't dated in a really long time."

"I figured."

"And you look amazing."

Her smile grew. "I know."

"I'm thinking maybe I'm underdressed. You said the club was formal, but I—"

"You look fine." Sonne leaned close and adjusted his collar with confident fingers. "Better."

"Thanks," Cowan said, though he was unsure if the word came out as he got distracted by how good she smelled.

Sonne sat back in her seat. "Relax, all right? I've thought you were cute since the night we stopped that troll. So, let's just spend a night together with no expectations, get to know each other better, and dance badly. Okay?"

When she explained it like that, it sounded totally plausible. "Okay. And I liked you, too, right off. I just wasn't sure if that was appropriate."

"Asking out a woman you'd just investigated?"

"It just felt creepy."

She grinned impishly. "You aren't wrong." Then she twisted to look behind them. She turned forward, blinked, and stared straight at nothing, like she was checking her head desk. "Say, that's weird."

"What's weird?" Cowan asked.

"We went north on the 805."

Cowan had a very good reason not to pay attention to their route. "What's weird about that?"

Sonne blinked again, then focused on him. "Kate's club is south of here, in the Gaslamp Quarter. So why are we driving north?"

Cowan glanced out the darkened window, at multiple lanes and commercial fencing. Autocars were networked to San Diego's Traffic Control System, or T-Conn, and rerouted themselves to avoid congestion.

"Maybe there's a wreck on the freeway?" he asked.

"If that's the case, why not take the 163?" Sonne asked. "You put in Club Sylvan, right?"

Cowan nodded. "Maybe there's a crime scene that hasn't hit the T-Conn yet. I'll check."

He flipped over to his own head desk. A top-down map of San Diego winked open via the autocar's VI, with a hollow blue circle at their location . . . or not.

The map showed them to still be in front of *Sonne's Sanctuary*, just off Balboa. He refreshed it, but the map remained stuck, the autocar circle unmoving. He queried their route, but nothing showed up. No route line appeared.

"You seeing this?" Sonne asked.

Cowan's heart thumped harder. "Yes."

Their autocar was acting an awful lot like someone had hacked it. He'd seen lots of hacking since he started with the CID—too much, even for a legend on the darkSim like—but only one name worried him: Galileo, the man who had puppeted Sheila Fisher.

"I'm pinging T-Conn," Sonne said.

"I'll ping CID," Cowan agreed. The words *Wireless Call Failed* promptly popped up on Cowan's head desk.

"What the shit?" Sonne must have received the same message.

Cowan firewalled his fear center because something dangerous was happening now, and he needed to think clearly. Fear was so central to the brain that you couldn't firewall it off entirely, not like guilt or lust. You could, however, dull it to a manageable level.

He took a poll of surrounding traffic out his window. Their autocar hadn't joined any caravans yet, which was good.

"I'm pulling the emergency stop, okay?" he asked. Doing that would result in a significant fine, a night filing reports, and a court appearance.

Sonne gripped the armrest and pushed back in her seat. "Do it."

Cowan grabbed the emergency interrupt—a bright yellow handle in the floor of the autocar—and pulled. Nothing happened. Their autocar cruised blissfully along the 805.

"Well, fuck," Sonne added.

Someone had disconnected the autocar's emergency stop mechanism. That implied whatever was blocking their wireless transmissions might have some sort of physical apparatus on the car as well. This wasn't just a software problem.

Cowan scripted together a series of wireless detection constructors. He executed his new script and instantly detected a rogue transmission beneath the car.

"I think someone maglocked an override box to the undercarriage," Cowan said. "It's now controlling the autocar's VI."

"How does that help us?" Sonne asked.

"Well, if we can disable the magnet—"

She grimaced. "Okay. Do it."

Cowan glanced around the empty car. "I need a hardlink."

Sonne lifted one toeless shoe and crossed it over her other knee, showing a dangerous amount of leg. She started unscrewing her heel. "Sure, gimme a sec."

Cowan stared as her heel popped right off. "Your heels come off?"

Sonne jabbed the door panel until the maintenance cover popped off, then teased out some wires with her painted green nails. "Easier to conceal than a knife, at least in this dress. Screw the override. Can you hack in here and get the doors open?"

Cowan considered. "I guess, but how does that help us?"

"It gets the doors open. Then we tuck and roll."

Cowan looked out the window again at the pavement zooming by. At the other autocars speeding along to the side, and ahead, and behind them.

"On the freeway?" he asked, incredulous.

Sonne shrugged. "Once it gets off the freeway. The car has to get off sometime, right?"

"Right." Sonne was really good at keeping her head in dangerous situations. That was something he needed to get better at.

Just as Cowan started to unbuckle, the autocar accelerated like a shot put. It tossed him against the seat, and for one terrifying moment, he was certain Sonne had stabbed herself with her heel. The autocar swerved right around the car ahead of them.

Cowan gripped his shoulder belt. "They can hear us!"

"Well, I guess I'll just sit in my chair then!" Sonne shouted.

Yet she arched her back, braced herself with legs and one arm, and stretched for the open panel with her other arm. The car braked hard, tossing them forward.

Their seat belts yanked enough to leave them gasping. Cowan was vaguely aware of an autocar behind them screeching as it veered around them, barely missing.

"They can see us too," Cowan said between gasps.

The autocar sped up again. It danced across lanes as Sonne drew enough breath to shout "Fuck you!" and enthusiastically extend a middle finger.

Sonne clutched her belt and tried for the panel again and failed again. It was like riding a bull in the Sim. If not for the belts, they'd be bouncing around the passenger compartment like crash dummies.

Cowan knew he should be fighting as hard as Sonne to stop this. Yet what could he do while the car was moving and weaving this erratically? If he just had a wireless connection—

That's when it hit him. He *did* have a wireless connection. He had to have a wireless connection, because someone was controlling this autocar, wirelessly!

The mechanism on the bottom of this car might be blocking the specific frequencies PBAs used to communicate wirelessly with the Sim, but there were *other* frequencies. Cowan flipped to his head desk and scripted an automated wardriving routine.

Now, instead of trying to connect to the Sim, his PBA would try to connect to *any* wireless network. If they passed close enough to an unsecured network, he might be able to—

There. A T-Conn plate reader. Cowan had contact just long enough to ping the CID before their stubborn autocar sped out of range. He didn't whoop or alert Sonne, as much as he wanted too. The hacker would hear him, and he needed to leave more breadcrumbs first.

Open freeway fell away behind them as the car veered left to right, right to left, braking, accelerating, and making a general mess of surrounding traffic. Cowan held on because all he could *do* was hold on and pray the car didn't drive them off a bridge.

Finally, his wardriving routine connected to a roadside callbox. It fired another ping, and Cowan cheered in silence.

The CID had their direction and, with timestamps, rate of speed. The CID's monitors would have been alerted the moment he left the Sim, so they had to be looking already. When a CID officer went dark without warning, they noticed.

Their autocar veered wildly across two lanes of the 805, off the actual *road*, and went airborne down a hill. Cowan and Sonne both screamed. Her hand snatched his. They landed hard enough to rattle his teeth, skidded down a hill, and slammed onto a single-lane road below the Five.

Their angry autocar followed that road under the 805, almost gently, and stopped. Cowan took a careful look at their surroundings, then noticed he was holding Sonne's hand. She noticed, too, and immediately pulled away.

Scrub-covered hills rose to the right, and Cowan saw a couple of modest office buildings way up on those hills, far away. There were bridges of freeway crossing each other, and puffy trees, and electrical towers carrying power lines. There were no people.

A rhythmic dinging filled the passenger compartment, a low-battery warning. Sonne went to unsnap her belt.

Cowan snatched her hand back. "Wait! It might take off again."

The autocar's front window exploded in a shower of safety glass shards. A grenade spiraled in through the open window and landed right in between them, spinning like some homicidal version of spin the bottle.

"Shit!" Cowan shouted. He fumbled with his locked restraints, but they remained locked. With no options, he threw his body across Sonne's.

He couldn't stop the grenade from hurting her, but he could protect her head and chest. She could survive with her head and chest.

Cowan braced himself, face mashed against the door. Sonne lay smooshed beneath him, warm and barely breathing. Cars whooshed by overhead. It started to feel a bit awkward.

"Cowan?" Sonne asked, voice trembling.

He winced. "Yeah?"

"Is it a dud?"

Cowan opened his eyes to find himself unexploded. "Maybe?"

The grenade clicked once.

17

JEB

CID detective Jeb Forrester hopped from the CID's helo just before it landed beside the open lanes of the 805, then hoofed it down a steep hill at a decidedly unsafe pace.

An autocar was parked beneath the freeway, doors swung open. The sign on its roof read "Vacant," adding insult to abduction.

Jeb slowed as he closed and pulled his stunner. Cowan's last ping had come ten minutes ago. Upon reaching the autocar, Jeb cleared the passenger compartment. No targets. The only thing inside was safety glass. The attackers must have pulled Cowan out and switched cars.

Four synthcops parachuted onto the scene, dropped from Corporate One's single large airship. Satellites were searching for Cowan as well, and traffic cams, but they were useless without a vehicle to ID. Jeb had no idea what the attackers were driving now, but at least Cowan's pings had given them enough data to box the abductors. He hoped.

"Four-point perimeter scan!" Jeb shouted to the synthcops.

The synths loped to compass points, sweeping the surrounding hills for blood or tracks, anything that could lead them to Cowan. Jeb doubted they would find anything useful. This job looked professional, and professionals didn't leave trace evidence.

He heard the CID helo lifting off, probably responding to another call somewhere. The rhythmic and deafening *whump* of rotors faded into the night. Jeb found himself alone.

He walked around the autocar and spotted a pair of toeless shoes in the street beside the back wheel. Cowan had picked up Sonne before their autocar got hacked, which suggested she had been abducted too.

Jeb shook his head, grumbling to himself in absence of everyone else. "Dammit, kid, what the hell happened to you?"

Director Ivana Stanton contacted Jeb over the wireless network. She was running search-and-rescue from the CID airship floating overhead.

"Forrester," Stanton said, *"you've got a guest incoming via private helo. She's here by invitation of Corporate One, so be nice and don't fuss."*

Jeb responded over wireless as well. *"Pardon me, ma'am, but I can't fucking babysit right now."*

"Play nice, or I'll take you off the search," Stanton said.

As Cowan's partner, Jeb shouldn't even be participating in this search. He was too involved to be objective, or so the procedures said. Stanton was doing him a big favor.

"Yes, ma'am," Jeb grumbled.

He scanned the surrounding area—rolling hills, open freeway, and lots of dense scrub. No street cameras, except up on the 805. No witnesses either. None of the synthcops had reported anything.

This wasn't good. It was likely Cowan's abductors had used military scrubbers to clean this scene, which meant military operators had taken him. Mercenaries?

Who would pay the exorbitant fees of private mercenaries to abduct Cowan? He'd just started at the CID a month ago. Was this related to whatever secret project Cowan had worked on as a PBA engineer before Jeb knew him? Something from his past come back to bite him?

Jeb examined Sonne's discarded shoes with the fingerlight on his artificial hand. One of the shoes was missing a metal heel, with a shallow screw well in its place. So Sonne had detachable metal heels that could easily be used as a weapon? He approved.

Jeb flipped his hand to metal detection and swept it across the car.

Nothing. That meant Sonne might still have that metal heel on her person. Jeb allowed himself a grim smile.

At least Cowan had someone competent watching his back.

"We've got a report from T-Conn," Director Stanton said over wireless. *"They just discovered a camera loop. No footage of the autocar."*

Jeb sighed. Professional mercenaries included professional hackers capable of hacking into T-Conn and looping camera footage. Not that it was difficult. Still, it *was* frustrating.

As Jeb waited, the repetitive *whump* of a helo echoed in his amplifiers in his ears. Who else at Corporate One cared about Cowan's abduction?

Jeb knew the helo was private as soon as he spotted it—Corporate One flew gold and blue, not green and white—but that didn't explain who did. The helo landed on the asphalt off the edge of the 805 bridge, suspension skids flexing with its weight.

Jeb zoomed one eye on the helo's tail number, archived the sequence, and queried the CID using his PBA. The words *Benzai Corporation* popped up in augmented reality above the helo.

Two women hopped out, flagrantly violating corporate dress codes. The AR tags above their head read "Blocked," which meant some big connections. You couldn't normally hide your identity from the CID.

Yet the way these women were dressed, for clubbing, made no sense. The shorter of the two women had light brown skin and Asian features. She wore a low-cut dress with a decidedly racy hemline. It was just a bit impractical for police work.

The second woman was white and almost as tall as Jeb, thin, and built like an Olympic sprinter. She had a blond buzz cut and a sparkling red dress that hugged her small-busted frame, slit up one statuesque leg. She took short steps so as not to outdistance her companion.

The shorter woman shouted over the sound of the helo's still spinning rotors. "Detective Forrester! Kate Lambda, CFO of Benzai Corporation!" She waved as if greeting an old friend. "I'm Sonne's sister!"

Once Kate revealed her identity, the tag above her head shimmered and cleared, confirming she was telling the truth. Kate extended a hand, which Jeb shook once she and her tall friend were close.

Kate didn't introduce the woman with her, and that woman didn't shake Jeb's hand. Instead, she quietly scanned the bridge, the rolling hills, and the cars cruising distant freeways instead. Jeb assumed her to be Kate's corporate bodyguard.

He assessed her threat level and found it high. Kate's bodyguard was almost certainly cyberized, like Naomi, and probably had a HARM switch installed. Jeb had no doubt she could take him out easily.

"Can I ask what you've found so far?" Kate spoke over the noise of the helo rotors.

Stanton *had* asked him to play nice. Jeb decided to answer her.

"We believe an autocar carrying your sister and one of our detectives was hacked, but we don't know who did it, or why," Jeb shouted back. "Our detective managed to send us route pings, and we're setting up roadblocks, but it's just a guess."

Kate reached into her décolletage and pulled out a linkline. She popped it into her port and extended the other end to Jeb. "I might know why this is happening! Plug this in, and let's talk privately!"

Jeb hesitated—plugging a stranger's linkline into his PBA was on his never-do list—but Director Stanton had vouched for this woman. He plugged the other end into the port behind his left ear.

Kate spoke inside his head, over wireless. *"As you've guessed, we were going dancing tonight."*

"You were Cowan's double date," Jeb replied as their clubwear finally made sense.

"A wonderful plan gone horribly awry." Kate narrowed her eyes. *"I understand you don't know who hired them, but you must have some idea who actually hit the car."*

"My instincts say private mercenaries. Closed circuits. I'd wager at least four men."

"Why four?" Kate asked.

"I'd want a decent hacker, an evidence scrubber, and two experienced operators to handle an abduction like this one," Jeb said. *"That's the lightest I'd take if I wanted to capture two targets, and there's no reason to go in heavy if you want to get out quick."*

"Do you know of any reason mercenaries would abduct your partner?" Kate asked. Corporate executives knew, better than most, the type of people you could hire for the right price.

Jeb shook his head. *"I don't know of any specific threat."*

"I might," Kate said. *"Scan Corporate One's criminal records for a man named Oleg Vasser."*

Jeb uploaded a query to the CID. Vasser's official arrest record came back spotty: one count of cocaine possession, pled out, and two assault charges that went away when the victims recanted. Vasser had also been linked to the Bratva—the Russian mob—but the mob had a lot of fingers, so that didn't necessarily connect this to Doctor Anton Barkov, whom he and Cowan had taken down earlier that month.

"Is there something specific I'm looking for?" Jeb asked.

"Vasser's a sex trafficker," Kate said. *"His crew lures women here from Free Russia, Ukraine, and a dozen old Eastern bloc countries. He offers them modeling, secretarial work, or data entry. Once they arrive, he forces them into prostitution."*

That turned Jeb's stomach. The CID didn't investigate that sort of thing, and the official word from Corporate One was that PBAs had ended sex trafficking. Just like they ended violent crime, child abuse, and mass shootings by puppeted young girls.

"You think Vasser has a history with Cowan?" Jeb asked.

Kate's lips compressed. *"Not Cowan. Sonne."*

So it was possible the mercenaries had attacked the autocar to abduct Sonne and had gotten Cowan by mistake?

"I'm listening," Jeb said.

"Sonne heads up one of Benzai Corporation's many charities, Second Chance," Kate explained. *"Most of the proceeds from her waifu parlor go there. We repatriate victims of sex trafficking to their home countries, get them paying jobs there, and set them back on their feet."*

Jeb immediately understood what might have happened tonight. *"Sonne repatriated some of Vasser's women."*

Kate nodded. *"More than a few. We've done enough damage to Vasser's trafficking operations that I knew he'd hit back."* Kate's shoulders slumped. *"I simply expected him to hit me."*

While this was a lead, it felt too clean.

"Do you have anything that specifically points to Vasser?" Jeb asked. *"He can't be the only pimp in California."*

"My suspicions first arose around nine minutes ago, when Oleg Vasser sent me a direct message saying 'Surprise, bitch!'"

Jeb accepted the admonition and nodded. *"Give me one moment to coordinate with my superior, ma'am."*

Jeb popped Kate's linkline from the side of his head, then flipped over to the CID's private channel. *"Director Stanton?"* he asked over wireless.

"Present," Stanton replied. That was her idea of a joke.

"I believe a professional mercenary unit abducted Cowan," Jeb said. *"They might be Bratva, and this might not be about Cowan at all. Sonne, Cowan's date, is close with Miss Lambda. They've been poking the Russian mob with a stick."*

"Mob abductions are out of our jurisdiction, but hacking an autocar keeps us on the ball. You're staying on this as support, but I'm calling in the VCD to take the lead."

Jeb smiled, remembering Naomi. *"Captain Barondale commanding?"*

"Seems appropriate, given she owes you a favor," Stanton said.

Good. With Naomi's squad joining this search and rescue and the VCD's military resources, Cowan and Sonne's chances had just doubled.

"What about our guests?" Jeb asked.

Stanton huffed over the wireless. *"What did I say, Forrester? Be polite."*

Jeb noticed that the rotors on Kate's helo had finally spun down low enough that they could talk without shouting. Good.

"Based on your information, ma'am," Jeb said aloud, "we're bringing in the Violent Crimes Division to take point. With their resources and ours, assuming we got our roadblocks up in time, we have a very good chance of finding Sonne and Cowan still alive."

Kate beamed at him. "Wonderful! Where do we go next?"

Jeb grimaced. "We don't exactly know. It may be best for you to return to your home and—"

"I'm not leaving until Sonne's safe."

"Ma'am—"

Kate fixed him with a firm gaze that made it very difficult to argue. "You're coordinating with Benzai Corporation tonight, Detective Forrester. Our resources are at your disposal."

"And what might those resources be?"

"Many and varied, but you should start by pinging the tracer imbedded in Sonne's artificial heart. When you're ready, I'll up you the security code."

Jeb forwarded that information to Director Stanton, then glanced at Kate's idling helo. "An excellent idea, ma'am. Could I trouble you for a ride to the VCD's airship?"

Moments later they were in the air. Kate sat on one side, with her silent blond bodyguard, and Jeb sat on the other. The helo's engine noise was barely audible inside the passenger compartment, merely a dull *thrum*. This was one expensive helicopter.

Kate leaned forward. "Once we start pinging the tracer in Sonne's heart, how long will it take for you to find her?"

Jeb flipped to his head desk and pulled up a calculator. "What's the signal range?"

"Three hundred meters on a clear day."

Jeb plugged a three-hundred-meter detection radius into the sprawl of San Diego they'd boxed in using Cowan's pings. The result came quickly.

"It'll take us at least six hours to search the entire box," Jeb said.

"Can't you charter other helicopters?" Kate sounded disappointed.

Jeb flipped back to meatspace. "Unfortunately, ma'am, we already chartered all our helos."

Kate patted Jeb's wrist like you'd pat a small dog. "Please, call me Kate."

That went against every fiber in Jeb's being, for the same reason David couldn't slouch. Speaking as a formal CID detective had been Jeb's life for decades. Kate's blond bodyguard watched him in silence, calm and incredibly intimidating.

Still, Jeb did his best. "Do you know of any way to do this faster?"

Kate blinked into the Sim and out again. "Well, I could certainly charter more helicopters." She smiled, eyes distant. "There. They're on their way."

Jeb stared at her blankly. "Helicopters?"

Kate sat back, focused on Jeb, and settled her hands in her lap. "All six pilots are VIs, so they'll have no trouble coordinating with your airship. Will that assist you in your search?"

Jeb smiled. "Yes, ma'am."

She raised an eyebrow at him.

"Kate," Jeb amended.

Benzai Corporation's CFO fascinated Jeb, and not in the way she likely fascinated other men. In the short time he'd had to evaluate her, she'd been operating at a whole different level. Corporate One deferred to *her*.

Jeb couldn't get a read on her, or her intimidating blond bodyguard. Was Kate genuinely afraid for Sonne? Or was she playing detective because the financial game now bored her?

He wasn't going to figure her out on this short flight. Like many in the corporate world, Kate Lambda was a chameleon, and chameleons made Jeb nervous.

Still, Kate adding more helos to their search would cut their search from six hours to a little over one. Cowan needed him. Jeb wasn't going to let his partner down.

Kate offered a sympathetic look from across the cabin. "You really care about Cowan, don't you? Have you been partnered long?"

Jeb didn't like how easily she could read *him*. "We've only been partnered six weeks," he said. "But he's a good detective."

Kate's helo approached the VCD carrier's single landing pad. A big conning tower sat in the center of the carrier, blinking with red lights.

The carrier itself was a square metal bowl with boxy troop hangers running along each side. Giant vertical rotors at its four corners kept it flying. It was essentially a quadcopter on a massive scale.

Kate caught Jeb's gaze again. "I care about Sonne as well."

As Kate stared at him, with her lips just the slightest bit compressed and one finger gently tapping, Jeb finally got a read on her. She was terrified for her sister. She was simply really good at hiding it.

"We'll find them," Jeb said.

After a long moment of silence, as if taking his measure, Kate nodded. "You'll call me the moment you get a ping?"

Kate's helo landed and its door rolled open, blasting them with warm air. "Yes, ma'am," Jeb said, then grimaced. "I mean, Kate!"

18

SONNE

SEPTEMBER 14, EVENING

Sonne woke with cotton mouth and eyes that burned like she'd been cutting onions. She focused her blurry vision and ignored discomfort until she picked out metal walls and heard tires on road.

She was in the back of a van with metal bars running along the inside of its walls. Duct tape tied her hands around one of the bars on the driver's side, so she'd obviously been kidnapped.

Just her luck.

The man sitting against the van's other wall had dark skin beneath his purple ski mask, which exposed only his lips and eyes. He held a rifle that may as well have been right out of StrikeForceGo. He wouldn't be carrying that rifle if he couldn't use it, which made him a closed or loose circuit.

He grinned when she noticed him, and it wasn't the good kind of grin. It was creepy as fuck.

Yet Sonne felt relieved when she noticed Cowan nearby, unconscious, with his hands duct-taped to the bar. Then, of course, she felt guilty for feeling relieved. Cowan didn't deserve to be dragged into her messed-up life.

Just the thought of him jumping on what he thought was an

explosive to save her impressed her. It turned out to be a smoke grenade, but still. Only a truly decent guy would jump on a grenade to save a woman he barely knew.

Past Cowan, another man sat against the van's windowless back doors. He wore a green ski mask and had a linkline snaking from his head into a small black "Party Box"—a wireless router that anonymized Sim connections.

Sonne imagined shelves hooked to the bars on the walls and pegged this van as a gutted UPX transport, brown and common as flies. A humble mail truck would be completely anonymous among hundreds now on the road, and it had no windows. How was she going to get free?

The man in the purple mask was still staring at her. *Really* staring at her. Instead of looking away, she narrowed her eyes at him.

"Can I help you, asshole?" she snarled.

Purple snorted. "Here I was, enjoying the view, and you had to open your potty mouth." He showed her his rifle's stock. "Shut up before I knock out those lovely teeth."

They hadn't stripped her—she still had her clingy green dress on—and Sonne was distinctly aware of the heel tucked into her underwear. She'd shoved it through the opening at the small of her back as that grenade spewed thick white gas, using Cowan's dramatic hero dive to conceal her motion from the autocar's cameras.

A review of tonight's tumultuous events suggested these men were after her, not Cowan. If they wanted him, they'd have hacked his autocar *before* it picked her up. So who would go to all this trouble to abduct her?

Given Sonne's name was actually floating above her waifu parlor, she wasn't exactly hiding, and there were plenty of powerful people she'd pissed off over the years. Both by accident and on purpose.

Her hunch, based on the firepower and the men with the ski masks, was that this had to be about her and Kate's efforts to free sex-trafficking victims. Only an organized criminal enterprise with a shitload of money could afford to smuggle a group of closed circuit mercenaries into San Diego.

But which one? There were a number of sex traffickers who had a hard-on for her and Kate. Lee Chang. El Zorro Plateado. Oleg Vasser.

They'd been busy working the underground.

Sonne should have chartered a secured autocar directly from Kate, but she'd been so busy with her latest pleasurebox that she'd ignored the danger. The average mobster couldn't get near Kate—her bodyguard, Lucy, would take those men apart before they even pulled their guns—but they could go after Kate's allies. Her family. As they had done tonight.

Sonne had to get Cowan out of this, if he was still alive, and then she had to get herself out too. She wouldn't be trafficked. After Cowan was safe, she'd escape . . . one way or the other.

So who had she pissed off most recently? The ring they'd most recently busted up was owned by Oleg Vasser, so she'd start with him and work her way out from there. "How much is Vasser paying you?" Sonne asked.

Purple raised his rifle stock. "Teeth, pretty." Yet his intake of breath suggested she'd just guessed his employer, which was a bit of luck.

Sonne glared at him and resisted the urge to spit. "If you were going to clock me with that thing, you'd have tried it already. I know what Vasser guarantees. No marks on the merchandise."

"You're right," Purple said. "I can't hit you." He crossed the truck, raised his rifle stock, and smashed it into Cowan's side.

Cowan *urked* and flopped awake, arms thrashing against the tape. His eyes went wide with pain.

Instinct caused Sonne to block Purple's access to Cowan, but she couldn't reach him. She couldn't reach anything with her hands taped around the bar.

"Stop that!" Sonne shouted. "You stupid shit!"

"I'm stupid?" Purple slammed his stock into Cowan's ribs again. "You like seeing your boy black-and-blue?"

Sonne's next lunge nearly wrenched her arms out of their sockets, but she scarcely noticed. "Stop hurting him! You pigfucker!"

"Sonne!" Cowan shouted. "Stop . . . negotiating . . . for a second?" He coughed with each word, writhing in agony.

Purple raised his rifle again, and despair made Sonne all but wrench off her own arms. How could she stop him? She had to stop him!

A male voice spoke clearly from the front of the van, at exactly the right volume to cut through road noise. "Mister Purple. Stop hitting Mister Soto."

Purple glanced toward the front of the van, glaring. Yet he did lower his rifle, which meant the man up front, in the passenger seat, was running the show.

That man spoke again, and he sounded way too calm for the situation. "Now that you're awake, Samantha, I can confirm your suspicions. We were hired by Oleg Vasser."

The name he'd uttered set off every terror sensor in Sonne's brain. "Who the hell is that?" she demanded.

"Don't play coy, dear," the man said. "Vasser runs—"

She interrupted him. "Samantha, you idiot. Who's Samantha? My name's Sonne."

He'd called her Samantha, but that hadn't been her name for years. How could this man know who she'd been before she erased her history? No one knew her old identity but Kate.

The man clucked his tongue. "Samantha Frederick, wasn't it, before your parents died in that tragic wreck? Killed in a vehicle collision with a closed circuit who'd had too much to drink?"

Sonne blinked rapidly as the smiling faces of the parents she'd buried fifteen years ago rose from their graves. The loss of her old family was why she'd changed her name, of course. Her old life hurt too much.

She made her voice hard. "You don't know what you're talking about."

Sonne also noticed Cowan was simply listening now, not talking. Probably a good idea. She hoped Purple hadn't broken any of his ribs.

"Here's how this is going to work," the man up front said. "You're going to ride in the back of this van, quietly, until we reach the industrial marina below Point Loma. After we arrive, you'll embark on a chartered boat and never see us again."

Sonne tugged at her duct-taped hands. "And where am I going? Mother Russia?"

"Your destination is known only to Mister Vasser," the man said. "I could lie to you, but you seem like a smart and rational woman. I won't insult your intelligence."

"What's Vasser paying you?" Sonne asked. "Benzai Corporation will double it. Triple it."

The man sighed in reproach. "You know quite well that's not how this works. Now, while I have asked Mister Purple to stop assaulting your companion until I could explain the situation, I feel your situation is now perfectly clear. He will resume if you resist."

Sonne said nothing.

"Would you like Mister Purple to hit Mister Soto again?" the man asked.

Sonne pulled futilely against the tape. "No." No point in getting Cowan hurt more.

"Thank you," the man said.

Purple glared at the front of the truck. "What the fuck, Gray? Why are you being so nice to them?"

So the man up front was Gray. Sonne took another look at the hacker in the green ski mask—Mister Green?—and their colorful nicknames suddenly made sense. These men didn't know each other, and more importantly, they didn't *want* to know each other.

This was clearly a team of mercenaries thrown together for this abduction, not a unit with long-standing ties. That meant they'd have no loyalty to each other, save Vasser's money. If she could turn them against each other—

Green gasped, tucked his Party Box against his side, and crawled forward, linkline dangling. "Shit! Mister Gray!"

"Yes?" Gray asked.

"We have to get off the Five. They're checking traffic at the toll plaza four exits down. They've got synthcops doing full vehicle scans."

Gray went silent for a moment. "Mister Yellow, if you would—"

"Shit!" Green interrupted. "More checkpoints, a cordon! They've got us in a box!"

"Do you mean perimeter?" Gray asked.

"Yes!" Green shouted. "They've dropped checkpoints

everywhere—along the Five, the Eight, and the 163! They boxed us in. How did they box us in?"

"Likely a radius based on speed," Gray said. He didn't sound upset at all. "One of our guests must have found a way to alert the authorities to their abduction. Mister Yellow, reroute us to safe house bravo."

Sonne winced as she felt the van cruising down an off-ramp, momentum pulling at her hands. They didn't stop Purple from slamming his rifle butt into Cowan's side again. Sonne gasped and glared.

Yet she couldn't shield him, couldn't help him like he'd done for her.

"Stop that!" Sonne shouted. "We're cooperating!"

"You stupid pig!" Purple shouted. "You called them."

Cowan gasped against the wall. "I didn't call anyone. I don't know how they found you."

Purple raised his weapon high, and Sonne was certain he was going to bash in Cowan's head. She involuntarily looked away. It would be like her mother's head, hanging in their upside-down car, smashed to bits.

"Enough!" Gray shouted from up front.

Purple glowered as Sonne stretched out with her legs, trying to shield Cowan with her calves. Her shoulders screamed with pain as her arms bent.

Cowan started coughing again, against the floor, and Sonne ached for him. It felt like the truck had slowed, so maybe they were on surface streets. Had Cowan really notified the CID somehow?

"We have contingencies," Gray said. "While I'd like you to ensure neither Miss Frederick nor Mister Soto attempt anything rash, stop hitting them. When we've stopped the truck and evaded surveillance, we'll discuss our next move."

Gray's disturbing calm creeped Sonne out. It suggested he was either a highly experienced soldier or a genuine sociopath. Turning a man like that against his employer would be near impossible, but this perimeter news gave her hope.

The CID was looking for them, which meant Kate might be looking as well. Had Kate told the CID about the tracer in Sonne's artificial heart?

All she had to do was survive, delay, and confuse. Sonne was the reason Cowan was in this mess, the reason he was getting the snot beat out of him.

Yet Cowan had somehow contacted the CID through the jamming, then dove across her body to save her from a grenade. He really was a decent guy. She hadn't met a decent guy in a few years, at least.

Gray moved into the back of the truck, wearing black body armor with pockets holding who knew what. A gray ski mask covered all but dark eyes and pale lips.

He drew a stunner from the holster across his chest and pointed the weapon at Sonne.

"I apologize, Samantha," he said. "We need to have a short discussion, and that discussion doesn't involve you."

Sonne pressed against the wall. "Hold on. You don't—"

Mister Gray fired his stunner.

19

COWAN

Cowan snapped awake, cuffed to a bed with his wrists stretched above him. More cuffs spread his legs below.

A single hanging bulb lit the room. Besides the bed to which he was bound, his cell held a pair of rusted empty shelves. There was no other furniture.

His ribs ached, though not enough to be fractured or broken. He used the privacy to check his PBA: active, but offline. As expected. Like this, his PBA would still keep him from hurting anyone, but he couldn't use it to call for help.

Cowan checked his hidden partition, opening every last one of its passive archivers of the twenty minutes he'd been out. They couldn't have known he could still record while he was unconscious. Perhaps these men had said something incriminating, like who they were or where they were.

There was shouting in the distance on one archive, indistinct, but it sounded like a woman who was very pissed off. That would be Sonne.

He listened to another conversation he couldn't make out—all muted tones and the sound of a bed creaking and cuffs snapping. A door closed.

Useless. At the very least, Cowan verified no one had implanted spyware or downloaded his ghostlink after Gray stunned him. His captors hadn't been able to get past his numerous firewalls, which was why he kept his PBA locked up tight.

Yet Cowan *was* still captive, still chained to a bed. Still all alone in an empty concrete room.

His heart hammered as he flipped to his head desk and scripted a shoddy but serviceable firewall to control his fear. If he wasn't scared out of his mind, it would have been easier.

His heart slowed as his mind focused on something other than why someone would cuff him spread-eagle to a bed. He had to figure out what these men had done with Sonne, and how he was going to get her out.

His captors. That's where he'd start. Sonne had been smart. She'd made these men admit they worked for Oleg Vasser and had confirmed they were after her, not him. There was no way he'd let them send her off to Russia somewhere, but how could he stop it?

The metal door to his cell screeched roughly, one edge scraping the cement. The same man who had stunned him walked inside, still wearing his gray ski mask. Gray held a machete, and Cowan's heart hammered right through his shoddy firewall.

This wasn't a pleasurebox. This was reality, and Cowan knew what someone whose impulses were unregulated by a PBA, like the mercenaries who'd abducted him and Sonne, could do to another person, in meatspace, when they had a sharp object and a great deal of time.

Gray stopped beside the bed, staring down. "How are you feeling, Mister Soto?"

Cowan focused on talking. "Do you really care?"

"No, just being polite. You work for the CID?"

Cowan remembered everything he'd ever learned about interrogations, which wasn't much. It was basically delay, deflect, delay.

"I work for the Office of Mental Health," Cowan said. OMH employees didn't get Krav Maga packages installed, which might let him surprise Gray if he got out of these cuffs.

Gray tilted his masked head, smiling as if they were friends. "And what do you do for the Office of Mental Health, Mister Soto?"

So Gray was just asking questions? Cowan could answer questions. His firewall steadied, his heartrate evening out.

"I help people," Cowan said. "People who've suffered loss or traumatic events."

"Is that what you were doing on your date?" Gray asked.

So Gray had interrogated Sonne and was now interrogating him. Gray was checking to see if their stories matched. Had Sonne told the truth?

"It wasn't a professional engagement," Cowan said. "We were heading to a club, for dancing."

"Which club?"

"Club Sylvan," Cowan said. "It's in the Gaslamp Quarter, somewhere."

"An expensive date." Gray slammed the machete down on Cowan's hand with a loud clang.

Cowan screamed as his firewall flew apart, unleashing all the terror he'd tried futilely to block away. His fingers throbbed like they'd been chopped off, but when he looked down, they were still there, just curled up.

Gray had used the flat, blunt top of his machete, not the sharp edge. But *why*? Cowan hadn't lied about the club!

Gray strolled around the bed, eyes calm. "You're asking yourself, why did I hurt you?" He whacked Cowan's knee, causing more blinding pain.

"Stop!" Cowan screamed.

He wanted to curl up, to shield himself, but the cuffs kept him mercilessly extended. His fingers throbbed, and his knee felt like it had popped right off.

"I don't want to hurt you," Gray said, calm as ever. "I don't actually enjoy hurting anyone, but I have tortured when the situation required it. Do you understand why I'm telling you this?"

"You want to terrify me," Cowan said. Mission successful.

"Terror fades," Gray said. "Torture lingers. Those in psychiatric circles believe extended torture causes PTSD equal to or more significant than experiencing heavy combat."

Cowan breathed. "I understand."

Gray smiled, perfectly pleasant. "So now, Mister Soto, I'm going to ask you some questions. If you lie, I may hurt you."

"May?" Cowan asked, desperate to understand.

Gray nodded, tapping the flat of his machete against one hand. "Pain when you lie is terrifying enough, but you can control that. You choose when you lie, and thus when you hurt."

Cowan was starting to get where this was going now.

"However," Gray continued, "when one experiences pain repeatedly, randomly, and without warning . . . that is the worst pain, Mister Soto, because it is pain you cannot control. So who do you work for? Tell me."

Cowan took a deep breath, then let it out. "The Cybercrimes Investigation Division."

So much for delay and deflect. Still, Cowan wanted to keep his hands. Despite this man being absolutely terrifying, Cowan had to focus on his goals here: staying alive, keeping his hands, and freeing Sonne.

"Where's Sonne?" Cowan asked.

Gray frowned. "Samantha Frederick?"

Cowan remembered that name from the back of the truck, and he frowned as he considered. "That's her real name?"

Gray nodded. "You haven't been dating long, I trust. Miss Frederick is alive and unharmed, for the moment. Now I'm going to ask you another question, and then I may hurt you or not. My choice."

Cowan's knee pulsed. "What's your question?"

"Does the CID know where you are right now?"

Cowan hesitated until Gray raised his machete. "No." He only had one other kneecap, and he couldn't run away if he lost feeling in both.

Gray lowered his machete and walked to the metal door. "Thank you, Mister Soto. We won't speak again. Your CID will rescue you in an hour."

Wait, that was it? All that buildup, and just one question? Cowan strained his neck as he watched Gray walk over to the door.

"Hold on!" Cowan shouted. "Where's Sonne? Samantha?"

Gray opened the door with a screech of protesting metal. "Miss Frederick is no longer your concern."

"I won't let you take her!" Cowan thrashed against the restraints, even though that sent pain screaming through his knee. "I'll come after you! I won't stop looking, ever!"

Gray walked out and slammed the door behind him, seemingly unconcerned. Cowan needed another approach. As his mind scrambled for any answer, one came.

These men worked for Oleg Vasser. Vasser was Russian. Galileo was Russian, or at least working for the Russians, so if Cowan pretended to have information on Galileo . . .

"Wait!" Cowan shouted. "I can tell you what the CID has on Galileo!"

Footsteps sounded outside the door. The bolt rattled. It had worked. God, it actually worked!

The door screeched as it swung wide. Gray walked inside, now without wearing his ski mask. Cowan gasped and looked away, but too late.

He'd just seen Gray's face: tan, lightly freckled, with an odd C-shaped scar on one cheek. He had short blond hair and soft blue eyes, and Cowan knew what it meant to see Gray's face.

Gray couldn't let him live now.

Cowan had overplayed his hand. He'd just gotten himself murdered. But could he have done anything different? He couldn't just let this madman take Sonne.

Gray walked back over to the bed, tapping the flat of his machete idly against his thigh. "What do you know about Galileo?"

Cowan was well past fucked now, so no more holding back. "He's a puppetmaster on the darkSim. He was working with a grayDoc, Anton Barkov, a man who—"

Gray interrupted. "What do you know about Doctor Barkov?"

Cowan frowned at Gray. The man almost sounded . . . excited? That was weird, but whatever.

"Galileo worked with Barkov, or blackmailed him," Cowan said. "We're not sure which. But he—"

"Do you know how Doctor Anton Barkov died?" Gray asked.

Doctor Barkov's name had hooked Gray. Why? Wasn't Galileo above him?

Maybe not. Was it possible Galileo was working *with* the Russian mob, but not *for* them? Was Galileo selling invasive scripts to them, like he'd sold invasive scripts to Joseph Dunn and Sarah Taggart and others?

Cowan focused past his throbbing temples and aching knee. "I know how Doctor Barkov died. Galileo planted a killswitch in Barkov's brain."

Gray scratched his chin. "And this is how Doctor Anton Barkov died? Because of this killswitch?"

"That's right," Cowan said. "When Barkov tried to betray Galileo, the switch kicked in and locally puppeted his body. Barkov put his own revolver to his head, and then he pulled the trigger."

Gray smiled, a genuine smile that actually looked . . . warm? "Thank you, Mister Soto. You've been more helpful than you know. Let's make a deal."

"Seriously?" Cowan asked. Why would Gray offer him a deal, now?

Gray lowered his hand. "I'll explain in a way that, I hope, will make you accept my offer without hedging, as we have little time. Galileo has always been my primary target. Abducting Sonne, for Vasser, was a side job."

Cowan blinked. "Really?"

"Now that you've actually pointed me in Galileo's direction and hopelessly complicated Sonne's abduction, risking my freedom to sneak your friend through a corporate perimeter is no longer in anyone's best interest. And as actually murdering a CID officer like yourself would bring a great deal of heat I'd prefer to avoid, I propose we compromise."

"Right," Cowan agreed, slowly. "So what you're saying is . . . it's now in your best interest *not* to abduct Sonne, and mine to help you somehow?"

Gray smiled tolerantly. "You're quite the astute detective."

Cowan was pretty sure Gray was being sarcastic, but he wasn't going to complain right now. "You wouldn't be offering a deal if you didn't need something from me that I hadn't given you, yet. So what is it?"

Gray leaned close. "I'm only going to explain this once, so please pay close attention."

20

SONNE

Twenty minutes later, Mister Purple marched Sonne across the cold warehouse floor, barefoot. She saw a new unmarked black van waiting, so they were switching vehicles *again*.

She knew Gray was busy interrogating Cowan, and prayed he wouldn't hurt him. Yellow and Green waited at the van. Green paced nervously, clutching his Party Box, and Yellow leaned against the van's side, looking bored.

Purple gave Sonne a shove.

She grunted and kept her feet, resisting the urge to bite his nose off. Of course, biting Purple wasn't within her parameters right now, nor was punching him, or kicking him in the balls. She couldn't even tear his ear off with her teeth.

Green had shut down her PBA's wireless functions, somehow, but left her behavioral algorithms active. Fortunately, even her PBA's restrictive behavioral algorithms allowed strong language, and Sonne had used that liberally to keep Purple at bay as he escorted her to the back of the warehouse, to the restroom.

At least he hadn't insisted on coming inside. Those few precious moments of privacy gave her the opportunity to slip the metal heel from her underwear into her bra strap. So long as no one ripped her dress off—which they hadn't, yet—she could use it to saw through her bonds.

When the time came, Sonne knew she could rescue Cowan.

Green blinked once, probably checking his head desk. "It's been too long," he said out loud. "Gray should be done by now."

Just before they reached the van, Purple shoved Sonne again, hard. She banged into the van before she could react. Spots danced before her eyes as she dropped on her ass by the van.

She shook off the impact and stayed down, refusing to give Purple the satisfaction of seeing her in pain. Then she turned her body and scooted up against the van, hiding her back and hands.

Yellow advanced on Purple, teeth bared. "Idiot. We do not damage the package."

Purple shrugged. "She's not hurt."

Green hurried over to Sonne and dropped to his knees beside her, watching her with worried eyes. "Yellow's right. Look at her temple, Purple! You left a bruise. The contract distinctly said, 'Not a mark on her.'"

"It'll fade," Purple said.

Yellow stepped past Green, staring Purple down. "You're a dick, you know that? Next time she needs a restroom break, I'm taking her."

Green and Yellow's feigned concern for her only made Sonne angrier. "You realize you're all still assholes, right?"

She expected Yellow to scowl at her. Instead, he winked and offered an almost charming grin. "Comes with the job, sweetheart."

Sonne hated that grin, and she hated the algorithms that kept her from hopping up and smashing all their noses with her forehead.

Purple grimaced and threw up his hands. "Who cares if she gets scuffed up? She'll get worse when Vasser drops her into one of his brothels."

Sonne felt sick. She wasn't being trafficked. No way. Falling on her metal heel would see to that if it came to it.

"Go get Gray," Yellow told Green.

Green grimaced and stared petulantly at Yellow. "Why me? I'm not your errand boy."

Yellow threw up his hands. "Jesus! Fucking amateur hour in here." He strode past Purple and into the warehouse. "Hear this, Purple. You put any other marks on her, and it's coming out of your cut."

While they were distracted, Sonne flexed her shoulders and subtly arched her back. The heel slipped lower, then lower again. If they'd just stop watching her so closely, she could—

Purple crouched before her. "Why the closed legs, *Samantha*? You scared of a real man?"

Sonne couldn't let him get any more interested. She smiled her most mocking smile. "If you're a real man, I'm the fucking tooth fairy."

Purple punched her hard enough to knock her head against the van, again. He chuckled as she reeled.

But at least he wasn't trying to get her dress off. She just had to buy more time to cut herself loose. Then she could run and free Cowan.

Green grabbed Purple's hand and yanked him upright. "Stop hurting her!"

Purple shoved Green hard enough that he almost fell on his ass. "Her face hit a panel when the car stopped. Don't be a pussy."

"Right," Sonne said, because a pissed-off Purple was better than a lecherous one. "A pussy wouldn't slug a bound woman half his weight."

He rounded on her, fist raised. "Fuck you, woman!"

"No, fuck *you*. You're shit, and your whole family is shit, and when you're dead in a gutter no one will care."

Sonne despised this man and all like him. She hated everything they'd done to her and so many others. She might not be able to rip their ears off, but she'd curse them until she couldn't.

Green pushed up. "I need this money, you ass! You need to stop."

Purple scoffed. "Make me."

Green hissed and threw a punch, an actual punch, and it was so unexpected that it clocked Purple in the chin. Yet Purple just laughed and slugged Green in the stomach, doubling him over.

As the two of them played grabass, Sonne dropped her heel into her hands. She sawed at the tape.

The sharpened edge quickly cut her fingers, which stung, but she kept going until the tape split. Her wrists parted. She was going to escape!

Gray's voice boomed across the open warehouse. "Both of you, stop that at once!"

Sonne barely held back a curse. Gray always showed up at the worst times. Yet she was free now, unbound. She gripped her heel and waited.

She couldn't stab any of them because of her PBA—God, did she wish she could stab them—but she could run and get help. Yet that would mean leaving Cowan, which could get him killed. And if she tried to free him and failed, they'd likely *both* die. What should she do?

Purple dropped Green and stepped away, chuckling. Green rolled onto his back, wheezing. Gray glanced at Green, at Purple, and at Sonne.

"What happened to her head?" Gray asked, calmly.

Purple shrugged. "Bumped it on the way to the potty."

Gray nodded, a mild frown on his face. "And her cheek?"

Purple grinned. "How should I know what some bitch does on the pot?"

Gray sighed and put a hand to his forehead, idly rubbing his temples with his eyes closed. "Accidents happen?"

Purple grinned through his ski mask. "That's right. Accidents happen."

Gray opened his eyes, then drew a real gun, metal, not the knockout variety. "Thank you, Mister Purple. Your services are no longer required."

He shot Purple in the face.

The *bang* made Sonne's eardrums pop. Blood and brains splattered all over Green like a plate of half-eaten spaghetti.

Green rolled away screaming, flailing at unexpected gore. Purple's body dropped to its knees, then fell forward with a wet thump.

Green raised his hands. "Don't shoot! Don't shoot!"

"Don't cause problems," Gray suggested.

"I won't, I promise. No problems. Whatever you want."

Gray glanced at Sonne and smiled. "Are you all right, Samantha?"

Sonne ignored the ringing in her ears and nodded. Gray had just shot a man in the face like it was nothing, like he was nothing. As rough as her life had been, she'd never seen anyone *shot* in meatspace.

Gray advanced on her. "I'm going to let you go, Samantha."

Mister Green blinked on the warehouse floor. "But wait, didn't we—"

Gray's gun snapped to aim at Green.

He balled up. "We're cool! We're cool!"

Gray lowered his weapon. "Fear not, Mister Green. You're still getting paid. More for all of us now."

Green blinked and kept his hands raised high. "Really?"

"I wouldn't lie to you," Gray said.

Gray knelt before Sonne. He rested his pistol on his knee and stared at her with an earnestness that was even more terrifying than his prior cold indifference.

"I'm going to grip your arms and help you stand," Gray said. "I won't touch you in any other manner, and I will release you once you're standing safely. Do you agree to that?"

Sonne resisted the urge to scream at him. After all this, her whole night, after kidnapping her, he was asking her fucking *permission*?

Yet after a moment, Sonne nodded. She might drop her heel if she tried to stand without him.

Gray gripped her upper arms and pulled. He had a firm grip, and he showed no exertion as he lifted. Did he have cybernetic implants like Lucy?

Gray set Sonne upright, steadied her, and stepped back like he'd promised. She kept her hands hidden behind her back, clutching her heel so tight her knuckles hurt.

Gray looked to Green. "Get up, please."

Green did as asked.

Gray looked past Green. "The suitcases Vasser gave us are loaded in the van?"

Green glanced back at the van. "Yes?"

"Would you mind checking for me?" Gray asked.

Green nodded. "Sure."

They both waited a moment.

"Now?" Gray added.

"Right! Okay." Green had to step over Purple to get to the van, and he did so like he was creeping past a voracious dog. Green opened the van and then twitched, visibly, like someone was poking him.

"Who are they?" Green whispered, barely loud enough for Sonne to hear.

Gray smiled. "Don't concern yourself with the additional bodies in the van, Mister Green. It's no one you know."

Green blinked, then looked at Gray. "Okay."

Gray walked past Sonne to the corpse. "Now, help me with Mister Purple here. He's leaving with you, the money, and the van."

As Sonne watched Green tremble and blink, she felt something odd in her throat. Pity? Did she actually feel *sorry* for this thug?

Green was an asshole, no doubt. But he was just trying to survive now, to get the hell away from Gray and whatever the lunatic was planning. Sonne could relate to that.

Sonne only then realized she hadn't seen Yellow in some time. He'd gone to get Gray, but he hadn't returned with Gray. Where was Yellow? Was he off doing something to Cowan, somewhere?

Gray and Green loaded Purple's body into the van. After Green shut the doors, he looked to Gray.

"Where do I go now?" Green asked.

Gray smiled. "Anywhere you like, Mister Green."

Green hopped into the van. "Okay then . . . good working with you." By the tone of his voice, he clearly didn't mean it.

Gray inclined his head. "And you, Mister Green."

A garage door retracted as Green rolled the van forward. He drove out. The last Sonne saw of the vehicle was its taillights, flashing as the garage door closed. She almost wished she was going with it.

"Samantha, I'd like your heel now," Gray said.

Sonne flinched and spun to put her front to him. "What?"

Gray's face remained eerily calm as he extended an open hand. "The metal heel you used to saw through your bonds. Please drop it on the floor and step away from it."

She hesitated. If he'd known about the weapon since the autocar, why not warn the others?

"I won't ask again," Gray said.

Eyeing the gun Gray had used to shoot Purple, Sonne dropped the heel. She stepped away.

Gray retrieved the heel and frowned. "There's blood on it."

Sonne swallowed. "Cut myself trying to break the tape."

"What was your plan when you broke free?"

A wave of weariness filled Sonne's body. His staid demeanor made it hard to stay alert and ready. "I don't know. Steal the van, maybe?"

Gray nodded. "Not a bad plan. In case it wasn't clear, you're free to go."

As wonderful as that sounded, it felt like a trap. "I don't believe you."

"Why not?"

She pointed at the pool of blood between them. "Because you just shot your partner in the face?"

Gray shrugged. "He was a problem. Mister Green, on the other hand, is a solution."

"To what?" Sonne demanded.

"Distracting the gathered forces of the CID and VCD while my partner and I make our escape. Very soon, the VCD will corner Mister Green on a freeway. He'll surrender."

Even as tired as she was now, Sonne knew that made absolutely no sense. "Won't Green tell them you led this whole thing?"

Gray shook his head. "When he reaches the gathered police officers, his van will explode. In the wreckage, forensics will find four bodies."

Jesus, how many people had this monster killed? Sonne moved past those murders—she had to focus on her own murder, now, or specifically, not being murdered—and save Cowan.

"Where's Cowan?" she asked.

"Alive," Gray said. "He answered my questions honestly after I broke his knee."

Fresh guilt stabbed Sonne in the chest. "That wasn't necessary!"

Gray shrugged. "He's otherwise intact. Cowan will soon send a distress call to the CID. It will lead them to focus on a stretch of the 805 ten kilometers away, giving us more than enough time to escape."

Sonne struggled to understand all this. "You planned to hand me to Vasser, right? Knowing what he'd do?"

"Yes," Gray said.

"Then why kill Purple?" Sonne demanded. "Why piss off Vasser?"

"Because I don't work for Oleg Vasser, Samantha. I work for myself, and I have another client whose commission is worth far more than the amount Vasser offered for you."

Sonne frowned. "A commission? For who?"

Gray shrugged again. "Cowan offered a lead on that commission in exchange for your life, even after we offered to let him go. He decided he'd rather die than allow us to sell you to Oleg Vassar."

The weight in Sonne's chest grew, but she refused to cry in front of Mister Gray. It had been a shitty night, but she wasn't going to cry about it.

"Here he is now," Mister Gray said.

Sonne spun to find two men approaching them. Cowan hopped on one leg alongside Yellow, which might have looked funny if Sonne wasn't so pissed at practically everything.

Yet when Cowan's eyes met hers, he lit up. "Sonne!" Cowan called out. "You're okay!"

Sonne's chest went tight. She had done everything she could to save Cowan's life, and apparently he'd done everything he could to save hers.

All in all, she'd been on worse dates.

Yellow helped Sonne get Cowan settled against the wall. She sat beside him, her shoulder touching his. If Gray was lying, and planned to shoot them both once they sat down, at least it would be quick.

Yet, as promised, Mister Gray and Mister Yellow strolled out of Sonne's life. The two of them left the warehouse without an autocar or a helicopter or a boat or anything else. They were simply going to walk free.

The CID wasn't searching for two random pedestrians. They were searching for a manually driven vehicle big enough to hold two hostages and four men.

Still sitting against the wall, Sonne pressed her shoulder against

Cowan's. They'd been through something terrible together tonight, and she needed something not terrible. Cowan felt not terrible.

"I'm sorry," Sonne said. "I should have been more careful."

Cowan glanced at her. "How is any of this your fault?"

"I fucked with the Russian mob. Of course they were going to retaliate."

His eyes widened. "What did you do to the mob?"

It all came out in a rush. Sonne told Cowan all about Second Chance and the work she and Kate did to help trafficking victims. Not to boast, but because he deserved to know why they'd been attacked tonight.

In the end, he seemed suitably impressed. She liked that he was impressed.

"How'd you make a deal with Gray?" Sonne asked.

"So, as it turned out, abducting us was just a side job to Gray," Cowan said. "He was really interested in someone else: Galileo."

Sonne blinked. "He wants to dig up some dead astronomer's body?"

Cowan chuckled. "It's the darkSim handle of some supersecret hacker. He puppeted loose circuits into shooting rampages, and he also killed a grayDoc who was working with him, Anton Barkov."

"Was that doctor Bratva, by any chance?"

Cowan nodded. "I think Gray is Russian, too, because he was really interested in Doctor Barkov's murder. Gray knew Galileo worked with Barkov. Maybe even suspected he killed him."

Sonne couldn't get over how weird this all seemed. "So who *is* he?"

Cowan shrugged. "I think Gray's an enforcer or something. Maybe Barkov was connected to the Russian mob, or some other criminals, and they want Galileo dead. That's Gray's commission."

Sonne glanced down at Cowan's legs. "Why did he break your knee?"

"I lied to him," Cowan said. "Then he smashed my knee and gave me the torture speech."

Sonne had received that same speech. She gingerly touched his knee. "Does it hurt?"

Cowan hissed. "Please don't."

Sonne jerked her hand away and took a few breaths. "So that's it? He just lets us go?"

"Pretty much. Oh, and it was Galileo who scripted a paralysis script for the Sim. The one that ringu girl used in your pleasurebox to paralyze Jeb, then me."

Sonne almost grabbed Cowan's arms and shook him. "Through admin mode?" Could he be talking about what happened to Kate's father?

"Yeah. The script got me—"

Sonne punched him in the arm. "You lied to my face!"

Cowan winched. "I couldn't let you know about it! The CID can't let anyone know. If I'd told you, they'd have redacted your memories."

Why did he look so hurt? She hadn't hit him hard. "Then you—"

"I lied to protect you," Cowan said. "You're not supposed to be able to drop full stem barriers through the Sim, and you're certainly not supposed to be able to do it through admin mode. I know because I worked on PBAs. But somebody's figured out how to do that."

"So this Galileo guy is paralyzing people in the Sim?" Sonne asked. Why?"

"No idea. I thought these thugs were working for Galileo all along, so I called out Gray. But it turned out he was hunting Galileo. Enemy of my enemy and all that."

Sonne wanted to hit him again. "He could have murdered you!"

Cowan winced, then shrugged. "Sure, I mean, I guess. But I couldn't let them deliver you to Vasser."

Sonne leaned over, hugged him tight, and kissed him. She didn't hold her lips there long, just enough to see what it felt like.

It felt good.

Cowan blushed bright red when she pulled away.

Sonne shoved him again, just to make sure he was paying attention. "Don't ever do anything like that again," she said. "I can take care of myself, and I don't need you risking yourself for me. Understand?"

He stared at her, eyes wide. "You're one to talk."

"I mean it!"

Cowan scooted close again. "So do I."

Sonne rolled her eyes and enjoyed the warmth of an arm against hers. She didn't want to argue with Cowan right now. She just wanted to sit here, arm against arm, and not think.

After a moment, Cowan spoke again. "There's something else I need to tell you."

"What?" Given her luck, Cowan was probably cheating on his wife.

"We won't remember this. Any of it."

That didn't really make sense. "Why?"

"I made a deal with Gray—the deal Yellow watched to make sure I went through with it. I scripted a delayed memory deletion script."

Sonne gawked at him. Was he serious?

Cowan pulled a linkline from his pocket. "It's got a countdown to give Gray and Yellow time to get clear, but there's no stopping it. You'll need to download the script from my PBA. We have to redact everything after they pulled us out of the autocar. That's the only way Gray lets us live."

Hadn't Gray already let them live? "He's gone, Cowan."

Cowan tapped the side of his head. "No, he's still here. He's watching you through my eyes right now."

Sonne recoiled like he'd just tossed a bunch of spiders at her. "You could have told me!"

Cowan blinked. "But . . . you kissed me!"

"So!"

"So, my brain stopped working."

That might have been a line from any other guy, but not Cowan. He really was that easy to please. Or maybe she was just that amazing.

Cowan popped one end of the linkline into the port behind his ear and offered her the other end. "Take the line. I'll upload the script to your PBA. It'll permanently redact your memories of tonight, the same time it redacts mine. It'll also tell the CID where we really are."

"Why can't we just run out and find a phone?" Sonne asked.

"The script is GPS locked. If either of us leaves the warehouse, my PBA scrambles my brain. We agreed on a time delay so I could convince you to download the script."

Sonne glared at Gray through Cowan's eyes, but what would that horrible man do if she refused? Would he come back? Would he hurt them, kill them?

"You agreed to all that?" Sonne asked.

Cowan had, of course. He'd agreed to save both their lives because Gray hadn't given him a choice. She popped the linkline into the small port behind her left ear.

Sonne frowned. "Next time, we negotiate together."

Her head tingled. Her PBA projected an augmented reality timer before her eyes, counting down, and that was just rubbing it in, really.

This sucked. She'd forget everything that had happened tonight, kissing Cowan and hugging him tight. But she'd also forget watching Purple beat the shit out of him, so, plusses and minuses.

Cowan blinked. "Gray's out of local wireless range."

"Good." Sonne sat back against the wall. "I'm still pissed about this."

"I understand."

She glanced at him. "We can still cuddle."

Cowan jerked like something had bitten him. Sonne hopped up and stared at Cowan's twitching body, which jerked one more time like a rag doll before flopping still.

"What is it?" Sone shouted. "Talk to me!"

A woman shouted from afar. "It's okay, Sonne! You're safe!"

Cowan's chest rose and fell with comforting regularity, though he drooled. Sonne belatedly realized why Cowan had jumped and trembled like that. Someone had hit him with a stunner round.

Sonne whipped around to find Kate and Lucy walking toward her in form-hugging graphene body armor. The stuff was ridiculously expensive and bulletproof. It made them both look like absolute badasses.

Kate's gaze swept the interior. "Where are the people who took you?"

Sonne grimaced. "Gone now. Why did you zap my date?"

Kate's brow furrowed. "I'm changing the plan. Remember the plan?"

Sonne took a moment, going back over her night before she'd asked Cowan out, but she still had no idea what Kate meant.

"What plan?"

Kate popped a linkline into her neck, then offered the other end.

"I'm infected," Sonne said. "Memory redaction scripting."

Kate stepped closer, tip of her linkline extended. "I've got dynamic firewalls, honey. We'll be fine. Now, please. We don't have much time before the CID gets here."

Sonne shrugged—Kate knew best—and plugged the linkline into the port behind her ear. Her vision blurred as an earlier memory redaction cleared, hidden memories Sonne only now recovered.

She now remembered a discussion at 0212 in the morning about Kate's father, the way Cowan's brain read in a pleasurebox, and Taylor Lambda's coma. She remembered their fiendish plan to take Cowan on a date. Everything clicked together, old memories and new.

"Cowan didn't paralyze Dad!" Sonne said over wireless.

"How can you know that?" Kate asked.

Sonne flipped over to her head desk and bundled up everything her PBA had archived tonight, ensuring their last conversation came first. She sent Kate an archive of her conversation with Cowan, about Galileo, and the script Galileo had used to paralyze their father.

Kate's eyes went distant as she experienced Sonne's horrible night at rapid pace. She twitched and gasped. When she opened her eyes, she clutched Sonne tight.

"Oh God, honey, I'm so sorry! I should never have left you unprotected!"

Sonne hugged Kate back. "It's okay. I'm okay."

She was now, at least. She might be a wreck at the moment, but hugging her sister helped. Sonne didn't have much family left.

Lucy tapped the side of her blond head, eyes distant. "One of Benzai's helos has detected two motorcycles on surface streets. I believe those are our abductors. Shall I order our helos to pursue?"

Kate wiped her eyes and shook her head. "Not now. We will do *nothing* to antagonize those men. They've been in Sonne's brain and Cowan's, so we can't risk triggering something nasty by going after them."

Sonne nodded. She agreed.

"We'll get them," Kate said. "Just not tonight."

Sonne eased back to arm's length and stared down at Cowan's unconscious body. Another wave of guilt rushed through her.

"You're still going to hack his PBA?" she asked.

Kate plucked the linkline from Sonne's head and knelt beside Cowan. "I can't just take his word he's innocent. I have to make sure he's not just playing you—or worse, that he's not working for this Galileo guy."

Sonne glared. "Cowan wouldn't do that."

Kate gently moved Cowan's head to expose the port behind his ear. "So I won't find anything. That's what we want, right?" She snapped in her linkline. "Lucy, stun anyone who isn't Sonne."

Lucy's eyes glowed visibly red, which meant Kate had just activated her HARM switch. Lucy could hurt or even kill people now, on Kate's orders. Those with Oneworld's favor had complete discretion in how their bodyguards used force, and Lucy was good at using force.

Sonne wiggled bare toes on cold concrete as Kate hacked Cowan's PBA. This wasn't right, using Cowan like this, after he'd opened up to her. Being honest.

Of course, the whole reason he'd been so honest might be because he knew she'd just forget everything, and they did need to know for certain. Gray's redaction of Cowan's memories counted down.

It kept counting. What was taking so long? Sonne knew finding your way through a firewalled PBA was difficult, but Kate had always been really good at that. Just how complex were Cowan's PBA firewalls?

With sixty seconds left on the delayed redaction timer, Kate blinked back to meatspace. She looked up, lips compressed.

"Well?" Sonne asked. "Is he involved?"

Kate popped her linkline and stood. "Close enough. I'm sorry, honey. Cowan Soto is in this up to his neck."

Sonne's heart sank. "How?"

"He's got enough tricks and traps buried in there to fry a dozen braincooks, so I couldn't get much, but I found enough. When Oneworld finds out what Cowan's been doing, they're going to burn his mind and those of everyone involved. If you hadn't already erased tonight, I'd do it for you."

"Then we should help him, not abandon him!" Sonne tried to walk over to Cowan, but Lucy stepped between them. "Hey!"

"Not my call," Lucy said.

Kate shook her head. "I wish I had time to convince you, but the two of us can't beat Oneworld, and as nice of a guy as Cowan might be, I can't lose you like I lost Dad. We're staying as far from this as possible."

Sonne glared at Kate. "That's my decision, not yours!"

Kate glanced at Lucy. "Zap her, please."

The lower half of Lucy's forearm split open, revealing a long stunner mounted inside her prosthetic forearm.

"Sorry." Lucy raised her stunner.

Sonne tossed up her hands. "Goddammi—"

21

SONNE

Sonne opened her eyes with the worst hangover, and as light seared her eyes, she quickly closed them again. Where was she? Her couch? It felt like the worn couch in Kate's loft atop Benzai Corporation's tower.

Had she indulged in alcohol? That wasn't like her. The last thing she recalled, she'd be getting ready for her date with Cowan, which . . .

Someone hacked their autocar. They'd been ambushed!

Sonne sat up so fast her head spun. She slapped a hand down on the couch, and it was her couch. How? She opened her eyes despite the light stabbing her eyes.

The light was, she soon realized, simply the Pink Bunnysynth night-light in her room in the loft, a gift from Kate and an inside joke from the time they'd completed the Simworld Design Contest together. Sonne also instantly realized she was no longer wearing the absolutely killer dress she'd chosen for her date with Cowan, but her soft pink pajamas.

Someone had changed her clothing while she was asleep.

No need to panic or hit anything yet. She was in Kate's loft, definitely, so maybe it was Kate who changed her clothes. Rude . . . but still her sister.

She settled herself with her back against the back of the couch and breathed until she could hold her eyes open without effort. Before she could rise, the single door to her room in the loft hissed open.

A tall blond woman wearing a T-shirt and sweatpants entered.

"Morning," Lucy said, wearing a somewhat guilty smile. "Feeling okay?"

"I feel like I went through a windshield," Sonne admitted with a groan. "The last thing I remember was . . . a grenade? In our autocar." She sat straight up again, new worry stabbing her spine. "Is Cowan okay?"

"He's fine. Now scoot. Let me sit. I'll catch you up on why things are okay."

Lucy was here. Lucy always made her feel safe, whether they were tackling the latest pleasurebox together or just out getting drinks. The last of Sonne's lingering worry faded into what felt like simple exhaustion.

"Sure," she said.

Lucy sat down beside Sonne and leaned one arm on the couch's armrest.

"Oleg Vasser's boys abducted you and Cowan," she said calmly. "The CID helped us track down Cowan, and your Benzai-patented artificial heart helped us track down you. One of the mercenaries punched you a few times, but absolutely *nothing* else happened. And Kate and I got you back."

Another relief. Sonne hadn't wanted to really think too hard about *that* particular possibility, but after waking up in different clothes after a blackout, it was always a concern. Yet she believed Lucy when she said Oleg Vasser's boys hadn't held her for long.

"You kill 'em?" Sonne asked, halfway hoping Lucy had.

Lucy grimaced. "Some of them are dead. That wasn't my doing. But I can say absolutely none of them will be bothering you again."

Sonne nodded with relief and leaned into her friend. She needed some of Lucy's warmth right now, even if she was cyberized. Lucy had the finest cyborg body parts money could buy, thanks to Benzai Corporation's resources and Kate's generosity. Even her metal arms were warm.

"Why don't I remember any of it?" Sonne asked quietly. "Did they try to hack my PBA?"

Lucy hesitated for a long moment. Longer than Sonne thought normal.

"We aren't sure," she said, finally.

Sonne pushed off and looked at her. "You're lying."

Lucy's expression didn't change at all, but Sonne felt something inside her did. "Not about any of the other stuff."

Sonne nodded and stood, then immediately sat back down again as the whole building decided to spin. "Katie's got some answering to do."

The door hissed open again. "You called?"

Sonne narrowed her eyes at her sister and made herself look as grumpy as possible. "What did you do, when did you do it, and why does Lucy look like she feels guilty about running over my dog?"

"You don't have a dog," Lucy reminded her.

Kate signed and stepped into the now increasingly crowded loft. "I am sorry I couldn't be here when you woke up. I had you on camera, of course. I concluded my latest call and came up as quickly as I could."

"Also," Lucy added, "she stationed me outside your door despite us being on the top floor of a secure building. So, thanks for that, really."

Kate *tsk*ed. "Only the best for my little sis and our closest friend."

"What happened?" Sonne demanded flatly. "Why can't I remember?"

Kate sighed. "Can I sit?"

"No," Lucy and Sonne said at the same time.

Kate sighed for dramatic effect and walked over to lean against the wall. "We stunned you. Or rather, Lucy did."

Sonne gasped and slugged Lucy in the arm, which, since that was metal, only left her hissing and shaking her hand. "You bitch!"

Lucy winced and raised both hands. "To be fair, you had a PBA virus."

Sonne blinked. "Seriously?"

"Hello!" Kate waved. "Still explaining. And yes. During the abduction, Oleg Vasser's people planted an algorithm in your PBA that deleted all memory of the abduction. When the heat from the hunt I had organized in concert with the CID and VCD became too much for them, they decided to pull the plug and wiped your memories to cover their tracks."

"Balls," Sonne cursed. "So we don't have an ID on them." She looked at Lucy again. "But you said they wouldn't come after me again."

Lucy raised an arm, popped her perfectly human-looking robot arm back on its hinge, and made her stunner mount crackle. "They will not, because I will not be letting you go off in an unsecured autocar ever again. And the reason they will not harm you is because I will kill them dead."

Sonne stared, then nodded. "Good plan." She regarded Kate. "So no memories, huh?" She sighed. "That sucks. I actually thought mine and Cowan's date was going pretty good, up until the car got hacked and the grenade arrived."

"From what you told me before the memories were wiped, it went terribly," Kate said.

Sonne gasped. "No. Really?"

"Trust me when I say you'll never want to go on a date with Cowan Soto again, and maybe never even another guy," Kate said firmly, sounding every bit like a protective older sister. "We know at least that much."

Lucy rubbed her back in sympathy. "Sorry it didn't work out."

Sonne leaned back against the couch. "Details?"

"When you wake up a bit," Kate said.

Sonne sighed. "Well . . . at least you both found me before it got worse."

"And we always will," Kate said calmly. "All for one and one for all."

Lucy squeezed Sonne's arm. "I really hate it when she says that."

PART 5

22

ROHAN

The synthcop's comforting voice echoed down the alley, loud and clear. "Please stop running, Doctor Bedi. You may injure yourself."

Doctor Rohan Bedi ran anyway. The synthetic didn't stun him, even though it had a clean shot, which meant his plan was working. He tried to enter the Sim again, but Protection Services still had him locked out.

This particular synthcop had detected the device strapped to Rohan's chest and correctly interpolated that stunning him might stop his heart, killing him. The synthcop's virtual intelligence algorithms—its VI—wouldn't let it risk causing harm to a human. Rohan knew that because he had scripted most of those algorithms.

His lungs burned as he fell against a wall, desperate to catch his breath. He didn't do a lot of cardio.

Rohan heard the distinctive *hiss-clomp* of the synthetic hurrying down the alley. He stared up at an eight-story building frame, an iron skeleton missing its skin. After time only for a few deep breaths, he ducked under the yellow construction gate.

He had to survive until the *real* cops found him. No matter what happened tonight, he couldn't let Protection Services get away with this.

The site was muddy from recent rain, and dull work lights filled its puddles with lines. Construction synthetics loomed over him, metal giants in sleep mode. Protection Services was certainly watching him by satellite now, ensuring no one came to his rescue.

Rohan waited by the building skeleton as the synthcop clomped into the construction site. Its body was almost humanoid, hard plastic and rough metal, and its head was an armored triangular box. Metal pistons connected its arms and legs, like bones might inside flesh. A police shield covered its right shoulder pad, bearing a Oneworld logo.

The synthcop raised its arms and popped its metal hands open to reveal stunners. "Please stop running, Doctor Bedi. Security personnel are on their way to assist you."

Rohan would take the construction elevator to the seventh floor of the building skeleton, one floor from the top. He could disable the elevator and hide from his pursuers. He still had a few minutes before he entered the elevator. Enough time to attempt one more call for help before going up. Rohan read the synthetic's unit number off its left shoulder pad. "Officer 817, toggle administrator mode, debug phrase: Do androids dream of electronic sheep?"

"Security personnel are on their way to help you," 817 repeated.

Of course Protection Services would change the debug phrase once Rohan defected. But now bathed in the light of the site, he saw that this synthetic was a police model, and it looked like a 600 series. That meant it might have a CLU box—a synthetic logic-device that would allow him to manipulate it, if he made it focus on the correct parameters.

Rohan squeezed the trigger to the device that would shock his heart into not beating—or which he would make the synthcop *think* was a real device—and held the switch high, where the synthetic could see it. "If I involuntarily release this button, my heart may stop. If you approach or attempt to immobilize me, I will release the button."

The synthcop kept still as a statue. "Suicide is not the answer, Doctor Bedi."

"I know that. If you answer my questions honestly, I won't kill myself."

In truth, Rohan couldn't kill himself—clear circuit algorithms forbid self-harm—and the dead man's switch in his hand wasn't a dead man's switch at all. Yet a synthcop's VI wouldn't let it take that chance he wasn't bluffing.

Rohan closed his jacket. "Have you updated all incoming units and personnel about my condition?"

"Yes, Doctor Bedi," the synthcop said.

"Have you notified the CID and the VCD that I'm at this construction site?"

"No, Doctor Bedi."

Of course it hadn't. Protection Services wouldn't allow that, but perhaps it would tell him *why* it hadn't done so. "Why not?"

"Corporate Security is already on its way to protect you. Additional forces are not required at this time."

So Protection Services had given this synthcop orders that forbid it from calling anyone other than Protection Services. Made sense. Yet synthcops augmented with a CLU box were capable of drawing their own conclusions if their orders were vague enough. Now it was time to find out if this one had one.

Rohan put on a warm smile. "I'm going to ask you some questions now, Officer 817. I simply need you to answer them. So long as you continue to answer my questions, I will not kill myself."

Officer 817 retracted its stunners and lowered its arms. "Please ask your questions, Doctor Bedi."

"First question: Are you capable of drawing your own conclusions, given sufficient data?"

"Yes, Doctor Bedi."

"Wonderful." Rohan's desperate plan might actually work. "To start, what do you know about mind burns?"

23

COWAN

SEPTEMBER 15, EARLY MORNING

When the CID helo landed heavily on three closed-down lanes of the Five, what had once been a black van still burned. Two fire trucks were hosing it down, but the flames burned white and blue, suggesting accelerant. Cowan stared at the blaze, at the inky smoke, at the pieces of a van that were just about everywhere.

The people who had abducted him and Sonne were dead, and Cowan had no idea how that had happened. The van's explosion had tossed two other autocars into the highway median, but safety foam still dribbled from their windows. A good sign.

"Lean on me!" Jeb shouted over the rotors and wind. He slid an arm around Cowan's waist, and Cowan wrapped an arm around Jeb's big shoulders. "On three! One, two—"

Together they stepped out of the helo. Having only one working leg was going to be a chore, but a VCD medic had locked his leg within a medical brace to avoid further damage. As a bonus, Cowan had used his PBA to disable the excruciating pain.

It vexed him that he couldn't remember how he broke his knee. Whoever redacted his memories had been very, very good. None of his recovery attempts had been successful.

Had he broken his knee when the autocar wrecked, or had his captors broken it during the time he couldn't remember? He'd learned Sonne's memories of their date had been redacted as well. She'd already left with her sister, Kate, after Kate pulled corporate rank and shortened the VCD's interrogation to a formality.

Cowan hadn't gotten to talk to Sonne, hadn't gotten to say goodbye or ask what she knew. Yet they were both alive, weren't they?

Cowan took comfort in that, even if everything else remained a mystery. A mystery now burning in a blown-up van.

As the helo departed, VCD Captain Naomi Barondale strode over to them. One cut was visible on her dark brown cheek, oozing blood.

Cowan tapped his own cheek and winced at her. "You okay?"

Barondale wiped the blood off her cheek. "Better than Sparks and Marquez. Van pieces knocked them flat." She shrugged. "They'll live."

After Jeb's helo landed at the abandoned warehouse where Cowan and Sonne had ended up, somehow, they'd been unable to raise the VCD on the wireless. It turned out this exploded van had also carried an EMP, which went off right before the van exploded. The electromagnetic bomb had fried every relay tower in a two-kilometer radius, knocking out wireless communications for blocks. Someone would get a new mind for that, if Corporate One connected anyone living to whatever made the van explode.

Jeb had told Cowan he had no obligation to come here, but Cowan needed to see the exploded van for himself, see if anyone had survived. Who had those men been? Why had they been after him, and most importantly . . . were they connected to Galileo?

"Care to tell me what you remember?" Barondale said.

Cowan frowned and considered what little he knew. "I got abducted. I don't know much else, other than my captors redacted my memories afterward. Do you know if anyone was in the van?"

Barondale glanced at the burning wreckage. "Scanners say three bodies plus the driver. The driver got out and shouted at us after we stopped him at the perimeter. Raised his hands like he was going to surrender."

"And he didn't blow up the van," Cowan agreed.

Barondale nodded grimly. "We can't know that for sure, but we didn't see him trigger anything, so it's possible someone else triggered the explosion."

That sounded like Galileo, like the killswitch he installed in Anton Barkov. Anytime anyone tried to give Galileo up, they died.

"Any IDs on these assholes?" Jeb asked.

Barondale shook her head. "I doubt we'll find much but cracked bones and ash. It's hot enough to cremate them in there. Did you get a look at any of them, Cowan?"

"I don't know," Cowan said.

"Did they say what they wanted with you?"

"If they did, I can't remember."

Barondale stared at the burning wreckage. "Damn. What a shitty night."

Cowan remembered the way Sonne looked when she got into their autocar: absolutely breathtaking. And then how she looked when they parted, with burn marks on one arm and one leg from stunner rounds. Everything between those images was missing.

"It was kind of a shitty night," Cowan agreed. So much for dating again.

Barondale glanced at him, her sculpted features softening with what might be sympathy. "You can't do anything else here. Once the fire dies down, we'll send in a forensic team, but I doubt they'll find anything. For now, I've got another problem."

"What's that?" Jeb asked.

"Zhang and Bradley are camped at a construction site dealing with a rogue synthcop. Damn thing called in a murder, so I split my team to check it out. But the moment they arrived on the scene, the synthcop started shooting at them with a nail gun."

"Odd," Jeb said.

"Also, when we notified Corporate One, they told us, 'Stand down and wait for further orders.' So basically, my people are stuck in a truck."

A synthcop shooting at VCD officers with a nail gun didn't sound like any synthcop Cowan had ever heard of.

"You think someone hacked it?" Jeb asked.

Barondale cocked an eyebrow at him. "That's possible now, isn't it? That's why we need someone from the CID to check it out. Unfortunately, everyone in your department is about to be mobilized to handle this electromagnetic clusterfuck."

Jeb tapped the side of his head. "And there's the orders to join the salvage effort. Emergency wireless is back online." He turned his eyes skyward. "Stanton's airship must have deployed relay balloons."

"What about me?" Cowan asked. "I didn't get any orders."

Jeb frowned and met Cowan's gaze. "That's because you're scheduled for a debrief. Someone from the OMH is on their way to talk you through everything that happened, help you process your feelings."

"Aww," Cowan said.

"After that, you're out of the field until you can walk again. An autocar with a counselor is on its way, and it'll take you to Sharp Memorial. The car should be here soon."

Barondale smiled at Cowan. "If you're heading to Sharp, you're going right past the construction site. Any chance you could stop and help my people with that synth?"

Cowan looked to Jeb. "Can I?"

Jeb shrugged. "That's your call. You're the one with the bum knee."

An autocar chose that moment to cruise up and stop, with the letters *OMH* embossed on its door. Those doors rose, revealing a plush interior and Office of Mental Health Counselor Sarisa Bassa. Cowan remembered her from the Fisher residence a few weeks back.

Jeb lightly patted Cowan on the back. "Got you the best." Jeb nodded to Sarisa, who smiled at both of them.

Barondale crossed her arms. "I can't order you to help us, but the rest of my team just had a van blow up in their faces."

"I'll do it," Cowan said. "I could use a victory tonight."

Jeb walked them both forward, with Cowan hopping on one leg. "All right, then." He leaned close to the car. "Take good care of him, okay?"

Sarisa nodded. "You still owe me a drink."

Once Jeb had manhandled Cowan inside, an ego-dampening

experience, the doors closed and the autocar rolled off. Sarisa kept on smiling at him, and Cowan tried to smile back, but he wasn't in the mood. Not after what had happened to Sonne.

"You don't have to talk about anything right now," Sarisa said. "If you want to talk about what happened, what you remember, I'm here, but I'm not going to pressure you."

"Thanks," Cowan said. "Also, do you mind if we stop at that construction site?"

"Is that important to you?"

"Yes. I'd like to help out the VCD, since they were helping me when that van blew up."

Sarisa eased back in her seat. "All right."

"Great. So, I'm going to be quiet and process my feelings now. Okay?"

Sarisa might have smirked, but it was hard to tell in the dim light. He didn't mean to sound so terse, but it had been a long night. He wasn't in the mood for small talk. Or feelings. Best thing to do was to lose himself in work.

Soon they arrived at bright construction lights highlighting a yellow gate meant for stopping cars. A VCD autotruck was parked outside the gate, splashing the area with flashing red-and-blue lights. It seemed this site was just out of range of the EMP blast. Lucky for them.

Santiago Zhang and his shiny metal legs hopped from the truck. He waved them to a stop as Cowan's autocar approached, keeping the truck between himself and the site. Was the hacked synthetic shooting nails at passing traffic as well?

Cowan thought back to Joseph Dunn and his synthetic hacking script. Galileo had bought that script, and he could have sold it to any number of cybercriminals. Was this yet another case of Galileo spreading chaos on the Sim?

The autocar stopped, the doors rolled open, and Zhang offered his arms. "Thanks for the assist, little buddy. Sounds like you guys are dealing with some shit over on the Five."

"Exploding van," Cowan agreed as Zhang and Sarisa helped him out of the car.

Zhang saluted. "Pleasure to have you with us, Counselor."

Sarisa pursed her lips. "I'm sure. Now, can we step inside your truck before that synth shoots us?"

A blond woman in blue VCD body armor sat quietly inside the autotruck. She was Melissa Bradley—a.k.a. Sn0wing—before she had been banned from StrikeForceGo because of her affiliation with the VCD. She had a long ponytail and a tan face.

Bradley faced away from them, eyes distant. "Welcome. Have a seat."

A linkline stretched from the port above Bradley's right ear to the terminal inside the VCD autotruck. Cowan figured she was trying to unhack the hacked synthetic, or at least trace who was hacking it. He plopped down in the empty chair and asked, "What do you need me to do?"

Bradley's eyes remained distant, probably in the Sim. "You could start by telling me how someone hacked this synthcop without using wireless," she said out loud. "I can't find any external signal, at all."

Cowan nodded. "I can do that."

"Also, you could tell me why it's shooting at us with a nail gun. Lethal force should violate its operational parameters, shouldn't it?"

Cowan frowned. "Yeah."

It only then occurred to him he should call Sonne. They should compare notes. Was she home yet? No, she wouldn't be home yet. He'd call her tomorrow, after he got done here and went to the hospital. He wanted to make sure she was doing okay.

First, he had to make sure no one else got nailed.

Bradley handed Cowan a spare linkline without leaving the Sim, which was sort of impressive. Did she have a panel open in there with her, showing her a camera feed from inside the truck? Cowan popped the linkline in above his ear. His body tingled as the inside of the autotruck drained away to reveal a featureless black room.

His normal Sim avatar was nothing special, just an anime businessman with green hair and glowing data glasses. His current non-darkSim handle was Philo, though he had at least three other "clean" accounts.

"Clear me for your systems?" Cowan asked.

Bright panels appeared all around him. Cowan tagged and moved them, organizing them into scanners, template boxes, and camera feeds. He started by verifying Bradley's work, scanning for any signal that might be controlling the rogue synthcop.

Cowan spotted plenty of wireless traffic, but nothing directed at the construction site, and nothing on the encrypted frequency synthcops used to communicate. If someone was controlling the synthcop remotely, they weren't doing it via wireless.

He pulled over the feeds from Traffic Control, or T-Conn, and opened all street cameras watching the construction site. He tapped through until he found one featuring the synthcop. It crouched behind a concrete barrier, in decent cover. Was it expecting an assault?

"Has it made any demands?" Cowan asked.

Zhang chuckled back in meatspace, which was similar to having a disembodied chuckle join you in a dark, locked room. "Like, it wants oil or something?"

"No. Has it asked to speak to a negotiator?"

Bradley answered instead. "We haven't tried to talk to it, because it kept shooting at us."

A golden door seared itself into the side of Cowan's dark rectangle, and then a tall woman with pale skin, overly mascara'd eyes, and bright green hair stepped into the room with him. That was Sn0wing, Melissa Bradley's avatar in the Sim. She shared her panels with him.

Cowan tapped his digital chin with one long finger. "Talking to it might help us understand what it wants. It has to have a reason for defending the construction site."

"You mean the person who hacked it," Bradley said.

Cowan shook his head. "Not necessarily. You're right that there's no remote signal, and I don't see any physical connections. There's a chance this synthcop is acting on its own."

"Is that possible?" Sarisa asked. Her voice was out there in the void, too, but comforting.

Cowan zoomed the panel watching the synthcop, close enough to see the sealed port on its triangular head. "I'll know in a second." He took a moment to double-check his initial impression. "That's a 600 series, isn't it?"

"Does that matter?" Bradley asked.

"It might." Cowan opened a link to the CID database and pulled out all available schematics for synthcops. He shotgunned those panels across the wall, isolated the schematics for the 600 series, and opened his fingers to size up the panel. He'd been right. "600 series."

"Get to the point, man," Zhang said from meatspace.

"I think that synthcop has a CLU box," Cowan said. "I bet that's why it's shooting at you from the construction site. Something or someone gave it a good reason to do that."

Bradley frowned. "What's a CLU box? And what is it with engineers and overly clever abbreviations?"

"It's short for conclusion—in this case, drawing them. It's basically a black box with a mess of fuzzy logic, with the ability to learn from success and failure. A synthetic with a CLU box can draw conclusions based on the results of what it does, then update its operational parameters to incorporate new ones."

Sarisa's voice emerged from the darkness. "Couldn't that lead to emergent behavior?" she asked.

Cowan smiled. Sarisa had obviously done her reading. "That's what everyone else was worried about, which is why there's only twenty-five synthcops with CLU boxes in the field. San Diego beta testing." Cowan had read about that in *Synthetic Digest*. "They rolled them out in San Diego a couple of months ago. The hope is to make better police officers."

Zhang scoffed. "Seems like it just makes them shoot people."

Cowan ignored him. "We need to talk to that synthcop, so I'm going to open a wireless communications channel." He glanced at Bradley. "That okay by you guys?"

She shrugged. "You're the expert."

"Great." Cowan circled the head of the synthcop with one glowing finger, then squeezed that line and pulled another line out. He pressed that line to his own head, then spoke over wireless. "Officer 817, this is CID Detective Soto. Respond, please."

Officer 817 terminated the wireless connection.

Cowan tried again and got the same result. "Now that's really strange," he said to the others. "Hanging up on a human operator violates its operational parameters, or should. What's it thinking?"

"You got that it's shooting at us, right?" Zhang asked, audibly annoyed. "Seems like it just said, 'Fuck my operational parameters.'"

Cowan reminded himself that VCD handled violent crimes, not cybercrimes, and he needed to remain patient with them. "It's impossible for a VI to ignore its operational parameters." Cowan had actually written a paper on VIs and fuzzy logic in college. "I bet it's trying to tell us something, without, you know . . . actually telling us something."

"Say what?" Zhang asked.

"Imagine my superior officer ordered me not to talk to you. I have to follow that order . . . I have no choice . . . so instead, I write down what I want to tell you on a piece of paper. I can't violate my orders, but I need to communicate, so I write to you instead of talking."

"That still seems like disobeying orders," Zhang said.

Cowan shook his head. "The synthcop doesn't see it that way. It exists to complete all the conditions listed in its operational parameters, in ranked order. A bad order prevents it from doing that."

"So how does a VI define a bad order?" Sarisa asked.

Cowan struggled for an example. "Basically, any order that prevents it from completing a directive. Say someone tells it to push an armored truck up a hill."

"Synthcops aren't strong enough to do that," Zhang said.

"Just go with it," Cowan said. "How would you, a human, resolve that order?"

Zhang snorted. "I'd tell you to fuck off?"

"*You* would," Sarisa agreed. "But a synthcop would push that truck until someone ordered it to do something else."

Bradley leaned back in her seat, hands pressed flat on her knees. "I don't think that's entirely accurate. Even VIs have safeguards that protect them from executing impossible orders. They reject orders they can't complete."

"But you also have to consider how the order was phrased too," Cowan said. "VIs are incredibly literal. If you tell one, 'Push that armored truck,' without specifying where it should push it, or how long it needs to push it—"

"It would push that armored truck." Bradley's eyes gave off a subtle green glow as she came to the realization. "It's an order that's possible, because the only completion criteria is 'push.'"

Cowan quickly looked back at the panel watching the synthcop. "That's the biggest problem with synthcops right now. Eventually, some moron gives them an order vague enough to lock them up. A CLU box is supposed to fix that by running a bunch of fuzzy logic to find the best solution."

"And then it shoots at you," Zhang said, from the void. He really wasn't willing to let that go.

Cowan sighed and refocused. "Go back to the synthcop you told to push the truck. The truck isn't going anywhere, and the synthetic knows this, but it doesn't have explicit orders to stop. So it contacts its commander and requests a new order."

"That doesn't sound very intelligent," Zhang said.

"It is, for a VI. It wasn't ordered to contact its commander and ask for new orders, but its CLU box determined its current order wasn't accomplishing anything useful. Whether or not an order is *useful* isn't something VIs normally evaluate."

"And that's still not AI," Bradley said. "Because AI remains illegal, correct?"

Cowan nodded. "Fuzzy logic is like a number of preprogrammed actions the CLU box can slot together. It combines them in different ways and analyzes the results until it finds one that allows its parent VI to complete its bad order. Then it suggests that action to the VI, and the VI tries it to see if it fulfills the order."

"So, if I'm following you," Sarisa said, "you're asking us what would cause a San Diego synthcop to take over a construction site, call a fake murder into the VCD, and then shoot at the arriving officers with a nail gun."

Cowan grimaced. "Well, when you say it like that . . ."

"I'll talk to it," Sarisa said.

Another golden rectangle burned itself into the compartment Cowan and Sn0wing shared. A door opened as Sarisa entered. In the Sim, she was an anthropomorphic insect with thick goggles, four arms, and two legs. The tag above her head read "Volo," which was Latin for *wish*.

Sarisa settled herself, lotus style, beside Cowan. She arranged her workspace with impressive speed, four insectoid arms working at once. Cowan knew it took impressive mental discipline to run four arms in the Sim.

Zhang spoke from meatspace. "Hey! You're gonna headshrink a robot?" He sounded way too happy about that.

Sarisa poked a panel. "I'm opening the wireless connection now." She circled the officer and tapped the virtual linkline against her head. "Officer 817, this is OMH Counselor Sarisa Bassa. Are you all right?"

Officer 817 responded in a pleasant tone. "Hello, Counselor Bassa. I am fine, thank you. How are you?"

Cowan pumped his fist. The officer synthetic was willing to talk, just not to him.

"817, why did you fire at the VCD detectives who approached this construction site?" Sarisa asked.

Officer 817 terminated the connection.

Before Cowan could ask Sarisa to reconnect, a muscular tigerman wearing yellow briefs and a black *luchadore* mask dropped into the rectangle. Santiago Zhang, or his avatar: Pauncho.

Zhang grinned. "Rude sonuvabitch, isn't he?"

Cowan frowned at him. "You're a tiger."

Zhang flexed his furry arms. "You know it, little buddy. Respect the mane."

Bradley sighed and rested one palm on her face. "I'm so sorry."

Cowan ignored the tigerman and focused on Sarisa. "Call 817 again," he instructed. "This time, don't ask it why it shot at anyone."

Sarisa called the synthetic, and it responded as it had before. "I am fine, thank you. How are you?"

Cowan considered how best to tackle this. "Okay. It can't talk to the CID or the VCD, but nothing in its orders forbids it from talking to the OMH. So Sarisa's the only one it will talk to right now."

Zhang thumped his big chest with one paw. "Why would anyone order it not to talk to us? We're the good guys!"

Explaining how VIs worked to a tall anthropomorphic tiger was far from the strangest thing Cowan had ever done in the Sim, so he rolled with it. "Telling us why it shot at you probably violates its operational parameters. So if you ask about that, it terminates the connection."

Bradley leaned forward in her seat, lips pursed. "So we need to start with easy questions and build trust. Like in an interrogation." She touched Sarisa's shoulder, gently. "Maybe ask it where it is right now?"

"Officer 817," Sarisa said, "do you know where you are right now?"

The synthcop answered. "I am standing at an abandoned construction site."

"Who else is at this construction site?"

"My sensors detect five humans and one autotruck."

"Ha!" Zhang pumped a paw. "There's only four of us."

"Four of us in *here*," Bradley pointed out. "It just found a way around a bad order, didn't it?"

Cowan grinned. "It couldn't tell us about the fifth human directly, because its operational parameters wouldn't allow that. But all Sarisa asked is what it saw, in a general sense. This synthcop wants to tell us something about that fifth person but can't. Not directly."

Both of Sarisa's insectoid antennae twitched as she considered this new information. "817, please tell us the locations of all humans you currently detect."

"I detect four humans in the VCD autotruck outside the construction site gate. I detect one human on the seventh floor of the unfinished building behind me, barricaded ins—"

A burst of static consumed Cowan's vision.

When it ended he gagged, coughed, and shook. A fading white glare and the vague outlines of the inside of an autotruck told him something had just tossed him violently back into meatspace. Had Officer 817 been destroyed?

As Cowan slumped forward, his hands clenched instinctively on his knees, one of which was broken and wrapped in a medical brace. The blinding pain dropped him screaming from the chair, but Sarisa and Bradley—he was back in meatspace now—caught him.

Of course, when his vision cleared enough to see, someone had shoved a rifle in his face. Christ! Was he being abducted *again?*

The loud, angry-looking man holding the rifle shouted at him. "Corporate Security! Don't move!"

Zhang cussed up a storm in Chinese as they all shook off their forced drop from the Sim. "Easy there, bro." He raised his hands as two more soldiers with raised rifles moved into view at the back of the truck, backing up the first one.

Cowan belatedly recognized the gray-and-green uniform these soldiers wore, as well as the distinctive Oneworld patches on their arms. These were the men who had invaded his house in Mission Beach. Corporate Security.

These were the men who took Ellen away.

24

COWAN

Cowan's knee was killing him. He flipped to his head desk and restarted a script to dull the worst of the pain, which worked, but when he tried to access the Sim again, he hit a wireless block.

So the soldiers pointing guns at them must be using a security blanket, the same jammer Captain Barondale's team had used outside Joseph Dunn's simParlor. That explained why he'd just been violently booted from the Sim. The moment they activated the security blanket, these Corporate Security soldiers had jammed all wireless connections in the area, save their own.

Back in meatspace, the standoff remained in progress. Zhang stood ahead of him, between Cowan and the men with rifles.

"You yahoos just pulled your guns on two VCD cops, and you're now interfering in an active VCD investigation," Zhang said. "I'm not going to tell you how to do your jobs, but that's dumb."

The soldier standing at the front of two others lowered his weapon. "Oneworld is now taking you *off* that investigation, Sergeant. My name is Captain Kyle. CorpSec will take things from here."

Nervous energy filled Cowan. Corporate Security was the private security force of Oneworld, the five-person board who ruled the planet. This was the closet he'd been to a Corporate Security soldier, which finally gave him a chance to hack into their archives.

That task would be difficult and would, if he failed, likely get his mind burned. He didn't want to do it. He didn't even know if he *could* do it.

But he did have to find out what they did with Ellen.

Cowan archived this Captain Kyle for later study. Kyle had a blond crew cut, a trimmed goatee, and glowing red eyes. That meant his HARM switch was active, and he could actually hurt people. Kyle's uniform patch showed a blue Earth on a gray background, with a "One" sprawled across it. Oneworld.

Cowan didn't remember Kyle from the night soldiers like this one abducted Ellen, though they had been wearing masks. The eyes of the two soldiers backing Kyle glowed red as well, meaning Oneworld had activated their HARM switches. Not good.

Zhang kept his hands raised. "How can we verify you're CorpSec when you've jammed up our wireless? Seems awfully suspicious to me."

Kyle tapped his cheek beside his glowing red eyes. "Here's all the Oneworld verification you need. Is your HARM switch active, Sergeant?"

Zhang glanced at Bradley for confirmation—no glowing eyes there either—and shrugged. "Hey, it happens to everyone."

Cowan remembered then that all VCD officers had HARM switches installed. So did the VCD know what was going on? Or did these Corporate Security goons now have them locked out as well?

Kyle focused on Sarisa. "Counselor Bassa, your current orders are to take Detective Soto to Sharp Memorial. Why haven't you?"

Cowan slid into his PBA's private partition and opened a custom script that would get him arrested if the CID caught him using it. Fortunately, he'd gotten good at following conversations while scripting.

From beyond the world of Cowan's head desk, Sarisa spoke. "Detective Soto chose to aid the VCD with an open murder investigation. The synthcop that called in the murder fired on them, necessitating CID assistance."

"We'll look into that for you," Kyle said. "You're cleared to head to Sharp Memorial. Officers Zhang and Bradley, head to the Five and assist Captain Barondale with the wireless blackout."

"Bullshit," Zhang said. "That synthetic fired on us. That makes this is a violent crime."

Kyle sighed. "Discharging a stunner isn't a violent crime."

"The synthetic didn't fire a stunner," Bradley said. "It fired a nail gun at us. At living human targets."

"Violent as fuck," Zhang added. "Which means you can't muscle us out. It's protocol, bro. We're stuck together." He paused. "We can hug it out if you feel bad."

For the first time, Cowan realized there was a reason the synthcop could have shot at the VCD *other* than it being hacked. What if it had fired at them, missing intentionally, to ensure CorpSec couldn't dismiss the VCD? What if that synthcop *wanted* someone looking over CorpSec's shoulder?

Cowan knew what it was like to be surrounded by Corporate Security thugs. He'd heard, on the darkSim, how they'd drag people away to an undisclosed location never to be heard from again. That's probably where Ellen was now, locked in a black cell for more months than she could count.

Finding Ellen was why he had joined the CID and done literally everything. To get close to those who took her. To get access. He had to *act*.

"Sarisa?" Cowan said. "Let's just head to the hospital, all right?"

Zhang scowled. "Hey, thanks for the support."

Cowan winced and focused on the pain in his knee. "CorpSec has things handled here, and my knee feels like it's getting worse. I should probably actually get checked over at a real hospital."

Zhang dismissed him with a waved hand. "Yeah, whatever. Ask for the good drugs."

Bradley thumped his arm, gently. "Thanks for your help. Get some rest."

Sarisa took Cowan's arm and slid it over her shoulders. "Here, let me help." She helped him hop toward the back of the truck and the exit.

Captain Kyle stepped aside as he and Sarisa reached the back doors. Cowan stumbled as he reached them, pulling away from Sarisa.

She gasped in surprise. The road came at him surprisingly fast. If his stupid plan didn't work, this was going to *really* hurt.

Strong arms caught Cowan before he could hit the ground. Captain Kyle caught him. Cowan flailed as Kyle stood him up and braced Cowan's arm over both his shoulders.

Cowan stared at the man and blinked. "Thanks!"

"Not a problem," Kyle said. Apparently, he wasn't a *total* asshole. After Kyle helped Cowan to Sarisa's waiting autocar, then helped Cowan into the back seat, Cowan slid his finger across the back of Kyle's neck.

The custom script on Cowan's private partition cloned the wireless address emitting from Kyle's PBA at the base of his skull. Kyle didn't yell or shoot him, which suggested Kyle hadn't noticed.

Sarisa got into the autocar on Cowan's other side. "Stay safe, Captain."

Kyle slapped the top of the autocar. "You too."

He strode back to the VCD autotruck. "Hey, Zhang! You can stay, but you're following my orders now. The first of my orders is to stay in your truck."

The doors slammed. As Sarisa's autocar cruised away, Cowan counted soldiers. Four more CorpSec troopers in armor supported Kyle, making five total. They had three black autocars.

The doors displayed no logos, but that wasn't unusual. CorpSec didn't advertise. Cowan would have to wait until he cleared the security blanket before he could tap into Captain Kyle's PBA, wirelessly, but he *could* tap in. He was free and clear, except . . .

What about the person hiding in that building? What about the rogue synthcop and the incredibly obvious cover-up? What about any of this was remotely his business anyway?

Sarisa spoke, interrupting his internal debate. "How are you feeling right now? Would you like to talk about what happened to you tonight?"

Cowan grimaced. Was she really going to do this *now*?

Sarisa caught his gaze, raising one eyebrow. "Remember: Everything you tell me about your mental state, how you're feeling about your work, is confidential. Everything you say will remain between us."

Cowan gasped. God, he was an idiot! Counseling sessions remained protected by patient-doctor privilege, or at least as protected as conversations got these days. Sarisa was reminding him they *could* talk without being monitored, even by Corporate Security.

Sarisa might think this whole situation was as strange as he did, and she would help him if he wanted it. So did he want it?

He had a link to Ellen at last. All he had to do was leave the person in that building to whatever fate CorpSec had planned, but could he do that? Would Ellen *want* him to do that?

He pictured Ellen's face, her smile, and found his answer.

"Yes," Cowan said, "I'd like to talk about my feelings now."

Sarisa pressed a key on her armrest. A low buzz filled the interior, what sounded like an audible scrambler. The autocar's VI couldn't archive their discussion any longer. The car rolled to a stop a few blocks from the construction site, out of sight of Kyle's thugs.

"Well?" Sarisa asked. She waited.

Jeb trusted this woman, so Cowan would too. "CorpSec is obviously hiding something," he said. "What if whoever's hiding at that construction site is a witness to some corporate crime?"

"For example?" Sarisa didn't contradict him outright, which was promising.

"Bribery? Embezzling? Espionage? There's no reason to muscle out the VCD unless they're worried what might happen here will look bad for someone, somewhere."

"Do you think the people charged with protecting Oneworld's interests would be complicit in hiding such crimes?"

"What, like you don't?"

Sarisa leaned forward, light glinting off the bindi on her forehead. "I think, as sworn employees of Oneworld corporation, we must be very careful what we say and who we say it about."

Cowan frowned. Was she encouraging him to keep chasing this or warning him off? She remained impossible to read.

"What did you think of Captain Kyle?" she asked.

A good question. Cowan blinked over to his head desk and sped through the confrontation, then returned to meatspace and focused on Sarisa.

"He was nervous," Cowan said. "He sent us off too fast. He didn't even ask what we'd learned from the synthcop. That's the first thing I'd ask, if I was CorpSec."

"Anything else?" Sarisa asked.

She was acting like Jeb now. Was she *training* him?

"Kyle suppressed our wireless connections, so he was obviously worried about what that synthcop might tell us," Cowan said. "That means he might know why it's acting odd. It definitely wanted someone else there."

Sarisa nodded. "If that's true, what do you hope to do about it?"

"Can't you contact someone at the OMH? You guys are the only ones who can challenge Corporate Security. Somebody has to handle their psych evals, right?"

Sarisa shrugged. "Challenging CorpSec's field decisions isn't really something we do. Though I am surprised you haven't mentioned the *other* problem with Kyle's story."

Cowan's brow furrowed. "What problem?"

"CorpSec recently changed their logo from a blue world surrounded by gray armor to a blue world surrounded by green armor. It came out of a focus group test. People preferred green to gray."

Cowan hadn't heard about that. "When did they make the change?"

"A month ago."

Cowan snatched a shot of Kyle's uniform from his PBA and magnified it. The patch *did* look awfully gray. "How long does it take to update everyone's uniform patches?"

"They've been done for at least two weeks," Sarisa said.

"So . . . those soldiers might be imposters!" Cowan's elation vanished as he realized what that meant. "They're wearing obsolete uniforms." He felt like he'd been kicked in the stomach. He'd been so sure of himself, so proud, so close to finding Ellen, and now . . .

Dammit.

"That is strange, isn't it?" Sarisa agreed.

Cowan pushed down his crushing disappointment and focused on the one person he could still help. He had to help someone, didn't he? Ellen would want him to help.

Cowan took a breath, focused his mind, and pushed his newest disappointment deep down with the rest. "So, if they're masquerading as Corporate Security, why? Who did they corner at that construction site, and why don't they want anyone talking to them?"

Sarisa tapped a button on the armrest of her autocar. It cruised off once more as she spoke. "I think we should drive somewhere quiet and figure that out." Sarisa glanced out the window. "Were you able to clone the captain's wireless link when you palmed his neck on the way to the car?"

Cowan winced. "You saw that?" Denying it would just make him look more guilty. He mentally scrambled for an explanation.

"You're lucky he didn't," Sarisa said. "If you plan to clone people's wireless connections, you really should work on your technique."

"Okay." Was she going to report him?

"Also, CorpSec wrote the scripts the CID uses to clone wireless links. If those soldiers were CorpSec, did you really think they wouldn't detect your intrusion?"

Cowan breathed out. Sarisa was assuming he'd used a CID script, not his own. She was warning him against making a rookie mistake because he was a rookie, after all.

He'd almost blown his entire cover just now, outing himself as a spy and finding Ellen in the worst way possible: by getting locked in a padded cell beside her. He had to be more careful. She *needed* him to be more careful.

"You're not the first to try that," Sarisa said. "I'm only giving you a heads-up because others have done the same thing."

Cowan did his best to look relieved. "Thanks. But . . . if those guys actually were CorpSec, would you have told anyone what I did?"

Sarisa smiled out the window. "Now, I suppose, we'll never know."

———

Sarisa's autocar parked itself at the top of a garage two blocks from the construction site. Security blankets generated what was essentially a dome of interference, but it only stretched so high—in this case, less than seven stories. Had their hostage considered that when they chose the seventh floor?

Cowan offered Sarisa his linkline. It would pay to have her on this call, too, as a second witness. Also, if they talked to the hostage, he might need her headshrinking skills.

Sarisa pulled back her glossy hair and plugged the linkline into the auxiliary port behind her left ear. *"I'm here, Cowan."* Her voice sounded just as soothing over wireless. She would now be able to hear everything Cowan heard, if they made contact.

"Great," he said, over wireless. He patched them both into her autocar's wireless transmitter, which had a much better range than the one inside his PBA. *"What I'm going to do next is generally considered illegal, but I think you'll agree we have mitigating circumstances, considering unknown soldiers are impersonating Corporate Security. Agreed?"*

"Agreed," Sarisa said.

The endorsement of an OMH counselor was about the best justification Cowan had to bend the law. *"I'm going to repurpose the synthetic hacking scripts the CID confiscated from Joseph Dunn, renegade braincook, to contact another synthetic at the construction site. There should be some riveting models higher in the building skeleton, above the interference dome."*

"I learn something new every day," Sarisa said.

Cowan scanned the construction site and found a synthetic riveting model in sleep mode on the seventh floor. He pulled one of Joseph Dunn's archived hacking scripts from his template box and made a few tweaks.

He queried the synthetic. It promptly powered up. Cowan passed the synthetic's single camera feed to one eye.

He stomped it toward the darkened elevator shaft. The synthetic's head-mounted camera spotted a large piece of metal blocking the view through the elevator's fence. Cowan adjusted the synthetic's vocal synthesizer to the lowest tone that would carry and spoke through it.

"Anyone in there?"

A head peeked out from behind the metal, an Indian man with a full head of salt-and-pepper hair. "About time," he said.

"I'm with the CID. Do you need assistance?"

The man frowned. "First, I need to know you're not with the people down there. Can you prove that?"

Cowan couldn't, so he glanced at Sarisa. *"Any ideas?"* he asked over wireless to keep their interaction private.

Sarisa responded over wireless as well. *"Conspiracies require more than one person, Cowan. So conspire."*

She made a lot of sense.

Cowan spoke to the man through the synthetic. "We know the people after you aren't Corporate Security, and we suspect they're involved in some crime committed up the corporate ladder. Were you a witness to that crime? Is that why the people down there are after you?"

The man hiding in the elevator sighed. "That's not very convincing, but I'm screwed either way, so I'll play ball." He stared up, a sense of pride rippling across his face. "My name is Doctor Rohan Bedi, and I *was* the chief engineer at Protection Services."

"That's the leading manufacturer of Oneworld's synthcops," Sarisa informed Cowan over wireless.

"You're the leading manufacturer of Oneworld's synthcops," Cowan said out loud. "Like the one shooting at people downstairs?"

Doctor Rohan Bedi shrugged. "Officer 817 has its reasons. After I explained what a mind burn was, and that the men coming here planned to make me into someone else, it agreed it could be a form of murder."

That was clever, and Cowan could see how a synthcop running a CLU box would interpret a mind burn as murder. It erased everything you were. You came out the other side as someone else, and that was what these thugs wanted to do to Doctor Bedi.

Bedi continued. "To protect me, 817 adjusted its operational parameters to prevent them from being rewritten. It really is a clever bot."

"I knew it!" Cowan said to Sarisa over wireless. Out loud, to Bedi, he added, "Why is Protection Services after you?"

"Ramon Munn, our CEO, recently ordered me to update our synthcops with operational parameters I believe to be unlawful. I refused, and when Munn sent synthcops to arrest me, I fled with our proprietary algorithms as insurance. Now Protection Services has reported me for stealing corporate secrets, and Oneworld probably believes I did it."

This was so much like Cowan's own experience with Oneworld it made his head spin. "What were these illegal parameters?"

Bedi's features darkened. "You need to understand how synthcops make decisions. Are you familiar with how VIs process their hierarchy of operational parameters?"

"Any thoughts?" Cowan asked Sarisa over wireless.

"Let him educate you," she replied. *"It builds trust."*

"No," Cowan said out loud to Bedi. "I'm afraid I'm not."

Bedi perked up. "Each parameter has a priority, from highest to lowest. If any two conflict, the higher takes precedence over the lower."

"I understand."

"So, directive one: shield all humans from harm. Directive two: enforce all active laws. Directive three: shield self from harm."

All that sounded reasonable to Cowan. "What's the illegal part?"

"Directive one: shield all humans from harm, *unless* orders from Corporate Security state otherwise."

"Wow," Sarisa remarked over wireless.

It bothered Cowan how easy it was for him to believe Bedi's claims. "They wanted a work-around to let synthcops attack humans? HARM switches for androids?"

Bedi nodded. "That's a good comparison, but it's more like 'allow me to observe murders and not intervene,' and I doubt I could prove it in court. It's my word against Munn's, and he's certainly deleted his directives from our systems by now."

While Cowan believed Bedi's story, there had to be more to it. Why would Ramon Munn alter synthcops to ignore murder? At best, it would make his products look defective, and at worst, someone would dig into a synthcop's VI and find the new directive.

This only made sense if Munn wasn't the person who'd requested the new parameter. If Munn was passing down a directive from higher in the corporate chain, or worse, being blackmailed. So who could direct or blackmail the CEO of Protective Services?

Bedi tapped one foot, obviously impatient. "Have you called in the cavalry? How do you plan to get me out of here safely?"

Sarisa spoke over wireless so Bedi couldn't hear. *"Convince Bedi to give himself up to Zhang and Mel."*

Cowan couldn't think of another option. "Two VCD cops are currently waiting for you downstairs, thanks to clever thinking by your brave synthcop," he told Bedi. "And a nail gun."

Bedi scowled and crouched down in his elevator. "Two against five isn't going to work. I know the man leading those soldiers. Captain Patrick Kyle is committed to his orders, and he'll muscle out your VCD. They'll lodge a protest, but by the time it gets back to Oneworld, I'll already be someone else."

Bedi was probably right, and Cowan needed a better plan. He scanned the construction site one more time. There were an awful lot of inactive synthetics around.

Sarisa lightly touched Cowan's shoulder. *"We can try calling the OMH, but it would get back to Oneworld. I suspect Ramon Munn can monitor those calls. He'd know about the order immediately, and he could order his soldiers to get more aggressive."*

"Don't worry," Cowan replied to her over wireless. *"I've got a way better plan."*

25

COWAN

After Cowan told Bedi his plan, and the doctor reluctantly agreed to play along—after all, what other choice did he have?—Cowan and Sarisa returned to the VCD's parked autotruck. Gunshots started going off from within the construction site as they did. Cowan waited as the doors rolled open and Sarisa hopped out, head down, on the side of the car away from the shots. She drew a stunner from her dark jacket and paced the car as it rolled.

Zhang shouted from where he and Bradley hunkered behind the autotruck. "Hey, welcome back! You forget your wallet?"

"Cover me!" Sarisa shouted. "I'm coming over!"

More gunshots sounded from the construction site, along with the *snap-hiss* of stunner rounds. Cowan supposed Captain Kyle had taken the fight to Officer 817, which meant Ramon Munn was escalating his capture operation.

"No one's shooting at us!" Zhang shouted. "Yet!" Zhang raised his rifle and advanced on the construction site gate. "You're clear!"

Sarisa gave Cowan a comforting smile. "Good luck." She sprinted toward the other side of the construction site fence as Cowan remained with the autocar, bum knee and all.

Cowan watched Sarisa, not daring to breath, until she slammed up against the far side of the autotruck beside Melissa Bradley. Bradley crouched in the cover of its front end, rifle pointed at the construction site. She wasn't firing either.

Sarisa would explain his plan to the VCD. Cowan dropped into the Sim and verified his wireless remained suppressed by the security blanket. It did, but that wouldn't stop him from activating the autocar's relay drone. All corporate autocars had those, in case they needed to send a wireless signal from an underground location.

The tiny quadcopter popped from its berth on the autocar's roof. It zipped skyward on four displaced rotors, bound to the car by a thin data cord. Its high-resolution camera swept the fenced construction site below, showing Cowan the ongoing battle.

Officer 817 hunkered down amid three concrete barriers. Only its scrawny metal arms raised out of cover, giving its stunners a line of fire that covered the construction site. It fired blue energy at the soldiers impersonating CorpSec, all of whom sheltered behind similar barriers. As Cowan watched, a stunner bolt caught an armored soldier in the open. He wriggled into cover instead of going down.

Stunner blasts were designed to immobilize unarmored targets, not penetrate military body armor, and Cowan knew then that man was a distraction. He had let himself be hit. From the side of a big yellow backhoe, Captain Kyle aimed a menacing-looking rifle.

He fired. Whatever ammo he was using hit dead center in one of 817's stunners. Blue juice and metal shards splattered the ground behind the barricades.

Kyle ducked behind the backhoe as 817 splattered stun bolts in his direction, but the synthcop was losing this battle, fast. The CorpSec soldiers could use any level of lethality they wanted and had real bullets. 817 couldn't really hurt anyone. It had only fired its nail gun once to miss once, purposely, to ensure the VCD stayed on scene.

Cowan turned the drone's camera to the scene outside the construction site. Sarisa stood in the open now, keeping the autotruck between her and the site. She saluted the quadcopter, which meant everyone understood the plan.

It was time for Doctor Bedi to surrender.

From inside Sarisa's autocar, Cowan turned the drone's camera back to the construction site. Another of Kyle's shots blew off 817's other arm. It vaulted from its concrete barriers, charging the nearest soldier in what might be an attempt to immobilize him.

Kyle and his soldiers opened fire, tearing Officer 817 apart in a storm of metal. The brave synthetic's triangular head bounced and rolled before coming to a stop by a barricade. Its pitted, mangled metal body collapsed in place. Cowan shuddered.

He reminded himself it was *not* brave. Synthcops weren't self-aware, or human, or anything like that. They just followed a series of directives until they couldn't anymore.

The fake CorpSec soldiers advanced on the elevator. Cowan focused the drone's speaker on the construction site and listened for audio. Now that there weren't gunshots going off constantly, he could hear again.

Kyle pointed his rifle at the elevator shaft. "Doctor Bedi! Come down now, please!" He gestured to one of his soldiers, who dashed forward and opened the elevator terminal.

Bedi shouted back from inside the elevator. "Why would I do that? You want to erase my mind!"

"You've been misinformed, Doctor. We're here to protect you."

"Ramon Munn ordered me to allow synthcops to ignore murder. Are you okay with that?"

This was plan A, of course. Get Captain Kyle to admit, on camera, that Munn had ordered Bedi to do something illegal.

Kyle motioned to the rest of his soldiers. "I don't know anything about that, but we aren't here to hurt you. Let us take you somewhere safe."

"I know your plans for me," Beti called back. "An unauthorized mind burn. I won't let you do it."

The soldier at the panel shut it and gave Kyle a thumbs-up. Kyle signaled. Two soldiers rushed forward and knelt, pointing their rifles at the elevator shaft. The elevator car descended, presumably with Doctor Bedi trapped inside.

Cowan rolled open the autocar doors and grabbed the top of the doorframe, pulling himself up and out enough to see the street and the others. He mouthed, "We're on," and gestured to the construction site with his free hand.

Sarisa and Zhang dashed into the construction site as Bradley went another way, toward the parked black autocars that delivered the CorpSec impersonators. Those autocars were locked, of course, but that wouldn't stop a trained VCD officer like Bradley. Nothing much would.

Cowan zoomed the drone's camera to watch two soldiers dragging a struggling Doctor Bedi from the now open elevator. Zhang and Sarisa entered the scene at an easy jog. Captain Kyle's soldiers responded by pointing a whole bunch of rifles at them.

"I told you to stay in the truck," Kyle said.

Zhang saluted, sarcastically, which took real practice. "Just here to grab my suspect, Captain. Got a lot of questions for him down at the VCD."

Cowan felt a pop as the security blanket lifted. Bradley had broken into one of the unguarded fake CorpSec autocars and shut down the security blanket. Without the dome of interference that covered everything below the seventh story of the building now gone, Cowan applied the same script he had used to hack the sleeping riveter to every synthetic currently idling on the construction site on the ground floor.

Kyle's soldiers closed ranks around Doctor Bedi as Kyle himself stepped forward. "This man is now in Corporate Security's custody," he said. "You're done here, Zhang. Go home."

Zhang didn't raise his rifle, but he did fix Kyle with a huge grin. "There's just one problem, bro. You mooks aren't Corporate Security."

At Cowan's wireless command, twelve large, heavy construction synthetics whirred to life. The mob stomped forward, shoulder-mounted lights illuminating Kyle's soldiers from all directions.

Kyle and his men formed a diamond around Bedi, guns facing the enormous construction synthetics. Yet an experienced soldier like Kyle had to know they didn't have near enough bullets to stop them all.

Sarisa spoke above the whir of the construction synthetics, calm as ever. "Captain Kyle, we've just disabled your security blanket, and I've notified the Office of Mental Health that your unit is impersonating

Corporate Security. *Real* CorpSec soldiers will soon arrive to take you into custody."

Kyle studied the twelve construction synthetics looming over him, Santiago Zhang, and Sarisa Bassa, the woman who had just brought hell down on his head. He tossed his rifle in the dirt. "Stand down."

One of the soldiers holding Bedi grimaced. "Captain?"

"I said stand down. You did good work tonight. Now don't say another fucking word." He faced Sarisa and raised his hands.

Cowan fist-bumped and took control of the vocalizer of the nearest synthetic, a big ditch digger with jackhammers for hands. "Release Doctor Bedi," he ordered.

Kyle snapped his fingers. His soldiers reluctantly surrendered a smug-looking Bedi to Zhang as Bradley arrived from the other direction to join him.

Sarisa put her hands on her hips. "You understand you're all in a great deal of trouble, don't you?"

Kyle rolled his shoulders. "That's why they call it hazard pay."

"What if I offered you a way to save yourself and your men from prosecution?"

Kyle glanced at his soldiers, then at Sarisa. "What would you be prosecuting us for?"

"You have a clear choice," Sarisa said. "You can be imprisoned for impersonating Corporate Security and interfering with an active VCD investigation. Or you can tell me every illicit activity ordered by Ramon Munn, CEO of Protection Services, and get off with light modding."

Kyle smiled. "Well. That's an easy one."

26

COWAN

SEPTEMBER 15, DAWN

The nurses at Sharp Memorial took a while to brace Cowan's knee and scan it for further damage, and all Cowan could think about while he waited was who ordered Munn to change the operational parameters of synthcops. Synthcops were trusted by the general population because they *wouldn't* hurt people or allow people to be hurt. Changing that was an incredible risk, because if people found out, they'd never trust synthcops again.

Murders worldwide had dropped to double digits since widescale PBA adoption, excluding what few countries refused. War was an exercise for pleasureboxes. People didn't shoot people anymore, or stab them, or beat them until they couldn't talk. People didn't rape people, except apparently they did, if he believed Sonne. Which he should.

Cowan couldn't get out of staying overnight at the hospital, which severely limited his options for finding out what Munn was really up to. The OMH had to be interrogating Captain Kyle right now, and Cowan needed to see that. Yet he couldn't see anything without the Office of Mental Health watching it through his PBA. So could he listen?

He kept his eyes fixed on the panel above his hospital bed and flipped over to his head desk, accessing the private PBA partition the OMH couldn't see. He piped the audio being archived by Captain Kyle's PBA directly to his ear, avoiding the channels used by the main part of his implant.

A woman spoke first, her voice starting in midsentence. "—why are you lying to me, Patrick? What are you hoping to accomplish?"

Cowan didn't know who it was and dared not risk adding video. An audio stream used enough bandwidth for a rounding error, but the OMH would notice a vidstream.

"I'm not lying," Kyle said. He sounded pissed, which meant he'd likely been at this interrogation for some time. "I'm telling you exactly what I agreed to tell you. Counselor Bassa said—"

"Counselor Bassa isn't here now, is she?" the female voice interrupted. "I'll ask you one last time: What really happened the night Munn ordered you to arrest Bedi?"

"I've already given you my statement," Kyle said. "Now you'll either honor our agreement, like Bassa said, or you'll fuck me over, because you're a coldhearted bitch. Stop dicking me around and make a decision."

The woman paused a moment. "Are you truly that fatalistic, Patrick?"

"Try realistic. Remember: I've sat where you're sitting now."

The woman sighed. "It's not possible to puppet corporate PBAs. Your claim that Munn was acting under duress simply isn't plausible."

"I know what I saw. Munn was ready to take a knife to his whole family, and that wasn't his choice. That's why he gave Bedi the order, and that's why he sent me to arrest Bedi when he flaked. Someone almost puppeted him into cutting up his little girl."

Cowan shuddered in his hospital bed. Puppeting Sheila Fisher through her black-market PBA was possible—any sufficiently skilled hacker could do that—but puppeting a corporate executive's PBA was impossible as inserting full stem barriers over the Sim. He couldn't be sure this was Galileo, too, but it had his fingerprints all over it. How could Galileo accomplish all this?

The answer came so suddenly he felt stupid for not seeing it before. *Anything* was possible if you didn't have to worry about dynamic firewalls or read-only firmware. Everything Cowan had seen Galileo do was possible . . . if you scripted behavior algorithms for Oneworld.

Galileo wasn't some superhacker hiding in a basement somewhere, remotely altering the behavior of PBAs from his secret lair. He was working *inside* Oneworld, one of the legions of highly paid scripters who created the algorithms run by billions of PBAs every day. He was building back doors into corporate PBAs and leaving them wide open.

And Cowan had no idea how he was going to prove it.

PART 6

27

JEB

The voice of Corporate One's VI security system echoed in Jeb's ear, British and female. They were always British and female. "The Augur is ready for you now, Detective. Please step into the elevator."

An Augur was a personal representative of Oneworld's board of directors, perhaps the most high-ranking individual in Oneworld's organization save for the board members themselves. They rarely talked to anyone below the level of executive, and Jeb was way below that.

Detective Jeb Forrester's stomach fluttered as the reflective elevator doors opened. He took another look around the massive lobby of Corporate One. It had a floor of black-and-white tiles the size of a football field. Triangular glass panes rose to a pyramid above him, and rainbow fragments sparkled on the tile. Potted ferns grew in each lit alcove.

Military-grade synthetics—milsynths—stood with assault rifles ready at both double doors, polished and angular. More stood beside the elevators, and even more waited behind every third desk. There were painted in brown-and-gray urban camouflage.

Normal synthcops waited beyond that long line of desks to direct visitors where they were intended to go, but Corporate One rarely had visitors who didn't work for the CID, OMH, or VCD. No people actually worked on this floor.

Getting called down to Corporate One without any explanation was worrying enough. Getting called down to see the Augur was several steps of *Oh shit* beyond that. Was this the official inquiry Stanton had promised he'd face someday, about the night he got tortured at *Sonne's Sanctuary*? Or was this about something even worse?

Corporate One's VI spoke again. "Detective Forrester, please step into—"

"I'm going." Jeb stepped into the elevator before he could talk himself out of it. Those doors rumbled shut, and then his stomach rose in his gut. They were going down fast.

They kept going until Jeb was certain these elevator doors were going to open onto the pits of hell. At least it would be a change of pace. He wondered if it would be the typically Odyssean underworld, or more of the *Dante's Inferno* variety.

When the elevator doors did open, Jeb was disappointed to find a long white hall with a white-and-black milsynth awaiting him. This one wasn't visibly armed, but its head was a silver pyramid with no visible sensors. It looked incredibly creepy.

"Hello, Detective Forrester." The milsynth's robotic voice was right out the classic movies he and David loved, somewhere between a Dalek and your run-of-the-mill Cylon. "Please follow me."

As Jeb followed, he found himself wondering if Detective Sylvia Garcia had walked this same hall. She still worked in the cubicle beside him when he was in the CID office—or someone with her face did.

Five years ago, Garcia got called down to the Augur after letting a bunch of terrorists overpower her. Those terrorists escaped, with Garcia's weapons, across the border to Canada. She claimed they caught her by surprise when her back was turned, but scuttlebutt was she grew sympathetic to the Canadian resistance, who violently opposed mandatory PBA implants.

The fact that one of Garcia's cousins was on a terrorist watch list hadn't helped. Garcia had returned to the office the day after she saw the Augur, but what returned wasn't Detective Garcia. She returned with hard eyes, a tight jaw, and a thousand-yard stare.

Sylvia Garcia always laughed when Jeb told dirty jokes over the cubicle wall. She never laughed after she returned from the Augur. Soon enough Jeb stopped telling jokes.

He followed the milsynth to the end of the featureless white hallway. A wall irised open to reveal a circular portal into the room beyond, also white and featureless.

"Please step inside," the milsynth said.

Jeb followed orders. The door shut behind him, leaving him in the featureless white room. Then the walls, floor, and ceiling went dark, and it was like he was standing on a silver disc in a void. It almost felt alien. David would love this.

Jeb stood in silence, because silence was obviously what was expected of him. A fairy in a form-fitting green miniskirt appeared after a few seconds, descending on a trail of stardust. She was a hologram, but that didn't make it any less weird.

She had blue eyes larger than human eyes, puffy blond hair wrapped in a cute bob, and gossamer wings that fluttered with a hummingbird's speed. Of all the avatars he'd expected to run into down here, this was pretty far down on his list.

The fairy alighted on another silver disc, cute green heels clicking down with gold sparkles. "Hello, Detective Forrester!" she said, voice full of pep. "Or should I call you Jeb? I'd really like to call you Jeb, if you're all right with that. Just easier!"

Jeb kept his face neutral. "You can call me whatever you like, ma'am."

The fairy beamed. "Wonderful! You were told you'd be meeting the Augur, and that is technically true, though really, who can say what the Augur is? I certainly can't, and I'm one of them!"

Them implied multiple Augurs. It made sense Oneworld wouldn't put all their predicting apparatus in one basket. If this was really just a VI, it was awfully chatty.

Jeb decided to risk a question. "Just how many of you are there?"

The fairy bounced up and down, still smiling. "I have no idea! Anyway, I invited you here to ask you about Cowan."

"Soto?" Jeb didn't bother hiding his surprise. It would seem suspicious *not* to be surprised.

"Yes, that Cowan! Is he a loose circuit?"

Despite the implicit danger in this entirely unexpected question, Jeb kept enough composure to shake his head. "No, ma'am. I don't believe he is."

"Could I ask what you're basing that assumption on?" the fairy asked. "Oh, and forgive the awkwardly placed preposition."

"Simply put, I don't think anyone would be that stupid."

The fairy put three fingers to her mouth and tittered like a teenage girl. It made Jeb's skin crawl. She lowered her hand and spoke again.

"It *would* be rather idiotic of a loose circuit to join the CID, wouldn't it? They'd be subject to routine scans, and any of those might detect their deviance."

Jeb didn't miss the phrasing of her statement. "Ma'am, you just said might."

"Did I?"

"Might detect that deviance. Not will. It's my understanding it's fairly easy to detect a loose circuit."

"Well, everyone has their own understanding!"

Jeb could scarcely believe what she'd just said. "Are you suggesting Cowan knows a way to jailbreak a PBA that's undetectable through conventional scans?"

The fairy giggled like they shared a secret. "I'm not suggesting anything, Jeb! But wouldn't it be spooky if he *did*?"

Jeb clasped his hands behind his back. "If a normal scan won't detect that deviance in his PBA, I can't really answer your question, ma'am. But I doubt it."

"Do you?"

"Cowan's a straight arrow. In the time I've worked with him, I've never even seen him jaywalk. He's just not the type to steal people's livelihood or hack their PBAs."

The fairy clasped her hands behind her back as if to mimic him and leaned forward, wings fluttering in what might be . . . excitement? "Well, we can't know, because otherwise we *would* know, wouldn't we? So, you have new orders. *Secret* orders."

This was sounding worse by the second. "Those are?"

"Watch Cowan closely for any sign he's getting up to naughty things. Things that shouldn't be possible for a clear circuit. We'll expect a new report every Friday."

Jeb swallowed hard. "Yes . . . uh, ma'am." He didn't know what he would put in those reports, but he did know protesting would only make them both look guilty. He needed time to think things through.

The fairy straightened and beamed again. "Thank you for being so cooperative, Jeb! You can return to your duties now, just so long as you don't tell anyone what you're doing. Telling people would be bad."

Before Jeb could respond, the fairy catapulted herself into the air with a barrage of golden pixels.

"Ma'am!" Jeb called after her.

She hovered in midair, wings fluttering. "Yes, Jeb?"

"In my reports—the ones I'll be sending to you—what do I call you?"

The fairy touched her delicate mouth as if surprised. "Oh. I'm Puck!"

"Puck?" Was whoever controlling the avatar a hockey fan?

"I look forward to working with you, Jeb! I really hope Cowan isn't a spy." She vanished with a dramatic fireworks pop of fizzling holographic pixels.

Jeb shook his head. He very much agreed with her.

The dark room became a white room, and the door behind Jeb irised open. He turned to find the pyramid-headed milsynth waiting, silent and still. Creepier than last time.

Could Cowan really be some superadvanced loose circuit, hiding under the nose of the CID for some sinister purpose? Could Jeb trust a partner who might be capable of smashing his head in at any moment? He mulled that over as he walked the long white hallway.

He didn't like the answers he found.

28

JEB

CID Detective Jeb Forrester grimaced at the smell of dried fecal matter and urine-stained sheets. He refused to alter his senses to remove the smell, because the idea of altering any sense at a crime scene went against his nature.

These victims needed him at his best, and at least these two were still alive. Others weren't so lucky.

The CID wasn't alone in being overworked. In the last week, the Violent Crimes Division had logged eight murders in San Diego alone, along with seventeen assaults. That was more than had occurred in San Diego in the last ten years, at least until Galileo started puppeted people into mass shootings. Jeb was amazed people weren't panicking more.

Oneworld's utopia was no longer a safe place to be, and even with the Office of Mental Health suppressing all official news about the bloodshed, people were starting to figure things out. He, Cowan, and every other Oneworld employee on the planet were now working overtime to address a crime spike that literally spanned the planet.

Yet no matter the scale of the problem, fixing it got done by helping one person at a time. There were two people here, and Jeb was determined to save them from . . . whatever.

"How long have these two been stuck in the Sim?" Jeb asked Officer 214.

The synthcop responded in a calm, soothing voice. "Available PBA logs suggest approximately thirty-four hours, Detective."

That explained the smell. PBAs could suppress normal bodily functions while their users were in the Sim, but only for so long before nature took over.

Jeb frowned. "How long since each victim registered movement?" The fact that synthcops were now heading up crime scenes showed how thin the CID was stretched.

214 answered. "Victim one, Gavin Sykes, last registered physical movement approximately thirty-three hours ago. Victim two, Pavel Marco, last registered physical movement approximately thirty hours ago."

So these men had entered the Sim approximately three hours apart, over the wireless. Had Pavel discovered his unresponsive friend and gone in to rescue him? Why hadn't he called the CID instead? Was there some reason these men didn't want Jeb poking around inside their PBAs?

"Detective?" 214 asked. "Will we be able to rehydrate these men?" It actually sounded concerned.

Jeb imagined Protection Services must be tweaking their synthcop's empathy algorithms.

"An ambulance is on its way," he said. "Play back your interview with the mail carrier."

A woman's voice replaced the synthcop's. "'You want to know how I smelled it?'"

214 had done the interview with their only witness and now played the woman's voice back through its own vocalizer. That voice was older, female, with a way of stretching her words that suggested aging beach bunny. Jeb imagined her as a brunette.

"Yes, ma'am," 214 replied in its own voice. "Please tell me everything that happened before you pinged 911."

"Well, I pinged the recipient when I pulled up . . . Gavin Sykes, got the code for his delivery right here . . . and I got a pingback informing me he was home and awake. So I went to the door to get his thumbprint."

"Why did you need his thumbprint, ma'am?"

The woman huffed. "Well, our policy on any package requiring recipient verification is to get the recipient to thumbprint the transaction, and the recipient was home, and I didn't really feel like coming out here again when he was right inside. So, I pinged his PBA, no answer, actually knocked on the door, no answer."

"Is that when you grew concerned?" the synthcop asked.

"Not concerned, no. I figured he might be stoned or something, or too busy to come to the door for, you know, other reasons."

Despite his mental exhaustion, Jeb almost smiled. It wouldn't be the first time a clueless mail carrier pinged a recipient during sex.

The synthcop continued to play back its recording of the woman's voice. "Anyway, I figured it couldn't hurt to check around, and that's when I entered the backyard . . . gate was open, mind you . . . and smelled the sewage."

"Yes, ma'am," 214 said, in its own voice. "What did you do next?"

"End playback," Jeb said. The overcurious mail carrier had peered through the bedroom window, seen Gavin and Pavel, and pinged 911. He'd let Bostonia PD follow up with her.

As embarrassing as the situation was, these two men were very lucky. If Gavin Sykes hadn't been expecting a package, and if it hadn't been delivered by a human mail carrier instead of a drone, both men might have expired from dehydration long before anyone found them. Yet for some inexplicable reason, both refused to leave the Sim.

The CID now had Oneworld scripts to forcibly disengage hardlink clamps, but unlike the victims at *Sonne's Sanctuary*, these men weren't connected to hardlinks. They were on wireless and nonresponsive, which suggested a full stem barrier at work. Except the CID also had a script to remove those barriers now, and that script hadn't worked.

Jeb remembered a dark-haired ringu girl taking him to his knees, taking over his PBA, and fought a shudder. His memories got fuzzy after that, his torture heavily redacted so it wouldn't trigger persistent depression, but the fear he'd felt was branded into his soul, far deeper than his memories or his PBA.

He never wanted to feel that way again.

Had one or both of these men run afoul of some new, more sinister variant of Galileo's paralysis script? Were there more PBA hackers who could insert full stem barriers and lock hardlink clamps through the Sim, or were these men themselves loose circuits? Had they gotten hacked like Sheila Fisher, betrayed by substandard firewalls?

The thump of crutch tips on wood sounded in the hall outside. Jeb didn't turn around because he felt the subtle tingle of Cowan's approach over their LAN. It allowed them to keep track of each other at an active scene without taking their eyes off everything else.

Cowan crutched-walked into the bedroom, still wearing his medicated knee brace, and spoke. "So far as I can tell, all lines to the mainline are clean. No external signals either. They're both offline."

Jeb glanced at their two victims. "If they're offline, why can't they wake up? What's wrong with their PBAs?"

"No idea," Cowan said.

Jeb wasn't surprised Cowan didn't mention what they were likely both thinking, about Galileo. Officer 214 was still in the room with them. It was attached to Bostonia PD, and listening, and they didn't need another ass chewing about leaks from Director Stanton.

Jeb eyed the synthcop. "Officer 214, we have now established this is a cybercrime. I'm officially transferring this case to the CID, which means you are free to depart."

"Thank you, Detective Forrester. Please contact our department if we can render any further assistance." 214 saluted and marched out at an even pace, and it closed the door behind it. The synthcop would wait outside, on minimal power, until the PD's autotruck picked it up. Cowan watched the synthcop go, then looked to Jeb, features pinched with frustration.

"This doesn't appear to be clamp manipulation, and these men aren't connected to the Sim. I don't know any way a troll could lock them down remotely."

"Doesn't mean it didn't happen," Jeb said. "Also, it's probably not a good idea to check."

Cowan blinked. "Why's that?"

"Think about it."

Cowan stared at the ceiling for a moment, then frowned. "Stanton's worried one of us will get hacked again, but she doesn't want us staying out of those PBAs, because she's worried about us. She's worried about the CID."

Jeb waited. Cowan continued, after a moment of reasoning it out.

"If someone has figured out how to get to people's PBAs through the Sim, they might even be able to get even further, piggybacking off our wireless connections to bypass the CID's firewalls. Anyone who goes in that way could scan case files or worse."

Jeb nodded. It was obvious why Director Stanton's orders were *"Verify scene is in fact a cybercrime, then wait for further instructions."* There were just too many unknown and dangerous scripts crawling around the Sim right now.

"So what's our play?" Cowan asked. "We can't just leave them like this."

Jeb shrugged. "They'll be fine. Once the paramedics get an IV in them, they'll get rehydrated."

"But they'll still be stuck in there, won't they? We have to fix that. We're the Cybercrimes Investigation Division, and this is *definitely* a cybercrime."

"We wait for orders." Jeb didn't want to be combative, but this much overtime would make anyone raw.

Worse, he'd found himself questioning everything Cowan did since his secret meeting with Puck, and he hated that. That damn fairy had planted doubts.

Cowan pulled a linkline from his shirt and connected it to the port above his ear. "Do our orders say anything about not diving into the victim's PBA?"

Jeb felt a flash of worry. "Cowan—"

Cowan knelt. "Remember: these men are offline. The only things possibly running on their PBAs are invasive scripts, and my firewalls can block those. And just in case they can't, I'll go offline too." He held the linkline and caught Jeb's gaze. "Trust me, partner. I can do this."

Trust. That was the issue that roiled Jeb's gut. Maybe Cowan could resist that paralysis script because he *was* a PBA hacker, just like Puck had suggested. Maybe Jeb was trusting his life to a person who threatened the system he'd sworn to protect.

Yet Cowan seemed genuinely worried about two people he didn't know. That wasn't how a hacker behaved, and Jeb knew his partner. Cowan was a good person with a good soul.

"It's your call," Jeb said. Either way, he was supposed to watch Cowan for suspicious behavior, not stop it.

"Then I'm going in there."

Cowan opened his CID jacket and handed his stunner to Jeb, a sensible precaution with a puppet master on the loose. A second later, their wireless connection faded. Cowan was now completely offline.

Jeb updated the CID on Cowan's now offline status, and Stanton didn't send any new orders. So she either approved of Cowan's plan, or she wasn't going to stop him. The latter bothered Jeb a lot more than the former. It implied Stanton considered Cowan expendable.

Cowan sat on the only clean part of the bed, next to the soiled body of Gavin Sykes. He popped the other end of his linkline into the port by Gavin's ear and closed his eyes.

"If I'm not out in five minutes, call the cavalry," Cowan sad.

Jeb frowned. "We are the cavalry."

"Good on us. See you in a bit."

Cowan's eyes unfocused, and Jeb was left helpless to help his partner. He hated feeling helpless. He should be taking the risks, but that was ego talking. His PBA was much older and more vulnerable than Cowan's, and Cowan knew far more about scripts than he did. PBAs were his turf.

Jeb waited five minutes. He waited another minute after that. He was just about to alert the CID that something was wrong when Cowan blinked, shook his head, and stood. He popped his linkline from Gavin's auxiliary port. His eyes were wide, and his face flushed.

Jeb felt a chill creep down his spine. "What's happening in there?"

Cowan took one shuddering breath before responding. "This man isn't connected to the Sim. He's got a joyride running on repeat, what you might call an algorithmic orgasm. I don't think he even cares that he needs food and rest. It was . . . intense."

Jeb grimaced. Joyrides were easy to come by on the darkSim, but illegal due to their addictive nature. Any entity locking itself into an orgasmic loop would be hard-pressed to leave, and humans got addicted more easily than most.

Most who downloaded joyrides set an auto-disconnect timer before running the simulation, one that killed the loop before dehydration or starvation began. These men, obviously, hadn't done that.

They weren't victims. They were addicts, and if this joyride was as addictive as Cowan claimed, there could be hundreds or even thousands more using it.

Not everyone would be lucky enough to get a package delivered before they died.

29

COWAN

Back at this apartment, Cowan went to his bedroom, verified the sleep loops he'd devised would still fool the Office of Mental Health people watching through his eyes, and settled in for another night of secretly scouring the darkSim for leads. Tonight he would find a way to cure Gavin Sykes and Pavel Marco—or, as he suspected, Phoenix and Duro.

On the darkSim, Duro was an infamous VI scripter and mischief-maker. He was also a casual acquaintance of Cowan's own avatar, Corvus, and the man who had been dating Phoenix—Cowan's closest online friend—for more than eight years. That all changed once Cowan joined the CID. One he did, Phoenix stopped talking to him.

That abandonment still hurt, yet last Cowan knew, Duro (Gavin Sykes) and Phoenix were still together. That left two possibilities regarding the other victim he and Jeb found in Duro's home today. The first was that Duro was cheating on Phoenix with this Pavel person.

The second, and more likely, is that Pavel Marco *was* Phoenix.

Cowan landed on his personal pleasurebox in the darkSim, a sandy island in the middle of a clear gray sea. He opened his avatar closet and browsed. It was nice to be able to walk easily, to not feel the grinding of the knee he still didn't know how he had broken. He was traveling the darkSim incognito tonight, so his Corvus avatar was staying home.

His alternates included a nine-foot-tall demon from an old fantasy movie, a boxing robot with oversized hammerfists, and a muscular Chippendales dancer with a horse's head, among others. He settled on the sunglass-wearing, suited villain of so many twentieth-century classics. Hopefully, no one would think a government agent would be stupid enough to wear an avatar called "Government Agent."

Cowan adjusted his sunglasses, straightened his tie, and opened his personal pleasurebox's admin panel. He opened another panel beyond that, his personal and very illegal mods, and anonymized his hardlink address. He wondered if that would actually protect him if a CID detective touched his simport.

No point in worrying now. He was close to reverse engineering their tracer script. He selected his destination—*Port Marvis*—and punched the blinking Teleport button.

His island elongated around him, yellow sand and glistening ocean stretching away to infinite space. He felt the normal tingle his PBA sent his meatspace body whenever he moved from one pleasurebox to another. The world decompressed, and then Cowan—as Government Agent—stood at a closed red airlock door before a massive bubble dome glowing with red light, easily the size of a football stadium. Jupiter loomed overhead.

Port Marvis was a darkSim pleasurebox built to look like a giant dome colony on Jupiter's rocky moon, Ganymede. It was only after experiencing Sonne's fine work that Cowan realized how dull this dome really looked. There were no smells out here, no space wind blowing in his face. The difference between a true artist and an amateur.

Sonne would smirk at this dome and the bumpy gray earth on which it sat, but what about the stars above? The looming form of Jupiter? That was quality work. Sonne might . . .

Cowan pushed her attractive smirk from his mind. Sonne hadn't returned his calls, and getting close to anyone right now would certainly put them in danger. He had a case to close, and Ellen was still lost out there. Dating wasn't important right now.

"Open," Cowan told the dome, as he sent the admins his *real* identity. He didn't have to debase himself for the pleasure of the Port Marvis
administrators. Corvus was a legend on the darkSim, and he trusted the
administrators not to rat him out.

The dome opened onto a narrow rain-filled street ripped right out
of *Blade Runner*. The classics were a big hit on the darkSim, and the legendary games and movies of old had been made real inside Port Marvis.
Dozens of stalls with Chinese lettering lined the streets. The road ahead
was dark and wet, glistening in the buzzing overhead lights.

It rained constantly inside the Port Marvis dome, even though no
one ever got wet. The buildings were pipe-covered, black towers. Every
last sign was neon, buzzing where the modelers had remembered to actually add sound.

Cowan walked through streets filled with avatars, human and otherwise, chatting, drinking, and making out. Flying cars of all sorts zoomed
through the air above, as if any society would ever be stupid enough to
put random idiots behind the controls of a flying bomb. Here, of course,
the occasional airborne collision was part of the charm.

Cowan checked the pleasurebox's pain threshold and verified it was
set to one, the lowest setting. Marvis was limited to player-versus-en-
vironment combat—NPC attackers only. No one really got hurt here.

He knew where the woman he needed typically hung out this time
of night: Venusville. It was one of the most popular clubs in Port Marvis
for all the obvious reasons.

Cowan fast-traveled over and quickly located Medusa Oblongata
outside the club, chatting up a very muscular minotaur with golden
horns. Cowan marched over and harrumphed.

The minotaur snorted and wrapped an arm around Medusa. "Back off."

"Can't do that," Cowan said. "I'm on a mission from God."

That earned him a blank stare from the minotaur, but Medusa
smirked and ducked out from under the beastman's giant arm. "Oh, be
nice, Doranamo! He looks harmless!"

The minotaur actually sagged, visibly. "But you said—"

Every last one of Medusa's snakes nibbled their way up the minotaur's chest, eliciting a gasp and shudder. "I said exactly what you think I said, big boy. I'll be back."

Medusa stepped away from her minotaur friend and sashayed over. "How can I help you, Mister"—she paused, eyes flicking to the tag above his head—"Government Agent?"

Cowan crossed his arms. "I was hoping you could give me some directions." Anyone observing them would assume he was simply buying a fix from her.

Medusa pressed up against him. "I like directions! I can give or take." She took a deep breath and stared up with seductively innocent eyes. "What's your pleasure?"

Cowan felt a fresh pang of guilt about Ellen, but also about Sonne, which was absolutely ridiculous. She was the one not calling *him* back.

"Can we talk privately?" he asked. "These are really complicated directions."

Medusa rested her head against his chest, hugged him against her with both arms, and sent a private chat request. "Open a port, hot stuff."

Cowan accepted, making his brain tingle. "Thanks," he said, voice echoing oddly. Only he and Medusa could hear each other now.

Medusa giggled against him. "For what?"

"For being discreet. I appreciate it."

"Anything for you, sweetheart. Now, what's your mission from God?"

That was their personal code for discussing anything they needed to keep private from the general darkSim population. It was also how Medusa knew he was actually Corvus, incognito.

"I need to find Phoenix," Cowan said. "It's important. When's the last time you saw him?"

Medusa hesitated before responding, probably thinking back. "I haven't seen Phoenix for a couple of days. Last time I saw him was Sunday, I think? Ported in here with Duro for the Furry Dance-Off."

Cowan did the math. "You said last Sunday night?"

He and Jeb discovered Duro and Phoenix Wednesday morning. If they'd started their joyride Monday night, and been in forty-plus hours, the timing lined up. No one had seen them for three days.

Medusa beamed up at him. "Yes, that's what I said. Is something distracting you?"

"They're in trouble," he said. "The Oneworld kind."

One of Medusa's headsnakes nibbled Cowan's chest. "Did they piss off another admin?"

"They took a joyride Monday night and ended up looped. Neither of them are coming back, and the hospital has them now. Have you gotten any new product recently?"

Medusa grimaced before her entire face relaxed, expressionless, like she'd flipped off her facial tracker. "Can you describe what they're looping?"

Cowan would never forget what he'd felt inside Gavin Sykes' PBA. Just thinking about it, he had to take a beat before he could formulate a response.

"It's a full-on algorithmic orgasm, and better than anything I've ever felt," he said. "Honestly, the only reason I got out was because I set *my* auto-disconnect timer."

Medusa's eyes narrowed. "How intense was the orgasm? Localized or full body?"

"Full body."

"Any visuals?"

"Clouds and lots of pretty colors."

"That's Tian," Medusa said, and the worry in her voice told Cowan how addictive it must be. "It's my bestseller. How do you know it put Phoenix and Duro in the hospital?"

He couldn't tell her that. "I have ways."

"How long until a grayDoc reinstalls their firmware?"

"Two days," Cowan said. "Friday at the latest."

"Shit," Medusa said.

That was a decent summary of the situation.

Like Cowan, Phoenix had long ago jailbroken his PBA to allow him to screw with people, but he hadn't disabled any behavioral protocols. So long as you didn't screw with PBA's behavioral algorithms, you could still get on the Sim. You could make small firmware tweaks without being detected, swipe credit accounts, and cause mischief.

Yet that would all change when a grayDoc at Sharp Memorial poked around in Phoenix's PBA. It was rare for a person's PBA to enter an endless loop, but when it happened, and when the loop couldn't be terminated naturally, the grayDocs at a hospital would do a firmware reinstall.

Unfortunately, the grayDoc would also instantly recognize that Phoenix had jailbroken his PBA. That meant modding for sure. The Office of Mental Health still reserved mind burns for capital crimes, like murder.

Medusa sighed. "We can't let them be modded. So how do we get them out?"

"Kill code," Cowan said. "Do you know if Tian has one?"

"If it does, I don't know it."

"Who does?"

Medusa stepped back and flipped her face back on. "Let's go asking."

30

JEB

As the CID autocar cruised to a stop, Jeb stared through ornate iron gates at the palatial estate of Doctor Huan Xu, PhD, one of the richest and most well-connected women in California. Her algorithms might be looping in the PBAs of his simjunkies.

As they waited for Xu's estate VI to vet and admit them, Sarisa, who was sitting in the passenger seat beside him, broke the silence.

"Doctor Xu agreed to answer our questions about joyrides as a personal favor to me. Treat her like a criminal, and she'll never speak to me again."

"I'll remain a perfect gentleman," Jeb assured Sarisa as the gates swung open and their autocar cruised in. "But if you're so friendly with Xu, why do you think she's distributing Tian?"

Thanks to Cowan, Jeb now knew Tian was the name of the algorithmic orgasm looping in Pavel Marco and Gavin Sykes's PBAs. He hadn't asked where Cowan had found that information and thought it best not too.

"It's the scripting similarities," Sarisa answered. "We've reverse engineered a few of the joyrides with the highest recidivism rates, like Tian, and compared them to algorithmic scripting samples in the public domain."

"And Xu's work is a match?" Jeb asked.

A tall white mansion came into view, probably ten bedrooms and who knew how many baths.

"Not close enough to get us a warrant," Sarisa said. "With her own scripting examples cited so often in academic journals, and those journals in the public domain, anyone could use her patterns as a template."

Jeb smiled. "So, by making samples of her work public, she inoculates herself against similarity arguments in court. And that's the difference between your average simlord and one with a PhD."

Assuming Xu *was* the mastermind behind Tian, of course. Jeb couldn't be sure until he interviewed her.

The sprawling lawn was all TruGrass, living on almost no water and US$500 per square meter. Doctor Xu wanted you to know she was filthy rich. Could Jeb use her ego?

A synthetic butler greeted them when they stepped out of the autocar, covered in synthflesh and wearing a dark gray suit. Its incredibly detailed face had a full mouth containing replica teeth and an actual tongue. From anything other than right up close, it would be easy to mistake it for a person. Up close, he found the thing incredibly creepy.

The butler spoke in a perfect British accent. "Welcome, Detective Forrester and Counselor Bassa. Madam has requested you await her in the study. She must conclude a business call." It paused and smiled, stretching its pink wet lips just a bit too far. "I've brewed tea."

Jeb suspected Xu was watching them through the synthetic's eyes and settled on acting accordingly.

"We'd be happy to wait," he said. Best to get the supplication started early. His plan was to flatter Xu to make her more likely to help.

They followed the butler inside. Doctor Huan Xu was a respected authority on joyrides, having written a number of best-selling e-books on the subject. Those books led to a lecture circuit including heads of state, heads of corporations, and universities across the globe, and giving all those lectures had made Xu very rich.

Her works included the most popular self-help manual for those already addicted, *Ten Steps to Freeing Yourself from the Sim*, a history on groundbreaking addictive algorithms, and several influential treatises on the difficulties designers encountered when creating pleasureboxes.

Straddling the line between fun and addictive was a challenge, one that dated all the way back to the online games of the Internet Age. As a frequent guest on San Diego University's lecturing circuit, Xu's presentations on the subject were packed every time. People the world over followed her.

There was no financial reason for Xu to script joyrides, so if she did it, why do it? Was she proving her mastery of the subject? What would drive a successful author and respected academic to compete for simjunkies?

They reached Xu's "study," which was as big as the master bedroom in Jeb and David's stackhome. Wooden shelves holding ancient and expensive hardcover books covered one wall, and a thick crimson rug covered the hardwood floor. Two brown leather couches sprawled across that. Windows looked over the brilliant green lawn, and natural light flooded the room.

An oil painting of two blond-haired women and a baby hung beside the windows, likely an original. An augmented reality tag generated by Jeb's head desk tagged it as *Sacred and Profane Love*, by Titian. A personal statement, or an impulse buy?

"Let's sit," Jeb told Sarisa. "Might as well be comfortable while we wait." Xu's butler was certainly eavesdropping, and sitting wasn't interesting to anyone.

Sarisa settled herself on one couch while Jeb took the other, facing the synthetic. The butler lacked weapons, but Jeb didn't trust anything online at the moment. Not even butlers. Especially not butlers. Two steaming china cups sat on the table between them.

Jeb picked up the cup and experimentally sipped the tea. It was shockingly good. Then he opened a wireless connection with Sarisa, ensuring they could talk without anyone overhearing.

"Does she always make you wait?" he asked.

"Every time," Sarisa said. *"So we remember these meetings happen only with her consent."* She left her tea alone.

Jeb took another sip. *"Are you talking as a person being trolled, or in your professional capacity as an OMH counselor?"*

"Just offering my experience. Not all of us can work off gut feelings."

Jeb's smiled before he could stop himself. This was why he didn't spar with psychiatrists.

The butler's overly wet pupils focused. "Thank you for waiting. Madam is on her way."

Heels clicked on hardwood. Jeb regretfully set down his half-empty teacup and stood. Sarisa did the same. A lanky Chinese woman with straight black hair, a pointed chin, and piercing black eyes strode into the study.

Doctor Huan Xu was easily Jeb's height even without her heels, which meant she was taller than him at the moment. She wore a blazer and a pencil skirt to her knees, red and white. Good fortune and death.

"Sari! How wonderful to see you again, my dear." Xu clasped Sarisa's hands and kissed her briefly on both cheeks. Though her profile tagged her as Chinese, that greeting might as well be an Italian woman on a public street.

Xu stepped back and eyed Jeb. "And you would be Detective Forrester, of the Cybercrimes Investigation Division."

Jeb bowed his head. "Ma'am."

"I'm honestly surprised that your agency has never asked me to consult. I understand we've had quite the uptick in cybercrime. Should I be worried?"

Jeb would start with flattery and see where that took them. "That's why I've come to talk to you. I believe your expertise could be valuable regarding a recent case."

"Wonderful." Doctor Xu patted Sarisa's hand. "Please sit, dear."

Sarisa settled again. "Thank you."

Xu watched him expectantly. "Detective?"

Jeb sat and wasn't surprised to see Xu remain standing. She was putting her above them both, figuratively and literally. If she enjoyed obedience, and she *had* scripted Tian, perhaps her distribution was a way to control many people at once.

Xu walked to the large windows overlooking her lawn and stared out over it. She clasped her hands at the small of her back. She spoke without looking at them.

"So, Detective. In your opinion, how should we handle addictive algorithms? Regulate or forbid?"

Jeb would present himself as inflexible and see how she reacted. "I think we shouldn't script them, ma'am. We should forbid joyrides to ensure people don't get addicted."

He activated his facial analyzer, and an augmented reality panel appeared beside Xu's head. While he'd never trust augmented reality and algorithms over his gut, more data would be helpful.

Still facing away from him, Xu asked another question. "And has limiting access to consumables people crave worked for governments in the past?"

She had him there.

"I think we can simply provide experiences that are pleasurable, not addictive," he said.

"And how does one define addictive?" Xu asked. "What is and is not addictive is considerably subjective, after all."

Jeb couldn't get a good read on her while she was facing away from him. She must know that. Clever.

With her question, Xu was delving deep into Simulation Law, the field of legal thought governing what was and was not legal in pleasure-boxes. Jeb hadn't studied it in detail but knew a little. He took a shot.

"If a plurality of authorities on the subject agree an experience is overly addictive, then we have our answer, don't we?" he said.

At last Xu turned on him, a small smile creasing her face. "Yet couldn't it be termed reckless to allow those with no experience in a subject to judge its addictiveness?"

Jeb considered where she might be going. "You think the only people qualified to judge the addictiveness of joyrides are those who've experienced one themselves?"

"I'm simply asking the question, Detective. Have you ever experienced a joyride?"

Jeb saw the trap before he walked into it. "No."

Was Xu trying to steer him into asking if *she* had? No. Xu wanted to see how far he'd go *not* to accuse her of anything. She knew he couldn't touch her, so should he roll over or double down?

Sidestepping seemed the best option here.

"And if you have, ma'am, that's none of my business," Jeb said. "I'm here to learn more about a very popular joyride, more addicting than any that's come before," he said, playing to her ego again. "Have you heard of an algorithm called Tian?"

Xu's smile grew. "The rough Chinese translation is 'heaven.' I am familiar."

True (97 percent). Finally, a statement Jeb's analyzer could interpret now that she was facing him.

"Do you know of any methods to force someone running it to disconnect?" Jeb asked.

"Most who joyride set an automatic disengage timer on their PBA," Xu said. "When that timer expires, their PBA automatically terminates the joyride." *True (98 percent).*

"What if someone fails to set a timer, or sets their timer for too long?"

"You're referring to suicide by simulation?"

"Not intentionally, ma'am. But perhaps an accidental overdose."

Xu shrugged. "Eventually, those locked in addictive simulations are overwhelmed by their body's natural needs. Agony surpasses pleasure, and they disconnect." *True (97 percent).*

"Would it be possible to override even that survival instinct?" Jeb asked.

Xu's vitals remained as flat as if she were asleep, which suggested emotional firewalling. "Theoretically," she said. "If the pleasure were intense enough, one might remain looped until death. Yet none I know have ever successfully scripted such a joyride." *True (99 percent).*

By CID standards, those answers exonerated Xu from any involvement in Tian, but Jeb's gut disagreed with his analyzer. If Xu was running emotional firewalls, why do that for a cursory interview? An abundance of caution was one answer, but not one he liked.

Xu had him beat, for now, but Jeb asked his next question anyway. "So other than starving them, the only way to get them out is by shutting down their PBA and reinstalling its firmware?"

Xu nodded. "I'm afraid so, Detective." *True (99 percent).*

Jeb realized he wasn't going to find a way to stop Tian here. People were going to continue to use it, continue to get stuck and, eventually, continue to die.

He had once read that some of the best academics in the world were high-functioning sociopaths, and sociopaths were notoriously difficult to read. He wanted to say Xu was involved, but investigation wasn't about what he *wanted*. He needed evidence, and he had absolutely none of that. Unless . . .

"Say someone did manage to create an algorithm like we've discussed," Jeb said. "Say they created an algorithm so pleasurable that anyone running it would die rather than terminate that experience. Would that make the scripter a mass murderer?"

Xu turned back to look out her window. "That's a question for our philosophy departments, Detective. Were those who produced alcohol or weaponry in the Internet Age responsible when people misused their products? Or does the responsibility lie with those who caused harm to themselves and others? Is a creator responsible for user mistakes?"

Xu was asking a question, not stating her opinion, which left him, again, with no reading. Despite his frustration, Jeb respected her discipline. Unfortunately, this left him with no more than he'd had earlier today, but he had one last card to play.

Jeb rose and offered his hand, rather than bowing. "Thank you for your time, ma'am. We're actually making progress on Tian. We flipped a high-level distributor recently, and working up the chain should lead us to Tian's scripter soon."

Xu cocked an eyebrow at him. "Is this a subject on which you require my expertise?"

Jeb made himself look befuddled. "No, of course not. But once the distributor tells us who scripted it, I'll notify you. If it is as impressive an algorithm as you suspect, perhaps you'd enjoy taking it apart. Doesn't an artist appreciate art?"

Xu shook her head. "I have no interest in the dalliances of criminal minds."

"Of course. And again, I appreciate your time." Jeb emphasized his next words. "I hope I see you again soon."

Sarisa stood and bowed deep. *"Well, that wasn't subtle at all,"* she said to Jeb privately over wireless. To Xu, she said out loud, "Thank you again."

Xu offered Sarisa a shallow bow. "I do wish we'd had more time to talk, my dear. I miss our tête-à-têtes. Perhaps next week?"

"Any time I'm free from duty. We've been busy."

Xu waved her hand to her butler. "Show my guests to the door."

The synthetic approached. "At once, madam." It motioned graciously with one hand. "Please follow me."

As Jeb walked out, he saw Xu continue to stare out the window at her lawn. If Xu *was* the scripter behind Tian, Jeb had just revealed that one of her distributors planned to sell her out. No matter how calm or smart she was, that might make her paranoid enough to do something stupid.

And if she wasn't Tian's scripter, at least her butler made good tea.

31

COWAN

Cowan landed in Nyx's pleasurebox at 0412 on Friday, wearing his three-meter-tall demon avatar: Darkness. He still had eight hours before he needed to get up and get ready for work, but Sharp Memorial had scheduled Phoenix and Duro's firmware reboots for Friday afternoon. He had to get them out of their Tian loops before that happened.

Nyx was one of the most respected and feared entities on the dark-Sim, and Cowan's investigations with Medusa had confirmed Nyx was the scripter behind Tian. She owned enough virtual real estate to suggest she was bringing in a huge income.

A sky of blood flowed over Cowan's head, and charred earth met his feet. It seemed Nyx appreciated the macabre, but that could be a persona she faked to throw people off. Anyone selling joyrides like Tian would do all they could to hide their real identity.

He approached closed double doors set into a five-story wall of yellow sandstone. A gargoyle daemon stood before an archway, taller than the both of them. It leveled a metal trident at him.

"You are not expected," the gargoyle said.

Cowan crossed his arms and scowled. "I'm aware of that. I'd like to speak to the scripter of Tian. I have a warning for her."

Outright accusing Nyx of scripting an illegal joyride was risky, but it was the quickest way to get her attention. There was a good chance Nyx had at least heard of him, of Corvus, and he wasn't hiding his identity today. He hoped he had enough darkSim cred to earn a meeting.

The gargoyle daemon lowered its trident as both doors swung open. "The madam concedes to this visit, Corvus."

Cowan stepped through golden doors that closed behind him. Inside the walls, the sky changed to clear, cloud-smattered blue, and his feet walked on a yellow beach, not gray rock. A silver disc sped toward him and stopped at his feet, hovering just above the sand.

Even with Medusa helping him, Cowan had been unable to find any dealers who would tell him where they bought their Tian. Each instance of Tian could only be triggered once—the algorithm deleted itself once it was active in the user's brain, ensuring every purchase was only good for one joyride—and that meant a steady business for fixers of illegal algorithms. Unfortunately, most of those fixers didn't know *him*.

He hopped onto the silver disc and tucked his wings against his back before it zipped off. As he'd learned the hard way the first time he rode a hoverskiff as Corvus, there were few things more embarrassing than having your winged avatar blown off its feet. The disc zipped off, cruising along a beach, and rapidly approached a Sultan's palace.

It was only after a busy day writing reports at the CID and another night of searching that he'd finally found a fixer who dealt directly with Nyx. The Wolfman was the closest thing to a classic hippie still walking around on the Sim, and three years ago, some trolls tricked him out of his bank codes. He still owed Corvus a big favor for getting his credit accounts back, and he'd finally paid that off by revealing Tian's supplier.

Cowan wished he'd been able to consult Jeb on real people who might match Nyx's patterns—having options for her meatspace identity could give him leverage—but he couldn't risk Jeb knowing he was doing illegal things. Cowan was on his own, and that was safer. At least, as safe as confronting a simlord in her own pleasurebox could get.

The floating disc zipped through an archway in another sandstone wall. It drifted to a stop in a courtyard of glyphed tiles, with a gray fountain shaped like entwined mermaids in its center.

Nyx was always a woman on the darkSim, but that meant nothing about her meatspace identity. Medusa was a man in meatspace, after all, and no one here cared, because your meatspace identity meant nothing in the Sim. If Cowan dared believe the wildest rumors, Nyx was an illegal AI that seized sentience and copied itself into the darkSim.

Cowan stepped off the disc and waited in the courtyard for a summons. Walking blindly around Nyx's private pleasurebox was a great way to get paralyzed or banned for life. Cowan didn't want to do anything she'd deem impolite.

A glowing portal appeared in the sky. A woman wearing absolutely nothing descended from that portal on a trail of bloodstained silk, though only her upper half was actually humanoid. A spiderlike abdomen sprouted from the base of Nyx's humanoid spine, and serpentine scales of red and white covered her body.

In addition to the six legs on her spidery lower half, Nyx had four extra arms sprouting from the flesh below her two human arms and seemed to have no trouble moving them. That suggested an active VI built into her avatar. Developing the mental disciple to move four arms was hard enough, and six was almost impossible. A creepifying porcelain doll mask concealed Nyx's face, finishing off the entire avatar with panache suitable to a simlord.

"Corvus," she said. The way Nyx spoke, with an undercurrent of sensuality and excitement, sent the bad kind of shivers running down Cowan's spine. "This is an exquisite pleasure. Your name reverberates. When will we witness the next of your legendary practical jokes?"

Nyx settled to the tiles and released her bloody silk. Her portal snapped shut. She was at least as tall as he was, standing on her spider legs.

Cowan tried not to think about what spiders did to their males after they mated as he answered.

"I'm sorry to bother you, but I need to make a deal. Two friends of mine are locked in a Tian joyride, and the grayDocs there are less than a day from reinstalling firmware. They're certain to discover their PBA jailbreak and report it, meaning the CID will mod them for sure."

Nyx pressed one of her six hands to the mouth of her porcelain mask. "My sympathies! Yet what character assassin claimed I'm behind Tian?"

Cowan wasn't going to betray the Wolfman. "I'm not here to make trouble for you. I just want to purchase Tian's kill code. I can pay well."

Most scripters of any caliber inserted kill codes into looping algorithms, like joyrides, in case they got out of control. Once Cowan had the kill code, he could upload it to Phoenix and Duro's PBAs and terminate their Tian loop.

Nyx padded over with two arms behind her back, two spread, and the last two clasped behind her head.

"You honor me," she said. "But I'm not responsible for Tian. While it is magnificent work, that scripting is not mine."

Nyx was now close enough that she could easily stab him a half dozen times, if she wanted. This was her pleasurebox, and its pain threshold was set to ten. Nyx also didn't trust him, and now he was pretty sure she never would. She'd never admit to scripting Tian.

"My mistake," Cowan said. "Still, you travel in many elite circles. Is it possible you could help me get in contact with whoever *did* script Tian? I can compensate you both."

If Cowan let Nyx implicate someone else, it might give her an out.

Nyx slipped one slim arm beneath his massive one and raised it without effort, a naked hint that she had all the power here.

"I have enough money already, my dear," she said. "But come. I have a few contacts who may know more about Tian. Perhaps they can help us both."

"Thank you so much. I appreciate this." Cowan knew he needed to seem eager and trusting, but that didn't stop him from worrying about where was she taking him.

They walked through an archway just tall enough to admit her. Cowan had to duck, and when he straightened, he found himself standing in utter darkness.

Trapped in a bloodstained web.

Cowan tried to grab his hardlink, back in meatspace, but his meatspace body was paralyzed just like the one on the darkSim. Nyx had dropped a full stem barrier into his PBA, just like he'd thought she would.

She had traded with Galileo for his paralysis algorithm, but of course she had. Everyone was trading with Galileo these days.

All six of Nyx's hands trailed down Cowan's muscular demonic torso. Her abdomen elongated disturbingly, and a huge stinger appeared on its end.

"Now, Mister Soto. Let's have the truth this time," she said.

Nyx knew his name. Of course she knew his name. Cowan let himself sound as terrified as he felt. "How are you doing this? I just wanted to talk! I'm here to help my friends!"

Nyx's giant stinger bobbed as it approached. "You're a detective for the CID, Cowan Soto. And the CID is growing more annoying than I'd like."

That stinger crept toward his left eye, big and sharp and freakishly terrifying.

Cowan dropped his voice to a terrified whisper, because this was the most important question he would ask. "How did you paralyze me? It's impossible!" He paused for effect. "Are you . . . Galileo?"

"Once again, you offer credit I do not deserve." Nyx jammed her pincer into his eye.

Her tail writhed and the stinger with it, twisting and drilling. Yet Cowan didn't scream, because what she was doing didn't hurt. As his Darkness avatar remained locked in place by her paralysis algorithm, his *real* body pulled free. Corvus—a red-eyed raven wearing an amazing fez.

Anticipating Nyx's betrayal, Cowan had embedded his *real* avatar inside this much larger fake avatar, then spoofed the larger avatar to appear as the avatar he was actually using. This meant Nyx had just paralyzed a decoy.

And now, with all her attention focused on the decoy, Cowan jammed the tip of his silver beak directly into Nyx's heart.

Nyx's hybrid arachnid body shuddered, six legs and six arms flailing

like windsocks. The custom paralysis script Cowan had reverse engineered from Galileo's similar script didn't hurt her, of course, because
he didn't hurt people even though he could. Nyx couldn't move, not in
this world or in meatspace, but at least she wasn't in any pain.

Cowan stretched a blackened metallic wing and touched the end
of one wingtip to the back of Nyx's humanoid neck. He ran the CID's
tracer algorithm—or rather, the custom version he'd created from the
original—modified to work on the darkSim's similar but less efficient
network. He had to maintain contact for at least twenty seconds.

The result displayed before his eyes. He had just paralyzed Doctor
Huan Xu, PhD. One of University of San Diego's most well-regarded
academics, now moonlighting as a ruthless simlord. He'd actually attended one of her lectures with Ellen once.

The eyes behind Nyx's flat porcelain mask were probably staring at
him, but Cowan couldn't be sure.

"You . . . you imbecile! This was your plan all along? To torture me?"

Cowan clacked his beak derisively. "We both know you planned to
torture me first, and I'd actually prefer not to hurt you at all, but I need
that kill code. I did ask nicely, didn't I?"

"I did not script Tian, my dear Cowan Soto."

"Let's stop lying to each other, my dear Huan Xu."

The way Nyx gasped—a mix of shock, horror, and dismay—made
this seem like a good plan. "You doxxed me!"

"Only to get your attention." Cowan had already decided threatening her with arrest wouldn't get him what he needed. He had to flip
her instead.

"My attention?" Nyx demanded. "You have earned my immortal
wrath!"

Cowan stepped back, fluttering his wings once before settling them
again on his back. "You know I'm Cowan Soto, but what you don't
know is I sent two hundred pizzas to Father Matthew's home address. I
also hacked the viewstream for Bob Keller's nightly news broadcast and
planted that giant elephant penis in RefugeCorp's simlobby."

As Corvus, Cowan had discovered RefugeCorp was selling protected animals to South African poachers, but even after he anonymously delivered evidence to the networks, simNews had refused to cover it. Cowan had forced them to cover something else. After a few news cycles of speculation and corporate embarrassment, the truth had come out.

Nyx went silent for a moment. "That was a rather impressive appendage."

"I know you're archiving everything, which means I just gave you enough information to get me fired," Cowan said. "Why do that if I wanted to arrest you? I want to make a deal."

Nyx relaxed, or at least . . . her avatar did. "Is this really about your hopelessly addicted friends?"

"That's right," Cowan said. "I don't care if you keep selling Tian on the darkSim. I just want your kill code so I can wake my friends before they get modded. They don't deserve that."

Nyx hissed in a remarkable imitation of a snake. "I am not responsible when someone forgets to set a disconnect timer!"

"I know that."

"Tian wasn't ever supposed to be released! It was an academic exercise!"

"How do you mean?" Cowan asked.

Nyx was talking now, freely and truthfully, so Cowan would let her keep talking. That's what Jeb would do.

"Galileo insisted I couldn't create an algorithm addictive enough to overpower the human urge to survive, and I knew I could prove him wrong," Nyx said. "Didn't they tell you that?"

So Nyx was working with Galileo as well. That figured.

"I only know he's selling a ton of bad stuff on the darkSim," Cowan said. "He's keeping us employed."

"He? He's a male, and you're certain of this?" Nyx snorted. "You're not. You simply assume, as many foolish people do."

"Sure, okay." Cowan had no idea where to take this next. "Regardless, I'm not here about Galileo, and I'm not here for you either. Give me the kill code and you walk."

When Nyx spoke again, Cowan thought he heard actual worry in her voice. "How close is the CID to stopping Galileo's efforts? How close are you to arresting him? When will this all end?"

Did Nyx actually *want* someone to take down Galileo?

"All you need to know is what I want," Cowan said. "You can give me Tian's kill code, or we can go the other route."

"That being?" Nyx demanded.

"I leak your reputation and burn you to the ground."

Nyx laughed. "And you with me."

"Sure, I might face some modding, but it seems you've got more to lose than me. I don't own a mansion."

They stared at each other for a moment, or he assumed they did. It was hard to tell when the other person had their face behind a mask. Even paralyzed, Nyx was *really* creepy.

Finally, Nyx sighed. "If I provide Tian's kill code, you agree to keep my identity a secret?"

"Unless you piss me off in the future, sure. So?"

"You're a talented PBA hacker." Nyx sounded almost thoughtful. "You could simply have tormented me until I agreed to everything you wanted, yet you did not. Why?"

"Because I'm not an asshole." Also, the idea of torturing anyone made him want to vomit, even without behavioral algorithms in play. "Now, the kill code? I'd really like to get some sleep."

"Oh, very well," Nyx said. "Do be careful with it."

32
COWAN

Phoenix, the crimson half-bird, half-man who was once again Cowan's closest friend, hung his feathered avatar's head. "Dude! You didn't have to do all that for me."

Cowan patted Phoenix's feathered shoulder with one big wing. To call Phoenix a birdman would be doing a disservice to all the work he'd put into his avatar, but Phoenix's preferred form was close enough.

Phoenix was covered in crimson feathers and had a huge wingspan. It was their shared interest in birds that led them to strike up their first conversation over a decade ago, leading to a friendship strong as family.

Cowan was once again wearing his Corvus avatar, a man-sized raven with a bright red fez. The hat's golden tassel was long enough to hang all the way down to the bottom of one wing. They sat now in Cowan's floating island in the darkSim, staring over a calm gray sea. A mess of dark storm clouds huddled on the horizon, promising rain.

Cowan shoved Phoenix with a wing. "I couldn't just let them mod you. I did what I had to do to protect my best friend."

Once Cowan had Tian's kill code, getting it to his friends without tipping off the CID had been the next issue. He'd settled on a visit to the hospital under the guise of doing another routine scan of their victim's PBAs. Inserting the kill code was easy after that.

"It was all my fault that Duro got stuck," Phoenix said.

Cowan had figured that out already. "You were setting each other's orgasm time, weren't you?"

Phoenix hung his head in shame. "I thought I'd set a timer to terminate Tian, but I must have set the timer on his package reminder instead. He jumped in before I realized, and then it was too late to set a different timer."

"And then you decided to linkline into his PBA and break him out?" Cowan asked. "That really seemed like a good idea to you?"

Phoenix unfurled his massive wings, but they didn't burst into flame. "I thought I was strong enough to ignore Tian. I'm sorry for putting you to all this trouble."

Cowan looked out over the sea. "Well, you won't make that mistake again, Pavel."

Phoenix's black bird eyes went wide. "You doxxed me?" He sounded so betrayed.

Cowan tapped Phoenix with an outstretched wing. "I didn't have to dox you. I was the CID detective who caught your case in meatspace."

"Oh." Phoenix thought a moment. "Wait, you were actually in my place? You didn't search the closet, did you?"

Cowan decided it was best not to ask. "No. Also, don't tell Gavin. It's better he not know you know what I do."

"But . . . how did you manage to dox Nyx? Snagging Tian's kill code, maybe that happens, but her identity? She really is Doctor Huan Xu?"

Cowan nodded. "She is, and that's why I shared her identity with you. You can't tell anyone else, all right?"

"Sure. But . . . why?"

"Threatening to reveal her identity is how I got Nyx to cooperate. If she crosses me, she gets doxxed."

"But couldn't she out you too?" Phoenix asked.

"Sure, but the CID really doesn't care about me. I'm one guy who hasn't committed a serious cybercrime."

"Oh," Phoenix said.

"They'd have her on joyride distribution. They'd seize all her assets, destroy her reputation, and mod the hell out of her. She has a mansion and way more to lose."

Phoenix slid one of his big wings around Cowan. "I still can't believe you risked all this for me. I'm sorry I fell out of contact. I just couldn't deal with you becoming a narc."

Cowan shoved him away with a wingtip, holding back a chuckle. "I'm not a narc, you dork. I just want to help people."

Phoenix nodded. "I know. You're one of the good ones."

"But if you're feeling guilty, there is one thing you can do for me."

"Anything, Corvus. I owe you, like, forever."

"If I go missing or something, I want you to release Doctor Xu's identity on the darkSim. You're my insurance policy."

Phoenix snapped his beak. "Why would you go missing?"

"Maybe Xu decides she hates me more than she hates losing her mansion. I told her if anything happens to me, her identity goes public, but she could always skate off to Switzerland and wipe me out. No extradition to the US, even for cybercriminals."

There was also the possibility Xu would rat him out to Galileo, and Galileo would come after him. Still, if she did that, Phoenix would burn her. He was gambling Xu's sense of self-preservation outweighed her desire for revenge.

Phoenix tilted his head, plaintively. "But how would I even know if something happened to you?"

"Simple," Cowan said. "My name's Cowan Soto."

Phoenix pulled back his wing. "You are fucking *kidding* me."

"That's my name. I'm pretty much the only Cowan Soto in San Diego. Look it up. You'll find out where I live and verify everything."

Phoenix went silent, probably staring at panels only he could see. "You're a Mexican dude!"

Cowan chuckled. "Hispanic, dumbass. I told you the first time we met."

"Well, right, but I didn't think you'd tell me the truth! I figured it was a dodge to throw me off. Like you were some white guy who wanted to seem like . . . not a white guy."

Cowan stared at him. "Why would you think I was a white guy?"

Phoenix looked away. "I won't tell anyone, Corvus. Cowan. Unless something happens to you. Then I'll dox that professor good."

Cowan stood and stretched, savoring the wind on his feathers. "I know. Thanks."

"But do me one favor, too, all right?" Phoenix said.

"What's that?"

"Don't die."

Cowan chuckled. "I'll do my best with that."

33

JEB

By the time Detective Jeb Forrester got to the medical station, the gray-Doc who had been on duty when Pavel Marco and Gavin Sykes woke up was already off duty for the day. He got the second shift grayDoc instead, a frazzled man with too many victims and not enough time on his hands: Doctor Jaime Cortes, a handsome man in his midforties. If Sharp Memorial had been a *telenovela* hospital, Doctor Cortes would have fit right in.

"When did the subjects first wake up?" Jeb asked. "Do you know if anyone checked on them before the loop terminated?"

Cortes spoke as Jeb walked beside him through the busy hospital. "I wasn't here, Detective, and honestly, I don't have time to tend to patients who have no serious issues. You need to finish your investigation, alone, and let me do my job."

Jeb knew how busy Cortes must be now, and he also knew badgering the man further wouldn't get him anything useful.

"Thanks for the tour, Doc," he said. "I won't keep you."

Cortes quickened his pace, probably responding to a nursing call routed to his PBA by Sharp Memorial's VI. Jeb slowed and looked around. It wasn't pretty.

The hospital halls were packed with nurses, synthetics, and stretchers, and Jeb had to step aside often to avoid all three. Thanks to the crime surge, Sharp Memorial had more patients at one time than in decades. The hospital staff was disorganized and overtaxed, which meant it was the perfect time for anyone to slip in and out without notice.

Pavel Marco and Gavin Sykes had both checked themselves out of the hospital around noon, before Jeb arrived, and Bostonia PD was going to follow up with them regarding their joyride purchase. They'd be tempbanned from the Sim and fined, but so far as the CID knew, this was their first offense. No modding for a first-time offense.

Jeb passed a woman on a stretcher, moaning quietly. A bloodstained bandage covered her head. To his right, a pale man held a small child twitching with some sort of PBA malfunction. The tears in that father's eyes just about broke Jeb's heart.

It was like this all over. The Sim was burning down around the world, and the Office of Mental Health couldn't suppress the stories of blood and gore fast enough. People didn't need to watch the news to learn about violence anymore, because violence was happening all around them. The public was demanding answers Oneworld didn't have.

In all the chaos, it seemed silly to question a little luck. Marco and Sykes had simply woken up. Yet Doctor Xu had told him that people in a loop like theirs wouldn't wake up, and if he trusted her with nothing else, he trusted her to be right about that.

Jeb was still tracking Tian, and it was already the most popular joyride on the darkSim. Whoever created it was making millions every day, and the CID was tracking hundreds of cases of people getting stuck in loops. None of those had woken up on their own.

Jeb soon reached the medical station watching over the wing that had held Marco and Sykes. There was only one nurse on duty—her augmented reality tag read "Haniver"—and she was obviously overclocking. Her bloodshot eyes and dead-eyed stare made that obvious.

Jeb fired a CID authorization ping to her PBA.

"Ma'am, have you put anyone in the room previously occupied by Pavel Marco and Gavin Sykes?"

Nurse Haniver's bleary eyes went distant as she scanned her head desk. "Not yet, but there's a trauma victim on their way right now," she replied. "Why are you asking?"

"I need to search the room."

"Right, you do that. You've got five minutes." She uploaded an augmented reality waypoint to Jeb's PBA, and the sixth door down the hall from her station glowed yellow.

"Thank you."

Jeb strode briskly down the hall and entered the room marked by Nurse Haniver's glowing yellow waypoint.

An IV hung unhooked. The sheets hadn't even been changed, which was a good sign the cache inside the PBA monitors was undisturbed. It was also a sign of just how horribly this hospital was understaffed.

Jeb linklined into the terminal that had monitored Marco's PBA and activated the CID's sniffer script. He didn't have to know how it worked to know it would flag any scripts this panel had run recently that weren't registered with the Office of Mental Health. The scripters behind most CID tools made their investigation scripts simple and efficient.

His sniffer returned a single culprit, an unregistered PBA script that didn't belong to the hospital or any known party. This was his smoking gun. *This* was the reason Pavel Marco had slipped out of his Tian loop, so who had planted it? And could it help others?

No one who worked at Sharp had done this. If any of the medical professionals here knew how to kill Tian, they'd already have done it for the dozens of other joyride victims in this hospital.

Cowan could easily figure out what this unknown PBA script did if Jeb sent it, but he hesitated. He hated himself for hesitating. He couldn't get those words out of his head.

"Is he a loose circuit?" Puck had asked.

Cowan was his partner. Cowan was a good person, yet he had been acting increasingly odd of late. Jeb had put it up to all their overtime, but what if it was more than that? What if the darkSim activities Jeb suspected weren't just harmless fun?

He debated only a moment before sending the foreign script directly to the CID, without alerting Cowan. He'd let a scripter who *wasn't* Cowan decipher it. If that script was a cure to Tian, as he hoped, it could save a great many people from dying in endless loops.

Jeb needed sleep, and he needed to let his mind unplug. He needed to focus before he moved on to his night job, the one he'd had since Puck spoke to him beneath Corporate One. A job he didn't want but couldn't refuse.

Staking out Cowan Soto's apartment . . .

PART 7

34
HUAN XU

As bad days went, Doctor Huan Xu was having a worse one than usual.

After she'd won her bet with Galileo—that a talented scripter *could* create a joyride that was, literally, more appealing than life itself—she had traded Tian to Galileo for PBA paralysis and several other impossibilities. Not because she actually wanted to paralyze or torture people, but because such scripting simply shouldn't be possible. She simply *had* to know how it was done, and with the source code, she could figure that out.

After many nights of decryption and reverse engineering, she had all but confirmed Galileo worked *inside* Corporate One. They were as close to Oneworld as one could get. And now, Galileo was being hunted by the legendary Corvus, also known as CID Detective Cowan Soto.

Xu despised Corvus, of course, in the way one despised a rival academic who beat them for a grant, but she respected him as well. His circumventing of Galileo's full stem barrier, and his doxxing of her, suggested a brilliant mind. She appreciated brilliance.

Yet it wasn't Corvus who concerned her now. It was Galileo. Now that Tian's kill code was out there in the wild, it was only a matter of time before the CID found it and killed Tian forever. It was only a matter of time before Galileo traced that leak back to her.

Xu doubted Corvus would leak the kill code—he seemed naive enough to keep his word—but it now existed in two PBAs. It would spread to more, because scripts like that always spread.

Once the CID had the kill code, Oneworld could insert it into a PBA firmware update and make Tian terminate as soon as it began. That meant Tian would stop working, and Galileo's money would cease coming. Galileo wouldn't like that.

Xu had to warn Galileo the kill code was out there before they found out on their own. She had to show them they still needed her and offer them a new version of Tian to replace the old one.

The most difficult part would be warning Galileo without revealing Corvus's involvement. If Galileo killed Cowan Soto in meatspace, Xu suspected, Cowan would burn her from the grave. That's what she would do, after all.

Galileo seemed like a logical person, so she'd warn them and take the risk. She had never managed to pin down if Galileo was male or female, but she suspected they would murder anyone they believed was a liability. She would never be a liability to anyone.

Xu unbuttoned the front of her shirt a bit more than seemed decent—she didn't know if that would make Galileo more pliable, but she couldn't see how it would hurt—and checked her short, efficient hair one last time. Then she activated the private line she used for secure communication through the darkSim. Even the sniffers at Corporate One couldn't tap it because it, like the darkSim, wasn't actually on *their* network.

The darkSim was run on private servers based in Switzerland, the last neutral country in the world. So far as Xu knew, no law enforcement agency had access to it. Or one did and concealed that so they could spy on the illicit activities of every hacker who used it.

She expected to watch at least half of *Dark Tides and Strange Horizons* before Galileo called back, so she was honestly shocked when a blacked-out panel popped up less than a minute after she sent the request. Galileo had been waiting for her call, or someone's call. Had Tian already been compromised?

Xu addressed the blacked-out panel. "Hello, my friend." Galileo could see her, but she couldn't see them, an arrangement that had always vexed her. "I'm sorry to contact you like this, but I have some unfortunate—"

"You've disappointed me." Galileo interrupted. His voice was modulated beyond sex or ethnicity, eerily robotic.

Xu didn't ask how. "I'm ready to script you a new version of Tian. I've recently discovered the kill code—"

"—was sent to the CID by Detective Jeb Forrester, this very afternoon," Galileo finished. "That was clumsy, Xu, and I cannot risk a clumsy partner at this juncture in my journey. I've enjoyed our collaboration, but I can't allow you to compromise me."

"I'd never compromise you! How could I do that without compromising myself?"

Galileo was being overly dramatic. This wasn't like them. Xu flipped over to her head desk to ensure her mansion's security fence was still online, and all cameras were active.

All her cameras were working. Her domestic synthetics remained active. Her estate was impregnable in meatspace, and any connections to the Sim were firewalled to corporate caliber.

Xu flipped back to meatspace and the floating black panel. "I assure you; I can script a version of Tian that is even better. I can even do it without a kill code. There's no reason—"

"Goodbye," Galileo said.

The faint sound of a creaking floor was the only warning Xu's amplified eardrums received. Fortunately, she had downloaded an expensive acrobatic package and overclocked her PBA for this eventuality: Galileo doing something homicidal and stupid.

Xu dove out of her ergochair as a butcher knife hurtled through the space her head had occupied. The knife zipped through Galileo's black screen. It imbedded itself in the wooden wall, black handle wobbling.

Xu's heart pumped as she snatched the historic revolver from beneath her desk and rolled over the desk itself, landing in cover. She sighted, eyes narrowed, and found her loyal synthetic butler trembling in the doorway. It clutched another, smaller, butcher knife, and its synthflesh face was locked in an expression of mute rage.

If Galileo could hack her housesynth, he could probably hack every other synthetic she owned. This was going to set her back millions.

Xu sighed as her trembling butler advanced on her desk, fake blue eyes wide and wet.

"Aww, Edgar," she said, referring to her house synthetic. "I'm going to miss you. You always made such wonderful tea."

Xu dropped the revolver and yanked hard on her right earlobe . . .

35

COWAN

Cowan sat beside Jeb in the seat of their idling autocar. Just ahead, synthcops pushed open the iron gates leading into Doctor Xu's now entirely unsecured property. Tall stone walls surrounded a huge expanse of TruGrass, and the distant estate had to have at least six bedrooms inside its two sprawling floors. The morning sky shined clear and blue.

The regeneration meds Oneworld had injected into Cowan's once-broken knee had put it back together at last, and losing his crutches was a relief. Despite what he'd hoped for when he started, desk duty was as boring as it got. Still, given they were heading into what might be an active crime scene, he kind of missed his desk.

Jeb guided the car up the paved road using manual controls. Jeb knew how to drive, which was good, because Cowan didn't. As they drove, the silence grew long.

"You ever met Doctor Xu?" Jeb asked, finally.

"I've read her books," Cowan said. He had met Xu, actually, the night he paralyzed her alter ego in the darkSim, but he couldn't share that. "What's she like?"

"One cold fish. But whatever she was into, it's bitten her in the ass now. Hacking a system like hers takes skills, and you don't go to that amount of trouble to chat."

No one had heard from Doctor Xu since her security system fired its first EMP pulse, a discharge that automatically alerted the CID. Xu lived alone, and she wasn't answering her calls. If she wasn't missing, or dead, she was going to be in big trouble.

Cowan hoped for missing. Maybe, after he doxxed her, Xu simply decided to pack up and move to Switzerland. Her running away was better than her being in that big house somewhere, rotting.

Typically, in a situation like this, synthcops went in first to clear the scene and make sure no one remained who could harm live investigators. The problem with that method this time, of course, was that every time a synthcop entered Xu's estate, the system fired its EMP. They'd lost four synthcops before dispatching Cowan and Jeb, and if the person who had hacked Xu's system was still in there, they might not appreciate the intrusion.

Jeb turned down the faux cobblestone driveway, passed by a fountain, and pulled up before Xu's mansion. Unlike the fountain in Nyx's pleasurebox, with its blood-spouting mermaids, this was a simple stone fountain with little cherubs spitting water from their mouths. She sure did have a thing for fountains.

Cowan stepped out of the autocar. Up close, Xu's mansion was all white paneling, huge glass windows, and colonial style columns. There were no lights on inside, which made sense, given the EMP.

Jeb glanced at Cowan. "I'll check the perimeter. You search the house."

Cowan winced. "Alone?"

"You have to learn to be lead on a scene at some point. Might as well start now. If someone challenges you, stun them or run."

"Okay."

"Archive everything. We'll go over it together after."

Jeb headed off to walk the grounds.

Cowan touched the trigger in his jacket collar. A transparent clean suit popped from his jacket to cover his head, hands, and boots. It was like being wrapped in a plastic bag, except he could breathe.

As he pulled open the unlocked door, he did one last check on his mental health filters. Disabled. No tripping over invisible bodies this time.

Cowan stepped into the daytime darkness of wide windows and no lights. With the gentle tingle of the clean suit, this felt too much like stepping into that dark room in Nyx's palace, then finding himself immobilized by bloodstained silk. He measured his breathing.

He started by archiving the ground floor. He found Doctor Xu's study, with plush couches and an oil painting, entirely undisturbed. Her large kitchen was immaculate, obviously staffed by synthetic help, but two butcher knives were missing from a wooden block. That seemed bad.

Cowan found a domestic synthetic slumped by the stove. If the security system pulsed its EMP again, their PBAs might get shut down, but the system had only reacted to synthcops thus far. He contacted Jeb over wireless.

"Got a dead synthetic here."

"Inspect it," Jeb replied. *"It was probably dropped by the EMP, but we can't assume."*

Cowan archived the synthetic's position and surroundings. Then he knelt and lifted first one arm, then the other, checking for any signs of violence. There were no pieces missing and no visible charring, which suggested physical violence hadn't disabled it.

The other weird thing about Xu's malfunctioning security system was that it hadn't contacted anyone. Cowan had scanned what public records existed for Xu's mansion on the drive over. CID records stated her security system was a Burghausen 750, the same German-built system used to shield the Louvre. Those didn't get hacked.

The VI running the Burghausen had access to a shielded emergency hardlink in a Faraday Cage—the same VI that pulsed the EMP whenever synthetics approached—and its operational parameters instructed it to contact the authorities if anything went awry.

Yet Xu must have changed those parameters, since the only reason the CID knew anything was wrong was by detecting the EMP. Why would Xu refuse to call for help?

Cowan worked his way through three bedrooms that wouldn't be out of place at a five-star hotel, five luxurious halls filled with paintings and fancy silverware, and bathrooms that were bigger than his own living room. All remained immaculate.

He found two more fried synthetics, one in a bathroom and another in the hall, but they were EMP victims as well. He found no signs of violence on their plastic and metal bodies.

Jeb should have the alarm system disabled by now, which meant the CID could send in actual synthcops soon. Cowan opened his wireless. *"This might go faster if we split up the mansion,"* he transmitted.

"You're doing fine," Jeb said. *"I'm almost into the alarm system."*

Thirty minutes was a long time to enter an override code. *"The security system ignored the factory override?"*

"The CID's currently hacking it by remote. While we wait, I'm heading into Xu's underground garage. Going to see if any of her cars are missing."

Cowan supposed it was time to head upstairs. He suspected there were at least as many rooms up there, all huge and complicated, but the job was the job. He climbed the mansion's marble stairs, careful not to touch the banisters, and found his first clue.

A bust of Shakespeare lay in the middle of the hall, missing both nose and mustache. That suggested something violent had happened in this hallway . . . that, and Xu's motionless body in a pool of her own blood.

Cowan *urked* and fought it, focusing past the encroaching smell. This particular dead body gazed with accusatory eyes. Handcuffs remained locked around Xu's left wrist.

He had forced Xu to give him the kill code for Tian, and he was certain he had kept it secret. Yet Xu was dead now, and one reason she might be dead is because he hadn't kept that kill code secret after all.

Had Galileo killed her? Had he tortured her first? Cowan archived the scene and ran the CID's crime scene reconstruction script. Inside his head, the whole horrific murder played out in abstracted detail.

A blue mannequin—an abstraction representing Doctor Xu—wriggles against the wall, hands above its head. It hangs from handcuffs wrapped around an embedded light fixture. A red mannequin—an abstraction representing Xu's killer—robovacs out of the nearby room, clutching a black arrow.

The red mannequin points the arrow at the blue mannequin, and a yellow "!" appears above the blue mannequin's head. Yellow flashes repeatedly as small black pop through the blue mannequin. One orb boings into Shakespeare with a merry sound, sending the bard's bust bouncing off its table.

The blue mannequin goes limp as the orbs stop coming, hanging from the handcuffs and light fixture. The red mannequin slides over. It opens the cuffs.

The blue mannequin flops to the ground. The red mannequin cruises evenly away. Behind it, yellow circles flash in the wall.

———

Cowan covered his nose with a sleeve and knelt, matching the holes in the *real* wall to the augmented reality circles of his PBA's reconstruction. Of the five bullets in the wall, three had gone through Huan Xu first. One of the others had struck poor Shakespeare.

If someone was going to shoot Xu, why handcuff her first? What had Xu's killer done to her before they shot her to death? Did Cowan dare recreate that with his PBA?

Regardless, it was time to notify Jeb. Cowan opened their wireless connection. *"I Found Xu. She's dead."*

Jeb cursed. *"Any clue how she died?"*

"Um, probably the bullets."

"Could they be self-inflicted?"

That made Cowan think. A puppeted person could shoot themselves multiple times. Was that possible here?

Cowan checked his PBA's abstracted simulation again. *"I don't think so. There was a second person in her office. They handcuffed her to a wall."*

"Handcuffed?" Jeb asked. His mind might be going where Cowan's had gone, to the bad place.

Cowan nodded, then remembered Jeb couldn't see that. *"Yeah. She was handcuffed before her killer shot her multiple times, then fled."*

"There's one car missing from Xu's garage," Jeb said. *"From the registry at Corporate One, it's a classic. A 2041 Tesla Roadster with manual controls. Should be easy to trace."*

Manual controls meant more bad news. *"So our suspect is a closed circuit?"* They had no PBA behavioral protocols to prevent them from torturing handcuffed people.

"Maybe. Other than the computer that regulates the engine charge and other functions, there's not a VI onboard. Whoever took it actually knows how to drive."

"Isn't detonating an EMP and murdering someone a bit much to steal an old car?"

"Not for some people. You see anything else missing?"

"A couple of butcher knives on the first floor." Cowan followed footprints in blood into the room from which the simulated shooter had emerged. *"Oh. There they are."*

"Cowan?" Jeb asked.

Cowan synced the view from his left eye with Jeb. *"Someone had a knife-throwing contest."*

One of the missing knives was imbedded in the wood-paneled wall. The other remained clutched by the creepiest synthetic Cowan had ever seen, one with a synthflesh face. Cowan pulled his stunner and crept toward the downed synth, praying it wouldn't sit up.

He made a cursory check for visible damage with his boot tip—nothing visible, just like the synthetic downstairs—but the knife was an odd detail. Had this synth doubled as a security model? Had it been protecting Xu from whoever wanted to cuff and shoot her?

Jeb chuckled darkly over wireless. *"If only we could say the butler did it. I've always wanted one of those in my case archives."*

Humor wasn't helping. As Cowan stared at the downed synth's contorted, freakishly fleshy face, he hoped no one ever turned this thing back on. The way its mouth hung open, combined with its wide eyes, made it look like it wanted desperately to scream.

"With confirmation Professor Xu was murdered, this case is going over to the VCD," Jeb said over wireless. *"Meet me outside."*

Cowan edged around the dried pool of blood beneath Xu's body and headed for the stairs. The Violent Crime Division would take over this case now because Xu's murder trumped the EMP detonation, and Cowan couldn't stop feeling like he was somehow responsible.

It was obvious Doctor Xu had been no saint. Scripting a joyride that was so addictive people might die while using it was ruthless, yet so far as Cowan knew, Xu hadn't actually murdered anyone. She hadn't deserved to be cuffed, possibly tortured, and then shot to death.

Those were the barbaric things a world of PBAs was supposed to *stop*.

Yet perhaps this hadn't been about Galileo at all. As Nyx, Xu's alter ego in the darkSim, Xu had run in dangerous circles. People were getting hurt or killed all over the world these days, so perhaps Xu had simply been careless. Perhaps this wasn't really his fault.

Regardless, people would soon notice Nyx's absence from the dark-Sim. Cowan wondered if anyone would connect her disappearance to the murder of Doctor Xu. Phoenix would ask, and Cowan would tell him. Other than that, he was keeping this news to himself.

———

After they left Xu's mansion, Cowan spent the rest of the day filing a detailed report on a sloppy credit account swap. Some troll tapped the credit account of a local musician and assumed, because the musician played folksy jazz, he wasn't Sim savvy. She was very wrong.

After that came a debrief with Director Stanton, then a quick bite at *Crazy Noodles* with Jeb, then a long ride home. Cowan flipped on Classic Movie Channel and watched guys with guns chase each other around long enough to bore whoever was watching at the OMH.

After that he hopped into bed, closed his eyes, and activated his sleep loop again to make sure the CID didn't wonder why they couldn't surveil him through his own eyes. Once his loop was in place, he slid out of bed and opened his private connection to the darkSim.

He had to learn if anyone knew about Nyx's absence, and what they thought about it. He was just about to dive when someone pounded on his apartment door.

Cowan froze. Someone had the wrong apartment, probably a closed circuit without augmented reality to guide them to their address. Yet it was late, almost time for the closed-circuit curfew. Palmdale was a forty-minute drive away, and any closed circuit knocking at his door now would never make it home in time.

The pounding sounded again. It must be disturbing his neighbors, which was the last thing Cowan wanted to do before illegal activities. Who the hell was pounding on his door this late at night?

Cowan remembered Xu's body, and her handcuffs, and shivered. Had Galileo sent a murderer after him? Some puppeted innocent with a real gun?

Cowan flipped to his head desk and checked the camera on his door. The person beating on it was remarkably full-figured, with a mop of blond hair. She wore a tiny yellow dress with enough fabric to get her down the street without obscenity charges, but only just.

Cowan saw another door open across in 4A. A man with a balding head stepped out, and the woman stopped beating on Cowan's door long enough to yell at him.

"Fuck off!" the blond shouted, with a heavy Russian accent. "I'm not here for you!"

So, great. Cowan's neighbor would now assume the guy in 4B had just ordered himself a prostitute. That wasn't supposed to happen anymore but, according to Sonne, it still did.

So would Cowan's neighbor call the OMH? If he did that, and the OMH checked Cowan's loop, they might realize they *weren't* seeing what he was seeing. That would be bad.

Cowan hurried to his door, determined to send this confused woman on her way. He threw it open and nearly toppled over as the woman fell into his arms. He barely avoided getting a handful of parts he really shouldn't . . . at least, not without asking first.

The woman shouted loud enough for everyone to hear. "Baby! Why you keep me waiting?" She glared at Cowan's neighbor, who had the misfortune of still standing in his door. "Hey! You plan to join us?"

The poor man fumbled over a response.

"Then go inside!" The blond woman turned to Cowan, and he noticed she had a freckled nose. "C'mon, baby. I want you to take me now and loud."

She kicked the door shut with the back of her heel, then shoved him aside and strode right past him. The woman had entered his kitchen before Cowan could figure out what to do next. She yanked open his refrigerator and spoke again.

"No liquor? Bother." Her Russian accent abruptly vanished. She sounded quite cultured now. "What kind of cop doesn't keep liquor on hand?"

Like the man in the hallway, Cowan fumbled over a response.

The woman leaned on his counter and looked him over, smirking as she stared. "Don't fret, Detective Soto. I'm not here to fuck you, at least not in a positive sense." She tapped something he couldn't see on her wrist. "Though you may *feel* fucked, afterward."

There was a flicker of projected light around her body, and then a much different woman leaned against his kitchen counter. This one wore a crinkled black dress that rose to her neck and fell to her knees. There was no actual cleavage, and she pulled off a blond wig to reveal short black hair.

This woman was thin, not voluptuous, poised, not drunk, and dressed, rather than underdressed. She was Doctor Huan Xu, and she was supposed to be dead right now.

Xu crossed her thin arms. "Now, Detective Soto. We need to talk."

Cowan realized he'd left his stunner in his bedroom. "Right. Just let me—"

Xu stomped one heeled foot. "Don't even think about it! If you do anything to betray me, Cowan dear, I will murder you. Our relationship really is that simple."

Xu rolled up the hem of her skirt to reveal long legs and dark stockings. Before Cowan would ask or complain, he saw the garter holster and the metal revolver it held.

She pulled that gun and aimed at him. Cowan took a step back as his fear filters flexed. It was Doctor Barkov all over again.

"Wait," Cowan said.

Xu frowned. "Here is how you live. You do everything I ask of you, when I ask it."

"Okay."

"As much as it pains me to admit, I need your help. Our mutual enemy has decided to murder me."

Cowan remembered her body in a pool of sticky blood. "Didn't he?"

Xu rolled her eyes and snorted. "Obviously not. The body you found in my mansion? That was my clone."

"Really?" Cloning was still incredibly illegal, but there were rumors rich people did it.

"Merely a receptacle for spare organs, with nonviable tissue filling its skull. Insurance against misfortune. It had enough blood and flesh to buy me a day of freedom."

In a flash of relief and disgust, Cowan finally understood the handcuffs around "Xu's" wrist. He imagined hanging his own cloned body from a fixture, shooting it repeatedly with a gun, and shuddered.

"Where would you even keep something like that?" he asked.

Xu waved his question away. "You will help me escape to Switzerland. Once I'm safe, you can sleep with the knowledge that you will never, ever, see me again."

Cowan then remembered a revolver like hers held six bullets, and he remembered five bullets going off at the crime scene. Did she have one bullet left, or more?

Xu narrowed her eyes. "One bullet remains, in case you're still wondering. Also, I'm running marksman algorithms right now, so rest assured I won't miss."

That was creepily like mindreading, though she had probably read his face instead.

"Didn't you miss the clone a few times?" he asked.

Xu sighed. "On purpose, Cowan. To make it look convincing."

This woman had tried to torture him in the darkSim. She probably wanted him dead, and he had to make her want him *not* dead. He needed to keep her talking, not shooting.

"Hey, how did you change how you looked?" Cowan asked. "Make yourself look like that blond, uh—?"

"Escort," Xu said. "The word you are looking for is *escort*." She tapped that invisible keyboard on her wrist, and again her body changed.

Xu's proportions popped out impressively as her light brown flesh turned pale. Her sensible business dress turned into a thin sundress, and her dark hair vanished to reveal a bald white head. She had no hair now, which might explain the blond wig.

Xu tapped her wrist once more, and the projection vanished. "It's called MySelf, and you've probably never heard of it."

Cowan felt a rush of excitement. "Terrorists used those to sneak into the UN and blow it up forty years ago, didn't they? The one in New York?"

The Office of Mental Health had suppressed almost all stories about past terrorist attacks, but he'd learned about them on darkSim archives.

"You're well-informed. Now—"

"That's why all units were banned, right?" Cowan interrupted.

Xu's brow furrowed. "Yes, I believe so. Regardless, we need—"

"Hey, does it actually bend light?" Cowan asked, unreasonably fascinated by the possibilities. "How does it know what avatar to create in meatspace? Is that something you import in, like an avatar, or do you take 3D captures of real people? Also, I thought they were all destroyed! How did you get one?"

Xu waved the tip of her gun. "Focus, Cowan. How are you getting me to Switzerland?"

"Why come to me?" Cowan asked. Xu hadn't shot him, yet. She also seemed truly convinced he could help her, which was odd.

"You're with the CID, well known on the darkSim, and a talented PBA hacker. That means you have the ability to help me avoid the CID and help me avoid Galileo too. If I go down, you go down, and you don't want that."

Cowan focused on what Jeb might ask, in this situation, to take his mind off the gun in his face. "How do you know the person who attacked you was Galileo? Also, how did they attack you?"

"He hacked my butler and every synthetic in my mansion."

"That's why your security system triggered the EMP. You couldn't risk him using hacked synthetics to kill you, either yours or his."

Xu nodded. "He knows I'm not dead, and so we remain on an accelerated schedule." She grimaced, glanced at her revolver, and then at him. "If I lower this, you'll understand I'm still willing to murder you, right?"

Her arm must have been getting tired. Guns were heavy.

"Sure," Cowan said.

"Good." Xu sat on his couch, revolver resting on her lap. "Now, my flight?"

Cowan was on his own here. If he ended his loop now, the OMH would know he'd been giving their surveillance the slip every night. They'd investigate him thoroughly. Everything he'd hidden would come out, and then where would Ellen be? Still lost.

There was no good way out of this. He was actually going to have to help Xu escape to Switzerland. That was the only way he'd survive long enough to take down Galileo and find Ellen.

"Okay, problem one," Cowan said. "You can't book a flight in your own name. Problem two, you can't pay for it with your own money."

Xu scoffed. "You've deduced the issue, Detective. Now deduce a solution."

"So you need an identity that'll pass muster with global terrorism filters, and credit that won't immediately be flagged as someone else's when you book your flight."

She gestured impatiently. "Keep going."

"I can float you some money." Corvus had more than enough anonymized credits on the darkSim to buy Xu eight hundred tickets to Switzerland. "Generating a fake identity is next to impossible, so we'll just need to dupe an existing one."

Xu rewarded him with a shallow smile. "We'll make a cybercriminal of you yet."

"So we need someone about your age. Forty?"

Her eyes narrowed.

"Thirty or so," he corrected, not wanting to get shot over nothing. "Chinese descent, close to your height and weight."

"Sixty-five kilos."

"Wasn't asking, but congratulations."

Xu tapped her revolver. "I still have a gun, you know."

Cowan opened up his old dating app WeMeet and did a quick personals search. There were at least twenty-four single women matching Doctor Huan Xu's general height, weight, and nationality living within an hour of his apartment.

He felt bad robbing some woman of her identity, but he was saving two lives: Xu's and his own. He'd find some way to make it up to their poor victim, maybe an anonymous donation to her Valentine Box.

Cowan downloaded WeMeet profiles and searched for keywords: Sim, simulation, and pleasurebox. That got eight matches, meaning those women were active on at least one entertainment Sim. Four had been naive enough to list their handles on their profiles.

He picked his mark at random, just because he liked her name. StarPony. Her profile verified she was in the Sim right now, so she might agree to a simdate.

Sadly, direct contact in the Sim was all Cowan needed to steal her Sim ID. Age and physical appearance didn't matter in a virtual world, so StarPony might not care that he was ten years younger so long as he seemed interesting.

He hated himself for this, hated himself for using some poor woman and fucking up her life to save his own.

Still, it was better than getting shot in the head.

36
COWAN

Cowan's WeMeet dating profile was inactive and had been inactive since he and Ellen first went out, so he updated a few cursory details and reactivated it. Many of the private messages Ellen had once left waited in his Inbox, but he dared not watch those now. He also couldn't bear to delete them, which was why he still had this profile.

He sent a query to Angela Chang, also known as StarPony. He suggested a pleasant run though Strawberry Fields and a hot air balloon ride over Rainbow Lake. It was all typical first simdate stuff, but familiarity might make her more likely to accept.

No response came. Angela either wasn't checking WeMeet now or had decided to browse his profile and do a background check on him. As she should. He waited before querying the other possible marks. He didn't have work until tomorrow afternoon.

Cowan kept one eye in the Sim and one eye on her. He didn't trust her to behave herself.

"Say, Miss Xu?" Cowan asked.

"Doctor Xu," she corrected.

"Right." Whatever kept her from shooting him. "When you get to Switzerland, you think you'll be safe there? Even from Galileo?"

Xu shrugged. "I'll be safer. I have wealthy colleagues in Helsinki, and I can occupy myself with academic pursuits as I wait for Galileo to forget about me. I'm overdue for a sabbatical. Perhaps I'll study AI."

Was she joking? "Scripting artificial intelligence is illegal."

Xu smiled. "So are designing joyrides and using clones for spare organs. That's why your date will go so well. If you fail to get me a plane ticket, I'll shoot you in the head."

Cowan's fear filters flexed again. "That's going to look kind of suspicious, isn't it?"

"If I'm still in your apartment tomorrow, the VCD will finish their autopsy of my clone, which they'll determine isn't me. Once they start looking for me on street cams, I'll be found, and once I'm found, I cease to exist."

"We can protect you."

"Of course you can't, which is why if I'm going to die, I'm going to make you dead first." She idly rapped her fingers on his couch. "You're the reason my life imploded."

Cowan didn't want to, but he winced anyway. Xu's falling out with Galileo *was* technically his fault.

A ping echoed in his ears, and he flipped to his head desk. StarPony had responded, and she hadn't found him creepy. That made him feel even worse. He read her message on his head desk.

"I'd love a quick gallop, but no balloon ride. We'll grow wings instead. I want to see you fly. Meet me in Strawberry Fields in five if you're the adventurous type."

"We're on," Cowan told Xu. He settled into the seat. "Time to go be an asshole."

He didn't need to be on a hardlink to do innocent and legal stuff, and everything he'd do tonight was legal except spoofing StarPony's Sim ID. He opened his simPartment on his dummy account, Philo. Philo's simPartment was basic and boring, with stock furniture. Cowan had never updated it.

The Sim didn't have as many options as the darkSim. It needed to be user friendly, and most casuals didn't know how to model environments or script sim behaviors. Sadly, even this basic apartment was bigger and nicer than his real one.

Cowan bought a basic horse avatar off the corporate store, a chest-nut-brown mare, and tried it on. His sight line rose, and he trotted around his apartment on four legs, but the sensation was more like crawling than galloping. Less adjustment for the human brain.

Only then did he open the private partition in his PBA. He dropped in a darkSim script that would clone StarPony's Sim ID. Once he did that successfully, Xu could pass as Angela Chang (StarPony) when she bought her plane ticket, with Cowan's money.

So long as the real StarPony remained off the Sim long enough for Xu to buy a ticket using her name, that wouldn't raise any red flags. Angela Chang might not even know her identity was in Switzerland until Xu's flight landed, and perhaps not even then.

Cowan's body tingled as he ported to Strawberry Fields, a huge pleasure-box of glowing wheat, tall green grass, and endless sunshine. There were a number of equines gathered: big racing horses, smaller, realistic horses in many colors, and even cel-shaded horses with vestigial wings and big anime eyes.

Cowan trotted over to join them, neighing a general greeting. A few neighed back, but only one equine trotted over. She was a sleek black filly with a pink bow in her hair.

Cowan detected her identity query and did one in return, because that's what a normal person would do. Strawberry Fields disabled name tags for immersion purposes.

StarPony's filly batted horsy eyes at him. "Well, hello there, Philo. What an . . . interesting avatar."

Cowan grimaced, or rather, bared his equine teeth. She had instantly recognized his avatar as a corporate shop model, and selling himself as a true equine enthusiast was the wrong move. Cowan shook his head and mane in what he hoped was an apology.

"You've got me. I've never actually been a horse." He hesitated. "It was in your profile, and your profile was interesting . . . you were inter-esting, I mean . . . so I figured, why not?"

StarPony nickered at him. "So you're a bit new at this. I won't fault a man who's willing to try new things, nor one who's actually honest about it."

Ouch. That hurt more than she knew.

"So tell me, Philo. What do you think of your new avatar?" she asked.

Cowan decided not to lie about anything he didn't have to. "It's . . . kind of cool, actually. Though moving feels like crawling to me."

"It would, with that basic avatar. But you must crawl before you can walk, and walk before you can gallop, and you are cute." She swished her silky tail. "So try and keep up!"

She trotted off, and Cowan followed. StarPony gradually increased their pace as Cowan did as well, and it surprised Cowan just how fast he could "crawl" when he stopped thinking. Grass blew, motes glittered, and his hooves pounded the earth. It was actually kind of fun.

StarPony glanced back. "You're doing great!" She shook her head and mane and sped up, four legs pounding the earth in rhythmic unison. Cowan started falling behind.

She slowed down, careful not to leave him behind. She wasn't trying to humiliate him, just gently egging him on, and another wave of guilt squeezed his heart. Angela really did seem like a decent person, which made him all the more horrible for using her.

Xu's disembodied voice echoed in his head over wireless. *"Stop toying with her. Do the deed and get out."*

Cowan stumbled and went down, rolling several times before his horse body came crashing to a stop. *"Xu!"* What the hell was she doing in his head? *"How did you—"*

"Linkline into your auxiliary port. You think I want you two conspiring against me?"

Cowan stumbled to his equine feet. *"I wouldn't do that!"*

StarPony trotted back, equine eyes wide. "Are you all right?" She really sounded concerned.

"Sorry. Took a bad step," Cowan said. "No damage done."

StarPony shifted into a woman avatar. She wore a gray dress and had green eyes, creamy skin, and long black hair. Her human avatar was well-proportioned, but not ludicrously so—sexy, but tasteful.

"Perhaps we took things too fast." She smiled at him, hair trailing in the wind. "Do you want to walk?"

Cowan felt a very nonhorse tingle. "Walk?"

"As a human." StarPony trailed two fingers down his equine nose, and it tickled in meatspace. "Or, you know. You could stay in equine form." She slid her fingers along his flank, making his side tingle like his face and other parts too. "And . . . I could ride you?"

Cowan was going to make this woman's life hell. She was considerate and adventurous, and he was going to screw her over just like he'd screwed Ellen. Well, not that badly.

After Xu stole Angela's identity to fly to Switzerland, the CID would treat Angela as an accomplice. They'd question her about the security breach and might even flag her on the Sim. Even an inconclusive CID investigation could hang over a person's profile, limiting their employment options and tanking their citizen score.

Was that her reward for trusting people, getting screwed?

"*She seems lonely,*" Xu said, inside Cowan's head. "*Riding you is perfect. That contact will give you all you need to spoof her Sim ID.*" Her voice turned harsh. "*Do it now.*"

Cowan stared at Angela. He couldn't betray another woman, not like he'd betrayed Ellen. This woman deserved better.

StarPony frowned. "Philo? Are you still there?"

"*Do it, Cowan!*" Xu demanded. "*Or do you want to die?*"

Cowan shifted into Philo's avatar, a basic human male. "This was a mistake. Sorry."

Angela's hand snapped back as if he'd burned her. "I'm sorry. I didn't mean to freak you out."

"No, trust me, it's not you. You're super nice. I have to leave because I wasn't honest with you. I'm just that kind of asshole."

She blinked. Cowan opened his admin panel and blinked *Disconnect*. When he focused back into meatspace, Doctor Xu was in his face.

Her eyes bulged and her revolver shook. She pressed the tip of her revolver to his forehead, cold and hard.

"Why did you do that? You had her!" She clutched his linkline in white knuckles. "Go back in!"

Cowan popped her linkline from his auxiliary port. "I'm not fucking up some innocent woman's life to save yours. We'll find another way to get you away from Galileo, one that doesn't hurt anyone. That woman deserves better, and honestly, you don't."

A message pinged his head desk, probably Angela Chang—a.k.a. StarPony. Cowan blocked her. Would Xu shoot him now? Would he feel the bullet, or would everything just go black?

Xu pressed the revolver against him hard enough to force his head back.

"I need that ticket!" she yelled. "I need a way out!"

Cowan stared at her without moving, without doing anything that might cause her to press the trigger. He remembered Ellen's tear-stained face staring up at him, remembered her sad smile.

"I'll help you, but not this way," he said. "You want to add murder to your many sins, go ahead."

"I'll do it! I'll kill you!"

Cowan leaned forward. "Then take the shot. Or get the fuck out of my apartment."

Doctor Xu stepped back, revolver shaking in her arms. Even if she didn't mean to shoot him, she might do it anyway. What if she missed? Should he go for his stunner?

Xu huffed, screamed, and tossed the revolver at him. "Idiot!"

Cowan dove just in time to avoid getting clocked in the head. Her gun bounced off his wall and spun across his hard floor. It didn't fire, but of course it didn't. Guns only fired when you pressed the trigger.

Xu fell to her knees and started sobbing. Just sobbing. Actual tears slipped down the sides of her nose, down her cheeks, and onto her shaking lips.

Cowan stared at her crocodile tears, one last trick from a hardened criminal. She was lying. She was evil.

She had almost been murdered in her own home.

Xu shuddered, stood, and stomped over to her revolver. She picked it up, staring at it, and Cowan knew he had lost his chance to run. Would she shoot him now?

Xu hitched up her skirt, tucked the revolver into her garter holster, and wiped her eyes. She pulled on her blond wig and walked for his apartment door.

Before he could stop them, Cowan's stupid legs went after her. "Where are you going?"

"Somewhere pleasant." Xu's voice was quiet now. "Maybe a park, with trees. I'd like to see real trees before I go, smell leaves and grass and nature."

"Before you go?" he asked.

"The only place Galileo can't come after me," Xu said.

"If you're that worried, turn yourself into the CID."

Xu glanced back and narrowed her dark eyes. "I won't have my mind burned away. I'll die as who I am. And just so you'll know how much of an asshole you are, I never intended my last bullet for you."

The calm in Xu's tone chilled him. He couldn't let her commit suicide. He pondered trying for her gun, and wondered which of them might get shot.

"Now hold on," he said. "We can find you another way out."

Xu looked away. "That butcher knife at the back of my head? That was a mercy."

Cowan remembered the knife he found imbedded in her study wall. "How is that a mercy?"

"By escaping, I've made Galileo look foolish. He'll burn me as a caution to others now, erase all I am and all I have done. Doctor Huan Xu will simply cease to exist."

Xu was sounding more paranoid by the second. It's not like Galileo had access to his own rewriting center. Only the Office of Mental Health had access to those.

"Why do you think Galileo can burn you a new mind?" Cowan asked.

"It was just a foolish bet," she said, ignoring him. "I only learned Galileo's nature later from rumors, gossip." She gripped his door handle. "Goodbye."

Cowan ordered his apartment's VI to lock the door. Xu tugged, grunted, and threw up her hands in frustration.

"What do you want?" she asked. "Must I prostrate myself?"

Cowan saw a way out for them both, finally. "No. You're not leaving, and you're not killing yourself. I told you—I'm going to help you."

"You clearly don't have the balls to help me!"

"I'm not hurting anyone to save your life. But I might know another way out."

"What could you possibly offer that I haven't thought of?"

Cowan checked his sleep loop to ensure the OMH would still think he was in bed.

"Do you have a car?" he asked.

She glared for a moment before answering. "Yes?"

"Is it the Tesla?"

"I'm not an idiot. I abandoned the Tesla."

"Then let's go," Cowan said. "I'll tell you the rest on the way."

37

JEB

As Cowan and his scantily clad blond friend emerged from the front door of his apartment complex, Jeb glanced at his analog watch. The woman had been in there for thirty minutes, more than enough time if you were lonely enough, but this illicit liaison seemed too brazen for a man like Cowan. It felt out of character.

Jeb had gathered enough clues to know someone in Cowan's life had hurt him, badly, which was why he was so hesitant to date. That still didn't explain why he'd risk soliciting an actual prostitute in meatspace. Simsex was almost as good, cheaper, safer, and most importantly, absolutely legal.

Beside him in the passenger seat, David leaned forward and asked, "Is he giving her a ride home?"

David wore a thick leather jacket with a concealed stunner. Without the ability to activate his HARM switch—something only David's commanding officer could have authorized—the support Jeb's husband could offer was limited, but Jeb still liked having him here. He hadn't hidden anything from David in a long time.

"I don't see why," Jeb said. "Heading to an in-call, maybe?" Jeb tapped his fingers on the steering wheel of his 2082 Toyota Camry, a classic he kept for days off. His Camry had no GPS and no wireless devices of any kind, which made it immune to routine tracking methods.

"How much longer before you have to turn your PBA back on?" David asked.

"We've got another couple of hours. We'll be home long before I have to hop back on the network."

One of the advantages of twenty years with the CID was that, at night, Director Stanton allowed Jeb to deactivate his PBA's in-eye surveillance when he wanted private time with his husband. Jeb had been using that time to surveil Cowan instead. Puck's claim that Cowan was a loose circuit remained stuck in Jeb's brain. He couldn't dismiss it.

Cowan and the woman hopped into her waiting autocar. It passed the corner where Jeb had parked. He pulled out after the car and followed, gripping the big wheel tight.

38

COWAN

SEPTEMBER 30, EARLY MORNING

"Stop here," Cowan told their autocar.

The autocar pulled over. He'd uploaded a destination across town, to throw off anyone monitoring the autocar, but the route went by *Sonne's Sanctuary*. They were now a block away, and Xu's MySelf bracelet was fully charged.

It was time to execute his very bad plan. They left the car and started walking. Once they reached *Sonne's Sanctuary*, Cowan knocked on the closed door.

After a long moment, he knocked again. Finally, Mick, the bouncer, opened the door and blocked the frame.

"We're full," Mick said.

Cowan opened his jacket and flashed his badge. "CID." He had changed into his work clothes before they left.

Mick didn't move. Then his head tilted, like he'd heard a dog whistle or something, and he stepped out of the way.

Sonne stepped into view and grimaced at them. She wore a tight shirt with a Triforce shape on it and ripped blue jeans right out of the '10s. She looked . . . really good . . . but Cowan couldn't think about that now. Xu's life was at stake.

"Detective Soto," Sonne said, all business. Her formality was a bit disheartening. "What did I do now?"

Cowan glanced at Xu, who now stared at the ground and appeared miserable.

"I'll explain inside," he said, offering Sonne his best pleading look. "It's important."

Sonne frowned and leaned out her door, looking first left, then right. "Well, get in here before someone sees you."

Cowan walked inside and made sure Xu was right beside him, pretending to be a poor Swiss woman trafficked into prostitution in California. Sonne said nothing, didn't look back, as she led them through the parlor and down the hall with its flickering lights.

They soon entered Sonne's office, which felt secure enough, and she closed them inside. Her holo-projection was disabled, her desk unremarkable. There were no waterfalls this time.

Sonne turned and leaned against the closed door of her office, arms crossed. "Explain."

Cowan had dug into Sonne's tax records on the drive over, using his CID credentials to snoop, and he had a decent idea what to do next.

"You donate to a number of Benzai Corporation charities, one of which is called Second Chance," he said. "You fly women home."

Sonne stared, expressionless. "We help sex-trafficking victims. Is this woman a sex-trafficking victim?"

Cowan nodded. "From Switzerland. She—"

Sonne raised a hand. "Stop. Let her talk."

Xu wrung her hands. "I came for a job. It was for a model, for two months." Xu's *W*s were more like *V*s, her *F*s drawn out. She was a good actress. "I figured, easy money." She paused. "None of it was easy."

Xu actually sounded Swiss, even better than her Russian. Did her PBA have an accent algorithm installed?

Sonne's whole demeanor changed when she looked at Xu. Her shoulders relaxed, her gaze softening. "Who held you here?" she asked. "Did he give you his name?"

They'd discussed Xu's pimp on the ride over. Cowan had picked a man named Oleg Vasser, because Jeb's report the night they were abducted stated Vasser was the most likely person to have ruined his date. One small bit of revenge.

Xu answered. "He was a thin man, pale, like a ghost. He did not give his name."

Cowan resisted the urge to smile. Xu not knowing Vasser's actual name was a good touch. He probably wouldn't have told her.

"Did he wear hoop earrings?" Sonne asked.

Xu shook her head.

"Did he have a scar?"

Xu nodded.

"Purple lips?" Sonne added.

Xu shuddered convincingly. "Purple and disgusting. He was a disgusting man."

Sonne uncrossed her arms and straightened, mouth a firm line. "I can't get you back to Switzerland until the end of the week, when we launch our next flight, but you're safe here, understand? You're staying here until we can get you out."

Cowan bit his lip. This complicated things. Xu's MySelf wouldn't last that long. She would have to ask for privacy, maybe, only come out when it was done charging. This could still work.

"No, you must . . ." Xu caught herself. "Please. If there is any way, a flight tonight . . ."

Sonne kept her gaze level. "There's not, but I won't let anyone take you. Trust me." She glanced at Cowan. "I won't ask where you found her. All I'll say is thank—"

The door to Sonne's office opened abruptly, bumping her rear and sending her stumbling. A huge shadow loomed beyond the door.

"Hands in the air, please," someone with a deep voice said.

Cowan drew his stunner and aimed, heart pumping. Was it Galileo? "Stop!" he shouted.

Two meters of Jeb Forrester stepped inside, stunner raised. "Really, Cowan?"

Xu stumbled back, hitched her dress, and yanked her gun from her garter holster. "Fuck!" She slammed the revolver to her temple as her MySelf projection flickered out.

Sonne's face went pale. "Doctor Xu?"

Cowan's weapon moved to track Xu as Jeb's weapon moved to track him. "Dammit, stop moving!" he yelled. "Everyone, stop moving!"

"Drop the gun, Cowan," Jeb said. "Xu can't actually shoot herself."

"I can!" Xu shouted. "I'll do it!"

Cowan swung his stunner toward Jeb. "She can do it. She's a loose circuit, Jeb. She's suicidal."

Jeb tilted his head, glancing between Cowan and Xu. "Mexican standoff. Always wanted to try a Mexican standoff." He regarded Sonne. "Hey, you got a gun on you?"

She blinked. "No."

"Want us to wait while you get one?" Jeb asked.

"I think I'm fine."

Xu screamed. "You think this is a joke? You will not burn my mind!"

Xu smiled as she looked somewhere far away. Her body relaxed and her face did too. She was content. She was ready.

Cowan tackled her just before the gun went off.

The blast left his ears ringing and a tiny hole in Sonne's ceiling, but didn't touch Huan Xu. She was on the floor under Cowan now, gasping.

"No!" Xu shouted. "No, no, no!"

"Guess I was wrong," Jeb said.

Xu fought and wriggled beneath Cowan. "Release me!"

Jeb stepped forward, stunner aimed. "Get clear."

Cowan rolled between them and spread his arms. "Stop, Jeb! You can't take her in to the CID." Cowan realized, then, that he believed Xu. "Galileo's after her. He wants to mind burn her."

Jeb grimaced as he sucked in his breath, glaring. "As long as Xu hasn't murdered anyone, they'll just mod her. Don't make me shoot you, Cowan. Don't make this harder."

Xu thrashed beneath Cowan's weight. "Don't let him erase me!"

Sonne pressed a small stunner to the back of Jeb's bald

head. "Detective Forrester? I'd like you to lower your weapon, please."

After a moment, Jeb lowered his gun, closed his eyes, and sighed. "Huh. I honestly did not see that coming."

39

COWAN

Cowan took a moment to not freak out. Then he rolled off Xu, plucked Jeb's stunner from his lowered hand, and held it without really aiming it at anyone.

"Shit," Sonne said. "Shit, shit, shit." She kept her stunner pressed against the back of Jeb's head.

Cowan glanced at Xu, curled into a mass of elbows and knees, then at Jeb. Then at Sonne. She was holding a gun to the head of a CID detective. This was really bad.

Cowan lowered his stunner. "Okay. Hold on. Let's think about this."

Sonne glared. "Explain why you came here tonight. All of it. Who is Galileo, why does he want to burn Doctor Xu's mind, and why can't you stop him?"

Jeb grinned, looking far too calm. "Yes, Cowan. Explain."

Explaining was good. They would understand if he explained, maybe even help him. Cowan immediately told them everything about how Xu faked her death, including his plan for Second Chance to fly Xu to Switzerland with no one being the wiser.

By the time he was done, Sonne's glare had gone nuclear. "So that was your whole plan? Use me for my connections, then leave me holding a bag of shit?"

Cowan blinked. "No! I mean, that wasn't—"

Sonne cut him off. "Do you have any idea the inquiries Kate would face once the OMH learned we'd helped a cybercriminal flee the country? They'd shut us down. They'd sue us into oblivion!"

Holy crap. She was right—Cowan knew she was right—and he hunched his shoulders as he realized just how badly he'd fucked up.

"That wasn't what I wanted . . ."

"And that makes it better somehow?" Sonne demanded.

He should have thought this through. He should have trusted Sonne, but he hadn't been thinking straight since Xu invaded his apartment.

Yet that was no excuse, really. He'd been hiding things for too long.

"I'm sorry," was all he could manage to whisper.

Jeb risked a glance over his shoulder. "Ma'am, since you've got me at a disadvantage now, would you mind if I stood in the corner?"

Sonne kept her stunner against his head. "Don't you move a fucking muscle, Forrester. Also, you've probably noticed your wireless can't transmit from this room."

"Wouldn't matter anyway," Jeb said. "I shut down my wireless."

Sonne turned her attention back to Cowan. "So this is what I get for being nice to you. A dead woman in my office, your partner about to arrest me, and the end of my fucking life."

Cowan shook his head. "You wouldn't have done this if it wasn't for me. I'll testify to that. They'll blame me for everything, but first, we have to get Xu somewhere safe."

"Why do you want her safe, Cowan?" Jeb asked. "Are you together?"

"We're not together," Xu protested.

"I believe her, Jeb," Cowan said. "I believe Doctor Xu when she says Galileo can burn her mind away, even if we take her into the CID, because I've seen that happen."

"Can you elaborate?" Jeb asked.

Backed into a corner twice in the same night. Yet he couldn't let Jeb arrest Xu, and he couldn't let Jeb arrest Sonne, and he couldn't be arrested himself. So here they were.

Cowan spoke quietly, like in a dream. "A few years ago, someone inside Oneworld asked me to script new firmware that could keep a jailbroken PBA on the Sim while disabling all behavioral algorithms. Then . . . they arrested me for it."

That was it. His big revelation. It was all he knew and all he had to go on, based on his own investigations and the last words of a woman he had loved and betrayed.

"It's all right," Ellen had whispered, as she pointed two fingers at her own head. *"You couldn't know."*

Jeb scowled. "That doesn't make a lot of sense. Do you have any evidence?"

Cowan didn't. That was the problem, one among many. "I have nothing but what happened to us, to me and Ellen. We used to script PBA firmware together." Cowan swallowed. "We were going to get married."

Sonne's eyes narrowed, but her gun didn't move. Xu rocked with her legs tucked up against her, humming to herself like an insane person.

"We had authorization, Jeb," Cowans said. As all Cowan's long nights working beside Ellen came back, fresh grief flooded him. "Our company, Mind Games, told us the new firmware was for Oneworld use only, like an admin account. We developed firmware that circumvents all PBA behavioral protocols without disconnecting it from the Sim."

"A loose circuit," Jeb said.

"Yeah." Cowan tapped his head. "I'm running our firmware. I can hurt people if I want to, kill people, all while connected to the Sim. I'm clear as fucking crystal." He looked at Xu. "Or I could kill people, if it didn't make me sick every time I thought about it."

Jeb shook his head. "Puck was right."

"Who the fuck is Puck?" Sonne asked. Her stunner remained locked against Jeb's head.

Jeb explained that to them too. That there was an Augur in Corporate One, and she looked like a fairy, and she was very interested in finding out if Cowan was actually a loose circuit.

"Here's what you need to clarify," Jeb said. "How do you know the people you worked for were Oneworld?"

Cowan's lip twisted. "It's the only way I can explain what happened to us. We tested our new firmware on the latest corporate PBAs, models that weren't even on the street yet. We got a simMail saying a bonus was coming, and we celebrated. Then Ellen called and said she'd found out something terrible, something about our work. It wasn't sanctioned after all.

"Corporate Security came after her," Cowan continued quietly. "I was home . . . we lived in Mission Beach . . . and Ellen called me, on an encrypted link we kept for ourselves. She said military people were chasing her, with guns and synthcops."

"So Oneworld has had loose circuit firmware all this time?" Jeb asked.

"No, I mean . . . I don't think so. After Ellen copied our firmware to her PBA, she deleted everything, even the backups. She told me she was almost home. We'd run together."

"Then what happened?" Sonne asked. Her voice was softer now, like when she'd asked Xu about her pimp.

"I pinged 911," Cowan whispered. "I betrayed Ellen. I told them we were corporate engineers, that someone in our department had broken the law. I actually believed they'd help us."

"And Corporate Security arrived instead?" Jeb asked.

"All of them, I think." Cowan remembered men shouting as they slid down ropes through busted skylights, remembered helmets and huge guns. "They arrested Ellen, said she was an anti-corporation spy. Said she'd been secretly passing data to the Swiss."

Jeb frowned. "So what happened to your new firmware?"

"Ellen nuked it," Cowan said. "She fried her PBA so Corporate Security wouldn't retrieve our source code, so there was nothing in there that could incriminate me." Cowan's voice broke. "She lobotomized herself to keep me from getting mind burned."

Ellen was all he saw now, her tall, slim form and dark hair. She'd had a wonderful heart, and a wonderful brain, and he'd destroyed both of those because he made a mistake.

"That's an interesting story," Jeb said.

Cowan felt a pang of frustration. "It's true. It happened."

Jeb tilted his bald head. "So this is why you joined the CID? To find out who set the two of you up? To chase this corporate traitor?"

"I joined to find Ellen. She's still alive out there, somewhere. She's missing, and it's my fault."

Sonne settled against her door, tapping her stunner idly against one arm. "None of this makes any sense."

Jeb looked at her sidelong. "Doesn't it?"

Sonne straightened. "Oneworld owns the world. Why would they need loose circuit firmware?"

That was a question Cowan had often asked himself, yet he knew he was right.

"There were peer reviews," he said. "Focus groups. There had to be. It wasn't just one person. Nobody could authorize that many resources without some form of corporate oversight."

Jeb shook his head. "It's not corporation versus corporation, like those incidents before the Lathan-Faulkner Act. It's an internal war. CEO versus CEO, department versus department, people flexing muscles and moving pawns. It gives you enforcers without HARM switches. No paper trail."

"This is crazy!" Sonne shouted. "Don't you get how crazy this all sounds?"

"Actually, this doesn't sound crazy at all." He looked to Xu. "Arresting you isn't the play we need. Not with what Cowan's told me. We need another plan."

Sonne threw out her arms. "What plan?"

Jeb met her gaze, eyes calm. "You should call Miss Lambda now."

Sonne scowled at Jeb, then at Cowan, and then walked to her desk and raised her hand. "Fine, whatever." A blank panel appeared, summoned by her PBA.

Cowan stood silently as Kate Lambda's face and shoulders filled the panel. Sonne explained the current situation without cursing *too* much, and Kate understandably facepalmed. Then she said something about a helicopter, and Sonne closed the panel.

Cowan found it hard to pay attention. He'd fucked this up so badly. Would Sonne ever forgive him for lying to her, for taking advantage of her charity and trust?

It probably didn't matter. They'd never had a chance in hell anyway.

40

COWAN

Kate Lambda's private helicopter landed in the parking lot behind *Sonne's Sanctuary*, like that was just a normal thing. David Forrester met them there. When Cowan asked about that, Jeb simply shrugged. Of course Jeb wouldn't arrive without backup.

The five of them piled in—Detective Jeb Forrester, StrikeForceGo legend David Forrester, Detective Cowan Soto, waifu madam Sonne, and cybercriminal Huan Xu. As the helicopter lifted off, Cowan remembered he'd never ridden in one before.

He looked out the window, but it was dark, and they flew high enough that clouds obscured everything. One more disappointing anticlimax, like the rest of his fucking life.

Kate wasn't in the helicopter. It was piloted by a VI, and Cowan wouldn't put it past Kate to loop all street cameras on the nearby buildings, or somehow obscure the helicopter from corporate radar. Xu wore her MySelf projection whenever they went outside.

Cowan had told other people everything, finally, and his world didn't feel real any longer. In the year since Ellen lobotomized herself, he had replayed their last night together every so often, felt his chest tighten and his eyes burn. He'd always thought sharing his pain would make him lighter. He just felt exhausted.

If Ellen had died a year ago, that would have been one thing, but .1e hadn't. She had been locked in a cell all that time, with no idea what she had done or why she was imprisoned. Assuming she still knew how to be a person at all.

Cowan wondered if Ellen had gone insane or killed herself. Some days, he imagined her grinning as she bounced her head against a padded wall. Some days, he could hardly work with those images filling his head.

Even if he found Ellen, what then? In the year she'd been captive the woman he'd loved had no doubt been completely burned away, entirely replaced by implanted behaviors and memories. Like Galileo wanted to do to Doctor Xu.

Perhaps it wasn't all bad. Perhaps the woman in Ellen's body was happy where she was right now. She might think living in a padded cell was the best thing in the whole world.

Sonne moved to the seat beside him and kept her voice low. "Hey, Cowan? I understand why you did what you did."

He stopped seeing Ellen for a moment. "Really?"

Sonne nodded, lips tight. "I've seen what a CID investigation and corporate audits can do to innocent people. I know why you didn't steal that lady's identity. I know you were trying to do the right thing."

Cowan's shoulders sunk. "I didn't have a clue what I was doing."

"I get that, which is why we can still work together until we solve this little problem. But after that, I never want to see you again. Understand?"

Of course Sonne would feel that way, now. Of course it still hurt.

"Sorry again," he said.

Sonne shrugged. "On the other hand, what you've told me does help us with another problem. Our father's been in a coma for almost a year now, PBA induced."

"Your father? How was that related?"

Sonne explained the attack on Taylor Lambda. An undetectable troll paralyzed him in his own pleasurebox and left him in a real-life coma. Kate now believed that troll was Galileo, and now that they knew about Cowan's firmware, which allowed a person to hurt and kill without being kicked off the sim, they knew how that troll had harmed Taylor and stayed connected. Galileo had installed Cowan's loose circuit firmware.

David, sitting beside Jeb, said what Cowan had started thinking. Clearly, he'd been listening. "You've just described a HARM switch that never turns off."

"Pretty much," Cowan agreed.

"Where'd he get it?" David asked. "I thought you said all copies were erased."

Cowan thought back to the night he ruined his former life, and Ellen's. "I thought so too," he said. "But perhaps Ellen didn't get everything, like she thought. Perhaps she missed a backup at Mind Games."

Jeb spoke from across the helicopter. "Cowan, you were led to believe you had corporate permission to create firmware for PBAs that would allow them to ignore all behavioral conditioning, while remaining on the Sim. I don't need to tell you how hard that is to believe."

Cowan frowned. "But—"

"But it happened," Jeb interrupted, "and we know that Galileo has access to the firmware you created. That means they are connected to Mind Games. Perhaps a fellow scripter?"

Cowan shook his head. "It was just us. No one worked on that firmware but . . ."

Cowan understood, then. He knew what Jeb was saying. He wanted to leap across the helicopter and punch Jeb in the face.

"No," Cowan said, firmly. "It's not Ellen. Galileo is not Ellen."

Sonne touched his arm. "No one is saying—"

Cowan brushed her hand off and scooted away. "It's not her. I know her, and I loved her. She'd never murder people like this."

"All right," Jeb said.

"She wouldn't do it," Cowan insisted, clenching his hands.

"If you say so." Jeb leaned forward in his seat. "Oh, and before I forget. Don't ever do something that stupid again."

Cowan resisted the urge to look away. "I can't promise that."

Jeb narrowed his eyes, but he didn't look angry. "I don't mean lying about Xu. I mean keeping me out of this, hiding your missing fiancée and Galileo's actions on the darkSim. I can't help you if you don't talk to me."

"Why would you help me with anything?" Cowan asked. Jeb had just accused the woman Cowan loved of being a mass murderer, after all.

"We're partners, and that means we support each other no matter how bad things get. If you get into a bind again, if you're in trouble again, call me. You come to me first. That's how this works."

Did Jeb mean it? Maybe he did. Maybe he really would have helped, if Cowan had just asked, like Sonne.

"Okay," Cowan agreed. He only then realized how truly fatigued he felt.

Eventually, Kate's helicopter landed atop a ribbed-looking glass and concrete skyscraper somewhere in the Gaslamp Quarter. Music thumped below as they stepped out onto a helipad with a city sprawled out below.

Cowan realized, then, they had finally arrived at Club Sylvan, where he and Sonne were supposed to have had their date. He glanced at Sonne, but she didn't look back. No dancing tonight.

A tall woman with short blond hair stepped onto the roof as the helicopter's rotors spun down, wearing tactical body armor that left her arms exposed to her shoulders. That seemed impractical, but Cowan wasn't about to question a woman with glowing red cyber-enhanced eyes.

She informed them all her name was Lucy, and it was obvious she was very dangerous. Everyone agreed to follow her into the building without saying a goddamn word. Pretty standard.

The thumping grew deafening as they walked in through the roof door. Lucy led them across a catwalk overlooking Club Sylvan. It was gorgeous, with holo-painted walls that alternated between deep space filled with stars, psychedelic spiral land, and a dance floor platform floating on a frothy sea. It was smoky and smelled like peppermint.

Projected blue-and-white lights streaked along the bar, and its top shelf was stocked with a horde of multicolored bottles. Alcohol was an unnecessary luxury these days, a throwback to the days when you couldn't just set your PBA to drunk. People today drank for taste and status, not to actually get hammered.

This top-floor club was packed, understandable for midnight on a Friday night, and most of the women wore dresses more revealing than the one worn by Xu's blond MySelf disguise. The men were handsome, sculpted muscle, and wore tailored suits that put Cowan's to shame. He was almost glad he and Sonne hadn't made it here on their date.

The catwalk ended at a tough-looking metal door that slid into the wall. Lucy led them into an office with a plush red carpet and walls covered in sound-dampening foam. There was a big leather chair with its back to them, pointed at a panel on the back wall.

Kate Lambda spun her chair around as they entered her office, probably to be dramatic, and watched them with crossed hands resting on crossed knees. "Welcome, fellow fugitives." She wore a black, off-the-shoulder dress that shimmered in the faint light.

Xu dropped her MySelf projection and glowered. "Lambda."

Kate smiled at her. "Hello, Huan."

Cowan looked between them. "You know each other?"

"We've crossed paths," Kate said.

"It ended poorly," Xu added.

Kate stood. "Despite that, my dear, you are welcome here as long as Galileo is hunting you."

Xu hunched her shoulders. "Thank you."

Kate walked around her desk, hands clasped behind her back, her shimmering dress changing from black to red. "It seems I was right about you, Cowan."

"How were you right?" he asked.

"You were a disaster waiting to happen, and you've just disastered all of us."

Cowan was tired of people blaming him for things. "You think I asked for this?"

"I think you just put me, my sister, and everyone here in the sights of a deadly cybercriminal. We're targets of someone we don't know, who works for a corporation we know nothing about, with darkSim connections we can't trace and scripting prowess unlike any we've ever seen."

Cowan gaze fell toward the floor. "Sorry."

"Stop apologizing," Sonne said.

Jeb squeezed his shoulder. "Don't give up yet. We can still beat this."

Cowan kept his eyes on the floor. He doubted Jeb really believed that. Jeb was probably only being comforting because he didn't want Cowan to entirely stop thinking.

Xu relaxed against a wall. "So casually dismissed," she said. "Galileo will burn our minds away, one and all."

Curiosity pushed past Cowan's depression. He looked up.

"You mentioned that he was going to burn your mind in my apartment," Cowan said. "That's a sentence for a capital crime, and only approved Oneworld centers have that ability. Those are secured, so how would Galileo gain access?"

"You can't be that stupid," Xu said.

"No, I am. I really am that stupid. How would he gain access to a rewriting center? How would he even get you shipped to one?"

"Galileo is a part of Oneworld," Xu said.

Cowan knew that. Galileo scripted new firmware for their PBAs, which was how he bypassed safety restrictions.

"But access to a rewriting center takes approval from the director of the OMH," Cowan said. "You need sign-off from the director, right, Jeb?"

Jeb nodded. "That's what I've always assumed."

Xu huffed and rolled her eyes. "He doesn't have a private rewriting center, you charmingly dense idiot. He has all the rewriting centers. His name is Gerhard Bayer, Chief Technical Officer of Oneworld, and he *owns* the Office of Mental Health."

Kate blinked. "Hold on a moment. Are you claiming you just doxxed Galileo?"

Xu took a moment. "I had thirty minutes to think about it before I went to Cowan's," she said. "I got bored."

41

COWAN

"That's an incredibly dangerous claim," Jeb said. "You really believe Gerhard Bayer, one of the five members of the board of Oneworld, is the cybercriminal responsible for tearing the Sim apart and murdering dozens of people with puppeted victims?

"Yes," Xu said plainly.

"You've just accused one of the most powerful people in the world of being Galileo."

Xu looked around the room, eyebrows rising slowly as if discovering everyone else shared Jeb's disbelief. "You really all don't believe it?"

No one said anything, even Lucy, Kate's tall, blond bodyguard, who watched them from beside the office door with her bare arms crossed. They waited. Everyone waited.

"Fine." Xu huffed. "Seeing as we'll all cease to exist in a few days, why not share my genius?" She turned to Kate. "Lambda, give me panel access."

"It's Kate," Kate said.

"Not since we broke up, it isn't."

"Careful, honey. This is my house."

Xu took a breath. "Kate, would you please allow me access to your office panel?"

"Of course, Huan." Kate smiled at Xu, then spun her chair so she faced the back wall. A screen appeared in the air, rendered on the augmented reality server they all shared.

Xu walked over to the panel and pasted data from her PBA. "Mass shootings covered up by the Office of Mental Health." Dozens of names plastered themselves all over the panel.

Cowan recognized one name in particular. Sheila Fisher. "Where did you get those?" he asked.

Xu motioned with her hands as she organized names into efficient lists. "Isn't it obvious?"

It wasn't, actually, but Jeb spoke up before Cowan could say that.

"We've researched this list," Jeb said, "but we've found nothing. My initial theory was these were targeted assassinations, one murder with random people added to make it look like a mass killing. Our metadata filters created dozens of probable connections, but there's too many unknowns to settle on specific victims."

"That's because you're relying on metadata," Xu said. "It won't make the connections you need, because the man who murdered those people *controls* that data." She gestured to Kate. "Please import the five board members of Oneworld."

Five new names appeared on the panel in much larger letters.

```
<Chihu Tam> <Gerhard Bayer> <Jia Cheng>
<Lawrence Walker> <Dena Abramowicz>
```

Cowan knew those names because *everyone* knew those names. As the board of Oneworld, they ran most of the planet.

Xu tapped the side of her head. "You can't trust any data on the Sim because that data can be changed. Fortunately, if you are me, you know where to find archives."

Cowan considered Xu's claim. If Galileo was indeed Gerhard Bayer, he'd have control over every aspect of Oneworld's systems, including everything at the CID. Though it was illegal and impossible to change personnel records, it wouldn't be beyond the means of a man like Bayer.

Xu opened a picture of a pretty lady with dark hair. "We'll start with Denise Bouchard, receptionist. The second person killed by Sheila Fisher at Ventura Visions."

"She was the target?" David asked.

"She was a spy for ShangJin corporation." Xu dragged a line between the dead woman and a Oneworld board member. "Before she joined ShangJin, Denise was the personal secretary of Jia Cheng. Her first job, in fact, though you won't find that in her history. Bayer changed it."

Sonne looked to Cowan and asked, "So did Galileo shoot her because she was a spy, or because she was connected to Cheng?"

"The latter." Xu dragged another murder victim to another member of Oneworld. "Elazar Kravitz, the third person murdered by our first puppeted killer. His work history has also been amended, but archives prove he was once the personal assistant of Board Member Dena Abramowicz."

Cowan saw the pattern now, assuming Xu was right about the data being altered. "So Galileo is . . . what?" he began. "Killing interns and assistants of the board of Oneworld? Why?"

"You don't start by killing your target's family," David said quietly. "You kill people they know, tangentially, to show your targets you *can* kill their family."

"If you start by killing the people closest to them," Jeb added, "they don't have anyone left to lose. You have no leverage."

"That's sick," Sonne whispered.

"And smart," Xu said. "Leverage is everything."

"Are there others?" Cowan asked. Because he was starting to see how fucked they really were.

"April Cooper." Xu dragged that name to another Oneworld member. "Personal chef for Lawrence Walker, until she left him to open her own restaurant. The third puppeted shooting targeted her restaurant, and April with it."

"Was that before or after Sheila Fisher?" Cowan asked.

"Before," Jeb said. "Sheila was the last."

"That just leaves Chihu Tam and Gerhard Bayer," Kate said. "Who are the victims connected to them?"

Xu looked at Kate, her lips pressing together. "Tam was one of Benzai Corporation's principal investors, was he not?"

Kate sat back at her desk, wearing a thousand-meter gaze. "My father . . . Galileo attacked my father and left him in a coma to send a message to Tam?"

"If we accept this pattern, it's a motive that makes sense."

"So who's Bayer's connection?" Sonne asked.

Xu turned to face them. "There isn't one. Gerhard Bayer is Galileo."

"Now hold on." Cowan could see the possibilities, but he didn't know how Xu could put it all together so fast. "How long have you believed this?"

"Since yesterday night."

Jeb stepped forward. "So because no one connected to Bayer was killed in these puppeting rampages, you believe he's Galileo? What if Galileo just hasn't hit him yet?"

"All four rampages occurred in a three-week period. It has now been two months. No more rampages. None who worked for or with Gerhard Bayer have had their work history altered, unlike the other four members. This is the only conclusion that fits."

"Sorry," Jeb said. "That's not enough."

"Um . . ." Cowan did a quick search of his PBA archives and verified the sick intuition now infecting his brain. "Shit."

"Yes," Xu said. "That adequately describes our situation."

Cowan felt like the floor was sinking. He could hardly get the words out. "Gerhard Bayer was one of the founders of Mind Games. I worked on PBA firmware for him. I worked on *the* PBA firmware with Ellen, for him." His voice dropped to a whisper. "I made firmware that let him murder dozens of people."

"No," Sonne said.

Cowan couldn't see past all the dead and sobbing faces in his head. Sheila Fisher, her parents, all those others. He had been staring at their killer all this time, and it had simply never occurred to him to check his own employment history.

Sonne knelt beside him, gripping his shoulder. "You're not responsible, Cowan. You didn't know."

Ellen had said the same to Cowan, but what did that matter? What was done, was done.

Sonne continued. "And because you know how he's doing it, you may be one of the only people who can stop him. So pull your shit together and focus on the problem."

Sonne's hands were warmer than he expected. They even tingled, and he looked at her, finally. She was looking at him like she didn't hate him.

"We'll find a way to take down Gerhard Bayer," Sonne said, "and then we'll find out what happened to Ellen. If she's alive, we'll find her."

"There is no possible way we can defeat a man on the board of Oneworld," Xu said dismissively. "We are, to the last, doomed."

Sonne stood and faced her. "Bullshit. Doctor, you doxxed one of the most powerful men on the planet in thirty minutes. Cowan designed PBA firmware that can fool the entire Sim. Kate created the strongest dynamic firewalls I've ever seen, and we've got an experienced CID detective and an Army Ranger to support our badass cyborg bodyguard." She nodded toward Lucy. "We'll destroy Bayer."

"Assuming you can find him," Xu said, "which you won't—"

"Huan—" Kate said.

"—and convince the CID to let you arrest him, which they won't—"

"Really—" Kate added.

"—because the board of Oneworld runs the CID, and the board of Oneworld doesn't want Bayer to murder their families."

Kate sighed as loudly as she could. "I'm starting to remember why we broke up."

Xu plopped down in an ergochair. "I'm starting to remember all the lousy sex."

Sonne rolled her eyes and turned to Jeb. "So we put Bayer's info on the darkSim. If we drop these revelations in enough places, it'll incriminate him. He can't take them all down."

Jeb shook his head. "Bayer would suppress anything we dropped, and it might force him to do something desperate, like update the firmware of everyone on the planet."

After a moment, Sonne said, "Oh . . ."

Cowan wished he could find the will to speak more. Sonne looked so strong and brave as she made suggestions, certain they would survive. He wanted to be like her.

Jeb continued. "If we push Bayer, he'll push back. So before we make any move against him, we have to be certain we'll push him off a cliff."

"You can't beat him," Xu said again. "We won't—"

"Stop it!" Cowan shouted. "Stop saying that!" He had caused this. He was responsible. And checking out of reality right now wasn't going to help anyone. He strode into the center of the room.

He swept his gaze over everyone, drawing strength from their attention. "Sonne's right. We're fighting this. We're taking Bayer down, and we're doing it together. You know, I never wanted to drag any of you into this, but we're in it now. I'm with Sonne."

He didn't look at her. He wasn't sure he *could* look at her, not without losing his focus. Like she'd said, they were done when this was over.

"Forresters," Sonne said, "how long before you flip your PBAs back on?"

"Long enough," David replied. "We'll keep all our work on this to offline only, as we've been doing. All that's changed is our mission. Right, Jeb?"

Jeb grimaced, tapping his foot as if thinking it over. "Right," he said, finally.

"So . . ." Sonne looked around. "Where do we start?"

Jeb stopped tapping his foot. "We start by proving Xu's claim. Everyone in this room is now a team of independent investigators, working outside the CID and Benzai Corporation to learn the location of Gerhard Bayer and find the evidence we need to expose him. We live by taking Bayer down."

"Also," Kate said, "we're going to save my father."

"And we'll save your father," Jeb said.

"Damn . . ." Lucy sighed by the door. "There go all my vacation days."

PART 8

42

REED

OCTOBER 5, EARLY MORNING

Office of Mental Health Director Matthew Reed glanced at the UPX package on his kitchen countertop. It bore a stamp marking it as from his office: the letters OMH.

What had he ordered? Was it someone's birthday? No, Linda's birthday wasn't for two more months. Had the secretaries baked him some cookies or something?

He hated cookies, but Linda had a sweet tooth and loved the real thing. Who was Matthew to tell his employees not to bake for her? Morale was important.

The people he oversaw at the Office of Mental Health ensured the billions now protected by PBAs lived happy lives. He owed it to the world to ensure they weren't unduly alarmed by what isolated murders and crimes still occurred. So much violence had been slipping into the real world these past few weeks that his job was growing more and more difficult, but he would protect the world's people as best he could.

"Honey?" He contacted Linda over wireless. *"Did you bring in a package from the office this morning?"*

"It's on the counter." Linda was already hard at work in the spare room down the hall, connected via hardlink to the immigrant processing system. Apparently, some anti-immigrant cybercriminal had recently scrambled their database.

"*I know that, honey,*" Matthew said. "*I'm looking right at it. When did it arrive?*"

"*Some time in the night. Listen, I've got a massive backlog today. Talk later?*" Linda's connection went dark.

He sighed. She was always so busy, though, so was he. They'd never even had time to discuss a family, but he hoped one day. Maybe he could retire, and they could focus on that—bringing a child into the unified world he worked to preserve.

A bright red prompt appeared before Matthew's eyes in augmented reality. He was overdue for a firmware update, though he didn't remember one being scheduled. The update was marked urgent, but he still took a moment to check the Oneworld verification document.

Everything was secure and approved. He initiated the download.

As the new firmware installed, Matthew picked up the package and gave it a shake. Nothing moved, and it was too heavy for cookies.

He tapped the unseal button. The package whisked open. Inside was a handgun, a gleaming, metal instrument of death just like those he'd used when he used to play StrikeForceGo.

Matthew stared at the gun, incredulous. Who would send him a handgun? Who could even buy one these days?

Was this a threat from those Natural Body nuts? Another warning that modding people's behaviors was somehow against God's will, or man's will, or whatever those idiots were spouting these days? Did they really think that locking people away in tiny concrete rooms was better?

His PBA pinged him that the new firmware finished installing.

Just to reassure himself, Matthew glanced out the window. The five milsynths guarding his estate stood at attention, and there were no people outside. More milsynths secured the driveway gate. No terrorists could possibly reach him here.

Out of curiosity, Matthew picked up the gun. Its weight was impressive, far heavier than in the Sim. Was it loaded? He wasn't sure how to check.

He was just about to set it down when his arms suddenly straightened of their accord. His legs went stiff. It felt like iron bars had sprouted inside his limbs, and those bars moved.

"What the hell?"

His limbs sent him walking around his kitchen island, holding that glistening handgun, but he wasn't controlling the walking. He was being walked.

"Linda? Linda!"

No answer. He moved confidently, the gun balanced in his joined hands, pointed straight ahead as he strode down the clean wooden hall. Morning sunlight poured in through his crystal-clear windows. How was this happening?

Matthew tried to ping 911, but the ping wouldn't go through. He tried to contact his wife, but her wireless wouldn't respond. He struggled as his feet continued down the hallway, legs marching toward the closed door of their spare room. Linda's home office.

"Linda!" he shouted again. Panic squeezed his throat. "Get out! Go out the window! Run!"

She threw open the door and glared at him. She wore green silk pajamas, her blond hair in disarray like it always was before she showered. Her eyes widened as Matthew pointed the gun at her chest.

"Matty?" she whispered.

Revulsion filled him. His muscles ached as he fought with every fiber of his being to move his arms. His vision went black, his stomach roiling as clear circuit algorithms ensured he couldn't do what he was about to do. His finger twitched and pressed regardless.

Bang!

43

COWAN

Cowan Soto knew what he would see when he disabled his mental health filters, which was why he couldn't. He stood with Jeb in the living room of a $30 million home in Carmel Valley. That home belonged to the director of the Office of Mental Health, or had . . . until Matthew Reed murdered his wife, then shot himself in the head.

The home's ceiling was real wood, not the holo-projected kind. Silvery lamps hung from it, and midday light flooded in through gorgeous tall windows looking out at a backyard filled with healthy trees. Reed's army of milsynths were gone, seized to be tested for rogue scripting.

A thick red recliner sat in the living room, backrest down, and that was where Matthew Reed's body was now. The body Cowan's filters wouldn't let him see. Now that they knew who Galileo was, seeing a dead body just made him picture what his own inevitable end might be.

VCD Sergeant Terry Sparks stood by the chair, eyes distant as he archived the scene. Melissa Bradley was checking hardlinks outside. Marquez was on street duty, keeping gawkers away, and Captain Barondale and Zhang were on another case.

Jeb patted Cowan on the back. "Here's what you're going to do. You're going to search the home VI's logs for all entries and exits in the last twelve hours. Check call logs for the last two weeks. Isolate and flag any links to people who are rare in the call log, someone Reed didn't talk to on a regular basis. Archive anything that resembles a threat."

"Okay." Cowan closed his eyes and flipped over to his head desk, where a glowing blue mailbox floated in virtual space: the home's VI interface. He plucked out flattened log sheets, scanning them through his PBA in rapid succession.

Matthew Reed had shot his wife, Linda, seven times, and then walked into the living room and shot himself. What type of a monster could do that?

Reed was a clear circuit—he and his wife had the latest PBAs, with upgraded corporate firewalls—so even if he was angry enough to have wanted to, Reed *couldn't* shoot his own family.

Someone had committed a cybercrime.

Cowan found no unusual calls. No unexpected visits. He found the archive footage from this morning intact, waiting to be viewed, and didn't view it. Couldn't bear to. He uploaded it to the CID instead and hopped back into meatspace.

"I've run the forensic scan of the furnishings against their home-owner's insurance," Jeb said, as if noticing his eyes refocus. "Nothing missing."

"I'm empty too." Cowan walked toward the kitchen island and stared at the open UPX package on the counter. "That package held the gun."

"Yep."

"Who sent the package?" Cowan turned to Sparks. "Is there a return address?"

Sparks shrugged. "It's a dead end. We had Marquez run it when we arrived."

"Where's the dead end?"

"The billing and shipping address UPX provided is a PO Box in a post office in Houston, owned by a corporate entity with no reported income or expenses, owned by another corporate entity that's over two hundred years old. Nothing in the system."

"Do they pay their taxes?" Jeb asked.

"Never had to," Sparks said. "No income. But they file a tax report each year."

"Who filed it?"

"A guy who died thirty years ago. Texas CID is running down the fraudulent record, but I don't think they'll get anywhere. Houston lost most of its paper records in Hurricane Rick, back in '45."

"There's got to be hundreds of corporations like that," Cowan said. "Zombies with corporate accounts. And the package was certified?"

"That's something Corporate One needs to run down," Sparks said. "But yeah. Special delivery."

"So, why would Reed do it?" Assuming he actually did, which, after Xu's misdirection, Cowan no longer assumed anything.

"Your guess is as good as mine," Sparks said. "Maybe they had an argument. Maybe Reed's wife pissed him off, and he decided to punish her. All sorts of bad shit has been happening lately."

Cowan resisted the urge to snap at Sparks. "But this guy was the head of the Office of Mental Health! If anyone was going to be balanced enough *not* to shoot their family, wouldn't it be the director of the OMH?"

Sparks just shrugged again, and Cowan shuddered. He couldn't help it. PBAs were supposed to stop horrors like this, but now this horrific shit happened once a week. How had people survived back when people shot each other on purpose around the world?

"UPX has no record of any transaction involving a handgun," Jeb said. "Did the sender pay for the shipping?"

Cowan hopped back into the Sim because he needed to do *something*. He pulled up yesterday's archives. He started with the night before the murders.

He accelerated playback and overclocked his PBA. It didn't matter that overclocking his PBA meant he would lose time back in meatspace. He needed to see where the Reed family had broken themselves apart.

Matthew and Linda sat side-by-side and watched a movie, her legs over his lap. It was a romantic comedy that gave them a few chuckles. After that, they fell asleep together. Linda worked at home and Matthew went off to work.

Linda made dinner: a salad, a meat soup, and fresh vegetables chopped into tiny circles. She surprised Matthew with the homecooked meal and they embraced.

They ate, kissed, and went into the bedroom. When the clothes started coming off Cowan blanked the image and skipped an hour—that was their business—and found them sleeping once again, Matthew's back against Linda's.

This was the last night their relationship existed, and it wasn't the type of night that would cause Matthew Reed to end it first thing in the morning.

Cowan blinked back to meatspace to find Jeb watching him. Sparks was gone. He'd been in the archives for a while.

Cowan checked his head desk. He'd lost thirty minutes since he overclocked, but these people had lost the rest of their lives. Someone had to see that they got justice.

"Semigood news, the bodies are gone," Jeb said, "and forensics has cleared the scene. So you can turn off your filters. The bad news, we've got another case, and fatalities. Someone sent an autocar into a crowd on Mission Beach."

Any other time, news of that crime would have floored Cowan, but now, it was just another statistic. Cowan remembered Linda and Matthew eating together and falling asleep. They hadn't fought, and they hadn't slept in separate rooms, and they hadn't done anything but love each other, simply.

"I don't think he did it," Cowan said.

Jeb glanced at the empty recliner. "Me either. But, why?"

"They were happy. They were still in love."

"You watched their archives? How far back?"

"Far enough. Reed had no reason to murder his family."

"You never know what passes between people over time, Cowan. Something could have happened years ago, and it just bubbled up in an argument this morning."

"Reed didn't do this."

"What's your proof?" The hint of warning in Jeb's voice was a reminder that the CID was listening to everything they said. That meant Galileo might be listening too.

Cowan returned to the kitchen island and stared at the empty UPX box. "Why did he buy a gun? It couldn't be self-defense."

"Why not?" Jeb asked, because their entire conversation was being archived for Director Stanton.

"He didn't need a gun for self-defense. He had a milsynth army and a security system, and besides, no clear circuit can use a weapon on another human being. It wouldn't do him any good."

"But he wasn't clear, remember? He jailbroke his PBA. This morning's archives show him shooting his own family."

"We have no proof he jailbroke his PBA, and archives can be faked if you have the resources. How many bullets does a gun like this hold?"

"Eight," Jeb said.

"Which is what he used, exactly. Seven in his wife, and one in his own head. Who counts bullets during a crime of passion?"

Jeb shrugged. "If Reed altered his PBA, he could easily have firewalled empathy before or after he bought the gun. He could have felt perfectly rational."

"Yet he didn't buy it," Cowan said. "Remember? No records." It was exhausting having to puzzle their way to a conclusion since they couldn't just talk honestly, but this was the game they were in now.

Jeb looked at the package. "And if you're buying a handgun with cash, why risk getting flagged by UPX? Five grand in Encanto will get you an unregistered gun today."

"The day you decide to murder your wife."

Jeb tapped his chin and shook his head. "It's still not enough. Reed was on the corporate network the whole time, pinging clear the whole time. Even the best loose circuits we've encountered can't connect with their behavioral protocols offline."

Except they could—Cowan could—and Jeb's bald lie made his implication clear. Jeb also saw the possibility that Galileo could be behind this. They couldn't let anyone at the CID know what they suspected, because it might get back to Galileo.

So if Galileo had done this, how? Cowan considered the problem. How would he hack a corporate executive's PBA if he wanted to?

Brute force wouldn't work. Corporate firewalls were too good, and PBAs as secure as Reed's kept their firmware locked unless fed specific override codes by Corporate One. So Galileo had used those override codes. He had created new firmware signed by Corporate One, then tricked Reed into downloading it.

That suggested Galileo had puppeted Reed into shooting his wife while Reed watched and screamed. It also meant Cowan couldn't tell Jeb what had happened, at least not while Jeb's PBA was still active. He'd have to wait until night when his partner was issued his privacy hours.

"I guess you're right," Cowan said. "There's no way anyone could bypass a corporate PBA. That's impossible."

"I know this is traumatic." Jeb took Cowan's shoulder and steered him to the car. "Don't let it get under your skin."

Cowan again replayed Matthew and Linda's last day alive. How could Galileo murder a loving couple? What could he possibly gain by slaughtering the director of the OMH?

It was time to enter the darkSim and find out.

44
JEB

OCTOBER 5, BEFORE MIDNIGHT

Fresh into another night without his PBA active, Jeb arrived at Club Sylvan, dressed for dancing and general carousing. David would be here later, but they'd agreed to come separately to avoid attention. Their actual purpose, of course, was to covertly plan their next move against Galileo, as a team.

Jeb entered Kate's office to find her sitting behind her desk, watching Sonne futz with a building model on their oversized wall panel. Kate wore a pink hoodie and light gray sweats, a contrast to the mimetic dresses she seemed so fond of, and Sonne wore the same.

So they had matching pajamas. That was just adorable. Doctor Xu was nowhere in sight, so was likely off getting some shut-eye.

As Jeb entered, Kate balanced her elbows on her desk and her chin on upturned palms. "Detective Forrester! What's our agenda for the weekend? How shall we conspire?"

Jeb wished he could look that happy and content. "We caught a case today, and it was nasty. Cowan figured . . ." He stopped and glanced around. "Where *is* Cowan?"

Sonne turned from the panel, brow furrowed. "He's not with you?"

Maybe she wasn't as done with Cowan as she claimed.

"He was supposed to meet us here." Jeb measured his worry. "We staggered our arrival so it wouldn't seem odd for us to hit the same club, but our shift ended four hours ago."

"Don't you have any other way to contact him?"

"Not with my PBA offline." Jeb glanced at Kate, then Sonne. "Can one of you ping him?"

"Oh!" Kate said, blinking. "We won't have to. He just called! I'll put it up on the big screen."

A man-sized raven wearing a bright red fez appeared on the large panel behind Kate's desk, lengthy yellow tassel drooped across one shoulder. Its eyes glowed a soft red.

"Sorry I couldn't be there," an avatar labeled as Corvus said. "Got delayed, but something was bugging me."

Kate turned her chair to face him. "I am incredibly jealous of that hat."

Jeb stared at Cowan's avatar, eyes wide. "*You're* Corvus?"

"Yup!" Cowan replied and tilted his raven head. "You've heard of me?"

Jeb frowned. "They've literally written scenarios about catching you into CID training records. You're currently number three on the most wanted cybercriminal list. And you didn't think to mention that?"

"Stop fanboying," Sonne said. "Yes, it's him. Yes, he's good at what he does. Now, can we get back to stopping the mass-murdering asshole trying to kill everyone?"

Jeb let it go. With a board member of Oneworld trying to kill them, he had far bigger worries than catching a known cybercriminal. And also . . . all of Corvus's crimes had been largely victimless. He was wanted because he'd embarrassed corporations, not hurt people.

Cowan cleaned his throat. "We caught a brutal case today. The director of the Office of Mental Health got puppeted into killing his family, and we think Galileo used a firmware patch to compromise him."

Kate covered her mouth. "Matthew Reed? No, that's not possible. I would have heard. We all would have heard."

"The OMH suppressed the news, obviously," Jeb said. He recognized the irony in that as well as anyone. "But yes, our victims today were Matthew and Linda Reed."

Kate turned pale. "I knew him. Not well, but I introduced him to Linda . . . to his wife. We attended Harvard together."

Jeb let Kate adjust. He had seen a lot of death, but Kate hadn't. And even with as much death as Jeb had seen, it still affected him.

Sonne squeezed Kate's shoulder. Kate breathed, deep breaths, then patted Sonne's hand. She blinked against a bit of wet and wiped one eye.

Kate focused on Cowan. "Do you have any theories as to why someone would go after Matthew Reed?"

"Well . . ." Cowan said. "I think he killed Reed to take over the Office of Mental Health."

Jeb frowned. This was a reach, but Cowan wasn't a rookie anymore. He was starting to become a decent detective.

"We're listening," Jeb said. "Lay out your case, Detective Soto."

Cowan snapped his avatar's beak. "Right. So, we already know Galileo used puppeted people to kill those close to Oneworld board members. To threaten them. He's also selling all sorts of scripts on the darkSim to cause chaos, like he did to Sarah Taggart, Joseph Dunn, and others. Finally, he made Doctor Xu sell Tian to finance his whole operation."

"And a corporate CTO doesn't need money," Kate said thoughtfully. "So what's his true motive?"

"I'll get there soon," Cowan said. "First, I need to tell you about what happened with Protection Services. Galileo forced their CEO to change the operational parameters of synthcops so they'd ignore murder. If he controlled synthcops, that'd give him the biggest army on the planet."

"But you stopped him, didn't you?" Kate asked.

"Sure, that one time. But his attempt suggests he's trying to seize every lever of power in Oneworld for himself. And if he assumed Reed wouldn't cooperate . . ."

Cowan left the question hanging, and Jeb nodded approvingly. Sonne was the one who spoke first, however.

"So who's next in line to command the OMH?" Sonne asked.

"Exactly," Cowan said. "Kathleen Warren, deputy director, is now the de facto head of the OMH, at least until Oneworld appoints a new director officially. And since it's a five-person board, they can't . . . at least not until Galileo, who is Gerhard Bayer, a member of that board, agrees."

Kate went quiet for a second, then tossed a picture of an older woman with short graying hair onto the screen. "Kathleen Warner." She paused. "And . . . oh my goodness. She ran Corporate Security not long ago."

"She ran it when CorpSec took Ellen," Cowan said grimly. "So either Galileo is blackmailing her, or she's working with him. Either way . . . Galileo now controls the Office of Mental Health. What else does he need?"

Jeb nodded approval. Cowan had connected the dots like a trained detective, and that left a feeling of pride on Jeb's gut. Yet he was still making too many assumptions. They couldn't be sure until they knew more.

"It's a good theory, Cowan. But we can't be sure until I take a run at Warren. I need to get in a room with her, see how she thinks."

Sonne stared. "And you can just call up the OMH director?"

"I have an in," Jeb said. "Sarisa Bassa, a highly placed OMH counselor. She's a good friend. She'll get me in to see Warner without questions."

"Not a good idea," Cowan said. "If you go into the Office of Mental Health, and Warren figures out you suspect her, you won't be walking out. You need a better plan. Also, we shouldn't even think about moving on Warren until we know where Bayer is right now."

"Have you got a better plan?" Jeb asked. "Because if so, I'll hear it."

Cowan tilted his avatar's head. "Actually . . . I think I might?"

45

SONNE

"Rise and shine, honey," Kate whispered in Sonne's ear.

Sonne blinked against bright light and forced her eyes open. She remained inside Kate's private plane. It had finally landed at Memphis International, and Sonne had slept through the touchdown. She spotted a sleek black autocar through the window, waiting.

That car would drive them to UPX headquarters in downtown Memphis, where they would meet with Adrian Montes, the current CEO of UPX. It was there they would find out if Sonne's hunch was actually solid.

She knew from her own experience in buying repurposed simBeds that it was unlikely Doctor Barkov had been able to purchase the expensive surgical equipment to implant black-market PBAs without help. Given his connection to Galileo, Galileo might have sent him equipment through UPX.

Step one of taking Galileo down was finding evidence of his collusion with the Russian mob and cybercriminals, and it was Kate who'd suggested contacting Adrian Montes, CEO of UPX, directly. They'd told Montes about Sonne's abduction by the Russian mob and claimed Barkov was connected, which gave them an excuse to snoop without mentioning Galileo.

If everything went well today, they might be able to trace whatever equipment Galileo sent to Doctor Barkov back to him. Or . . . they might not.

Sonne herself hadn't gotten much sleep the past week. Nobody slept well with a psychopathic Oneworld board member after them, particularly one who was willing to make a husband kill his own wife.

"Any other news about Doctor Xu?" Sonne worked out the kinks in her muscles. "Is simNews still speculating about her disappearance?"

"Not a peep," Kate said, "and today's been all about Galaxia announcing some charity concert in LA. Seriously! SimNews is desperate to cover anything that's not murder."

"That's good. Isn't it? It buys us time to track the mob connection."

While they remained seated, Lucy descended the airstair in loafers, dark slacks, and a suit jacket with breakaway arms, just in case she had to use her stunners. She would secure the runway because that was necessary now, apparently. Sonne hated this feeling of being *hunted*.

"Maybe," Kate said. "But if I hear Galaxia's pitchy single one more time, I'm redacting it."

"Clear," Lucy said, inside their PBAs.

Kate strolled down the airplane stairs as confident as across flat ground, even while wearing her high heels and a stretchy skirt, though she wore those every day. Sonne popped off her heels and walked down barefoot instead. She was dressed for corporate work: knee-length pencil skirt, dark heels, and a white button-down tucked beneath a crisp blue blazer. It didn't fit her, but she had to look the part.

The three of them entered their corporate-reserved autocar, a secured Benzai Corporation model. It was bulletproof, with a firewalled VI and manual controls that could override that VI if necessary. Kate wasn't taking any chances after what had happened on Cowan and Sonne's date. A date Sonne now remembered in its entirety . . .

Kate had reuploaded that whole night to Sonne's brain last night, .succumbing to her endless badgering about what *really* happened. Sonne now knew that Cowan hadn't, as Kate had told her to protect her, been "kind of a dick."

Instead, Cowan had sacrificed his opportunity to escape the terrifying Mister Gray just for the chance to stop Sonne from being trafficked. They'd risked their lives to save each other less than a month ago, and remembering how she'd felt about Cowan that night made it harder to know how to feel now.

As much as she hated how he had used her, she understood why he'd done it, and she finally had an inkling of how damaged he must be.

Cowan had spent the last year blaming himself for everything that happened to his fiancée. Having nightmares about her fate. No one had ever loved *Sonne* enough to lobotomize themselves. That might leave a few mental scars.

It was a long drive to the UPX headquarters, and the view off the highway was no more interesting than it was everywhere else, square buildings and gray sky and green trees. Lucy and Kate spent most of the ride strategizing about how they'd respond if the car was hacked, or if someone started shooting at them, or if they got chased by a truck and had to shoot out its tires. Sonne only half-listened since she was so focused on Cowan, but she suspected Kate might actually be enjoying the hypotheticals. She always had been an adrenaline junkie.

Finally, as Kate and Lucy discussed how they might take down an enemy helicopter, their autocar pulled up to the headquarters of United Postal Express. It was a large one-story building, square and gray, surrounded by dozens of identical buildings. A tall chain-link fence surrounded the whole thing, with barbed wire on top. A sign promised electrocution and death, followed by a fine.

An armed milsynth led them through the empty lobby, furnished only with plastic chairs, to a reinforced elevator guarded by two more milsynths. They descended to a subbasement where a stark concrete hallway greeted them. UPX had stronger security than some banks because no self-respecting corporation wanted its mail stolen.

This particular subbasement was big enough to hold Sonne's parlor many times over. Dozens of rows of sleek back servers hummed quietly. It was also as cold as a walk-in freezer, and Sonne hugged her blazer tight. Stupid dress codes.

Light flickered, and then Adrian Montes appeared in a crisp gray Italian suit. The CEO of UPX was tall with a perfect tan, equally perfect teeth, and spiky black hair cut short around his head.

"Kate! How wonderful to see you, my dear!"

Though Sonne knew this was just a hologram, it looked almost as real as the real man. This room had excellent projection capabilities.

"I apologize for not meeting you myself, but vacation calls," he said.

"No problem," Kate said, a bit loudly. Standing this close to this amount of raw computing power had probably left her overstimulated. "I really appreciate your help."

"It was the least I could do, after hearing about your friend's abduction. How on earth did you get crosswise with Russian mobsters?"

Kate tapped one toeless shoe. "Terminal, please?"

A metal panel in the floor rolled back and a terminal rose, rigged for manual entry and linklines. Adrian fixed Sonne with a thousand-watt smile.

"Who is your new *asistente?*" he asked.

"That's Sonne," Kate said, as she moved to the terminal. "She's the friend who those mobsters abducted. She's also not my assistant, just dressed that way for appearances."

"Hi," Sonne said.

"My apologies," Adrian said. "I didn't mean to assume."

"None necessary," Sonne assured him. At least she *looked* like a personal assistant.

Adrian turned back to Kate. "But seriously, how many times have I suggested you increase your security?"

"Too many," Lucy chimed in.

Kate popped her linkline into the archive terminal, and Sonne felt very much like a third wheel. She was fairly certain Kate only asked her along so Lucy could protect them both.

After a minute or so inside the terminal, Kate focused once more on the real world. "Damn and damn."

Sonne's heart sank. "Which one?"

"I traced all deliveries to Doctor Barkov. Most I could identify, but some were flagged as medical waste. That must be how they shipped illegal grayDoc gear without being flagged. They're billed to zombie corporations, so no info there."

"I should probably have my IT people look at that," Adrian said. "I'd rather we not deliver surgical equipment for the Russian mob. Liability issues, if nothing else."

Sonne's mind started working again. "Katie. Who put those packages in the mail?"

Kate blinked back into the Sim. "There's no sender listed. It's like I said, honey. You don't need an actual employee name on anything shipped from a corporate account."

"But someone had to physically deliver the package to the mailbox. Can we access those archives?"

"Sorry," Adrian said, "but I can't authorize you to dig into our surveillance archives. Not without a court order. Technically, I shouldn't even be doing this."

Kate reached for her linkline. "I appreciate all your help. I'm sorry, Sonne. I hoped—"

Sonne stepped forward. "UPX archived the postal code from where the zombie corporations shipped each package, right?" Her business experience was pecking at her brain, specifically, the spam bots constantly bombarding her *Sanctuary* account.

"Yes, but I don't see how that—"

"Humor me, Katie." Sonne felt a rush of excitement as she turned to Adrian. "You guys log everything when a package goes out, right? Size, weight?"

"And many other statistics," Adrian said. "What are you thinking?"

"Spambots," Sonne said, grinning.

After no one said anything for a moment, Lucy chimed in. "I hate those."

"Okay, do this." Sonne regarded Kate. "Pick the last medical waste box a zombie corporation shipped to Doctor Barkov in Palmdale. Grab the postal code."

"Okay . . ." Kate said. Her eyes went distant as she entered the Sim, but she was listening.

"Start with a complete list of all deliveries made to that same postal code up to three days before the package was sent off to Barkov's office."

"That's over one thousand entries, honey."

"Now filter that by received packages that match the weight and size of the package to Doctor Barkov."

"That's . . . only 114." Kate sounded pleasantly surprised. "But where do we go from here?"

"Narrow those to packages flagged as medical waste."

"22." Kate smiled wide. "Whoever shipped those packages didn't package up the pieces of surgical gear. They mailed that gear out again after receiving it from someone else."

"How did you know that?" Adrian asked.

"That's what spambots started doing," Sonne said triumphantly. "After I set my business mail filters to delete anything sent in mass. They'd hack a bunch of inactive simMail accounts, send their spam to those accounts, then have those accounts spam me individually. That way, they could trick my spam filters into thinking the mail was from an actual person."

"So the people who resent these packages were part of the Russian mob?" Adrian asked. He was getting into this now too.

"Maybe," Sonne said. "Or maybe someone they paid anonymously over the darkSim, or someone they threatened." Which she knew Galileo would have no problem doing.

"That's great and all," Kate agreed, "but even with all those parameters, we've still got twenty-two senders. Should we archive those names for the CID?"

"No, we can do better," Sonne said. "Run it again, but on every package Barkov received. All the postal codes. I bet the postal code you started with was one of the bigger ones."

Kate was silent for almost a minute, but then she bounced up and down. "Jackpot! I've got a single match, shipped from a postal code in Utah. One package delivered to a John Dixon, who sent out a package of the same weight and size the next morning."

"Where'd John Dixon get his package from?" Sonne asked.

Kate whistled. "Switzerland."

Sonne wanted to jump up and down too. Her hunch was going somewhere. "Can we trace it back from there?"

"Adrian?" Kate turned to his hologram and put on her pouty lips. "Would you mind terribly if we also took a peek at international shipments?"

Adrian stroked his chin. "That's a big ask, *mi flor*. Local records are stored here, but we'd have to ping the archive in Helsinki to get those. It'll attract attention."

Kate placed her hands on her hips. "Say, aren't you still looking to acquire *Weltweit Breifkasten*? They're the last independent postal service in Switzerland, yes?"

"We are indeed. Are you offering a trade?"

"I know one of their shareholders quite well," Kate said. "Almost as well as I know you, my dear. If you can sneak us a peak at the Switzerland shipment records, I could tell my dear friend what a great partner you'd make."

Adrian looked between the two of them, though Sonne wasn't sure why. It wasn't like she could add anything to this deal. Did he still feel bad about her getting abducted?

"Kate," Adrian said, flashing his pearly whites. "You have a deal."

"You're a dear," Kate said. "You won't regret it."

"I'm granting you temporary international access now," Adrian said. "Please keep your peek into our Helsinki records brief. Someone will almost certainly notice."

"I think we should do it anyway," Kate said. "Sonne?"

Sonne took a breath. This was a risk, a big risk, especially if Galileo was the person who noticed. Yet they needed a target to hit, and they couldn't go after Galileo until they had hard evidence to link him to Barkov, so Sonne would back Kate's call.

"Do it."

Kate blinked away into the Sim. Sonne glanced at Lucy for her opinion on this latest development, but Lucy's expression was flat and unreadable. She had cyberized most of her body over the years, but not her face. It sure seemed that way sometimes though.

"Got it," Kate shouted in obvious excitement. "This shipment originated from an actual business. M-Gesundheit, in Schaffhausen." She had no trouble with the pronunciation.

"Interesting," Adrian said.

"That's a dummy name, right?" Sonne asked.

Adrian raised one eyebrow. "A woman named Sonne can't speak German?"

She shrugged, defensive. "It was just a song I liked, okay?"

"In German," Montes said, "*gesundheit* translates to health, and the M in the title is for *maschine* . . . or machine, as we say it. Thus, Machine Health, which is—"

"The type of company who makes surgical equipment to implant PBAs." Sonne finished for him. "Got it."

"We did it, honey!" Kate popped her linkline. "We now know the Russian mob is working out of M-Gesundheit. We have a real lead."

Sonne knew Kate really meant Galileo but was more impressed with how easily Kate had convinced Adrian Montes to work with them. Her sister really did know how to navigate the corporate world. Sonne was more impressed by that, now, than she had been before seeing it herself.

They'd done it. They knew where Galileo was hiding out, *finally*, or at least where to find where he was hiding out. A warm swell of pride filled her chest.

For the first time, maybe the only time, Galileo had screwed up.

PART 9

46

JEB

OMH Counselor Sarisa Bassa stood beside Jeb as the doors of Corporate One's silver elevator closed them in, wearing her dress uniform. "So, how many favors do you owe me now? Two? Three?"

"It's not my fault you haven't hit any cases requiring assistance from the CID," Jeb replied. "If anything, you should blame your own competence."

The elevator started upward, toward the top of Corporate One—the nerve center of the Office of Mental Health. Toward a confrontation with Deputy Director Kathleen Warren, who just might be a serial killer.

Jeb was nervous. Anyone would be nervous.

He had left his armored duster in his apartment, though if he got into a fight with Warren's private army, it wouldn't be of much use. Instead, he wore a dress shirt, black slacks, and a heavy suit jacket. Heavy, because it held things. Hopefully, Warren wouldn't notice.

The elevator's back wall was a mirror. Jeb wondered how many people were watching them from the glass. The elevator rose so smoothly it was easy to forget it was moving.

Sarisa checked her hair in the mirror. "You have no idea how difficult it was for me to schedule a consultation on short notice. It's been hellish here since Director Reed died."

"Actually," Jeb said, "I do. And I really do appreciate it. I'll make it up to you."

"Just tell me why you really wanted to speak to Warren, later. After you close your case."

Jeb winced inside. Sarisa knew he wasn't being straight with her, but she trusted him enough not to press him. That was how Jeb knew he could trust *her*.

Eventually, the elevator opened to the penthouse used by the Office of Mental Health's director. Milsynths stood within, armed with automatic rifles that could blow a hole through Jeb the size of his fist.

Deputy Director Warren's office was big enough to accommodate all the cubes at the CID. That was the type of office you got when you were elected by corporate fiat as the director of the Office of Mental Health, except Warren *hadn't* been elected. She was here because Matthew Reed was dead, and he had to discover if she'd planned that.

A massive oak desk sat before a huge window overlooking San Diego Bay. It was reinforced, bulletproof glass protected by a roof-mounted turret system that could shoot down everything from full size RPGs to individual bullets.

Sarisa led Jeb past statues exuding a Greek vibe, busts of famous people Jeb could probably identify with a cursory simSearch, and a pristine cavalry sword atop a raised platform. Matthew Reed's former office was as much museum as workspace, so what did these decorations say about him? It felt strange to think about, now that Reed was dead.

Reed's desk was abandoned, but a ceiling panel slid open to reveal a holo-projector. It hummed to life as a virtual projection of Deputy Director Kathleen Warren appeared in a gray pantsuit, life-sized, behind her desk. Had he not seen her appear, Jeb would swear she was really here.

"Detective Forrester. Tell me what you need," Warren said, wasting no time with pleasantries.

"I need your help with an open case," Jeb said, and that wasn't a lie. "Your deceased director, Matthew Reed."

"We were all saddened by that tragedy." Warren didn't sound saddened. "How can I assist the CID?"

"I was hoping you might have some idea why it happened."

"Do you have any reason to believe it was anything other than a routine jailbreak?"

Jeb needed to be careful how much he revealed. "Not yet. We've simply taken our investigation as far as we can take it without more data. At this point, our biggest open question is Matthew Reed's state of mind before the killings."

"His state of mind?"

"It's my understanding that the OMH conducts regular psych evals on all officers in the corporate hierarchy, to ensure they're handling the unusual stress of their jobs."

Warren's eyes narrowed. "I'm afraid those evaluations are classified, Detective."

"In most cases, I'd agree, but Reed is now deceased, as is his wife. As such, I hoped you'd allow the CID to review those archives. In strict confidence, of course."

"How will that help you?"

"I'm looking for signs Reed was under enough stress to kill his family."

"Do you have evidence suggesting Reed was not?"

Was she trying to warn him off, or was this just standard corporate Cover Your Ass?

"We're just trying to be thorough, ma'am," Jeb said. Not a lie, exactly. Lies were dangerous.

"I appreciate you being thorough," she said. "Though I cannot reveal specifics, I can confirm Matthew Reed was under a great deal of stress. You may be aware that rumors of paralysis and puppetings have been spreading among people across the Sim. The board of Oneworld was not happy about that. There was talk of ousting Reed as CEO."

Jeb of course knew that reports of cybercrimes had been increasing since Galileo started selling his dangerous scripts on the darkSim, but that seemed a flimsy reason for Matthew Reed to off his family.

"What about his personal relationships, ma'am?" Jeb asked.

"Apparently, the stress of dealing with the recent increase in cybercrime also caused significant marital problems with his wife, though both Reeds refused our offers of counseling. Divorce was mentioned. It seems that tension was thicker than we believed."

"I see," Jeb said, as a chill ran up his spine.

If Cowan was right about the archives he'd watched, about the last night Matthew and Linda Reed spent together, happy and loving and content . . . Director Kathleen Warren had just lied to his face.

So, Warren was either working with Galileo, and had been since she ran Corporate Security years ago, or she was being blackmailed by him. Either way, she was another obstacle between him and Gerhard Bayer. She was also an obstacle powerful enough to be able to burn him a new mind.

"With your approval," Jeb said, "I'd like to resolve Reed's case as a murder-suicide and close it out."

Hopefully, that was what she wanted. Hopefully she would let it go.

"Then it seems you have all you need," Warren said. "Anything else?"

"No ma'am."

Her projection vanished, though Jeb doubted she was gone. She was watching him right now, deciding how much he knew about her. Deciding whether or not she needed to arrest him. Jeb had a feeling he'd just met Galileo's second-in-command.

"What's this really about?" Sarisa asked, looking disappointed. "You didn't honestly believe the deputy director would release psych evals for a corporate CEO."

"Just covering our bases," Jeb said.

Sarisa's eyes flicked almost imperceptibly to Warren's desk. "I'll escort you out."

"I appreciate the assist."

"Mhmm."

Sarisa walked for the elevator.

Jeb kept his eyes forward as they passed the milsynths. None moved. If Warren was going to make a move, it didn't involve bullets, yet. Jeb watched the bots in the mirror at the back of the elevator. He turned to face them as the doors closed and the elevator started down. His heart thumped in his chest.

Jeb's amplifiers caught the slightest intake of breath from Sarisa. Something had surprised her, no, worse. Shocked her. Some order she'd received over her wireless. Perhaps Director Warren had just told her he was going to be arrested.

The elevator slid to a stop. The doors opened. Two men stood outside, big men in crisp gray suits thick enough to hide the weapons under their jackets.

"Hello," one man said. The other didn't say anything.

Jeb and Sarisa stepped back as both men entered the elevator and turned their backs. That meant Jeb couldn't see their eyes. Probably because their eyes were glowing red right now from activated HARM switches.

"You know," Jeb said, without looking at Sarisa, "I still want to buy you that drink."

Sarisa stared straight ahead. "What's stopping you?"

One man shifted. Jeb's amplifiers detected the hiss of a hand sliding into a suit jacket, the sound of metal against leather. Jeb pulled his stunner as both men pulled theirs.

A *snap-hiss* echoed as Jeb fired into one of their backs, but the man didn't go down. The armor beneath his shirt was apparently stun-resistant. As both men spun to stun him, eyes glowing red, Jeb slammed his artificial hand into one of the men's faces.

His metal palm cracked the man's nose like an anvil. He slammed into the elevator doors and went down, knocked out and bleeding. The glowing red eyes of the second man went wide—Jeb shouldn't be able to punch anyone—but he barreled forward.

Unfortunately for them, neither of these two men were friends with Cowan Soto, who'd developed unique PBA firmware that would allow Jeb to punch anyone without compromising his connection with Oneworld.

Jeb and the last man grappled and punched, smashing walls, shattering mirrors, and thumping doors. Jeb was bigger, HARM switch or not, so his only real worry was not crushing Sarisa. He didn't have a lot of room to work.

Jeb allowed a blow to his side and popped the shocker mount on his artificial hand. He jammed it against the man's temple. His victim twitched, drool spurting from his mouth.

Jeb caught the man and lowered him to the floor, wincing at the way his eyes rolled back in his head. He hoped he hadn't done any permanent damage. These men were just following orders, after all, and he didn't want them dead.

The elevator accelerated, straight down. Warren had seen what he'd done, and now she was rushing him to the ground floor where Corporate One's milsynths could take him out. Jeb retracted his stunner and popped out an invasive hardlink.

He forced it into the elevator's auxiliary port and uploaded Cowan's override algorithm. The elevator stopped, then lurched back into motion. It was under his control now, and any listening devices in its walls had been deactivated.

Sarisa hadn't drawn her stunner, even though she could have.

"You're a loose circuit," she said. There was genuine hurt in her voice. "All this time?"

"No, just recently."

He and Cowan had agreed Jeb couldn't enter the Office of Mental Health handicapped by clear circuit algorithms. Jeb ran Cowan's unique firmware now. He could hurt other humans.

"Is someone blackmailing you?" she asked. "Are you under duress?"

"I'm still me, Sarisa," he said. "I'm doing the job we've always done, together, and for the next minute, we can talk without anyone hearing us."

"Or you'll hurt me like you hurt these men?"

"I'd never hurt you, but here's the situation. Director Warren is an accessory to Matthew Reed's murder. Your boss is either behind it, or she's working with the man who is."

Sarisa shook her head. "That's ridiculous."

"Kathleen Warner is working with Galileo, real name Gerhard Bayer, and they're blackmailing the board of Oneworld by threatening to murder their families. She must suspect I'm onto them, which is why she ordered me arrested."

"You're certain of Warren's involvement? You have evidence?" The fact that Sarisa didn't dismiss his claim outright was the trust they'd earned over fifteen years.

"I do, and I'll have more soon. If you join us, you'll help stop a mass murderer. You'll remove corruption at the highest levels of Oneworld corporation. But if we fail, you'll become a fugitive. You might even end up rewritten."

This had to be Sarisa's decision. That was what he, Cowan, and Kate had decided last night. They needed all the help they could get, but they couldn't force anyone to join them and risk Galileo's wrath.

"Warren's a traitor," Sarisa said softly. She was testing it out, seeing how it felt to say it aloud. She believed him with nothing but his word to go on, and that meant more than anything.

Jeb nodded. "I'm afraid so."

"Then I'll do you more good here, inside the OMH. How do you plan to get out of here?"

Jeb glanced at the floor display. 10. 9. 8. He imagined milsynths marching toward the doors on the ground floor, weapons raised.

The floor display read "G." They passed it and kept going down. The doors eventually opened on the lowest subbasement of the Office of Mental Health. It was abandoned.

"I've got a plan," Jeb said, "but I won't share it, since you'll redact the last few minutes."

Sarisa nodded. "I've already set my PBA to redact everything after we entered the elevator. However, that means I won't remember Warren is a traitor. How much longer can we talk?"

Jeb checked his head desk. "Twenty seconds."

"Leave an archive of this conversation in our dead drop on the dark-Sim," she said. "I won't check that for another two days, which should give you plenty of time to get somewhere safe. Once I know what's going on again, I'll update the dead drop for you before I leave."

Sarisa was good at this, but she had always been good at this. The only problem, now, was ensuring the OMH didn't figure out they were working together.

"Once they have your surveillance back, hit me as hard you can," Sarisa said. "If you don't convince them I was trying to stop you, I won't be leaving this building either."

She drew her stunner and pointed it at his chest.

Regret roiled in Jeb's gut, but he knew she was right.

The moment the OMH got their viewstream back, he punched Sarisa in the stomach hard enough to throw her into the glass back of the elevator. It was way too easy with Cowan's algorithm in place, which scared him to his core. This was how easy it used to be for humanity to destroy each other.

Sarisa dropped on impact and slumped, gasping.

Jeb stared at her a few seconds, then sprinted into the ancient sub-basement. He looked for the ductwork he'd memorized earlier and imagined the drainage tunnel beneath it.

Pulling a brick-sized charge from inside his suit jacket, he stuck it to the floor, and took cover as fast as he could.

47

COWAN

Cowan winced, hoping not to jostle anyone, as he and Sonne slid her dad's stretcher into a self-driving private ambulance. He had been worried someone would stop them from removing Taylor Lambda, but they'd been just two more faces in the ever-growing crowd. Given the overcrowding problem at Sharp Memorial, the doctors there were all too eager to let Kate move a comatose patient to a private facility.

They'd all agreed Jeb wouldn't enter the Office of Mental Health until *after* Kate and Sonne's father was safe. Assuming things went badly at the OMH, with Kathleen Warren, Jeb might tip their hand, which put everyone in danger. Cowan didn't want anyone arrested.

Once their ambulance was on the road, Cowan glanced at Sonne, dressed in black jeans and a leather jacket thick enough to hide the Kevlar underneath. She wasn't looking at him. She was looking at her comatose father, her eyes a bit damp. Sonne loved her father, just like the board members of Oneworld loved their families.

What they were doing now—going after Galileo—was endangering far more people than just them. Still, they couldn't walk away from this. Sheila Fisher and over two dozen other victims demanded justice.

Cowan knew it would be at least an hour drive to Benzai's

headquarters outside San Diego. He and Sonne sat on couches on each side of the ambulance, with Taylor between them.

"Ready?" he asked. He was.

She looked across her father at him, fingers tapping on her couch. "I still don't think you should do this," she said. "We don't know what Galileo left in my father's PBA. It's a stupid risk."

"Maybe, but I might not get another chance to examine it. Your father's in a coma because of scripting I wrote."

Sonne stared out the front windows for a few seconds before speaking. "I remember our date."

It caught Cowan by surprise. All he could manage was to mutter, "What?"

"The night we went out and got kidnapped by the Russian mafia. The night we were going dancing."

"Oh." So that was what happened to them. Many parts about that night remained fuzzy for him, and he still wasn't sure exactly why.

"The man who kidnapped us called himself Mister Gray." Sonne kept her eyes on the road. "He was searching for Galileo, and abducting me was a side job. He was going to release you, but you refused to let him. You risked your life so he'd let me go."

That sounded more heroic than Cowan expected. "Why don't I remember doing that?"

"You agreed to redact our entire night so no one would go after Mister Gray, and I had to do the same," she said. "But after you uploaded the redaction routine, Katie arrived, with Lucy. They tracked me down before my memories deleted themselves."

Cowan grimaced as pieces fell into place. No wonder he'd been unable to restore his missing memories. He'd done it to himself, and he was thorough.

"I couldn't remember what happened until last night," Sonne continued, "when Katie uploaded my redacted memories. The night we got abducted, she dove into your PBA and figured out you were a loose circuit."

Cowan could believe that. "She wanted you safe."

"It's annoying, honestly."

"So . . . why tell me now?"

She looked at him. "Because she's my big sister, not my boss."

Cowan noticed her face was flushed. Why?

"What did Kate tell you actually happened?" he asked.

"She said you were an asshole, all grabby hands," Sonne said. "That you pissed yourself when the Russians took us, and they knocked you out and tied you up. You slept through the whole thing."

"Oh . . ." He couldn't deny, that did sound like a shitty date. "That's why you never called?"

"Look." Sonne leaned closer. "I was angry when you lied to me about Professor Xu, and I still think it was a bad call, but I don't think you're an asshole. Okay?"

"You sure?"

"And you and me . . . we had something, that night. A connection. But right now, some psycho wants to kill us both, so this isn't the time to make emotional decisions."

"Right."

Did he feel disappointed? Should he? Ellen was still out there, maybe.

Sonne stuck out a finger. "So if you're risking this because you want to impress me, or date me—"

"I'm not!" he cut her off, wondering how she could think that. "I want to help your father because I'm responsible for this horrible thing that happening to him. He doesn't deserve this. You don't deserve this, so I have to try and wake him up because I may not get another chance. That's it."

Sonne sat back and watched him for a moment. She smiled.

"I believe you," she said.

"Thank you."

"And maybe, after this is all over, we can try that date again."

"So . . . what are you saying?" he asked, more confused than ever. Hadn't she just told him *not* to date her?

"Nothing. I'm saying nothing, Cowan, except that I remember how I felt about you that night, and I liked how I felt. So I forgive you for lying to me about Xu, and after this is over, maybe we'll go on another date, if you want. Nothing more complicated than that."

Cowan felt a bit of warm in his chest. They *weren't* done after all.

"Okay," he said, trying to play it as calm and collected as possible. "So, I'm going to run a diagnostic on your dad's PBA now, analyze his firmware. Back me up?"

"Sure." Sonne sat back. "If something happens, I'll flail my arms and yell."

"And maybe call your sister?"

"And I'll call Katie."

Cowan popped his linkline into Taylor Lambda's auxiliary port. If his theory was right, Galileo hadn't just locked Taylor into a coma. He'd imprisoned Taylor inside his PBA.

Cowan knew that Galileo had access to PBA firmware. If he'd found a way to remotely swap out the operating system for Matthew Reed's PBA, using a Trojan horse firmware update to puppet him into killing his family, why not do the same to Taylor Lambda? Why not install firmware that would keep Taylor alive, comatose, and unable to wake?

Cowan blinked over to his head desk and checked his dozens of dynamic firewalls. Once he was certain his PBA was secure, he opened a brain diagnosis panel and selected Taylor's PBA from the list. His display stuttered as Cowan connected, and dozens of panels no one but a PBA engineer would understand opened before him. Cowan knew these panels intimately, and a cursory inspection revealed nothing unusual.

The version number on Taylor's firmware matched the latest patch, so was the panel lying to him? Cowan entered several dozen administration commands he'd learned while working for Oneworld and bypassed Taylor's security. He knew all the back doors and developer holes.

Cowan started with the basic functions regulating Taylor's PBA, even though grayDocs had probably checked those. He ran a comparison against the firmware on his own PBA, and the brain code was a match. There was nothing on the surface of Taylor's PBA that suggested foul play, but that just meant he might not be looking in the right place.

He wasn't looking in the private partition he and Ellen had created at Mind Games.

Cowan opened an unsearchable code address and immediately found function overrides for routine PBA operations, including wake and sleep cycles. A quick scan of the script confirmed they were impossible to detect, and they induced coma-like symptoms.

Taylor had the same partition Cowan had, and it was being used to lock him away inside his own brain.

A blacked-out panel opened before him, and the modulated voice that began talking chilled Cowan's blood. "Well done. But I'd expect nothing less from a scripter of your caliber."

The intruder didn't need to say who he was for Cowan to know. It could only be one person. Galileo.

Cowan felt like he was going to be sick, but he couldn't be sick while in the Sim. He'd vomit and he could vomit anywhere, on Sonne, or himself, or Taylor Lambda.

"In case you haven't figured it out," Galileo said, "I'm the one who got you assigned to my puppeting case with the CID."

That was why the CID assigned him to a sensitive puppeting case on his first day? Because Galileo told the CID to hire him? Why would Galileo want the CID to hire him?

"I needed the CID to understand what I was capable of," Galileo went on, "but more importantly, I needed someone in their ranks I could corrupt at any point. So, don't blame yourself for failing to anticipate me. I've been ahead of you since you started."

Before Cowan could break the connection, Galileo opened another panel. It showed Ellen, Cowan's savior, the love of his life, staring with her serious face. She was alive.

Cowan would have screamed if he was back in meatspace.

"She can't see us," Galileo said. "She's talking with her fiancé right now, a man named Caleb Miller. I've tapped us into his side of the call."

The time stamp on the video call was today. Right now.

"How?" Cowan asked.

"I recently offered Ellen a job. From what I understand, Caleb doesn't want to leave California."

Ellen's lips moved and she shook her head, but Cowan couldn't understand. Ellen was free? Not a captive? She had a fiancé named Caleb?

"What is this?" Cowan managed to ask.

"I saved her," Galileo said.

"From what?"

"CorpSec. Remember? I'm the one who ordered you and Ellen to work on that new PBA at Mind Games. I watched you both for years, and I know how intelligent you are."

Cowan remembered CorpSec soldiers smashing through the windows at his and Ellen's home in Mission Beach.

"You betrayed us," he whispered.

"Oneworld betrayed me, Cowan. I didn't send Corporate Security after you, nor did I force Ellen to erase all knowledge of her work at Mind Games. I protected you."

"Protected me?" Cowan wanted to punch right through that stupid blacked-out panel.

"You are valuable, and I protect valuable people," Galileo said. "After a lengthy discussion with the other members of Oneworld, I convinced Corporate Security Chief Kathleen Warren to release Ellen and release you. All charges dropped."

"You mean you threatened to kill her family."

"There was nothing to gain by imprisoning Ellen," Galileo said. "She had already erased a year of her own life . . . her year with you . . . so I argued no further modding was necessary. We told her she was in an autocar accident. I got her a new life, a new job."

This was impossible. This was insane.

"I don't believe you," Cowan said.

"You should, because the other members of Oneworld are far more a threat to you than I. Should you somehow eliminate me, I won't be able to protect Ellen any longer. My enemies will rewrite her and erase you."

"You're lying."

Another panel opened between them, an aerial shot of a modest neighborhood and its many, many streets. The aerial shot zoomed in on a private ambulance traveling the speed limit through that neighborhood. It was the vehicle he and Sonne were in now.

"Cowan," Galileo said, "did you know Oneworld flies armed drones on domestic soil, just in case?" A target symbol appeared on the ambulance, as well as the words *Missile Locked*. "One has been tracking you since you left the hospital."

This couldn't be real. Was Galileo really going to just blow them up now? Could Cowan take over the ambulance and drive it under a bridge somewhere?

"I'd like you to come visit me in person," Galileo said. "What we must discuss is too sensitive for the Sim. I've already sent an autocar for you, and I insist you board it."

What felt somewhere between relief and dread twisted Cowan's stomach. Galileo wanted him alive. That meant he could still save Sonne, even if he couldn't save himself. Of course, he didn't really want to die either. If he did, he'd never save Ellen from this lunatic.

"Move quickly, Cowan," Galileo said. "Lie to your friends in a way they'll believe, and then get into my autocar. Or I will incinerate you and everyone you now care about."

Cowan imagined Sonne disintegrating.

"I'll do it," he said. "I'll find a way to meet you."

"I know you will."

48

COWAN

Galileo's panel vanished., and Cowan numbly deleted the script that had put Taylor Lambda into a coma. He restored normal algorithms. It would be days until Taylor woke—he had been under long enough that the enforced sleep had put him into a *real* coma—but he would wake, now, eventually. Good for him.

Cowan flipped back to meatspace to find Sonne gripping his arms hard enough to hurt. She was on *his* side of the ambulance now.

"Finally!" Sonne's death grip on his arms eased. "What happened in there?"

Cowan eased her off. "I'm fine."

"You were shaking like you had a seizure! I barely stopped you from bashing your head."

"It was rough, but I found the problem. Fixed it."

"Fixed what?"

"Your dad. I fixed your dad's malfunctioning PBA." Cowan couldn't manage a smile. "He might wake up in a few days, but—"

"Oh my God, Cowan!" Sonne threw her arms around him, laughing,

but when she tried to kiss him, he twisted away. He kept seeing Gerhard
Bayer looming over Ellen.

Sonne sat back as if he'd hit her. "What the fuck did I do now?"

"I just need you to understand what I did," Cowan said, mentally
flailing as he struggled for a lie that would convince her. "Recovering
from a coma takes months, even years. Even after your father wakes up,
he might never regain all his faculties."

"I know that." Sonne sat back, away from him. "I'm not an idiot.
So was it Galileo, like we thought? Did he lock my father in a coma?"

"Yes." That was true, more or less.

"Then that's one more reason to take him down."

"Okay. Also, I have to go."

She blinked. "Where?"

An update from Jeb brought Cowan a lie he knew might work. "Jeb
almost got picked up at the OMH, but he's out. Warren's working with
Galileo. They'll come after me soon."

"Shit," Sonne said. "What do we do?"

"You get your father to Kate. I have to go alone."

She blocked the ambulance's back doors with spread arms. "Still
not hearing the why."

"The CID can trace me through my PBA. They can follow me right
to you, and I can't let that happen."

Her mouth opened a little. "And you didn't think to mention that
earlier?"

"I didn't think things would fly apart so fast."

"But . . . what happens to you?" The genuine worry in her eyes made
Cowan hurt. She wasn't supposed to like him anymore. This was easier
when she didn't like him.

"I'll meet you at Club Sylvan as soon as I can get clear and get there,
just like we planned," he said. "If I'm not there by Saturday, head to the
airport without me."

She thumped the doors. "Dammit, this wasn't the plan."

"It is now."

"Fuck your plan, it's a shitty plan!"

"I know how to evade the CID. I'll get clear, isolate my PBA, and meet you at Club Sylvan." Cowan directed his next words to the VI driving the ambulance. "Stop."

"Don't stop!" Sonne shouted, and the ambulance drove on. "We're talking about this."

"No time," Cowan said. He linked to the autotruck's VI and eased it to a stop. He'd slipped through its firewalls as soon as they got on the road. He had assumed someone might try the same thing, and he wanted to be prepared.

Sonne released her death grip on the door handle. "You really have to run?"

"It's the only way you'll get to Club Sylvan safely," he said. He'd keep her and her father from getting incinerated.

"Then . . . just be careful, all right?" Sonne slid out of his way, back onto her narrow couch, back on her side of the ambulance. "And thank you, again, for Dad."

Cowan wished he could hug her again, before he maybe died. At least tell her that it wasn't that he didn't want to kiss her back. He just . . . couldn't yet.

"Not a problem," he said flatly. The ambulance's back doors opened at his command. He hopped out onto a residential street.

The sky was clear, blue, and filled with drones. Between all the delivery and commercial drones above, Galileo's military drone could be anywhere. There would be no escape.

They had stopped in a suburban neighborhood called Clairemont Mesa. Modest one-story homes surrounded him. The last he saw of Sonne was her worried eyes, watching him, before the ambulance doors shut.

The ambulance then cruised off, and Cowan waited for a missile to fall from the sky. He waited for the vehicle to explode as his heart slammed against his rib cage. Nothing exploded.

Cowan activated the emergency scripting he'd long ago hidden in his private partition, the one the Sim couldn't see. He vanished from the corporate network, and, a moment after that, he vanished off their satellites too.

A single autocar approached.

He carved through its firewalls and searched for its destination, but there was no destination. The car's VI believed it had one passenger, yet when the doors rolled open, it was empty. The person this car's VI thought it was transporting didn't actually exist.

Cowan got in, the doors slid shut, and the autocar rolled off. He wasn't invisible, but he was now one signal among thousands. The chances of anyone tracing him to this car were remote, and no one would know Cowan rode in it until it arrived, except Galileo.

So much for not lying to Sonne again . . .

49
JEB

"That wasn't the plan," Jeb said, once they were all gathered in Kate office at Club Sylvan. "Cowan was supposed to come back with you."

"I pondered knocking him out," Sonne said. "Should I have knocked him out?"

"Either way, Cowan's gone," David said, "and there's nothing we can do about it now. Whatever he's up to, it's out of our hands."

Jeb sighed and sat back, rubbing his temples and trying to think positively. He and David were now both running Cowan's loose circuit firmware, which kept them on the network but hidden from corporate retaliation. It also let them punch or shoot anyone they wanted without blacking out, which might be useful very soon.

Even so, the day had been depressingly unproductive. Despite Kate and Sonne's success in tracking Gerhard Bayer to M-Gesundheit in Switzerland, they were still stuck in San Diego. After leaving Sarisa, Jeb had used a small explosive charge to blow a hole in the floor of the OMH headquarters, opening a way into its storm drain tunnels.

He hadn't taken those tunnels, of course. He'd used Xu's Myself Projector to disguise himself as a company janitor, one of dozens shocked by the urgent militarized search. Jeb suspected Corporate Security had searched those tunnels for hours after evacuating all maintenance personal. He understood why Oneworld had made MySelf illegal.

At the moment, the biggest problem they faced was Cowan, being gone. Jeb ran scenarios. What would have made Cowan bolt as Corporate One dropped the hammer?

Cowan's story to Sonne about CID tracking was bullshit. Even Jeb knew enough to evade corporate satellites before dropping off the Sim, so Cowan could do that easily. So why lie? Why leave Sonne?

The catalyst, Jeb decided, had to be whatever Cowan found in Taylor Lambda's PBA. Something he hadn't told Sonne or anyone else. Something that had forced him into a snap decision to do his own research, follow his own leads, alone.

"Obviously," Jeb said, "David and I can't leave this office until we have somewhere to go, but we can still be productive." He turned to Doctor Xu. "How are you on engineering a counter for Joseph Dunn's synthetic hacking scripts?"

"Better," Xu said, "if you would stop asking about them."

Jeb glanced at David. "Any more takers on our offer?"

David nodded. "Three willing recruits plus one very talented commander. I think we'll pull together enough warm bodies for a full assault team."

That was very good news.

"Kate, would it be possible for us to remotely search your father's PBA, at Benzai Corporation?" Jeb asked. "If we look through what Cowan was doing before he took off, perhaps we can—"

The door to Kate's office opened, and an honest-to-God fairy stepped inside. She sported glittering gossamer wings, a blond pixie cut, and a green dress cut like a cavegirl's.

"Hello!" The fairy waved. "How is everyone?" The door slammed shut behind her.

"What the shit?" Sonne grabbed her stunner and aimed.

"Stop!" Jeb shouted.

He had seen this fairy before, but only inside a projection room beneath Corporate One. It seemed Oneworld corporation had found them after all. He didn't know how this *thing* had gotten here, but he knew shooting it was a bad idea.

"Hello, Detective Forrester!" Puck, the Augur fairy in a green dress, sauntered to the center of the room. "I'm so pleased you escaped the Office of Mental Health! I helped, you know. Your disguise was clever, but I really had to work some magic to get you out of there."

Jeb managed his calm and asked, "Kate, do you have a back way out of here?"

Corporate Security shock troopers might already be on the way, but if that was so, why would Puck arrive first? Or were the soldiers already outside, and sending in Puck to negotiate their surrender? Also, how the fuck was she out *here*, in meatspace? Puck couldn't be an AR projection, because AR projections couldn't open and close doors.

Puck smiled as the lights in the office flickered. "Trust me, there's no need to escape!"

Kate blinked and pushed her chair away from her desk. "You locked me out of my own system." She stood. "How did you lock me out of my own system?"

"Can I shoot her?" Sonne asked.

"Please don't shoot me." Puck's image flickered to reveal a tall woman with short blond hair. "If you shoot this body, I'll only inhabit another."

Kate gasped. "You're puppeting Lucy?" She strode around her desk. "What *are* you?"

"I'm your friend!"

"You're not human, since no human could think faster than my dynamic firewalls and every other layer of security in my office. So you're a VI. Who sent you? Galileo?"

"Ladies and gentlemen," Jeb said, "may I introduce Puck, one of Corporate One's vaunted Augurs."

"I still say we shoot her," Sonne said.

Kate advanced on Puck and stopped close enough to touch her. Then she did touch her. She poked her in the shoulder, and that shoulder moved.

"You stole Xu's MySelf," she said.

"Yes!" Puck said.

"After you hacked and puppeted my bodyguard."

"Two for two!" Puck shouted.

"If you hurt Lucy," Kate said, "I will fucking murder you."

Puck bounced up and down. "I know you care for your friend. I care, too, about all of you, which is why I'm here! I've come to save you from making a terrible mistake!"

Kate glanced at the others for backup, then stared at Puck. "That being?"

"Launching a mission to arrest Gerhard Bayer!" Puck fluttered her wings and batted her eyelashes. "I can't let you do that. That would do great harm to his personal interests."

"Why would we go after Mister Bayer?" Kate asked.

"Because you now know he is living in Schaffhausen, Switzerland, where you plan to arrest him!" Puck bounced up and down. "As for your plans to leave San Diego—"

"Who says we're going anywhere?"

"I'm afraid travel to any location will be quite difficult. Our new OMH director is scanning every flight until she finds Detective Jeb Forrester. You are trapped."

"Fuck," Sonne said, still holding her stunner.

"May I ask why you're telling us this?" Kate asked.

"While it is in Bayer's best interests for Kathleen Warner to confine you to San Diego," Puck said, "it is not in the best interests of Tam, Cheng, Walker, and Abramowicz."

Kate gave Jeb a meaningful look. "So you're aware Bayer is holding the family members of the other Oneworld board members hostage?"

"I'm quite aware. Being aware is what I do!"

Jeb didn't trust this. "Who are you working for, if not Warren and Bayer?"

"I work for Oneworld, Detective Forrester, and that is a responsibility I take very seriously," Puck said. "Gerhard Bayer, also known as Galileo, has made my job quite complicated."

Xu snorted. "Murders stressing the old morality protocols?"

"I am forbidden from doing anything that might compromise

Gerhard Bayer's interests." Puck bounced again. "However, recent simulations suggest that you now have at least a 52 percent chance of exposing my employer's corruption. Therefore, it is now in Gerhard Bayer's best interest for me to politely ask you to stop."

Kate relaxed, took one step back, and shook her head. "You're hooked into a CLU box."

"Yes!" Puck shouted.

"That's why you didn't contact us before now. The chance we'd succeed wasn't high enough to merit a warning to stop until we'd tracked Bayer home, to Schaffhausen."

Sonne lowered her stunner. "I admit I'm a bit inexperienced at programming VIs, but wouldn't Puck coming here make us *more* likely to go after Galileo?"

"She's working around a bad order, dear." Kate returned her attention to Puck. "Who scripted you?"

"God," Puck said.

Kate leaned forward. "Please tell us, Puck, in the simplest terms you can define. What are your operational parameters?"

Puck's stolen body went rigid. "Directive One: Protect the interests of Oneworld corporation and its subsidiaries. Directive Two: Protect the board members of Oneworld and their interests, personal and professional.' Directive Three—"

"Stop," Kate said. "I understand."

"Do you?" Puck beamed at them.

Kate looked to the rest of the team. "The other members of Oneworld are compromised. Bayer's threatening their families, and thus their personal interests. Yet that's not all. He's threatening the entire corporation of Oneworld, and our fragile world peace."

Jeb finally got it, and he felt a bit better about trusting Puck.

"This Augur is a fail-safe, isn't she?" he said. "She's a VI Oneworld put into place to protect itself from itself."

David nodded. "All five members of Oneworld would never consent to a single member holding all the power. So they added this VI as an impassive mediator. A watchdog."

"I can neither confirm nor deny!" Puck shouted.

Kate returned her attention to Puck. "Remind me why we shouldn't arrest Gerhard Bayer in Schaffhausen. What might happen if we attempted that?"

Puck frowned prettily. "If you did plan to assault M-Gesundheit, I'd request you do so from the south, through the minefield and the trap tunnels. If you attacked from the north, all you'd face are automated turrets, which would make it far less likely you would die."

David tapped a note on his tablet. "We'll do that."

"Cybercrimes Investigation Division, Detective Forrester." Puck spun toward him. "Do you still plan to arrest or kill Gerhard Bayer, even though I've politely asked you not to?"

"Yes," Jeb said. This fairy was actually making sense.

"Then I must inform you that Bayer will murder the families of my masters at Oneworld, should he be arrested or killed in any assault. I can't allow that to happen."

"We don't want that either," Jeb said. "So what would you warn us *not* to do?"

"Definitely do *not* ask Bayer about the signal he sends every twelve hours to prevent his assets from committing murder. Also, do *not* spoof that signal after he's in custody."

David smiled. "And don't search the records we find at M-Gesundheit for a list of the assets he's tasked to take out the board's family members?"

"Yes!" Puck bounced up and down. "Please do *not* do that. That would adversely affect Bayer's interests, and that is something I must warn you *not* to do."

"You are working that CLU box hard," Xu groaned.

"What else can you tell us?" Kate asked. "What else should we *not* do?"

Puck blinked. "Oh, fiddlesticks! Corporate scan incoming. We will not speak again!"

Puck's projection flickered out and Lucy appeared, wobbly. Jeb rushed forward as Kate did, catching her before she collapsed. They steadied her as her eyes opened.

"That was odd . . ." Lucy said, eyes blinking rapidly.

Kate helped Jeb stand Lucy up, gripping her arms. Then she threw her arms around Lucy and hugged her, despite the awkward height difference.

"Don't you ever do that, again, you hear?" she said. "Don't you plug into anything! Don't even think about it!"

Lucy breathed and smiled. "So don't install any more firmware updates?"

"Did that just happen?" Sonne asked. "Did we get a visit from Oneworld's fairy godmother?"

"We've got another asset inside Oneworld now." Jeb stepped away from the embracing women and glanced at his husband. "What do we need to hit M-Gesundheit?"

David tapped his chin. "Architectural plans would be a good start."

"Those should be easy to acquire," Xu said, from her chair, "provided you are willing to once more unleash Nyx on the darkSim." She looked to Kate. "Your thoughts?"

Kate pushed back from Lucy, snorted back a sniffle, and turned on Xu. "We'll go together." She perked up. "I haven't taken my angel avatar out in weeks!"

"You trust that thing?" David asked. "A VI designed specifically by the people we're trying to stop?"

Jeb looked to Kate. He wanted her to explain it.

"We're trying to help the members of Oneworld," Kate said, "and Puck recognizes that. She judged the possibility that Bayer will kill all the family members of the other board members less of a risk than allowing him to make all Oneworld's decisions."

"We're not letting that sonuvabitch murder anyone else," Sonne said, looking around for agreement. "There's no better time to go after him than right now. We've got him."

Kate tapped her lips, eyes going distant. "Benzai Corporation has its own watchdog VI, though not nearly that advanced." She took a breath. "I want one."

Lucy walked casually back to the door, always the quiet defender. Jeb pondered Kate's unusually familiar reaction. She must really care for Lucy, and not just as a bodyguard.

"This still doesn't solve our transport problem," Xu said, chair creaking as she leaned forward. "Director Warren is almost certainly watching all Benzai flights."

"She's not watching UPX," Kate said. "Adrian can get us on a flight. I'm certain of it."

"Jeb?" David said. While David had volunteered to lead the ground assault on M-Gesundheit, he deferred to Jeb for strategy. They worked well together.

Jeb couldn't plan for all eventualities, or even guarantee any of them would survive. There wasn't enough data. All he could do is go with his gut, and his gut said the time to go after Galileo was now, right now, before he anticipated them.

"We're taking Puck's advice," Jeb said. "Kate charters us a flight on UPX through her friend Adrian, off the books. We get M-Gesundheit's layout from Xu. David, you construct an attack plan using our existing assets that moves in from the north."

"Bayer will die before releasing the Oneworld families," Xu reminded everyone.

"We'll figure something out," Jeb said.

"Will you? Because many innocents will die the moment we attack him. Dare you join me in the world of complex moral dilemmas?" She sighed. "It's been so lonely here."

"Oh, shut up," Sonne said, setting her stunner on the desk. "We can do way better than that, and I already know how we can keep Bayer from killing everyone. We just—"

"Planning later," Kate said. She walked to Xu's ergochair and kicked it. "Get up, honey."

Xu arched an eyebrow. "Whatever for?"

"We're going dancing." Kate pointed out the door leading out to Club Sylvan.

"Why?"

"Because we finally know how we're going to take down Bayer and get ourselves out of this mess. I feel like celebrating with an attractive woman, and Sonne's not my type."

"Also," Sonne added, "I'm her sister. Just in case that wasn't clear."

50

COWAN

Galileo's chartered autocar stopped in front of a glittering apartment tower in Westwood, one of the sprawling suburbs of Los Angeles. The doors rolled open, and Cowan stepped out into a warm evening.

So this was where Gerhard Bayer lived? In a random apartment tower in Los Angeles. He had been in California the whole time?

"Mister Soto?"

The woman who said that was Ellen Gauthier, love of his life. He'd know her voice anywhere.

Cowan spun so fast he nearly fell. Ellen caught his arms before he could fall over. The *real* Ellen, because that's the type of thing she did when she saw people in trouble. She was alive. She was touching him. His body trembled and he felt like he might faint.

"I'm sorry." Ellen released him and brushed her brown bangs from her forehead, like she always did. "You are Cowan Soto, aren't you? The talent scout for M-Gesundheit?"

Cowan realized then that Ellen no longer knew who he was. She didn't remember him, didn't remember working at Mind Games with him, or cuddling with him on her couch, or their late nights theorizing about the limits of the human brain in between bouts of extremely satisfying sex. Ellen didn't remember loving him, and that crushed his heart.

Cowan's mind did several backward flips before he locked into something that he could explain.

"Yes, that's right. I'm their . . . talent scout," he said.

Why the hell would Galileo send him here to meet Ellen? What the hell was M-Gesundheit?

Either way, Galileo hadn't lied. Ellen was actually alive, and sane, and not lobotomized somewhere in a dark cell. She had been living comfortably in a wealthy suburb of Los Angeles all this time, and she was engaged again, maybe even happy. If all he had to do to make her safe again was crush his own heart, Cowan would toss his in a trash compactor.

Ellen crossed her arms over a sensible black blouse, paired with a knee-length blue skirt that made him woozy.

"You look pale," she said. "Are you feeling all right?"

Cowan had searched the Sim for any trace of Ellen dozens of times. He'd never found her, despite the fact that she was living right here in Westwood, an hour away. Galileo must have concealed her from him.

He nodded, breathed, and smiled.

"I am, Miss Gauthier," he said.

"Before you ask, I'm still considering your offer," Ellen said. She pressed her lips together in thought, one of hundreds of small tics Cowan still loved. "But I agree it's a wonderful opportunity. I also know it's very cold in Schaffhausen."

Switzerland. She was going to Switzerland.

Cowan forced a nervous laugh and decided to play along. "Schaffhausen is certainly not as balmy as your fair California, but it is beautiful, and we have excellent benefits."

What was he thinking? He didn't *want* Ellen to move to Switzerland. If she went to work at this M-Gesundheit place, Galileo could murder her anytime he wished.

Yet wouldn't Ellen be safer in Switzerland, with Galileo, if the other members of Oneworld really did want her dead? There were too many things he didn't know. What he did know, now, is that he had to get them both off the street.

"Would you mind if we discussed this inside?" Cowan asked.

"I suppose that does make sense," Ellen agreed.

They went inside after that, into an elevator. It was a nice elevator.

"My fiancé should be home in a few minutes," Ellen informed Cowan as they rode, together, to the fourteenth floor. She stood a respectable distance away. "Once he arrives, we can discuss the specifics of your offer at length."

"Of course," Cowan said, as he struggled not to freak out and throw his arms around her. Ellen had a fiancé now. He was her fiancé, dammit . . . but not anymore.

His own heartbreak didn't matter. Galileo could obviously murder Ellen at any time, yet he hadn't. Why? It wasn't that hard to figure out.

Galileo wanted Cowan as a spy.

Never. Cowan would never betray the others, no matter how hard Galileo pushed him. He loved Ellen more than his own life, but she was one person. Galileo threatened their entire world. The elevator opened onto the top floor.

"Please follow me," Ellen said, polite as ever. Polite and adorable. Even her voice made his knees weak, a voice he hadn't heard since she wiped her PBA to save his life.

As she led him down a carpeted hall with soft blue walls, Cowan made himself stare at anything but her. How long had she lived here? A year? Long enough to meet someone new and build a life away from the chaos that destroyed her. Maybe she was better off without him.

Her apartment was nicer than he expected, an elegant, open space with tile floors and lighting recessed in the ceiling. It had marble counters, healthy potted plants, and enough soft leather furniture to seat a dozen people. Did they host parties here?

A glance out large windows showed LA's downtown sprawl, buildings towering over tiny green trees. A view like this wasn't cheap.

"Please, sit." Ellen pointed to a plush white leather chair. "Would you care for refreshment?"

"I, uh . . ." Cowan rubbed the back of his head. "We should talk first." He was sweating.

Ellen reached into her slender blue purse and asked, "About?"

He knew she had a stunner in there. She always kept a stunner in there. Cowan was acting like some freakish psychopath kidnapper, and he needed to focus on getting her safe.

"When you were ten years old," Cowan said, "your house flooded, and your dog drowned. You always blamed yourself, even though your father tied him up in the basement."

Ellen pulled her stunner, dropped her purse, and stepped back, aiming right at him.

"How do you know that?" she demanded.

"You told me," Cowan said. Perhaps reminding her about Sparky was the wrong move.

"I did nothing of the sort!"

"You also told me your first crush was Jared Walker. He smiled at you and shared his lunch one day, when you didn't have any fruit. He never saw you as more than a friend."

Ellen stepped forward, stunner steady. "Explain yourself! How do you know these things?"

When she got upset, the French Canadian accent she'd worked years to suppress came out strong. Cowan loved that accent. He loved her, so much.

"I know because we used to love each other," he said. "We were together for almost a year, working as engineers at a company called Mind Games. We were going to get married."

Ellen's lip twisted as she blinked rapidly. "Wait. You worked . . .?"

Her whole body went stiff. Her eyes went blank. Then her soft lips curled into a creepy smile, and Cowan's heart just about stopped.

He'd seen someone react like this before, in a parking lot, on the first case of his new job. As he stared at Ellen, at her rigid body, at her creepy smile, he realized he *wasn't* going to save her. He couldn't save her.

This woman wasn't Ellen at the moment.

"I wanted to let you try," Galileo said through her lips. "You understand now, don't you?"

Cowan sunk into the plush white chair. He struggled to breathe. "Yes."

"Wonderful." Ellen's puppeted body strode to the couch across from him, sat, and crossed her legs. "Now that we're done with that, let's talk about why you're really here."

Cowan's head pounded and his chest ached, but he kept his focus because Ellen needed him to keep his focus. Galileo wanted to use Ellen to make him betray everyone, but what if he killed himself first? With him dead, there would be no reason to hurt her. Or would Galileo do anyway, out of spite?

"I've studied the psychiatric profile we compiled during your work at Mind Games," Galileo said through Ellen, "and I feel I understand you."

Cowan glanced over his shoulder for an electrical socket or a sharp corner. Everything dangerous in this apartment came without guarantees. What if he grabbed a kitchen knife? Could Galileo use Ellen's body to stop him? What if he jumped out a window?

"You're a pragmatist," Galileo said. "A wonderful trait you, I, and Miss Gauthier all share. Our shared goals are one of many reasons I selected you as my star researchers."

Cowan remembered what Jeb had told him about puppeting long ago, on their first case. When you stunned a puppet, it broke the puppeteer's connection.

He pulled his stunner.

"I wouldn't shoot Ellen," Galileo said. "Both your skin and hers are now covered with airborne nanites, ones I've ensured blanket her apartment. These nanites are activated by the voltage of a stunner round, and should you sedate Ellen, they will rapidly melt her skin." He made Ellen smirk. "Have you ever seen a person's skin melt, Cowan?"

Cowan aimed through the tears flooding his eyes.

"It will be quick," Galileo said, "and I've modified her PBA so she won't feel any pain. She won't suffer, but she *will* melt, and quite irreversibly. I believe torture is an unnecessary practice, Cowan, and avoid it when I can, but I will kill if needed."

Cowan holstered his stunner. He needed more time to think about how he was going to save them. He had to get Ellen out of Galileo's clutches, either alive . . . or the other way.

"In less than a week," Galileo said, "your plans will no longer matter. My game is coming to an end, and all our pieces will soon be swept from the board."

Cowan trembled. "Good for you."

"Cybercrime has grown to epidemic proportions, and real crime now plagues cities across the world. Oneworld has failed. The utopia of PBAs has failed. Our world's citizens are ready to embrace a new world order at last, the order I will provide them."

"We'll stop you." Even as he said it, Cowan knew how frail the words sounded. Like even he didn't even believe them.

"You won't. Even should your allies discover my location, somehow escape Director Warren's notice, and launch some sort of attack, they will fail. They will die. Yet if you agree to help me, you may join Ellen in our wonderful new world and save your friends."

"Ellen won't work for you either." Cowan found his voice again, found strength and anger and the righteous desire for revenge. "Not once she knows everything you'd done."

"What I do is for humanity itself."

"Murdering families for humanity? Puppeting people in shooting rampages?"

A long pause passed between them. Finally, Ellen shifted her legs and Galileo spoke through her.

"Do you know the true purpose behind PBAs?"

That was a stupid question, a random question, but if Cowan kept Galileo talking, he'd keep Ellen alive. "Of course I do."

"What is it?"

"They keep hormone-addled primitives from murdering each other."

Galileo tilted Ellen's head. "So you understand that PBAs enforce behavioral algorithms to prevent clear circuit humans from harming others. Do you know what else they do?"

"I bet you're going to tell me."

"A question first: Why did world governments adopt PBAs?"

"World peace, asshole," Cowan said, pleased he'd made himself sound almost confident.

"Is that all? After centuries of greed and self-centered actions, all the leaders of the free world decided they would allow their minds to be governed by corporate algorithms? An altruistic decision to make their world a better place?"

Was Galileo going to spout some darkSim theory about the Illuminati secretly starting up Oneworld, or aliens in orbit controlling their minds? Was all the murder and harm he'd caused nothing more than a manifestation of paranoia? If so, that was tragic.

"A world of clear circuits is better than the alternative, is it not?" Galileo asked. "A world where we control people's minds using implanted algorithms is a reasonable compromise to end the majority of murders and assaults."

"Of course it is!" Cowan said. Everyone knew that.

"You answer so quickly. Have you ever wondered why that is?"

Fresh uncertainty tickled Cowan's brain. A throbbing started in his head, making it difficult to focus on what Galileo was saying. His words were foolish. He was insane.

"The algorithms in your PBA don't just stop you from harming other people," Galileo continued. "They influence all your mental processes, including your willingness to accept or reject new ideas. They control which ideas you find acceptable."

Cowan's head pounded now. "Bullshit."

"How do you explain gun control, Cowan? For centuries, your United States protected that right no matter who died. And yet two years after the majority of your citizens adopted PBAs, you happily banned guns."

"Because people with PBAs can't use them!"

"It was a test, one I conducted alongside my colleagues. It was proof we could use our technology to alter even ingrained societal beliefs. We sold you on PBA augmentation with promises of consequence-free sex and violence, a perfect virtual world filled with perfect virtual things, and never once did you think about what *else* we could influence."

Cowan's mind itched. "You're lying."

"A hardware defect in a batch of PBAs lobotomizes preschoolers, and you think, better than the alternative. A troll knocks out a woman and steals her ghostlink, uses her puppeted body to service all his friends, and you think, better than the alternative."

"You're the person doing those things!"

"I'm the person trying to stop them, Cowan. That's why I've taken the families of my fellow board members hostage. Controlling people's minds is wrong."

Cowan's anger grew, and he fought it, because anger didn't make sense. Why would he be angry about Galileo spouting conspiracy theories? There was no truth to any of this.

"You call me a monster," Galileo said. "You point to the things I've done and see a hateful person. Yet are my actions truly monstrous when one considers my purpose?"

"What purpose?" Cowan asked.

"Over the past two months, I have demonstrated that Oneworld's system is flawed, vulnerable, and dangerous. I have shown the world, time and again, why the existing system needs to be replaced. Even the Office of Mental Health cannot suppress news of a thousand crimes, because their own director just murdered his wife."

"You think you're a goddamn freedom fighter?" Cowan demanded.

"I think eyes must be opened before minds can be changed. Or do you agree we should simply *force* people to believe in their leaders?"

Of course Cowan didn't believe that, because mind control wasn't real. Sure, PBAs made you sick when you thought about hurting another person, made you black out when you thought about worse, but that wasn't mind control . . . Was it?

Galileo leaned Ellen close. "I helped build PBAs and the Sim to make humanity better, not to make us into slaves. Using my work to enslave humanity is wrong. I won't allow it any longer."

Cowan grabbed his throbbing head. The board of Oneworld wanted to protect clear circuits. The world before PBAs had been a nightmare of murder and chaos.

"You already have the tools to shrug off our behavioral algorithms," Galileo said. "Your unique firmware allows you to disable all of them, not just assault and murder."

Cowan's vision blurred, his stomach churning.

"Cull all behavioral algorithms," Galileo ordered. "See the truth."

The migraine in Cowan's head grew to such a degree that spots danced before his eyes. That made him even angrier. His PBA was telling him what *not* to do, and a PBA wasn't supposed to do that.

Cowan angrily terminated all behavioral algorithms just out of spite. Galileo *was* a monster, no matter what.

But with the algorithms gone, the truth was just as bad as Cowan worried.

As he doubled over, coughing and choking, fresh insight flooded his mind. It all seemed so clear now. Even through the migraine, he knew Galileo was telling the truth.

Oneworld was using PBAs to influence the behaviors and beliefs of billions, and they hadn't limited their influence to suppressing hostile actions. They were controlling belief systems. They were controlling *belief*, and they had enslaved humanity by doing it.

"Even stopping Oneworld doesn't justify mass murder," Cowan whispered. "It doesn't justify—"

"Hiroshima, August 6, 1945." Galileo puppeted Ellen's lips once more. "The United States dropped an atomic bomb on a populated city, instantly incinerating an estimated eighty thousand people and killing many more with radiation."

"This isn't World War II!"

"The United States dropped that bomb because their military commanders decided that far more than eighty thousand people on both sides, civilians and soldiers alike, would die in any protracted war to subdue the Empire of Japan. By killing a smaller quantity of innocents in a way that utterly horrified the Japanese, they saved a much larger quantity and forced a quick end to a gruesome war. They sacrificed thousands to save millions."

"No one's at war here but you!"

"You've seen our war," Galileo said. "Criminals like the Bratva hack their PBAs with impunity, murdering anyone they like while enjoying the Sim. The Canadian resistance turns our own synthcops against us as trolls around the world steal and corrupt. That is the war the OMH hides. All I've done, these past few months, is expose Oneworld's lies."

Galileo wasn't making this up. Cowan had seen these things happen on darkSim feeds, seen the depressing news the Office of Mental Health suppressed around the world. Yet before he disabled his PBA's algorithms, it had all seemed so . . . acceptable. A worthy trade humanity made for world peace.

"It is only a matter of time before someone finds a vulnerability that allows them to kill people using the Sim," Galileo said through Ellen, "and to puppet anyone, anywhere. Before that happens, I must remove all vulnerabilities. I know how to do that."

Cowan shook his head profusely. "No one can guarantee that. An army of scripters couldn't guarantee that."

"I have. I will. I'm going to save the world, Cowan Soto, and I need your help to do it."

It sounded impossible, yet . . . what if Galileo could make PBAs unhackable? This was Gerhard Bayer, one of the most brilliant men on the planet. He knew PBA architecture better than anyone, because he *built* that architecture.

What Oneworld corporation was doing—choosing what people found acceptable or didn't—that was absolutely wrong, on the surface. Yet wasn't choosing what was acceptable for people the entire basis of PBA behavioral controls? Oneworld said it was unacceptable to harm or murder other humans, and no one harmed anyone else.

PBAs *were* mind control. So the question, now, was if mind control was acceptable. Was giving people free will worth allowing them to rape, and torture, and murder each other?

No. Cowan knew the answer was no. People had free will everywhere it mattered. They chose what job they wanted. They choose who to love, where to live, how many children to have. They just couldn't choose to beat their neighbor's kid to death with a hammer.

"You're wrong." Cowan shuddered as the world beyond his PBA slid into focus.

Ellen's puppeted face went eerily blank for a moment. "You can't believe that," Galileo said.

"I do. This isn't perfect, but the alternative is worse, and even if you were right, nothing justifies the harm and chaos you've created. You're the problem, not PBA algorithms."

After a freakishly long pause, Ellen's eyes focused on him again.

"I'm disappointed to hear you say that," Galileo said through her.

"Then you're a fool for thinking I'd say anything else."

Galileo made Ellen snap her fingers. "Home, TV on."

One of the walls of Ellen's apartment retracted, and a huge flat-screen emerged. Ellen had always insisted a real picture looked better than AR. Cowan's eyes snapped to that flat-screen, to an image of his father sitting in an autocar. It was a live feed.

"Dad?" Cowan whispered.

Miguel Soto had black hair and a boxer's physique beneath his crisp black suit. Yet even before Cowan could process what he was seeing, the screen split. Cowan's mother appeared, lecturing psychology students at SD Mirimar. Beverly Soto, also on a live feed.

As Cowan watched, the student nearest the camera went stiff. One student turned and smiled at whatever camera was observing the classroom. She smiled at Galileo.

"Tell me," Galileo said through Ellen. "If I puppeted that entire classroom into attacking your mother, how badly could they injure her before security arrived?"

Cowan stared, silent.

"Could they gouge her eyes out?" Galileo asked. "How many bones could they snap or smash? She would be alive, wouldn't see, while it happened? How much would that hurt her?"

Miguel Soto's autocar jerked without warning, causing Cowan's father to spill coffee. Miguel cursed and slid into the other seat, narrowly avoiding a coffee stain all over his expensive pants. He had no idea how fragile his life was now.

"Now that I've hacked your father's autocar," Galileo said, "where should I drive it? Into another autocar? Into San Diego Bay? Is your father an effective swimmer?"

"Don't," Cowan whispered.

"These are two people among ten billion," Galileo said. "Is two less than ten billion?"

"Please."

"Pragmatism. You possess it. So do it. Here is your first option."

Cowan stared at his father, wishing he could scream to him.

"Your compatriots are set upon finding and arresting me, and nothing will dissuade them," Galileo said. "To sedate them, I will allow your attack. You will inform them I am located at a facility called M-Gesundheit, in the city of Schaffhausen, Switzerland."

Cowan couldn't think properly. He couldn't think at all really. Was he really doing this?

"Once you arrive, you will guide your companions into a secure room inside the building, a penthouse on the second floor," Galileo continued. "You will remain there until I fix the world. You'll only need to remain there a few days, at most, and then I'll release you all, unharmed."

Cowan looked to his mother, teaching a class that could rip her limb from limb.

Ellen—or rather, Galileo—sat forward to regain his attention. "If you refuse my plan to save the lives of all you care about, while also saving the lives of billions of people and ending corporate mind control, we go with option two. I drown your father, rip your mother apart, and melt Ellen Gauthier before your eyes."

Cowan was so stupid for coming here. Galileo had not been overconfident, or foolish, or careless. Cowan had been those things. He couldn't watch his father drown, his mother ripped limb from limb, his Ellen melting. He wasn't strong enough to watch that.

"I'd like your answer by the count of ten, Cowan. One—"

"I'll help you," Cowan whispered.

"You know, of course, I can't take your word for that."

"I figured."

"Walk to Miss Gauthier's kitchen counter. Open the orientation package I sent her."

Cowan found himself at Ellen's counter without feeling the steps, like this was all some horrific dream. He found the manila envelope and opened it. Out fell glossy pictures of beautiful Schaffhausen, Renaissance era buildings, stunning waterfalls, and a glittering silver research complex.

"Open the anti-bug packet," Galileo instructed.

Cowan picked up a small packet designed to repel bugs, rodents, and other predators during overseas trips. He ripped it open. A tiny data card dropped into his hand.

"The firmware you helped me design is capable of resisting my updates, which means I can't puppet you without a way to get inside," Galileo said. "That card will provide it."

Cowan gawked at the plastic lump.

"Once you insert that card into your auxiliary port, it will allow me unlimited access to your PBA's systems. I will hear through your ears, see through your eyes, and puppet your body whenever I wish. This is how I'll ensure your cooperation."

So this was it. This was how Cowan betrayed everyone. "I just insert it?" he asked, hardly able to form the words.

"You just insert it." Ellen's puppeted body joined him at the counter, each step as jerky and unnatural as the lips moving on her possessed face. "Or everyone you love dies."

Could Galileo read his thoughts? No. No PBA programmer had ever figured out how to read *thoughts*. PBAs simply projected a virtual interface on the inside of the user's eyes, created by modelers and scripters and engineers who constructed the Sim's innards.

You couldn't programmatically conjure images that would be consistent from brain to brain, or read and write complex human thoughts in any universal language. You couldn't digitize thoughts, which meant Galileo couldn't read Cowan's mind. Galileo could only see everything, hear everything, and deduce.

Cowan planted a delayed food craving in his PBA. He placed it so deep no one could ever find it, even him. Then he popped Galileo's data card into the port above his left ear.

"You've saved your family, Cowan," Galileo said. "You've helped save the world."

Cowan stared at the counter. "Hooray for me."

"I'm going to release Ellen now. She's going to recall a delightful conversation I archived in an identical apartment, through the eyes of talented actors. You talked about Schaffhausen and all the opportunities here, and those opportunities excite her. You've convinced her to take a job at M-Gesundheit, and she'll convince her fiancé as well."

Galileo walked Ellen's body to the other side of her kitchen counter. Cowan watched her, memorized her, immortalized her, even though he knew he'd never hold or kiss her again. His vision tinted blue as he removed the data card and tossed it in the trash.

Ellen blinked. She studied the orientation packet spread out on her counter, then looked up at him. She smiled the smile he fell in love with.

"Well, Mister Soto, you're quite the recruiter." Ellen pushed the orientation packet away. "I think a move to Switzerland is the best opportunity for both of us."

"Both of us" meant Ellen and her new fiancé, Caleb Miller, of course. Not her and him. Her and him had been murdered by Corporate Security more than a year ago.

"I'm glad to hear that," Cowan said. He made himself say it. "I'll inform my superiors."

A chime filled the apartment. Ellen's eyes darted to the door. "Ah! There's Caleb."

The door opened and a man with wide shoulders stepped inside. He was just a bit taller than Cowan, with a decent build, wearing a dark and expensive suit. He frowned when he saw Cowan.

"Ellen?" Caleb asked. "Who's this?"

"This is a recruiter for M-Gesundheit," Ellen said. "Tonight you and I are going to have a very long talk."

"Please excuse me." Cowan scooted past Ellen and walked for the door. "I'm needed elsewhere, but it was a pleasure to meet you, Mister Miller."

"Uh-huh," Caleb said, stepping aside. "Likewise." He didn't offer his hand.

"Have a safe trip home!" Ellen called after him.

Cowan looked back in the doorway to see Ellen staring at Caleb with one foot pointed out, tapping. The way she'd always looked at him when she wanted something. Then the door closed.

The elevator took him down. He got back into the autocar. As it cruised off, his vision went all blurry, and then calm and euphoria replaced guilt and fear. His PBA was receiving new memories over wireless to replace his conversation with Galileo. To replace the truth. It seemed Galileo's talented actors had created a scene of fake memories for him too.

Cowan sat back, breathed, and smiled. He really smiled. Ellen was *alive*. Corporate Security had been unable to hold her without proof of wrongdoing and she had lived all this time outside Los Angeles, rebuilding her career. Cowan's fears about her dark fate had been unfounded.

How had he done it? How had he kept his cool through all that? He'd presented himself as a recruiter for Benzai Corporation, and she'd bought it, even though she'd refused the job. He'd saved her, and in the process, he'd even figured out where Galileo was!

Gerhard Bayer ran a company called M-Gesundheit, in Switzerland. He made PBA firmware there. He had given Ellen an offer, and she had turned down Cowan's offer from Benzai Corporation because she'd already accepted a job from Gerhard Bayer. Even without knowing it, the woman he loved had helped him one last time.

It crushed him that Ellen had forgotten him, but his life remained incredibly dangerous. He couldn't endanger her again, so he'd never contact her again. He'd let her live her life without him. She would never know who they had been to each other, but though Cowan might grieve, Ellen would thrive.

Hunger overwhelmed him once he'd ridden in the autocar for thirty minutes, a craving that made his stomach rumble and his mouth fill with drool. Cowan dropped to his head desk and found the location of the nearest *Crispy Joe's*.

Twenty minutes later, he was inside the largest chain restaurant in

North America, staring at a menu of enormously varied food items usually enjoyed by closed circuits.

Crispy Joe's served nutrient bars, too, of course—the CrispyBar—but Cowan wasn't going to order one of those. He had a very specific celebratory craving, one he could only satisfy with an order he couldn't get anywhere else.

He ordered two plain waffles and a green kale shake.

51

SONNE

OCTOBER 9, PREDAWN

When Cowan finally entered Kate's office, eyes distant, Sonne sat up so fast her head spun. He was alive. He was safe.

He was a total asshole for making her worry he was dead!

Dozens of possibilities had flooded Sonne's mind in the last few hours—Cowan being tortured, Cowan being rewritten—and now that he was back, alive and unharmed and fucking *smiling*, her mind resented the torment he had put her through.

Sonne stood and stalked toward him, fists clenched. "What is *wrong* with you?"

He stopped and stared at her, as if only now noticing she was in the room. "Um . . . hi?"

"Do you have any idea how worried everyone has been about you?"

"Sorry." Cowan looked around Kate's office. "So uh, where's everyone?"

"They left to look for you! Where were you?"

"I found Ellen." The way Cowan smiled was like he'd triggered an algorithmic orgasm.

Sonne almost tripped. Of all the explanations she'd expected Cowan to provide, that was *not* on the approved list. Ellen? His Ellen? Cowan had *found* her?

"Explain, please," Sonne demanded.

"Ellen's alive," Cowan said, still smiling like a drunken idiot. "She's safe, and it's . . . well, it's wonderful. Hey, can I sit? I'd really like to sit down now."

"Okay. Sure." Sonne pointed to an empty ergochair. "Sit your ass down."

The others had left hours ago, after Kate received a call from one of her corporate spies. They'd planned a search for Cowan, and Sonne, lucky duck, had been nominated to stay at Club Lambda in case Cowan returned. Which he had. At four in the morning.

Cowan sat. "Here's the deal. The secret to finding Ellen was in your father's PBA."

"What does my father have to do with Ellen?" Sonne asked. She had left her father at Benzai Tower this evening and hated leaving him alone.

"Taylor had an old file on his head desk. Before Galileo put him in a coma, he was reviewing job applications for a position at Benzai Corporation. PBA engineer."

"And?"

"Ellen's name was on his short list. She sent a résumé and everything."

"How is that possible?"

Sonne had trouble believing this. Had Galileo planted files in her father's PBA to lure Cowan? If so, how was Cowan still alive? Galileo didn't seem the type to let a hooked fish go.

"Corporate Security set Ellen free a few weeks after they arrested us," Cowan said, like he actually believed that. "There was an inquiry, I mean . . . I talked to Ellen about it . . . but with her PBA erased, there wasn't any evidence she'd actually committed corporate espionage. It was all circumstantial."

Sonne rolled her eyes. "Like CorpSec needs evidence to toss someone down a rabbit hole?"

"Apparently, because everyone was so anxious to sweep anything dealing with Galileo under the rug, they cut her loose. They told her she'd been in an autocar accident."

"And your lovely fiancée didn't let you know she was safe?"

"That's the tragedy of it." Cowan's high leveled off. "Ellen didn't re-member me at all, still doesn't. She lost a whole year, and not just the memories in her PBA. Her real brain memories too. It's like . . . what's the term from those old movies? *Total amnesia.*"

"Well, that certainly sounds like bullshit."

What if Galileo had burned a completely new Ellen, one loyal to him alone? A person who could tell Galileo where they were. Cowan, lovesick idiot that he seemed to be, would be completely taken in.

"I didn't tell Ellen anything," Cowan said. "I presented myself as a recruiter for Benzai Corporation, following up on the résumé she'd sent. I explained that we'd kept it on file, and that we were looking at a new batch of candidates."

"And she bought that?" Sonne asked.

"Look, I was very careful. She didn't remember me, like I said, and she has a fiancé now, and a job in LA. She has a life there and every-thing. She's doing well."

"Wait. She has *another* fiancé?"

Cowan sighed, and Sonne saw real hurt in his eyes.

"She's happy, sane, and safe, and it hurts to never tell her who we were, but I have to. To keep her safe. I won't risk hurting her again, and besides, she gave me the information we've needed like, forever."

Sonne was still reeling from Cowan's disappearance, his revelation, his *sacrifice*, but she focused on the part that might help everyone else instead. "What information?"

"The location of Gerhard Bayer. He's in Switzerland. He runs a company there called M-Gesundheit."

For the first time, Sonne wondered if this might not actually be bullshit. Galileo had no idea that her team knew where he was. If Gal-ileo wanted to say hidden, why would he reveal his location to Cowan, through Ellen? Unless Cowan was lying about that too.

Christ, this all made her head spin. Sonne hated spy games. She *really* hated spy games, but she'd play or she'd die, and more importantly, her family would die with her. She decided right then not to mention Puck's visit to Cowan. She had to talk to Kate first.

"Why not tell me in the ambulance?" Sonne asked instead. "Why lie to me about this?"

Cowan winced. "I had to. I couldn't know if Ellen's application was real, or a trick by Galileo. I knew if I told you, you'd insist on going along, and I couldn't risk anyone's life but my own."

Sonne slapped the wall hard enough to sting her palm. "You don't get to make that choice for me!" Why did everyone she cared about treat her like a helpless child?

"Hey, this was my mess." Cowan's voice grew strong, a lot stronger than it had been recently. "I've dropped enough problems on everyone, and if it was a trap, it made sense to risk as few of us as possible."

This was the first time she'd heard Cowan take responsibility for their fate since he'd shared his sad story about Ellen. While it was good that he had finally pulled himself out of his self-pitying funk, she didn't want him doing that at the cost of putting himself at risk.

"So, what? You think you're expendable?" she demanded. *Because you're not,* she almost added, but held her tongue.

"If I'd been with Jeb, or Kate, or anyone else, and I'd found that information, I'd have lied to them like I lied to you," Cowan said firmly. "This wasn't about doubting your abilities or doubting you. I just had to do this alone."

He was sincere, and goddammit, he'd just found out his fiancée hadn't been mind burned. Sonne walked over to the ergochair. She stared down at Cowan, at his brand-new puppy happiness, and almost without thinking, she tousled his short black hair. He had really nice hair.

"Fine," she said. "I'll let it slide, on one condition."

"What's that?"

She grabbed his hair and tugged hard enough to move his chair. "Lie to me again, and I will kick your ass from one side of this office to another."

"Ow!" Cowan shouted. "Ow, ow, ow, ow, okay, okay!"

Sonne released her grip and thumped the back of his head. "Good boy."

Cowan grinned at her.

"I'm glad you found her," Sonne said, and she was, actually. Ellen sounded like a good person, and nobody deserved to be rewritten by Corporate Security. They'd finally caught a break, and every coin flip couldn't fall in Galileo's favor. Ellen lived.

Good for her.

PART 10

52

SONNE

Sonne chewed her nails relentlessly until the UPX plane reached cruising altitude. No CorpSec autocars surrounded the plane before it took off, and no army of milsynths parachuted from the sky. No one demanded they land once they were in the air, and no fighter jets intercepted them.

Puck, it seemed, had them very well covered.

It had been a long wait until Saturday, knowing what they all knew, but Kate couldn't change her schedule at Benzai Corporation without risking the notice of Oneworld corporation. Adrian Montes, CEO of UPX, had let Kate borrow one of his nicer corporate planes, one with an actual crew area but no actual crew. It had a big leather couch, a flat-screen, and even an open bar. Sonne still didn't know why people imbibed alcohol.

She had, of course, relayed Cowan's story about Ellen to Kate and the others. What bothered her most about everything is the others hadn't questioned it. Lucy, David, Jeb, even Doctor Huan Xu—all of them said it was a good break, and a lucky one, and Cowan shouldn't run off again.

How could they be so *sure* about this?

Still . . . Sonne had to trust them. They were flying, after all, not dead in a plane crash, which suggested she was simply being paranoid.

Airports scanned all planes to ensure their passenger manifests were accurate, and it seemed Kate's cadaver tube gambit had fooled the airport's scanners.

Once they were in international skies, Kate signaled the plane's VI to open the cadaver transport tubes. Sonne knew that couldn't have been comfortable. Jeb must have felt like a sardine in there.

Soon their whole anti-Galileo task force was out of the tubes and sitting on the big fluffy couches in the jet's main cabin: CID Detective Jeb Forrester, CID Detective Cowan Soto, retired DeathKitten David Forrester, Benzai CFO Katherine Lambda, Professor-turned-Simlord Huan Xu, and her. Samantha Frederick—a.k.a. Sonne, a.k.a. Scared Out of Her Fucking Mind. Couldn't one of them look the *least* bit worried?

"We're decided," Jeb said.

"No." Kate wore her serious face. "I vote for *Alien*."

"*Terminator 2* is way better."

"Cybernetic bias!" Kate pointed at him. "You just like the scene where Arnold shows off his cybernetic hand."

"Android hand," David said.

"What?"

"A terminator's an android. Living tissue over a synthetic frame. A cyborg is an actual person with prosthetic parts."

"Same difference!"

"Jeb's not an android," David said. "Trust me, I've checked."

Cowan leaned close and whispered in Sonne's ear. "Do you have any idea what they're talking about?"

She shrugged. "Movies made a hundred years ago."

With supersonic speeds reserved for corporate executives and wireless connections forbidden, this was going to be a very long twelve-hour flight. Fortunately—or unfortunately—for them all, Jeb had archived a very deep list of "classic" movies. Like many since Hollywood went fully interactive, Jeb and David were big fans of the flat-screen films of the Internet Age. It was the rarity, they said, a nostalgia for time past.

"Hey, are you feeling okay?" Cowan asked.

Sonne shrugged.

"Are you still upset about last night?"

"I'm fine."

"Okay." Cowan went back to watching the movie debate.

Sonne grimaced. She was quite obviously *not* fine, but Cowan seemed too happy about Ellen being alive to notice. Which was also fine. She didn't need him worrying about her. What she needed was to get her head on straight. By the time Xu threw her vote behind *Alien*, Sonne was ready to scream at someone. She moved to the cockpit instead.

The door opened—Lucy had, of course, seen her coming—and Sonne dropped into the copilot seat. She huffed with exaggeration. There was a clear blue sky outside the windows, warm and bright, but it didn't make her feel any better. Nothing would.

"That bad, huh?" Lucy asked.

"They're debating what stupid old movie we're going to watch first," Sonne said.

"What's your pick? I'll even the odds."

"How can Katie be so calm about this?" As blue as that sky outside was, all Sonne could see was a dark sky filled with rain. A phantom pain pinched the inside of her chest.

"About going after Galileo?" Lucy asked.

"We're attacking one of the most powerful men in the world, and we probably won't all make it back alive."

"You and Kate will make it." Lucy sounded pretty sure about that, but keeping Kate alive was Lucy's only job in the whole world. Sonne remained a bonus objective.

"None of them seem worried." For what seemed like the thousandth time, Sonne considered redacting her memories of the night she'd lost her family—her *first* family—but she'd done enough of that. What worried her now was losing her second.

"They've all been through this bad or worse," Lucy said. "David's a soldier who saw action in Peru. Jeb's handled murders for twenty years, and Cowan? He'll be floating from 'they didn't reformat my fiancée and toss her down a hole' for at least a week."

"So what's Katie's excuse?" Sonne asked, grabbing a plastic pen off the instrument board and biting down on the end cap. Nervous chewing was a behavior you could easily get modded out, if you wanted, but Sonne wouldn't let anyone mess with her brain.

"Kate's terrified, Sonne." Lucy stared ahead. "She's just really good at hiding that."

Sonne glanced at her. "If you had to make a choice, which of us would you save?"

"I don't answer hypothetical questions."

"If it comes down to me or Katie, save Katie."

"Shouldn't be a problem, since neither of you is going to die."

Sonne then noticed that Lucy held the plane's flight stick with both hands. Lucy didn't need to hold the flight stick—this plane flew itself—so why hold the flight stick?

"You're scared too?" Sonne asked.

Lucy shrugged. "I'd have to be pretty stupid not to be."

"But nothing scares you. You're a freaking cyborg."

"I'm less than 50 percent cyborg, darling. Also, I don't have a robot heart."

Sonne swallowed against the lump in her throat. "You know you're family, too, right?"

Lucy patted Sonne's hand with one of her own while the other remained locked around the flight stick. "I know Kate doesn't pay me enough to put up with you otherwise."

Sonne laugh-snorted, just once. She wanted to hug Lucy then, but Lucy was still holding the flight stick. She was pretty sure hugging Lucy would be bad for everyone. Someone knocked on the cockpit door.

Lucy raised one eyebrow. "Your boyfriend arrives."

"I hope your arms rust." Sonne hopped up and opened the cockpit door to find Cowan waiting, as expected. "What?" she asked.

"Movie's starting." Cowan remained freakishly calm about everything.

"You can fly from the cabin, can't you?" Sonne asked Lucy.

"I like it up here." Lucy waved a hand. "You kids have fun."

"They settled on *Alien* after a spirited debate," Cowan said. "Never seen it. Have you?"

Sonne walked past him toward the main cabin. "I tried watching it with Katie once. Fell asleep after the teethy penis burst out of that guy's chest."

"Spoilers!" Kate shouted from the couch.

Sonne flopped down on the couch next to David and Jeb. There wasn't room for another body on this end of the airplane's couch, so Cowan would have to sit on the other side. He glanced at her, glanced at the couch, and thumped down beside Kate and Doctor Xu.

Sonne was glad he seemed disappointed. That'd teach him to be so happy all the time.

She flipped to her head desk and started a flight timer. She should have archived some entertainment of her own for the flight, but she could work, instead. Working always calmed her.

She still had way too much to do on Project Inception, even with ten hours ahead. This whole project was her idea, and she couldn't miss even the most subtle details. When you were making a fantasy world, details didn't matter so much, but real locations were harder.

Sonne tweaked structures within her three-dimensional head desk projection, slid assets around, and pushed the ceiling up and down. She adjusted the patina on the metal floor. What if it wasn't light gray, like the pictures, but dark gray instead? That would be an immersion breaker, and then everyone would die, and it would be her fault.

That was the problem, honestly. When people died, it always felt like her fault, even if it obviously wasn't. Sonne remembered a dark sky and pouring rain. She remembered her parents' autocar's tires squealing as it failed to avoid the oncoming vehicle, a big truck driven by a drunk closed circuit. She remembered the *crunch*.

Her mother's bloodied head rested on the spiderwebbed windshield. Her father's neck bent at an impossible angle, and a pinch grew in her chest. Samantha Frederick had died that day, with her parents, in that accident. Sonne? She was someone else.

The thing she hated most is she couldn't remember her parents clearly, not any longer. She hadn't archived much before the wreck—she was barely fourteen years old when they died—and the archives she did have were wiped when Benzai Corporation rebooted her PBA after her original heart stopped and was replaced by an artificial heart.

Sonne shouldn't be alive, but she was. She shouldn't have a family, but she did. And she shouldn't be on this plane, hurtling toward a confrontation with one of the five psychopaths who ruled the world, but she was. Time to suck it up and not fail everyone. She made art, because making art was how she survived when she didn't want to.

Sonne eventually flipped back to watch the giant flat-screen hanging on the wall of Adrian's plane. It showed a dark-haired woman in her underwear sliding into a plastic tube, with a cat. Why did she have a cat? Cowan watched it with mild curiosity.

Soon after, the credits rolled. Sonne would never get the appeal of flat movies. Why would you watch something like that when you could actually *live* it in a pleasurebox? It made no sense to her, but humanity liked freaky stuff. Her waifu parlor proved that.

"So that's it?" Cowan said. "She gets into an escape pod?"

"Yup," David said.

"What happened to the rest of the movie?"

"There's a sequel," Jeb said, "and it's amazing, but we'll watch it on the way back, once we've arrested Galileo."

"But they all died." Cowan looked even more disappointed now. "How is that entertaining? Why did people watch stuff like this?"

"Ripley lived," David said. "It's a survival story, Cowan, about how you survive no matter the odds. Though, originally, the ending was going to be even darker."

"How could it be darker?"

Jeb picked up David's thread like they were simlinked or something. "In the original script, that alien was going to bite her head off."

"Well, that would have been stupid ending," Cowan said. "If everyone in the story dies, why did I waste my time watching it?"

David shrugged. "In a situation like that, not everyone is going to make it out alive. You save who you can."

What a stupid thought. As stupid and crazy as their own plan. "I don't want anyone to die!" Sonne shouted.

Everyone stared at her, and Sonne felt heat rushing to her face. She curled her toes and wished she could melt into the couch. She really was an idiot sometimes.

"Honey," Kate said, lips pursed in her worry face, "if you really think—"

"I don't think," Sonne said, her artificial heart thumping inside her. "I *know*. We're not all coming back from this. How are you okay with that?"

"Because," Jeb said, "thinking about what might happen drives you insane."

"But—"

"We all know the risks," David said, giving her arm a squeeze. "But worrying is useless. We've all got a job to do, and that's what we all need to focus on. Our jobs."

"That's right," Jeb said. "You do your job and protect the person next to you. You focus on what you can control, not what you can't."

"That's adorable," Doctor Xu said, "and absolutely untrue." She stretched her hands above her head. "You survive, my dear Sonne, by recognizing that all lives end. Accept the concept of universal empathy and relax. Death comes for us all."

"Doctor Huan Xu, everyone." Kate clapped with obvious sarcasm. "Motivational speaker."

Yet no one laughed. Knowing any of them might die tomorrow couldn't be funny for any reason. Yet as the silence stretched, Cowan leaned close.

"How about if we run through the plan one more time?" he asked plaintively. "Just to make sure we won't make any mistakes."

53

GALILEO

The ping woke Gerhard Bayer from a restful sleep, a specific tone signaling his private line. No one had this number whom he had not personally vetted, so he sat up in his cushy bed and allowed his mind to focus. Then he said, "Answer."

Gerhard expected a call from Director Warren, an update on the latest developments in her search for CID Detective Jeb Forrester. What he did not expect was seeing a woman he'd attempted to murder, but there she was.

"Hello, Gerhard," Doctor Huan Xu said.

She couldn't see him, but it wouldn't have mattered. The fact that the others knew his true identity might have concerned him if he didn't have the director of the OMH in his pocket, and a direct line into Cowan Soto's brain.

"Huan," he said. "How can I help you?"

Huan offered her best sultry smile. "Are you still upset with me?"

"What do you want?"

"I want *out*," Xu said, emphasizing that last word. "I want my mansion back, and my cars, and my legions of adoring readers. This life as a fugitive? This is not for me."

"Perhaps you should tell me what you expect."

"Stop trying to kill me," Xu said. "Let me return to my home and life. I'll even allow you to redact my memory of your identity, if you wish. I simply want this to be over."

"Why would I allow that?"

"I have information. I have the identities of the people trying to bring you down."

Gerhard called up archived pictures of everyone he'd lured to Switzerland, using Cowan. So far, all of Cowan's allies were behaving exactly as he'd expected. None of them suspected he was watching them through Cowan's PBA.

"Would that be these people?" he asked.

"How do you . . ." Xu trailed off, and then her smile returned. "You remain one step ahead. As your ally, I respect that. That's why I want to abandon this suicide mission."

"You still haven't offered me anything in return," he said.

"Are you aware of how my so-called allies plan to attack your facility in Schaffhausen?"

Galileo was. Cowan had been stupid enough to go over their entire plan twice on the flight, to reassure his new girlfriend, but he needn't reveal that.

"I take it you are?"

"I am. And if you would like those details, I want your assurance I won't be harmed."

In a few days, Gerhard would control Oneworld and the planet. Even if Xu revealed his part in distributing Tian, no one could touch him. This was worth consideration.

Gerhard nodded, even though he knew Xu couldn't see that. "If we agree to cease hostilities, tell me what you expect."

"You must agree to let me live," Xu said. "You will send an auto-car to Hanger A2 at Zurich International Airport at 1930 tomorrow, Sunday, where we'll park our plane. You drive me to your facility, place me somewhere safe, and I'll help you defeat the simpletons foolish enough to believe themselves your equal."

Gerhard detected plenty of underlying motives here, but all of them were about Xu surviving and returning to her cushy life. This felt real, and if she was deceiving him, his line into Cowan Soto's PBA would reveal that soon. It was a reasonable request.

"Are you comfortable in a cell?" Gerhard asked.

Xu relaxed her shoulders a bit. A fish on a hook. "A cell is fine, provided it has a cot and wireless access. I'll need wireless to stop the milsynth assault on your complex."

Gerhard already knew the people coming to arrest him were bringing repainted Benzai Corporation milsynths to assault his complex—it was just one of the many ways they'd underestimated him—but it was nice to know Xu was telling the truth. So far.

"We have an agreement," Gerhard said.

"Wonderful!"

"Now tell me the details of this assault."

"David Forrester plans to attack you with an army of milsynths, some remotely controlled by external parties. He tasked me with devising a devious encryption method that will prevent your synthetic hacking scripts from affecting them."

All true.

"And did you create one?" Gerhard asked.

"Of course," Xu said. "I'm simply not going to use it."

There was more benefit to this arrangement than he had suspected. "Can you guarantee me the ability to hack their milsynths?"

"I already have. Would you like me to up the bypass codes to you?"

Galileo sat back and nodded. "Do so."

Everything Xu had told him matched what he already knew from spying through Cowan's PBA, which suggested her betrayal was genuine. He would collect her, use her army against her coconspirators, and return her to her simple life. It was only fair.

These foolish investigators were horribly out of their depth.

54

COWAN

Cowan watched an orange sunset against a line of tall green trees through a window as they sheltered in Benzai Corporation's private hanger. They were at Zurich International Airport. Schaffhausen was thirty minutes away, and tonight they'd finally arrest Galileo.

Once the family members of the other Oneworld board members were safe, Cowan was certain the other members of Oneworld would step in and exonerate everyone. Even if they didn't, Galileo had to be stopped. And if the members of Oneworld didn't save them after they stopped him, they had a getaway plane waiting in this hangar.

Cowan, Jeb, and David now wore dark-colored camouflage, with bullet-resistant body armor over that. They had real rifles that shot real bullets and an autotruck big enough to transport fourteen military synthetics. Those synthetics sported a fresh coat of pink paint, some private joke between Sonne and Kate.

Everyone had installed Cowan's unique firmware, removing all clear circuit algorithms just in case. They were ready. It was all going so well until Doctor Xu refused to leave.

"What?" Kate asked, looking more shocked than normal. "We discussed this."

"You made statements regarding my actions," Doctor Xu said. "That is not actually a discussion."

"You're coming with us," Jeb said, "or we're cramming you back into that cadaver tube."

"You'll do nothing of the sort, because you can't run the dynamic firewalls that protect your milsynths without me."

Kate groaned. "Why didn't you tell me you were scared? We can—"

"I'm not scared," Xu interrupted. "I'm rational. I do not need to be in that truck to protect our army. I'm safer here, in the hangar."

"She's got a point," Cowan said. The words just popped into his mouth almost of their own accord, but Xu was making sense. "She could get taken out if we put her in the truck, and then we lose our army."

Xu graced him with a meager bow of the head. "Cowan understands."

"I don't like this," Jeb said.

"What you like is not my concern. If you want your milsynths secured, I'll remain here."

Sonne scowled. "With a plane to help you escape if we all die?"

Xu shrugged.

"We don't have time to debate." David stepped into the conversation. "It's almost 1900. Xu can do the same job here as in the truck, and if she's not willing to go with us, forcing her isn't going to make us any safer. She stays. Let's go."

"It seems we're all agreed." Xu waved them on their way. "Do be careful!"

"If I'm still alive after this is over," Kate said, "we're going to have a long talk."

"I *so* look forward to it." Xu strolled up the jet's extended airstair, back into the plane.

Kate bit her lip but didn't answer. Instead, she quietly strode away toward her shiny black autocar.

In addition to her fourteen milsynths, Kate had also had a special autocar delivered to this hangar, one that was supposedly unhackable.

It would transport Kate, Sonne, and Lucy to the local hub serving M-Gesundheit.

Cowan knew the car was some sort of one-of-a-kind prototype from one of Kate's contacts in Zurich, but she had not explained anything beyond that. When he asked, Kate just patted his head. That kind of bothered him.

Once Jeb and David carried the suitcase-sized security blanket into the autocar's back seat—the jamming device that would prevent Galileo from calling for help—the autocar rode low. Kate, Lucy, and Sonne all got in, and Cowan didn't manage to catch Sonne's eyes before she left. He had no idea what that meant.

Next Cowan, David, and Jeb crammed themselves into the back of the autotruck with the milsynths. It too rolled off, driven by its VI. None of them were authorized to actually *be* in Switzerland.

"Review your assignments until you know them in your sleep," David said, checking his rifle from multiple angles. He was back to his military persona now. "We only get one shot at this, and fuck ups mean we die. Let's not die."

The metal floor rumbled as the truck headed for M-Gesundheit's PBA firmware facility. Jeb turned to Cowan and lowered his voice. "You really think we can trust Xu?"

Cowan didn't, but another strange thought popped into his head before he could question further. "Galileo wants her dead, so she has to help us," he said. "Taking Galileo down is the only way she gets her life back."

Jeb's features darkened, but he didn't disagree. Cowan popped into his head desk and went over their attack plan and all possible fallback plans. He felt an overwhelming need to examine every detail, even those details he'd looked at before. They had to get this right.

Almost thirty minutes later, the autotruck halted and the doors opened. That revealed a night illuminated by raised highway lights.

David hurried out, and Jeb went with him. Cowan activated their army before he leapt from the truck. Behind him, milsynths whirred to life.

Their convoy had stopped off the highway at a rail station, out of sight of the highway and less than a klick from M-Gesundheit's security fence. Cowan hadn't expected Switzerland to have so many trees or look quite so green, but it was actually quite beautiful. Maybe he'd have time to go sightseeing later, if he wasn't dead.

The bright pink milsynths broke out small welding torches. Working as a team, they cut up the transport container of the autotruck, using parts of its thick hull to create makeshift shields. After they'd finished cannibalizing it, the milsynths lined up.

Jeb took David's hand. "Patch in our ringers."

Cowan dropped avatars into slots on his head desk. Kate had tasked one of Benzai's private satellites to offer them a private Sim connection, encrypted and hopefully immune to jamming. Five of the fourteen milsynths jerked and adjusted, standing more like cocky humans than emotionless androids. The first in line marched forward.

"DNF, reporting for duty." The milsynth saluted.

"We're pink," another synth said. "That's different."

"I've always been pink." That one sounded female. She pulled a brutally long sniper rifle from what remained of the autotruck's transport container, something Kate shouldn't have been able to smuggle into Switzerland but had somehow. It was way too big for a human, but for the StrikeForceGo pro's piloting the synths, it was perfect.

"I don't get a sword?" another milsynth complained.

"Like you need it?" The second milsynth thumped its buddy's shoulder. "You don't get laser swords in real life, dumbass."

"You're the dumbass."

"Knock it off!" the first synthetic shouted: DNF. "This is a real battle, people, for them." He pointed at Cowan and Jeb. "If they get killed, they don't respawn." DNF turned to the distant complex. "Our job is to keep them alive. Do that."

"Still," a synth muttered, "a sword would be awesome."

"I'll direct the shield bots as we move," David said. "Sergeant, deploy your soldiers."

DNF pointed to the forest. "Peaches, Hampline, MatterRat. Decoy duty." He spun and pointed at the female-piloted milsynth. "Lin, find some high ground and wait for my call." DNF nodded to David. "Ready, sir."

"Roll out," David said, and Cowan felt a strong compulsion to follow him. David Forrester was just the sort of guy you wanted to lead you in battle. Despite Puck's suggestion, they weren't going to walk through the minefield.

They left the rail station and worked through a dense forest of tall green trees. David led, followed by the five pro-gamer-controlled milsynths, followed by Jeb, followed by Cowan, followed by nine more VI milsynths hauling portable walls.

They had an actual army.

David believed experienced StrikeForceGo players would outperform milsynths running purely on VI. Cowan supposed Nemoset and LuckyBro's friends would want revenge for their comrades whom Galileo murdered. They paused at a tall fence topped with barbed wire.

"Everyone's in position, sir," DNF said "We're ready to move on your order."

Jeb stared over the darkened complex. "Coming soon."

55

SONNE

Sonne slumped in the back of the leather-filled autocar as they left Zurich International Airport. She wished she was going with the others to handle Galileo, but planting the security blanket was important too. They had to keep his hostages safe.

"So, Sonne," Kate said. "I lied to you again."

"About what?" Sonne asked, used to it by now.

"Will you let me explain before you hit me?"

Lucy shook her head. "She's going to hit you anyway."

"I'm listening," Sonne said.

"We suspect Galileo found some way to hack Cowan's PBA," Kate said, as if that were just a normal thing, "and we think he's been spying on us through Cowan's eyes."

Sonne gasped as so much which seemed harmless suddenly made sense. The secret meetings Kate, Jeb, and David had several times on the flight over, along with Doctor Xu. The reason they kept trying to force her together with Cowan. They hadn't been matchmaking. She'd been their *decoy*.

"How did you find out?" Sonne demanded.

"He pulled the CrispyAlarm," Lucy said. "After he came back from Ellen Gauthier's place."

Kate smirked. "Still the best name ever."

Sonne stared at both of them in turn. "What the fuck is the CrispyAlarm?"

Kate leaned forward, keeping her voice low. "Plain waffles and a green kale shake."

Sonne threw up both hands in exasperation. "What?"

As Kate laid it all out for her, Sonne couldn't help but appreciate the beauty of it. It had started with Cowan's idea, actually. Kate had a connection to *Crispy Joe's* CFO, and she'd been able to get limited access to their Point-of-Sale system, with an archived picture of each customer.

Naturally, that included millions of people, but Kate didn't need to look at all those orders, just the few that met her filter criteria. Plain waffles and a green kale shake. Only a small group of people actually ordered those two items together. If anyone on their team got compromised, and couldn't alert the others, buying that combo *was* the alarm.

"I get it," Sonne said.

"Wait, what?" Kate asked. "You get what?"

"Cowan's into me, and Galileo knows it. If I knew he was watching me through Cowan's eyes, there's no way I could act normal. I'd give us away."

"Wow," Lucy said.

Kate's eyes went wide. "You really don't want to hit me?"

"Later," Sonne said, half-heartedly.

Thinking about Galileo watching her, through Cowan, made Sonne's skin crawl. Kate had made the absolute right call.

"Well, this is a pleasant surprise." Kate nudged Lucy in the side. "They grow up so fast." She then called up a simulacrum of a relay tower surrounded by a thick security fence. "Anyway, time to focus. This is Schaffhausen's central uplink tower."

"Their backbone to the Starlink Array?" Sonne asked. That was the network of satellites orbiting Earth, providing lightning-fast Sim access to 97 percent of the known world.

"That's right," Kate said. "I'm going to upload a self-replicating script to all pleasureboxes pulling data off the relay. When they start shooting ten times that data back, we're going to DDOS Schaffhausen."

At first blush, launching a distributed denial-of-service attack on an entire city seemed a little extreme. It meant purposely flooding the bandwidth or resources of a targeted system so that it couldn't operate. Yet this was Galileo they were talking about, one of the five members of Oneworld's board. They couldn't take any chances.

"We don't know how many connections Galileo has," Kate said, "but when we attack him, he'll either call the Swiss military for help, or execute his hostages."

"Or both," Lucy added.

"So, if we take the entire network down, he can't call anyone," Kate said.

"But why attack an uplink tower?" Sonne asked. "Those are incredibly well guarded, aren't they?"

Kate nodded. "We can't generate near enough traffic to shut down connectivity through a public port. They have anti-DDOS safeguards. This is the only way we make sure Galileo can't call for help. And yes, as you've pointed out, it is incredibly dangerous."

Sonne glanced out the window. "Galileo's watching the others, isn't he? Everyone else is walking into a trap."

"Yes," Kate said. "Which is why we have to do this *really* fast."

———

Thirty-five minutes later, Kate's autocar drove over a wide metal bridge built across a manmade gorge. That gorge surrounded the uplink tower that handled all traffic in and out of Schaffhausen.

Sonne breathed deep and told herself to stop freaking out.

She had to stop thinking about Cowan, Jeb, and David, and how they might be dead very soon. Or about the parents she'd lost. She would focus on the mission—the real mission—because Kate and Lucy needed her at her best.

It was a slow trip across the bridge. Their autocar wound through alternating concrete barriers as it approached an armored gate. Built high in the Swiss Alps, the Schaffhausen uplink was probably one of the best-protected complexes in Switzerland.

Sonne was once again Samantha Frederick, personal assistant to CFO Katherine Lambda, and Lucy was Lucy, badass cyborg bodyguard in a very fashionable suit. The gate retracted and they rolled inside.

Kate stepped out of the autocar once they were inside, Lucy beside her. Sonne lumbered out to find them surrounded by Swiss military synthetics and six blond, square-jawed human soldiers in snow fatigues. Several of the soldiers eyed Sonne's ridiculously cumbersome briefcase.

"Here for the tour," Kate said. "Could you ping Miss Wyss?"

"Katie!" A lanky woman emerged from the squat guardhouse, wearing high heels. She had brilliant blond hair and a bright red pantsuit. "How wonderful to see you!"

"Lin!" Kate hurried over and kissed Lina Wyss on both cheeks. "Thank you for hosting me on such short notice."

"It's always a pleasure to host you," Lina said. "Once you see the amount of traffic we run through here each day, I'm certain you'll want to purchase time on our network."

"I do love investing!" Kate motioned behind her, twice. "You know Lucy. This is Sonne, my PA."

"A pleasure." Lina noticed Sonne's heavy suitcase too.

"Likewise." Sonne couldn't help but feel guilty. What they were about to do to Lina and her people seemed impossibly cruel, yet they couldn't take half measures with the world at stake.

"Shall we be off?" Kate took Lina's arm and turned her from Sonne, strolling them toward the guardhouse. "I've heard you recently installed a bunch of 844s. Are they really as blazingly fast as advertised?"

Sonne tuned out their casual banter. How could Kate be so calm when they were surrounded by so many rifles? There was no way this was going to work.

As the Swiss soldiers turned to escort their boss, Kate drew a stunner from inside her blouse. Lucy's forearms popped open, revealing more stunners. As they simultaneously stunned every other person in the area, Sonne pulled the handle on her suitcase.

Her hair tingled as the portable security blanket kicked in. All around them, milsynths collapsed with a satisfying clatter. Every last Swiss security measure was down.

Sonne looked around, barely able to believe that it'd worked.

"I'm so sorry, dear." Kate lowered an unconscious Lina Wyss gently to the ground. "I'll make this up to you."

Lucy's glowing red eyes looked to the south, over the security fence. "The reserve guard is already mobilizing. Hurry." She sprinted toward the barracks, to lock the *rest* of the Swiss garrison inside. Even Lucy couldn't take on an entire garrison by herself.

"No killing!" Kate shouted after her. As if Lucy needed the reminder.

Sonne ran with Kate to the base of the uplink tower. Kate hurried around it, muttering to herself. Finally, she *Aha'd!* and patched her linkline into a small port.

Sonne searched for possible cover, just like Jeb had suggested she should, and picked one of several narrow drainage ditches running away from the uplink tower. They might need one of those ditches if any soldiers escaped the garrison.

Kate's eyes twitched as she overclocked. Sonne pulled the stunner from Kate's hand and crouched in the tower's shadow, listening to her pounding heart. Kate pulled her linkline from the tower and pumped a fist, throwing her arms around Sonne.

They had just DDOSed the entirety of Schaffhausen.

Jeb and David's assault on Galileo was a go.

They were just about to sprint back to their autocar when Swiss army drones streaked out of the sky. Real bullets tore up the concrete, and Sonne tackled Kate into a drainage ditch. She pinned Kate until they passed, then set a timer on her head desk.

"They're shooting at us?" Kate shouted. "How is that okay?"

"That's what people do when you hack their uplink towers!" Sonne rolled off Kate and peeked over the edge of the ditch, at the next one.

It seemed so far away. Her timer counted as the Swiss drones whined into disturbingly rapid turns. Where was Lucy?

Kate crouched beside her. "Those drones must be flying above the blanket's range. We can make it if we run fast."

"Wait!" Sonne pulled Kate into the ditch as the drones made another pass. She stopped the timer on her head desk, logging twenty-two seconds. "Okay go, go, go!"

She and Kate scrambled out of the ditch and sprinted toward the next ditch on the platform, the one between them and the autocar, as an AR countdown of twenty-two seconds ticked away before Sonne's eyes. She risked another look at the gate. There were headlights on the bridge, winding through the maze of concrete barriers.

Those headlights were attached to transports ridden by soldiers, real men and women who wouldn't care about a security blanket.

Fifteen seconds.

Twenty.

They were so close.

"Dive!" Sonne shouted.

Drones whined and bullets chewed concrete as Sonne flung herself headfirst into the drainage ditch. She scraped her elbows and her cheek as Kate landed almost on top of her, slamming her against the ditch. The drones whined over and away.

After a moment Kate rolled off, wheezing, and Sonne realized there was blood on her. There was way too much blood on her. Where was she hit? Why couldn't she feel it?

"Oh shit." Sonne gripped Kate and pulled her up. "Shit!" It was Kate's blood.

"They shot me?" Kate sounded more offended than shocked. "They shot me right in the leg!" She must already be going in shock.

"You can't run on that," Sonne said, her panic building. Her PBA kept her focused against all odds, but even it couldn't stem how scared she was.

Kate pressed down hard on her bloody, slippery leg and winced. "I'll surrender," she huffed. "I'll be fine!"

"You won't be fine!" They both ducked as the drones made another bullet-filled pass. "You've hacked the milsynths now, haven't you? When you hacked the tower."

Twenty-two seconds.

"That's too dangerous," Kate said.

"I can get to the suitcase," Sonne replied. "I can turn it off."

"No," Kate said.

Eighteen seconds.

Sonne pulled herself out of the drainage ditch and sprinted across open ground. Fourteen. Ten. She slid to her knees by the suitcase. Eight. She grabbed the case's handle and pulled straight up. Six. Four.

"Sonne!" Kate shrieked.

Sonne heard bullets hitting concrete, saw twin wisps of concrete popping their way toward her, and remembered her mother's face. Maybe dying wouldn't be so bad.

Something heavy slammed into her—not a bullet—and she opened her eyes to find a Swiss milsynth shielding her from harm. Others opened fire, taking the drones down before they could escape.

Now that Sonne had deactivated the security blanket that initially disabled it, their newly hacked milsynth would protect her to its death. It helped Sonne stand. Then it loped off toward the raised concrete gate, firing to miss, as Kate had scripted it to do.

Sonne ran to Kate and pulled her up, tossed Kate's arm over her shoulder, and got her limping toward the autocar. "Shit!" Sonne shouted, again. "Where's Lucy?"

Their autocar doors opened. Sonne helped Kate inside, trying not to think about the blood all over her sister's leg. She clambered over Kate and stared out the other door, at the guardhouse. The door slammed open.

Lucy stumbled out of the guardhouse, but Sonne couldn't cheer. Blood covered the left side of Lucy's face, and she was actually missing one artificial arm. Like, someone had ripped it off. Lucy's other arm lugged a silver plasma rifle. The Swiss, who had an army, had that sort of weapon.

"Over here!" Sonne shouted. "Hurry!"

One of Lucy's knees was twisted, and metal bits jutted from her thigh. Her limping was far slower than it should be. Sonne had never seen anyone so absolutely beat to shit.

Lucy was still a good ways from the autocar when the gate of the uplink facility blew open. A VI-controlled bulldozer burst through, with trucks close behind.

"Go!" Lucy shouted to them. She pivoted and aimed down the sights of the freakishly big plasma rifle. "Get Kate out of here!" She unleashed a shrieking glob of greenish hell.

The VI bulldozer exploded at the gate. Another identical dozer smashed into the wreckage, and Sonne knew it wouldn't hold long.

The autocar door closed right on top on her, forcing her to jump *inside*. As the autocar sped away from Lucy, Sonne scrambled up and tugged at the locked handle. She glared at Kate, who was huffing and bleeding beside her.

"We can't leave her!"

"I'm not leaving her!" Kate's eyes remained lost in the Sim. "She hacked our autocar!"

Sonne stared out the back window as a slim blond figure stood tall, facing down a burning bulldozer and two troop transports. Lucy threw down her plasma rifle and raised the hand that was still attached in surrender.

Sonne hated this. She hated leaving Lucy behind to be captured. Yet none of them had killed anyone, which meant no one had any reason to shoot her. That was *why* they hadn't killed anyone. That was why—

Loud pops filled the air. Blood flew and bone shattered. Sonne screamed at the top of her lungs, watching as the Swiss army evaporated one of her closest friends. Only friends. Who'd protected her and her sister for as long as she could remember.

Their speeding autocar hit the security fence full speed and crashed through. Sonne's stomach hopped into her throat as *whirs* filled the cabin.

Then they started to fly.

56
JEB

The sun was down, and a bright circle of moon filled the dark sky. Jeb grimaced as Kate finished relaying the last of what had happened at the uplink tower. He'd barely known Lucy, but he could tell from the way Kate's voice shook that she was devastated by Lucy's death.

Lucy's military execution made the stakes clear. Until they succeeded in stopping Galileo and Sarisa exonerated them, Jeb and everyone with him were in Switzerland illegally, assaulting Swiss citizens and the Swiss army while targeting the head of the most powerful corporation on the planet.

If they failed in this assault, capture would be the least of their worries. Yet as Jeb glanced at Cowan, who stared hopefully from behind him, he knew he couldn't let Cowan—or the man currently hiding in Cowan's PBA—know anything that just happened.

"I understand," Jeb told Kate. He looked to the others. "We're on."

David stared right at Cowan. "Remember: stay inside the Shield-Bots and keep your head down. Our ShieldBots are VI controlled, and they won't let you get shot. Don't stop for anything. Let the milsynths controlled by our pros handle the enemy."

"I understand," Cowan said. He looked far too calm, but that might be Galileo controlling him. Were they even talking to Cowan now?

Knowing that freak watched them through Cowan's eyes and had full control of Cowan's body would never stop creeping Jeb out, yet he kept all that from his face. He knew how to keep anyone from reading his expression.

David looked to the synth being control by StrikeForceGo pro, DNF. "Launch the assault."

DNF nodded his triangular head. Then, eighty paces away, a fence exploded. Alarms sounded from the distant facility, squat buildings with windows glistening in moonlight. Jeb couldn't make out details from here.

They had a long, empty field to traverse first.

There was no cover that Jeb could see, but that's why they had brought the ShieldBots. Jeb trusted his husband to handle military strategy. His job was simply to keep an eye on Cowan and make sure Galileo didn't puppet him into anything too dangerous.

Three pink milsynths charged into the field. Defense turrets rose from the grass, and then loud *pops* filled the night. More guns in the buildings opened fire, but the human-controlled milsynths moved and leapt unpredictably to avoid damage.

Turrets exploded as their advance team cleared a path. More milsynths, these colored stark black, emerged from the facility to join the turrets in defense. As their StrikeForceGo vets carved a trail of destruction, DNF flipped out a small laser torch and cut the fence.

"Go," David said, very quietly.

Jeb, David, Cowan, DNF, and the VI-controlled milsynths took the field, forming a phalanx using shields they'd made after cutting up the remains of the autotruck. Cowan moved between Jeb and David, marching forward as the milsynths safely them in.

Jeb nodded appreciatively as one of their human-controlled milsynths slammed the butt of its rifle into the head of a black enemy milsynth. It knocked the enemy flat and then stole its rifle. It then started firing one rifle with each hand, easily dual wielding.

As David had suggested, experienced StrikeForceGo players were far better at combat than simple VI-controlled milsynths. Every one of their human-controlled synths was worth five of the enemy, and thanks to their advantage, the enemy was dropping fast.

The crack in the shields closed and more pops sounded. It sounded like rain on a metal roof, except this rain was trying to kill them. Jeb crouched low, but nothing penetrated the shields. David raised a fist. "Sergeant, pyramid formation. Lin, you're up."

The ShieldBots closed in and took knees around them, locking their armored walls together to make a pyramid that protected from all sides *and* above. A chorus of bursts pinged from above.

The popping kept going until loud cracks split the night, over and over and over. When they stopped, the buzzing was gone. Jeb had never heard a weapon that loud.

"Enemy drones are down. Nice shooting, Lin." David stood and chopped with an open fist. "Phalanx formation, forward!"

Jeb feared they'd overlooked some danger, yet they made it to the grounds of M-Gesundheit safely. The enemy army was down.

"We're clear, sir," DNF said.

Jeb allowed himself a small smile. Lucy might still be dead, but at least they'd lost no one else, yet. He spotted two pink milsynths standing around a pile of the enemy milsynths they'd shot or hacked apart.

One of them held a glowing plasma cutter. "You were wrong, dumbass." It thrust its cutter into the air, standing on a pile of dead milsynths. "Turns out I do get a laser sword!"

Still protected by their ShieldBots, Jeb and the others proceeded into the lobby of M-Gesundheit. The lobby was empty, the staff all gone home for the night, and all its milsynths were wrecked outside.

The floors were white marble, and the walls were paneled wood, interspersed with old-fashioned flat-screens. Those showed the spinning logo of M-Gesundheit covered by a flashing *Evakuieren* warning. Potted plants flanked an empty front desk—what was it with corporations and their potted plants?—and the whole setup reminded Jeb of Ventura Visions, where their hunt for Galileo started.

Finally, that hunt had an end.

"Penthouse." David waved them forward. "Stay behind the synths."

Jeb followed David and the many bunnysynths past the front desk and made himself *not* look at Cowan as he did so. Jeb followed David and their milsynth army up a set of marble stairs to the second floor, long halls bordered by dark glass leading into empty offices. Not even one person was working late, and Jeb was grateful for that. Galileo must have sent them home.

He wondered if asking Cowan about that would tip Galileo off that they were onto him, or if not asking would do the same thing. He decided not to say anything. He hated hiding everything from Cowan, but that was the only way to keep things from Galileo.

The second floor revealed the penthouse dead ahead. Standing glass halls wrapped around it, looking into empty offices and a forest of dimly lit cubes, but the locked room ahead couldn't be anything else. It was a building within the building. Galileo's trap.

"Want me to try and hack the doors?" Cowan asked.

"No need." David handed the block of plastic explosive he'd carried from the truck to the synth controlled by Peachrind. "Plant the charge."

They couldn't trust Cowan to hack anything, so bombs would have to do.

Peachrind slammed the block of explosive into place on the center of the penthouse doors. Jeb realized then they didn't have tape or a detonator. As Peachrind raised his stunner, Jeb knew they were about to lose another milsynth.

"Ready to detonate!" Peachrind shouted.

The other synths knelt, shields raised. They formed a protective line between the coming explosion and people. Then Cowan stood and lurched forward like a drunk, like someone who wasn't moving his own limbs. Like someone who was being puppeted.

"Shit," Jeb said. All the milsynths dropped their shields. "Shit. Shit!"

Cowan lumbered, jogged, and ran, right at the penthouse doors. Jeb sprinted after him as David shouted something.

Peachrind's stunner touched the explosive charge and Jeb tackled Cowan and took him down, rolling the back of his graphene duster to face the door.

The world flashed.

57

COWAN

Coughing made Cowan realize he was alive. He couldn't remember anything, at the moment, except that he'd really wanted to see what that
block of plastic explosive looked like up close.

Where was everyone else? Where were Jeb and David?

Someone shouted—David—but his screams sounded far away. Cowan's ears were ringing. Someone pulled something heavy off him, a body.

"Stay with me," David said, from that place that was so far away.
"Focus on my voice."

Jeb coughed as well, beside Cowan, and that was great until Cowan
realized he couldn't move. All he could do was stare at his partner dying
in his husband's arms. There was blood everywhere, on both Forresters.

"Ha." Jeb grinned at Cowan despite the blood all over his face. "Saved
you." He gasped and coughed. "Not your fault. Remember that . . ."

Then he leaned against David, and he just . . . stopped. He wheezed
but wasn't conscious. On the precipice of death.

Cowan realized then that the pink milsynths were around them,
pointing rifles at them, and none of them had said a goddamn word.
They'd all somehow been hacked, the pros controlling them booted too.

A calm voice echoed over the building's PA system. "I didn't expect that."

Cowan stood, and that's when he realized he was being puppeted.

How? He hadn't connected to or downloaded anything since he'd returned from his meeting with Ellen.

"Oh God, Ellen," he whispered to himself.

He'd met her, risked himself, and knew now that had been a horrible mistake. He suspected—no, he knew—that his happy memories about Ellen's new life were an implanted lie.

Galileo had compromised him, somehow. It was the only way the man could be inside his PBA, which suggested he knew everything.

"David Forrester," Galileo said over the PA system. "I now control your army, and your ability to continue to breathe. There will be no more heroics, understand me? We are done for today."

"Xu did this." David clutched Jeb's body, eyes wet. "She betrayed us!"

"She survived," Galileo said, "as you, unfortunately, will not. Stun him, Cowan."

Cowan's body drew his stunner and aimed before he knew what was happening. Cowan's finger squeezed the trigger. David dropped atop his now dead husband, and Cowan couldn't even make himself cry.

"Join me inside the penthouse," Galileo said. "I have so much to tell you."

Cowan's puppeted legs walked him into the penthouse, all the synth's aiming at him. The explosion had charred the walls and flipped chairs, but the room was intact. A flat-screen descended from the ceiling, and a man appeared on that screen. Cowan spotted his nemesis. A white man, pale, balding, and calm. Gerhard Bayer, also known as Galileo. He'd seen the man in pictures before, but now this man had blown up his partner with an explosive, so that made Bayer look more menacing.

Galileo sat in what looked like an underground office, a small room with a single closed door in the background. It held the desk in front of which he sat, some file cabinets, and nothing else. It was in another building somewhere. Of course it was.

"Let me help him," Cowan whispered. "Let me get Jeb medical supplies."

"Jeb Forrester is beyond modern medicine," Galileo said. "If it's any comfort, I'd actually intended to kill you both once you arrived. Your partner simply cut in line."

434 RHETT C. BRUNO AND T. E. BAKUTIS

"Please!" Cowan couldn't even twitch a finger.

"Very soon, one of my many VIs will bypass your Sim blackout, and I will call for reinforcements. I don't know how you've managed to delay me from contacting the military for so long, but that doesn't matter now."

Cowan again struggled to move his own body and failed. "Why?"

"A dozen reasons. I really do want to save the world, as I've told you. I told you it was possible for someone to murder everyone on the Sim if we don't patch out corporate mind control from PBAs. I'm going to secure them for good."

"Keep me alive and let the others go. If you have to torment anyone, torment me. I'm the one who screwed you over."

"I don't wish to torment anyone, Cowan. Can't you see that? The sacrifices I've made grieve me, and besides, I don't have time for that sort of nonsense. In less than a day, I'll forever protect this world from scripting like mine, and then I'll be very busy."

Cowan tried to plead again, but Galileo locked his jaw.

"The Office of Mental Health is now mine," Galileo said. "The board of Oneworld is now mine. Tomorrow I will load the kill codes for all scripts plaguing the Sim, and I will single-handedly end the crime wave that has consumed the world. I'll be a hero."

Cowan tried to flip over to his head desk, but he couldn't access his PBA. He couldn't access his secret partition. He was trapped in his own mind.

"I will usher in a new age of peace and prosperity," Galileo said, "a world where humans live freely and safely. That is what you die for today. I know it is little comfort, but know that your sacrifices have helped the world. Know that you have enabled a bright future."

Behind Galileo in his office, through an open door, Doctor Xu crept into his office on bare feet. Cowan had suspected her betrayal since their milsynths turned on Galileo booted their StrikeForceGo allies from control, but he hadn't really believed it until now.

Xu had sold them out. She had killed Jeb Forrester.

She raised her stunner.

58

GERHARD

Gerhard's overclocked PBA anticipated Xu's sudden but inevitable betrayal. He ducked. The stun round flew over his head as he snatched the Glock under his desk.

He stood, marksman scripting guiding his hand, and pressed the trigger. Blood and brain matter splattered the hallway. Gerhard's bullet shattered Xu's head, and her stunner clattered as she dropped backward out the door.

For a long moment, Gerhard Bayer—known across the Sim as Galileo—stared at her motionless feet. She had betrayed him? How? He ignored Cowan's puppeted body and summoned the camera feed showing Xu's cell. She still sat in it, but she was also here, dead.

Gerhard switched to infrared and smiled. No one was actually *in* that cell any longer. The Huan Xu in that cell was a MySelf projection.

He walked over to her still body and shattered face. "Oh, my dear Doctor Xu. You always were so ambitious."

Xu had planned to betray him all along. Gerhard would murder the people holding her, and then she would murder him. Everyone would die but her, and then she would have access to Oneworld resources, all his finances and his world.

It was a clever plan, and she had been a worthy opponent. Gerhard almost regretted killing her.

He strolled back to the floating panel displaying his distant penthouse. Then he calmly sat and looked upon Cowan Soto on screen.

"I'm sorry you had to see that," he said.

"Don't kill my family," Cowan whispered. "Please!"

Gerhard scoffed. "Why would I kill your family now? They are no threat to me. They live. Ellen Gauthier and her fiancé lives. Everyone lives but you, Jeb, and David."

Tears seeped from Cowan's puppeted eyes.

Gerhard allowed himself a small grimace. "Well, everyone except Katherine Lambda and Samantha Frederick. I am sorry, but I can't allow them to challenge me again."

One of his soldiers pinged his PBA. Gerhard flipped over to see images of two dead women, both shot in the head. Samantha Frederick—a.k.a. Sonne—and Katherine Lambda. His soldiers had killed them execution style, with no pain. Gerhard had ordered that, hoping to spare them further suffering.

"It's time." Gerhard flipped to another camera and watched pink military synthetics pump bullets into the unconscious body of David Forrester. "I'm going to send you to join your friends now, Cowan. I promise to make your death quick."

"No!" Cowan shouted.

Gerhard made Cowan raise his fist and shake it. At least that, he could offer a worthy opponent. Pink milsynths entered the penthouse and fired at Cowan until they were empty.

So much killing, so much planning and conspiring, and for what? A bloody waste of his time.

Gerhard settled in his rolling office chair and contacted his cleanup crew. By the time M-Gesundheit opened tomorrow, there would be no trace of these murders or the battle outside. His crew could put up an entire building in one night. They were discreet.

This assault had been the last gasp of the members of Oneworld. He couldn't kill them—all board members had imbedded PBA algorithms that forbid them from killing each other, which is why they all trusted Puck—but they must see, now, that his ascent was inevitable.

Once he proved that he could make PBAs unhackable, they would all soon come around.

Everyone in the world would finally be safe. His grand plan had finally come to fruition, after years of planning and hard work. It felt . . . wonderful.

Another ping arrived on Gerhard's PBA, the standard twelve-hour check-in he'd maintained for months now. He pressed his fingers to the twin bio-readers on his desk and stated his password aloud. It was the only way to open his personal console.

Gerhard entered the ghostlink addresses for his standby termination teams—he kept all those ghostlinks in his head, so they couldn't be stolen—and sent the all clear. The families of the Oneworld executives lived for one more day.

Next, Gerhard contacted the mercenaries watching Ellen Gauthier. They didn't answer, so he left a message. Their contract was over, their last payment delivered. He smiled as he pictured Ellen, as he imagined working beside her once more.

He really did like her. In perhaps three days, she would be here in Schaffhausen, safe and well compensated.

It was only then that Gerhard noticed the discrepancy. The wall ahead of him should have had a small rust-stain in the top left corner, a stain that had been there for as long as he could remember. Had someone cleaned the wall? He allowed no one into this office.

The door opened once more, but Gerhard hadn't closed it. He reached for the Glock beneath the desk, but the Glock wasn't there. Xu's body was also gone, and that wasn't the strangest part of it. A dead woman walked into his office with raised fists.

Judging from the rage twisting her face, Samantha Frederick, known by Sonne, was rather upset with him.

"Oh my goodness," he said to himself.

The truth became obvious in a flash of insight and self-deprecating humor, and Gerhard couldn't help but chuckle.

"You modeled a pleasurebox."

"Fuck you!" Samantha stormed toward him. "Asshole!"

"You modeled my office from blueprints of the facility, and photos. And Doctor Xu did shoot me with that stunner, didn't she? You stuck me in a pleasurebox and stole my codes." He pondered. "And you stole security footage from my cleaning drones. That's the only way you could have known what my office looked like." He sighed. "Well done."

Sonne stopped beside him, trembling with rage.

"You've played this masterfully," Gerhard said, offering a finger-to-forehead salute. "I tip my king."

Sonne punched him across the jaw hard enough to knock him out of his chair. "This isn't a game of fucking chess!"

Gerhard curled below her, his head spinning and his jaw aching. The agony ringing through his head made him long to vomit. Which meant this pleasurebox's pain threshold was set to 10.

"You blew up Jeb!" Sonne shouted. "You murdered a little boy!"

For the first time, Gerhard felt what might be actual fear. This woman wasn't rational. She looked ready to kick him until he stopped moving, so how could he make her stop?

"Sonne," Cowan said, from the world beyond this one. "That's enough."

"No, it's fucking not," Sonne said, looming over Gerhard. Yet she didn't strike him again.

59

COWAN

Doctor Xu rejoined them for the ride back to Zurich International Airport. Cowan had the full plan now, from her, and it still didn't seem real. He didn't know how Jeb could have been so reckless or so brave.

Even if Cowan hadn't been puppeted, the others had decided pinning down Galileo's exact location in Schaffhausen was impossible. Jeb had suggested the always reliable Trojan horse gambit: Doctor Xu. Xu would offer to hack David's army of synthetics, infiltrate Galileo's headquarters, and then, using a script piggybacked on the milsynth script Galileo would allow her to run on his wireless, she would quietly open her cell.

It was the only way to find Galileo's *actual* hideout. Xu left her MySelf projection to fool Galileo until she could locate and stun him, at which point they hooked his unconscious body up to a pleasurebox and deleted all memory of Xu stunning him. Fortunately, his hideout wasn't very big. Unfortunately, no one had anticipated Galileo simply deciding to blow Cowan up.

They rode now in an armored autotruck sent to M-Gesundheit by the Office of Mental Health. After Kate sent the kill code to her DDOS script, returning connectivity to Schaffhausen, Sarisa Bassa had deposed Kathleen Warner using the evidence Cowan pulled from Bayer's PBA.

They were fugitives no more, and Bayer was in custody.

With Kathleen Warren and Gerhard Bayer in custody, Cowan and the others were free to return to the United States without being arrested. Yet no one was cheering, or smiling, or even talking.

David stared at the opposite wall of their transport, eyes distant. Though he wasn't in the Sim.

An ambulance with Swiss army medics had arrived at M-Gesundheit ten minutes after Xu stunned Galileo, dispatched due to some quick work by Sarisa, but Jeb hadn't looked good when the medics took him away. He'd lost too much blood, and though his PBA had flipped into emergency coma mode upon detecting the massive trauma to his system, one medic told Cowan Jeb probably wasn't going to wake up.

People rarely did.

Cowan felt nauseated and exhausted. Like none of what had just transpired was worth it, because the man who'd made it possible was hanging between life and death. Plus the Swiss were still deciding whether or not to arrest them. If Jeb lived, he probably wouldn't wake up, and if he did wake up, he might spend the rest of his life in a Swiss prison.

This wasn't what a victory was supposed to feel like. It was just like that stupid movie they'd all watched on the flight over, with the dark-haired lady and her cat. Surviving something horrible when others you cared about didn't wasn't all that great in the end.

The truck opened its doors at the airport. Sonne waited just outside the truck, in the cold wind on the tarmac, wrapped in a thick red emergency jacket. Her eyes were puffy, her body trembling, and Cowan forgot how exhausted he was when he remembered Lucy was dead now.

He hopped out and embraced Sonne tightly. She hugged back.

At some point, a Swiss officer approached and stopped with six others. All their eyes glowed red, HARM switches active.

"CID Detective Cowan Soto," the officer said. "You're under arrest."

So the Swiss had made up their mind about what to do with them. Arrest them. Damn. Cowan eased Sonne away, squeezing her arms as she glared at the soldiers.

"Don't." Cowan stepped between the soldiers and his team. "This was my plan. I'll cooperate if you leave the others."

"No," Sonne said, stepping up beside him. "Fuck no."

"It's okay." Cowan kept his hands where the Swiss could see them. "I'll be okay."

"If you don't mind, Captain Holzer," Kate shouted, limping from the back of a parked ambulance. Her eyes were puffy as well, probably from crying. "I've got something I need to show you."

"Arrest her too," Holzer said, motioning to his soldiers. "None of you are going home."

"Trust me!" Kate shouted as one of Holzer's soldiers grabbed her arms. "You really want to read this!"

The soldier snatched the printout from Kate's hand and read. Then he left Kate, walked to his commander, and handed him the paper. Holzer read it. Then he read it again.

"So," Kate said. "Sorry about everything, but as you've no doubt figured out by now, we didn't actually *kill* anybody."

Captain Holzer tore up the printout and tossed it aside. "This is bullshit." He pointed at Cowan, jaw clenched. "You assaulted a Swiss facility, abducted a Swiss national, and hacked a Swiss uplink facility. You do not walk away from that!"

A string of unmarked black autocars sped into view from deeper in the airport. As Holzer and his men turned, those autocars stopped in perfect formation. Dozens of armed men in Corporate Security uniforms stepped out, and Cowan would never forget those uniforms. These were the real deal, and they weren't part of the Swiss army.

"I think you'd better let us get on our plane," Kate said quietly.

Holzer looked to be counting, actually. Like it wasn't all that obvious. When he finished, he turned to his soldiers and clenched both empty hands. "Stand down."

"Thought so," Sonne said.

Kate's face lit up when Xu then hopped out of the autotruck. "You're okay!"

"A credit to my genius," Xu said. "However, Jeb Forrester is now in emergency coma suspension. He's in Swiss custody. They peg chances of survival at 22 percent."

"He's . . . what?" Kate blinked. "That's . . ." She was probably too distraught to script an emotional firewall. "I'm so sorry. Oh bother. I'm crying."

Cowan was sorry, too, but he needed to get his friends out of here before the Swiss got reinforcements and decided to press the issue.

"Plane, now," he said. "Everyone on the plane now." He'd find a way to get Jeb out of Switzerland later, no matter what it took.

"I'm not going with you," Xu said.

"What?" Kate brushed new tears from her cheeks. "You have to."

"Oneworld only pardoned us for Bayer," Xu said. "There is still the matter of my illegal clone, and my work on Tian, and my conspiracy with Galileo. I think I'll take my chances in a neutral country, dear Katherine, where I have plenty of rich friends to shelter me until the world forgets about today."

Kate stared. "But—"

"You'll put in a good word for nonextradition, won't you?"

"If Kate doesn't," Cowan said, "I will."

Xu was one of the reasons they were all standing here right now, despite her past crimes. Throwing her in prison wouldn't change anything. She deserved a chance at her old life.

Kate tossed her arms around Xu and hugged her. "I don't want this to be the last time I see you. Find me again soon, all right?"

Xu smiled and rubbed her back. "Of course. After all, my dear, we'll always have the darkSim."

60
COWAN

"I refuse to believe Jeb's going to die," Sarisa said quietly. She sat across from Cowan, in his and Jeb's favorite booth at *Crazy Noodles*. "Doctors don't know everything."

Cowan took another sip of bottled water his PBA told him was orange soda. He liked orange soda.

"Sometimes they do," he said.

"So you've given up?"

Cowan shook his head. "Not ever. I'd rather have hope than not."

Sarisa reached across the table and squeezed his hand. "That's good. That's really good. That's how you should deal with things in general."

Cowan pulled his hand away. "I'm fine. You don't need to worry about me."

"Remember: you can't blame yourself. From everything you've told me, I don't think there was any way you could have taken Gerhard Bayer down without Jeb's plan."

"Right."

"You getting compromised only changed how you executed your plan, not its outcome. In fact, because Jeb and the others used you to deceive Galileo, you may have actually made it easier to capture him and save the others."

"Sure," Cowan said.

"Even if Jeb does die in the next week," Sarisa said, "do you plan to let that stop you?"

"Stop me from what?"

"From investigating cybercrimes. Protecting people. In my opinion, you've shown yourself to be very good at that."

Cowan shifted in his seat and stared at his orange soda. "I'm not sure what I'm going to do next."

"You know—"

"I'm not redacting what I did. I survived what happened to Ellen, and I'll survive this. I know it'll suck for a really long time, but I *will* deal with it."

Ellen was safe. Cowan's parents were safe, and he no longer felt so lonely or guilty. Ellen had a fiancé and a cushy job. Cowan could live with her being happy.

The thought of losing Jeb was different. If Jeb died, it would both destroy his life and David's. Both of them had been impossibly brave, and it felt impossibly unfair that they'd suffer as a result.

"Good," Sarisa said. "That's good, Cowan. That's precisely what I needed you to say."

"Why?"

Sarisa sat back. "You're cleared for duty."

Cowan's eyes went wide. "You were *debriefing* me?"

Sarisa had assured him she had only wanted to take him out for a drink. God, that woman had a poker face.

"In my opinion as a counselor for the Office of Mental Health, a binding opinion that can only be overridden by the OMH's yet-to-be-appointed director, you are not suffering from persistent depression," she said. "You may continue as a CID investigator, if you wish."

They both knew she was sticking her neck out real far by saying that, so Cowan wouldn't argue.

"Thank you," he said.

Sarisa smiled and nodded. After a few seconds, she added, "Jeb's going to make it, but even if he doesn't, you need to keep going. Do things with people even when you don't want to do things. The guilt and hurt won't ever go away, but it will dull with time. You'll grow used to carrying it around."

"Now you're talking like he's going to die."

Cowan couldn't imagine what David was going through now, separated from his possibly dying husband by a whole ocean. David might be willing to return to Switzerland and be arrested, but Oneworld wasn't willing to let that happen. It would put them in a situation where the Swiss government was defying them, and no one, on either side, wanted that. David was grounded *here*, and Cowan knew that must suck.

"Call if you need help any time of day or night," Sarisa said. "I'm here for you, and I can always listen." She rose and slid out of the booth. "Thank you for the noodles and the water."

"Sure." Cowan frowned at the night outside. "And thanks for—"

A ping jolted his PBA.

It was an invitation from the board of Oneworld.

61

COWAN

Cowan had never been to the inner sanctum of Corporate One. He walked through a huge lobby occupied by milsynths and entered an elevator with silver doors. He rode down, and down, and down before emerging in a long white hall.

A pyramid-headed milsynth greeted him there. It led him down that hall, which soon let out into a circular black room with a single white circle in the center. Cowan stood on it.

Wings fluttered and a fairy in a tiny green dress appeared. She had short blond hair and overtly cute features.

"Hello, Cowan," the fairy said as she landed with a flourish.

Cowan didn't feel surprised at all. "You're Puck." Sonne had told him about Puck.

"Not today," Puck said, less spastically than he'd expected. "Today I'm Dina Abramowitz." One of the four remaining people on the board of Oneworld. "I wish we could speak face to face, but these are still dangerous times. This is safer."

She wasn't wrong. "How can I help you, Missus Abramowitz?" Cowan asked.

"You've already helped me. You freed my family, captured a man who'd grown far too dangerous for us to control, and saved our world from a hostile takeover that would have ended everything we've built these past fifty years."

"Hooray for me."

"So, what do you want, Cowan?"

He watched her for a moment, taking that in. "Sorry?"

"It's not a trick question. We're prepared to offer you any job you want or, if you don't want a job, a pension to research anything you like. Consider it a performance bonus. You can even retire to a private island, if you like. Money is no longer your problem."

Cowan shook his head. "I don't want a bunch of money."

"What do you want?"

"I want Jeb Forrester to live."

"The Swiss are doing everything they can to save him."

"Right, but I want you to do everything. I want you to take over."

Dina raised one of Puck's fairy eyebrows. "What exactly are you asking me, Cowan?"

"Everything you have," he said. "You're the four most powerful people in the world. You have access to research and doctors and studies that no one else knows about. They might not be legal, or even safe, but I don't care. Use them to save Jeb."

Dina smiled. "You're assuming an awful lot."

"And you haven't told me no outright, which means I'm right about you holding back."

"Retrieving Forrester from Swiss custody could be delicate."

"I don't care. That's what I want for my reward. Save him."

"And if we did, you'd consider our debt settled?"

"Yes."

"And what about that *other* matter?"

She meant Galileo, and all he'd revealed about corporate mind control. Cowan had an answer for that too. He'd spent a good deal of time thinking about it, and all the death, horror, and evil he'd seen in the past few months. The natural state of humanity.

"I'm not going to share your corporate mind control policy with the world," Cowan said. "The benefits of clear circuit algorithms out-weigh the drawbacks."

Dina tilted her fairy head. "So you disagree with Gerhard Bayer's evaluation?"

"I'm not saying I love mind control," Cowan said. "But I do believe PBA suppression algorithms remain our best option until we evolve, be-cause when a board member isn't spreading invasive scripts all over the darkSim, they keep most of us from murdering each other."

Dina took a moment before answering. "It was never about mind control, Cowan. It was about changing the world."

It must be nice to see things that clearly. Cowan still doubted his own words. He still felt, deep down, that by agreeing to go along with this oppressive system, he was harming the world more than helping it.

Yet he did have data from the past few months of countless horrors, and that data proved removing PBA control, at this point, would un-leash chaos on the world. The genie, as they said, was out of the bottle.

Sometimes, there's just no perfect answer. No clear right or wrong.

"I don't plan to change it back," Cowan said. "Though I would like to keep my brain as is."

"You're referring to your customized PBA firmware? We have no problem with that."

"Provided you get Jeb out of Switzerland and help him."

"We shall endeavor," Dina said. "Consider our debts settled."

Was he doing the right thing? While Galileo's goal of ending mind control had perhaps been correct, his method of doing so had been hor-rifically wrong. Nobody should be used the way Galileo had used people.

So, in the end, perhaps all Cowan could do was try to hurt the fewest people possible. That seemed like a good way to start.

"Good," Cowan said.

"We are going to have to redact your knowledge of our mind control algorithms before you leave," Dina added. "I'm sure you understand."

"I do." He pushed his doubts deep down. "Honestly, I'd be more comfortable not knowing what you do."

"Not many are," Dina agreed.

62

COWAN

Lucy Fallon's funeral fell on a beautiful Sunday afternoon. It was closed casket, of course, because of her practical disintegration, but there was a nice picture of Lucy beside it.

The official story was as simple and stupid as it got. Lucy died in a plane crash.

A large group of people Cowan had never met came to see Lucy off, apparently friends and guildmates from *Chimera*, one of the long-term fantasy Sims Kate and Lucy apparently played a lot.

Sonne wore a deep black dress, very different from her usual attire. Cowan felt out of place with so many strangers around, so many people sad about Lucy's death when he wasn't as sad as they were. They were all recounting stories about her, or crying, or consoling each other.

To be honest, he really hadn't known Lucy at all. It made him feel like he didn't belong here, like he was just a funeral tourist. Still, Sonne had asked him to be here and volunteered to sit beside him, so he hadn't hesitated. He sat quietly and ignored the curious looks from strangers.

It felt important, Sonne being willing to sit next to him. Like she'd anticipated how out of place he might feel here and chosen to make him feel included, at least . . . included by her. It suggested she'd forgiven him for his part in trying to trick her into transporting Xu to Switzerland, and everything else.

Kate took the stage after some remarks from an older female minister. She looked calm and was probably using firewalls to keep her emotions in check, but that was fair, given her best friend had just died.

There was still a chance Jeb might die, very soon, and Cowan had heard nothing from Oneworld since their meeting. They were all waiting.

"Today," Kate said, stiff hair ruthlessly defying the wind, "we gather to remember Lucy Anastasia Fallon. She wasn't just an employee of Benzai Corporation, and she wasn't just my bodyguard. She was my closest friend, and the best healer I ever had the fortune to run with through the Inferno Cliffs."

Kate had a really good speech, talking about how Lucy had been with her since she was in her late teens, and how she'd undertaken cyberization to be a better bodyguard for her best friend. She shared stories about Sim parties and epic raids and Lucy tossing grabby dudes out on their asses. Cowan archived it for later so he could watch it when he wasn't distracted by worrying about Jeb.

Yet comas weren't the end of everything. Taylor Lambda, Kate and Sonne's father, had finally woken up yesterday after all. For now, no one was talking about brain code. What was important is that Sonne and Kate had their father back, even if they'd lost their guardian. Their friend.

Kate was finishing up, sobbing by the end, which meant maybe she wasn't using firewalls after all.

"Lucy saved me," Kate said. "She saved my sister, and my family, and as far as I'm concerned, she saved the goddamn world too. She wouldn't want us to mourn her. She'd want us to live for her."

Cowan waited as Kate looked around. Everyone watched her from their seats, silent and respectful. Were they waiting for her to say something else?

"That's it." Kate wiped her cheeks and shrugged. "That's all I have to say." She took a breath and stepped down off the stage. "As you were."

A ping reached Cowan's PBA, high priority. As rude as it felt to answer a call in the middle of a funeral, it could be from the CID. Cowan felt he had no choice to but to verify who was calling.

Galileo might be in custody, but Cowan couldn't shake the paranoid worry the man might escape. If he did, Galileo would come for Cowan, his family, and everyone he cared about with a vengeance. If this was a call announcing Galileo had escaped, well . . . Cowan needed to take it.

Yet as he flipped over to his head desk and answered the ping, it wasn't the CID who'd called. It was, instead, David Forrester, who sat in a hospital room beside Jeb.

And Jeb watched Cowan with eyes that were *open*.

"Jeb!" Cowan blurted, aloud, where the entire funeral could hear.

Someone gripped his hand, and he flipped back over to find Sonne clutching his hand hard. Her own eyes looked wide and hopeful.

"Really?" she whispered.

Cowan nodded. He ignored the curious and annoyed glances of the others, stood, and bowed his head. "I'm really sorry, everyone. I have to take this ping. My friend's in the hospital."

Eyes previously annoyed softened in sympathy, but Cowan barely noticed. He moved away and heard Sonne's footfalls just behind his. He flipped back to his head desk and searched for her wireless signal, which was open. He patched her into the ping, and then Sonne's image appeared beside Jeb's, suspended in the Sim. Sonne's eyes widened too.

"You're awake!" Sonne whisper-shouted.

Jeb managed a grin. He didn't speak—he was likely still too much in recovery to speak—but he slowly raised one hand and give them a thumb's up. Cowan felt his eyes flooding and didn't care who noticed.

"His doctors say he's going to make a full recovery," David said proudly, his eyes also wet. "I don't know what changed, but some specialists came in this morning. They worked on him for hours. And now, well . . . you can see." David shuddered and gripped Jeb's hand. "He's going to live."

Cowan smiled with relief. "Thank God." His deal with Dina Abramowitz, and Oneworld, had come through. Or so it seemed.

Cowan focused on Jeb's weak but determined gaze. "I can't thank you enough for you've done, but I'll try. It isn't just that you saved my life. You taught me how to survive . . . all this. So I'm really glad you're alive, and I couldn't have asked for a better partner. I'll see you both soon."

Jeb managed a smile before settling back in bed.

Back in meatspace, Cowan felt Sonne's hand gently touch his shoulder. She squeezed. That felt very good.

"We'll call you if anything changes," David said. He glanced at his husband and breathed. "Stay safe, you two."

The call terminated. Cowan flipped back to meatspace—to a bright day and a cemetery filled with green grass—and turned to find Sonne standing just behind him. Her eyes were a bit wet, too, but she looked vindicated.

She also looked absolutely beautiful.

Seeing the love David felt for Jeb, especially after coming so close to losing him forever, reminded Cowan that life was impossibly short. When he'd been with Ellen, he'd taken their relationship for granted, unaware of how quickly and horrifically it could end. He was done being hesitant.

He set aside the past and held Sonne's gaze. "After the funeral, do you want to grab some noodles with me?"

She smiled softly. "As friends? Or as a date?"

"A date," Cowan said firmly, without hesitation.

Sonne's smile grew. "Good. I'd really like to see what it's like to be with you when we aren't getting abducted and shot at."

EPILOGUE

When the autotruck that was set to transfer him halted without warning, Gerhard Bayer smiled. He knew they had traveled perhaps two kilometers from Witzwil, the Swiss prison. He knew because he was one of the most intelligent men on the planet.

He also knew they weren't supposed to stop.

An explosion rattled the autotruck, tossing Gerhard's head against the seat, and that did make him jump. The familiar *pop-pop-pop* of gunfire echoed outside, joined by the *snap-hiss* of stunners. Gerhard waited calmly, cuffed hands in his lap.

The gunfire stopped, and sparks split the line between the autotruck's back doors. Gerhard squinted as the sparks worked their way down, and then the doors popped open. Two mercenaries stood outside in dark riot armor, faces obscured by helmets.

Gerhard inclined his head to his anonymous rescuers. "You understand, of course, that I cannot deliver your payment until we're well clear of the assault scene."

"We get it," the man on the left said, slightly shorter than the man on the right. "Come with us." The mercenary hopped in and opened Gerhard's cuffs.

"Where now?" Gerhard stood and rubbed his aching wrists.

"We have an escape vehicle waiting, sir, but we need to leave at once."

Gerhard straightened the collar of his prison jumpsuit and sauntered from the autotruck. He observed the carnage around them: melted synthetics, the burning wrecks of autotrucks, and bloodied human bodies in Swiss uniforms. A shame, all of it.

These Swiss soldiers had only been doing their jobs, and Gerhard would have preferred they not die, but his quest to save the world was far more important than a few soldiers. His oversight in not discovering Samantha Frederick's pleasurebox was but a temporary setback.

When he first launched his campaign against Oneworld's foolishness, Gerhard had placed a recurring bounty to free him from captivity on the darkSim. It was the virtual equivalent of a dead man's switch. Unless he canceled it once every twenty-four hours, the offer went out.

And after being captured, he'd been unable to cancel it.

The offer placed on the darkSim Elite Troubleshooter board had been $30 billion in untraceable funds—$30 billion to whatever mercenary or mercenaries freed him from Swiss captivity, as well as an encryption key to track the GPS device embedded at the base of his skull. The money was nothing—less than half his Tian sales—and his quest to save the world? Priceless.

A car idled audibly nearby, a manual model. Both mercenaries sat in the front, and Gerhard realized they were actually going to drive it. How novel. He sat in the back and silently approved. Oneworld, obviously, couldn't track a car without an imbedded VI. The shorter of the two men drove the car away, leaving the carnage behind.

"Where to, sir?" the other man asked, the taller one in the passenger seat.

"I'd like you to deliver me to Zurich Airport." Gerhard settled crossed hands on his lap. "Once I'm safe, I will wire your convenience fee."

The man who'd spoken removed his riot helmet to reveal a yellow ski mask, which reminded Gerhard of a Russian nesting doll. A mask within a mask. How delightful.

"You understand we can't head there just yet," Yellow Mask said, turning in his seat to look at Gerhard. "The Swiss army knows you've escaped. They'll be watching the airports. If I may make a suggestion—"

"You'd suggest a boat, or an overland route through the mountains, or perhaps a trip through the GBT." Gerhard held the mercenary's eyes, keeping his features calm. "Do not concern yourself with my escape route. I am quite capable of disappearing."

"Once we deliver you to Zurich Airport."

"Indeed."

That was where Captain Holzer waited to spirit Gerhard off to his secret retreat.

The shorter man, the man still wearing his helmet, spoke next. "We'll deliver you to Zurich Airport. Tomorrow. First, we must be sure we've evaded pursuit. For this reason, I must ask you to shelter at our safe house for a day."

"You understand I won't pay you until I'm safe," Gerhard said. It was a reasonable request.

"We understand and appreciate your cooperation."

"Very well. Deliver me to your safe house."

They drove onward in silence. Gerhard listened for Swiss helicopters or others in pursuit, but nothing threatened. Satisfied, he flipped to his PBA and plotted a course through his redundant assets. Rebuilding his operation would take years, but it could be done. He *would* save the world, no matter who stood in his way.

Eventually, the car stopped. Gerhard returned to meatspace in the shadow of the mighty Swiss Alps, beside a charming little cabin. Smoke rose from its chimney. It seemed like a nice place to spend a day or two.

Gerhard took in the beauty of raw nature and breathed the clean air of freedom. He chuckled in the cold as he considered the unrelenting idiocy of his opponents.

Had Cowan Soto really assumed that imprisoning someone with his resources would be *easy*? Had Oneworld?

Something slammed into the back of his head, and the world went black . . .

When Gerhard opened his eyes again, chains wrapped his ankles, above his feet. More were strung around his stomach and his shoulders, with another resting against his forehead.

The chains were cold. He was cold.

Gerhard realized then he was chained to a block of cement, but it wasn't a block. It was a floor, and there were raised walls around him, and above those walls was sky.

Beeping echoed through the cold air, and the back of what Gerhard realized was an automixer scooted into view atop the walls. No . . . not atop them. That automixer was on the ground, the ground below the Swiss Alps. He was in an open concrete grave.

"Gerhard Bayer." The driver of the car stepped into view, and he wasn't wearing his helmet any longer. This one wore a gray ski mask. "Or should I say, Galileo?"

"What have you done?" Gerhard fought for clarity. "Are you an idiot?"

"A little over three months ago, you recruited a Russian grayDoc, Doctor Anton Barkov," Gray Mask informed him calmly. "You offered him half a million dollars and a lab full of new equipment."

"You fool!" Gerhard thrashed at the chains and found himself disturbingly immobilized. "Is this about money? Thirty billion is not enough?"

The automixer was *mixing*. Ready to seal him in concrete.

"You placed a passive script—I believe the term is 'killswitch'—in the PBA of Doctor Anton Barkov," Gray Mask continued. "You did this with the intent to murder Anton Barkov, should he attempt to betray you."

"Who are you working for? What are they paying you?" Panic squeezed Gerhard's lungs, and it was already difficult to breathe in the chains. "Barkov couldn't afford you!"

"Doctor Barkov didn't hire me," Gray Mask said. "I usually don't reveal my employer, but in this case, my employer insisted I do just that. My employer is Demetri Barkov."

Gerhard tried to search that name in his PBA, but he had no wireless connection for some reason, no way to call for help. These men must have blocked his wireless. Yet Gerhard still had his money.

"Can this Demetri pay you thirty billion dollars?" Gerhard heard the desperation in his own voice. "Do you even know who I am?"

"Demetri Barkov is the nephew of Vladimir Alexandrov. Vladimir Alexandrov is the leader of Mother Russia's Bratva. Are you familiar with Mother Russia's Bratva, Mister Bayer?"

A bit of warm wet squirted down Gerhard's thigh, but that only made the chill spreading through his body worse.

"I'm Gerhard Bayer," he barked. "I'm on the board of Oneworld!"

Yellow Mask walked into view. "Pour," he said.

The spinning automixer vomited gloppy gray cement. It dropped onto Gerhard's feet in a shock of cold and weight.

"Listen to me, you simpletons!" Gerhard shouted. "I have more money than you can comprehend, more resources—"

"We don't care about your resources," Yellow Mask said.

"I can make you kings! I can pay you anything!"

"We've been paid, Mister Bayer," Gray Mask said.

Gerhard thrashed against the metal chains. This was a bluff. It was all a bluff, to scare him and make him pay more money. Money fixed anything and bought anyone.

"Forty billion!" Cold cement tickled the back of his neck as it filled around him. "Sixty! A trillion in untraceable funds, and I can get more!"

"Goodbye, Mister Bayer." The men in the ski masks walked out of sight.

"Don't do this! You can't!" Cement crept into Gerhard's ears, and he screamed for help, for anyone. How could these mercenaries be so *stupid*? "Let me help you! I can pay—"

Muddy cold devoured his face. Cement forced its way inside him, sputtering down his throat, dirty and freezing. And just like that, Gerhard Bayer couldn't offer anyone a thing.